THE WIND REMEMBERS

by

Caroll Louise Shreeve

The Wind Remembers

THE WIND REMEMBERS

Dedication

This book is dedicated to those who always believed in me and my story and to the countless falconers and bird-refuge volunteers whose efforts have brought endangered raptors, particularly falcons, back from the brink of extinction.

THE WIND REMEMBERS

Every effort has been made to assure that all physical facts used in the creation of this fiction work are accurate. The author and publisher are not responsible for questionable information provided by consulted experts or for errors in the editing or printing processes. Though some concepts were borrowed from current events, all characters and plot inventions are purely fictional.

No part of this book may be reproduced in any form electronically or otherwise, except for the purposes of review and promotion, without the express permission, in writing, from the author, publisher or the author's representatives.

Shreeve, Caroll Louise McKanna, 1942–

    The Wind Remembers: Copyright © 2012 by Caroll Louise McKanna Shreeve. All rights reserved. Prepared in the United States of America.

    1. Fiction—Suspense
Caroll Louise Shreeve
ISBN# 1936434466   ISBN# 978-1-936-434-46-6

Published by Synergy Books
Available on various E-Book formats.

Cover illustration by Caroll Louise Shreeve
Cover design by David W. Smith

THE WIND REMEMBERS

Table of Contents

Prologue		7
Chapter One	The Hugging Tree	9
Chapter Two	Rattled	25
Chapter Three	Familiar Ground	43
Chapter Four	Felon, the Wind	52
Chapter Five	Charmed	65
Chapter Six	Secret Schemes	83
Chapter Seven	Wings of Promise	97
Chapter Eight	Unsettling Circumstances	127
Chapter Nine	Coming Together Coming Apart	159
Chapter Ten	Unraveling Tangles	196
Chapter Eleven	Dangerous Ground	234
Chapter Twelve	Dancing on the Edge	249
Chapter Thirteen	Raining Consequences	287
Chapter Fourteen	Solstice Sojourn	317
Chapter Fifteen	Coming into the Light	358

The Wind Remembers

THE WIND REMEMBERS

PROLOGUE

~ Friday the 13th of June

Searing desert winds flow across Great Salt Lake, suckle water suffused with lake stink, and conjure cumulus clouds. The burdened clouds collide with cold mountain air and roil thousands of feet high. Glittering with lightning they erase the moon. Thunder cracks. The roaring storm bursts upon the town of Farr—preying upon a farmhouse huddled on the bench below—extinguishing electrical power.

Suzanne Price slams windows against the rain. Lightning flits through darkened rooms—like the wings of a frantic bird trying to escape.

Mitzi, clutching her teddy bear, grips Suzanne's fingers so hard the wedding band bites into soft flesh.

"Mommy, this nighttime in our house scares Bear Lovins!"

Suzanne gropes the wallpapered hallway. A step behind, Gregory gasps a breath. The irritating click of his fingernails reminds her of a busy insect. She wishes he'd stop it. Wishes more for Steve who taught him how to make the incessant noise.

"Only a little way to go, kids."

She moves a sweaty palm from wall to swinging kitchen door, pushes it open, enters a freight train of storm racket. Rattling windows are alive with lightning and streaming water.

The Wind Remembers

"Okay, darlings? I'll get a flashlight. Stay close! Isn't this an exciting adventure?" She means to sound confident, but knows her raised voice comes out forced and strident.

"Mommy! Make our 'lectricity come back on!"

"Sissy baby!" Greg hisses. He pushes past them. "Dad would've made sure the lights didn't go out."

Wind-driven water drills the roof like rifle shots. Suzanne glimpses the bulky-branched cottonwood in the yard, its leaves whipping in the wind. A cracking shriek erupts like the earth itself splitting open. She pushes Mitzi to the floor, screams above the din, "Greg, get under the table. Cover your face!"

A ferocious scraping of leaves brushes the panes. Branch upon breaking branch collides with the ground. With the culminating crash of mighty trunk, the house shudders. Suzanne feels Greg at her side, hears his ragged breathing, reaches to hold him close. He clings, then shrinks away.

"Dad would know what to do if . . . if you hadn't ruined everything." He gulps air. His fingernails click faster than the raindrops pelting the cracked windows.

In the dark, they wait while the storm's momentum swirls beyond the orchard, up and over the mountains. The roar subsides. On hands and knees, Suzanne ventures to a
cabinet drawer, fumbles among its contents, switches on a flashlight.

"The worst is over. Everything's going to be all right now." She breathes a prayer of gratitude that they've been spared from huge branches, which could have come crashing through the windows, showering them with broken glass.

But of course—the worst is not over.

Chapter One

The Hugging Tree

Gregory Price

~Saturday the 14th of June

The boy was the first to see it. In dawn light the big tree was dead. Smashed to the muddy ground like some giant had tromped on it until it was nothing but broken branches. It would never stand up and let him climb to where he could see the top of the house roof, like when his dad told him where to put his hands and feet to be safe while he got his balance. Safe mattered to his dad even when he couldn't fix things anymore.

Now the tree could never scare the boy again like it did during the storm last night. It was all the way dead, just like his dad. Gregory felt safe—but he was angry enough to bust. He sucked air through his clenched teeth to make his heart stop pounding inside his pajamas. He crawled back into bed and pretended to sleep as if being without his dad and the climbing tree didn't matter anymore. Somewhere deep inside he knew he was just pretending. He just didn't know what to do about how much it hurt.

Gregory held still under the blankets until it was time for Suzanne to wake up. When he heard her go from her room to the bathroom, he jumped out of bed and raced to the kitchen. Getting there first seemed terribly important. Being first was more and more important about a lot of things. He didn't know why and he didn't care. It mattered. That much he knew and that was that.

He picked up the new book about insects and waited for her to come through the swinging door, before turning the pages.

Suzanne Price

~Saturday the 14th of June

"Morning, Greg." Suzanne tacked a pencil sketch to the fridge with magnets— mute testimony that the entire cottonwood lay in the yard. She'd hoped only a couple of huge branches had broken off in the storm. Inside she was simply sick about the loss. *I mustn't let the kids know how upset and frightened I am,* she told herself.

Greg banged a bowl on the table and scraped his chair closer to the old bureau where a crock of garden roses shared space with the portable TV.

"When will my shows come back on?" he whined, leafing through his new book on insects. He spoke without looking up at her.

Suzanne turned to the counter, made coffee and split bagels, glad the power, if not the cable, was restored. Her back was to him.

"I have no idea," she said, making an effort to sound ordinary before she turned to study him. *Something's bugging him that he's not ready to talk about. I'll have to tread lightly and get him to open up before Dee arrives.*

Greg scarfed Cheerios, his dark hair sticking up in tousled spikes. While the coffee brewed, Suzanne glanced occasionally out at the cottonwood. Without a job, she mulled over the daunting expense of having the massive tree removed. When Dierdre's visit was over, she planned an earnest job search for full-time work. *What I'll have to settle for will be a far cry from my drawing board.*

Parting lacy curtains above the sink, she studied the unbelievable mess of branches rising beyond the back steps. No longer shaded by the great tree, the windowpanes glared with sunlight. A few of them had glittery splits from top to bottom. *Thank God none of the old glass shattered in the wooden framework. They knew how to build things a hundred years ago.*

Mountain peaks above the bench surrounded the valley like a protective fortress. The rain-swollen Farr River gushed spray over the rocks along the cherry orchard. Pink-gold light glistened on green vegetables against moist black loam, perfect for a watercolor she had no enthusiasm to paint this morning.

Mitzi joined them and propped her teddy bear in a chair. His worn velveteen nose rested on the table. She went to Suzanne and raised her arms for a hug. Suzanne knelt and snuggled Mitzi close.

"Mmmmh, you smell good, Mommy."

"She's not our mom," Greg remarked.

Mitzi's smiling face clouded. "I can *so* call her Mommy. Daddy said."

Suzanne lifted the three-year old to reach the bowls in the cupboard. "It's not like you to be so rude, Greg. What's up?"

"You deserve it," he whispered.

"What was that again?" Suzanne asked, knowing full well what he'd said. *Is it no TV that's made him so sassy or the scary tree smash?*

"Nothing, I didn't say nothing."

"Good. If you can't say something nice, don't say anything. We have enough problems this morning."

Suzanne helped Mitzi with cereal and milk before going to her bedroom to dress. In white jeans and a blue cotton blouse, she checked in the mirror to see if she'd pass her sister's scrutiny. Hair would do. *Nothing to be done about my puffy eyes.*

She opened the bedroom shutters. Branches of the cottonwood twisted like serpents seeking shelter from the light. They ruptured the garage door, carrying the TV cable with them. *Ah, there's our TV problem, and I can't get to the Blazer. The whole cottonwood—gone.* It was hard to take in the truth of it, but the thought occurred that the tree could be sold for firewood. She returned to the kitchen feeling more hopeful.

Mitzi spooned make-believe cereal into her teddy bear's stitched mouth, all the while murmuring secret baby words. Greg's cheeks bulged with cereal. His finger traced a row of insect pictures. Suzanne set her mug on the table. He looked up at her, gulped his cereal down, and looked away before their eyes could meet.

"Kids, I've called a tree service to clear the garage door but it may take all day. We won't be able to drive to the airport to pick up your Aunt Dierdre."

"She's not our aunt, 'cause you're not our mom," Greg announced. "She's just your sister."

"I like Aunt Dreedra," said Mitzi.

"I didn't say I didn't like her," he added, "I just said she's not our aunt. Dierdre's okay. At least I can say it right, not like some babies I know."

"That will do, Greg." Suzanne rinsed last night's dinner plates and loaded the dishwasher, wondering what had been eating him even before the storm took out the TV.

A diesel truck crunched to a stop in the gravel driveway, prompting her to look outside. The driver climbed down from what appeared to be a shiny new truck. The door's fancy logo was spelled out in twig letters: ARMSTRONG TREE SERVICE—*Two Generations of Experience.* Recognizing the sandy-haired man, she nearly dropped a spoon, but wiped her hands on a dishtowel, tossed it on the counter and smoothed her hair with shaky fingers. She practiced a casual smile. Her heart pounded in her ears. *What is HE doing here? I expected his father or some employee!*

The Wind Remembers

***

Through the curtains of the door she watched him come, carrying a clipboard and a cell phone. He skirted the massive tree, inspecting the damage while he climbed through fallen branches and clouds of leaves to approach the back door. Just the sight of him after all these years was unnerving.

His curly eyebrows sun-bleached like his wavy hair, Taylor Armstrong was more than a good-looking man of thirty. He'd been her steady in college, and she'd broken it off. Not because she didn't love him—no—not because of that. The impact of seeing him again made her giddy, yet cautious.

"Who is it, Mommy?" Mitzi asked.

"A man from the place I called about our tree, Sweetheart. An old . . . friend."

Her face flamed. *When did he come back to Farr?* She opened the door. At twenty-eight, she felt as awkward as a schoolgirl.

"Mrs. Price . . . Suzanne!" she heard the surprise in his rich baritone. "It's been a *long* time." His easy smile quickened her pulse.

"Yes, yes it has, Taylor. I . . . I see your work is close to your forestry studies. Thought you'd never stoop to cutting down trees for your father. Said you'd rather plant them for the Forest Service way out in some wild over-logged back woods."

"So you still remember some things I confided to you." His smile was thoughtful.

Her insides were a muddle of confusion. She felt like rushing into his arms to feel their warm security enfold her again. Yet the urge to close the door and avoid dealing with her feelings about him made her struggle for composure.

"And do you still paint watercolors of trees?"

Mitzi tugged on her arm. "Mommy, can your man friend fix our tree back up?"

"I'm afraid not." Taylor looked back over his shoulder at the debris. "It's not good for much except firewood when it dries out. Lucky that old giant fell away from your house."

Time stalled for Suzanne. She took in the new and remembered shape of him, the muscular shoulders, arms, and thighs of the man she'd last seen in 1993, seven years ago. No wedding band circled his tanned ring finger. She chided herself for noticing.

"Mommy, your friend asked you something; don't cha hear him?"

Suzanne realized she'd been staring at Taylor's mouth, watching his lips form words, remembering kisses that tingled to her toes when those lips had flooded her with pleasure the first time he'd really kissed her, softly for so long she'd had to catch her breath when he pulled away. Not registering what he said, she felt unable to meet his eyes with her own. She brushed her hair back, feeling vulnerable and foolish.

"Taylor, can this tree be removed this morning? I'm stranded without my car. Dierdre's arriving this afternoon. You remember my twin."

"Who could forget Dierdre?" He grinned.

Suzanne sobered. This was the side of Taylor she'd never understood, never been comfortable with—*ooh, his teasing innuendos*. "What will it cost to remove the cottonwood?"

"Do you have wind-damage insurance?"

"What does that have to do with how much it costs?" *He still answers my questions with more questions. How annoying!*

His smile was all innocence, his voice a tease. He looked into her eyes. "You haven't changed your style one bit, Susie. All business when something's on your mind. Our price is negotiable, depending on whether we get our money the week we do the work, or if we have to wait for payment by an insurance-adjustment claim check, which might be whenever somebody gets around to it."

"Oh, of course." *He has a sensible reason after all.*

Mitzi went back to the kitchen.

Suzanne watched Taylor's eyes follow her. She remembered Taylor used to have a soft spot for his niece and nephew, probably grownups by now. *I wonder if he has children of his own. Perhaps he doesn't wear a wedding ring, especially when handling power tools. But then, maybe he's a roving bachelor. Why should it matter?*

"I still don't know what your base charge is," she persisted, trying desperately to concentrate before she gave her thoughts away on her face or in her voice.

"I'll have to survey the extent of the project, but it won't take but a few minutes. Come along. I'll explain or you can take my bid sheet to go over with your husband."

"I . . . we won't be able to pay you right away." Her awkwardness resurfaced. Inside she shrank to Mitzi's size, took a breath and blurted, "It may be necessary to sell the wood to pay for your labor."

Taylor shifted his weight from one foot to the other and looked back at the yard full of tree. He chewed at the inside of his lower lip. His eyes returned to hers. "We'll work something out."

The muddle stirred. She didn't want to be obligated, yet the needs of her family had to come before her pride. Being friendly couldn't hurt. Besides, he was a welcome break in her loneliness. "Perhaps when you finish, you'd like a cup of fresh coffee now that we have power again?"

"Um . . . You bet, I remember you make great coffee."

She flushed at memories of sharing more than coffee with him.

Taylor shoved his phone into a pocket of his denim jacket. He uncapped a pen and descended the porch steps, walked the perimeter of the sprawling tree and spent a long time at the place where the raw wound of the stump splintered up between the house and the garage. She waited outside the back door, watching him through the tangled veil of upended leaves. He assessed the garage door damage last, pacing off the distances while he made notes on his clipboard. Finally, he capped the pen and returned.

"Ready for coffee?" she asked.

The Wind Remembers

He hesitated, his face deeply serious. "I think I'd better talk with your husband as soon as he's home."

"That won't be possible."

"Then I think there's something you should see before I remove all the signs. In fact, it may not be wise for me to even do that . . . yet."

She nodded, apprehensive at his seriousness. "Okay, lead the way." *What on earth could make this problem worse?* She stepped down to the driveway behind him.

Following, she tried not to focus on the way his hips moved in his jeans. He squatted on the heels of worn leather cowboy boots. Rain-matted tufts of the tree's cotton clumped here and there in the damp grass. Where the massive cottonwood had risen whole and strong only yesterday, as big around as her family standing tight together in a hug, Taylor pointed to a fresh scar.

Suzanne and Steve had joked about the tree's family-hug size when they first moved in. Now her family was as fragmented as the tree. With effort she dragged her mind to the moment, knelt next to Taylor and studied the flat area of the jagged stump where he was pointing.

"Why, those are saw marks, aren't they?"

"That's right. I can't figure why someone would cut into an old mammoth like this and stop part way through. You're damn lucky whoever did this half-assed job started near the house, so the bulk of the tree fell away into the yard. It could have taken half your house down with it. I hate to think . . ."

Horrified, she choked, "I can't imagine." *Oh, Heavens! The kids could have . . .*

"Suzanne, from the consistency of the resin here, that cut isn't more than days old. If done very long ago, capillary action would have been interrupted and the leaves would have wilted from lack of water." His fingers traced the black circles. "These saw marks are fresh."

"I don't understand." She bit her lip. "This dear old tree wasn't even diseased. I loved it." Her voice quavered to a whisper. Tears gathered on her lashes.

He looked away, giving her time to come to grips with the gravity of the situation, before going on in an all-business tone. "A lot of people can't abide these trees for how they dirty up the lawn when their cotton comes on." He paused. In a softer voice he said, "Perhaps your husband forgot to mention he was having it cut down? Though no reputable pro would start cutting at the bottom of the trunk."

"We fell in love with this old place because of that tree. I just can't imagine who would do such a terrible thing."

"Susie, this trunk is cut nearly two-thirds through. It's mid-June. When it's hot and dry cottonwoods take on all the water they can hold. Each main branch weighs several tons. Come late summer, it wouldn't have taken more than an extra strong canyon wind to topple it, let alone a storm with 65-mile-an-hour winds like last night's. Of course, by then you'd have noticed the leaf atrophy where the branches wouldn't be getting any sap." He stood and looked at her. "Have you heard of any other destruction like this up here on the bench?"

She shook her head no.

"Does anyone have personal grudges against your family, your husband perhaps? Something that happened on his job?"

She defended, "No one has reason to harm us or our property. Besides, if it was cut so recently, where's all the sawdust?"

"Good observation. That's why the job looks deliberate." His fingers probed the long, damp grass around the humped tree roots. He brought up a sizable pinch of seed-studded cotton, rain-matted sawdust and fragrant splinters. "When I drove in, it seemed odd a tree of this size went over without ripping up many roots. You'd better have your husband report the vandalism before I start my clean up."

The porch door opened. Mitzi called from the top step, "Mommy, Greg won't share more Cheerios. You better come make him be good, or me and Bear Lovins will be starved!"

"Come on, Taylor. Let's save the day for Mitzi over a cup

of coffee and a cream-cheese bagel. Then I'll decide what to do."

Life had taken yet another bewildering turn. *Who could have done such a dangerous thing? Why? How could there be so many decisions to make?* Frustrated with Steve for leaving them, the familiar knot in her stomach returned with a vengeance. *I mustn't blame Steve, poor darling. It is what it is. With God's help I'll figure it out.*

She touched Taylor's arm, wanting to explain, but not too much. He looked down at her, waiting. Their eyes met. Her flesh prickled. "Please don't mention anything about this in front of the children. The crash of this tree was scary enough."

"Sure, whatever you say," he said. "But if I were your husband I'd sure as hell want to know who did it—and why. And I'd make them pay to remove and replace this beauty. Both jobs will be pricey."

"Yes, of course." *Pricey, oh lord.*

Taylor supported her elbow while she stepped over a tree branch so thick it came above her knees. His sure touch brought to mind times when being near him was exciting and comforting all at once. When she was steady on both feet, he released her.

Entering the back door with Taylor, feelings erupted with a power she'd never allowed herself to experience for more than a few anxious moments when they'd come so close to being lovers. Instinctively, she inhaled the man scent of him and nearly reeled. Passionate memories filled her with as much apprehension as remembered desire. She shook her head to clear it and led the way into the kitchen.

Greg looked up from his book with a mouth full of cereal, reminding her of a squirrel stashing pine nuts, lately hoarding his pleasures as though if he looked away they might disappear.

"Good morning, son," Taylor said.

"I'm not your son, mister."

"Greg, be polite, please. This is Mr. Armstrong. He's come to help with our fallen cottonwood."

Suzanne watched Greg stare boldly at Taylor, one arm firmly wrapped around the Cheerios box.

"It's not fallen," he said, biting out the words. "It's all the way dead now!"

Suzanne prayed he wouldn't say something else rude to show his distain for her in front of Taylor. She wanted everything to look as if her life was going exactly as it should, *without Mr. Taylor Armstrong, thank you very much.*

"Greg, share the cereal with Mitzi, please."

"And with Bear Lovins," Mitzi insisted.

"And with Bear Lovins," Suzanne repeated, lifting a pair of blue and yellow mugs out of the cupboard. She poured the coffee above the sink with her back to Taylor, so he wouldn't see how badly her hands were shaking. Hearing the cereal box being shoved across the table, she sighed with relief.

"Sit in Daddy's chair, Mr. Armfrong," said Mitzi.

"Thanks, Mitzi, but I've got too much work to do on that big tree in the yard. I need to go soon and check on some other peoples' broken trees, too."

"Still like it black?" Suzanne asked, "or do you add cream and sugar now?" She turned and handed him a mug. Their fingers touched. Electric waves flowed up her arm.

"Black is fine."

Pretending not to notice how Taylor's voice had gone husky, she poured Mitzi's milk and some dribbles into Bear Lovin's bowl. She hurriedly toasted a bagel and brought cream cheese and jam from the fridge. Yanking the silverware drawer open in the old bureau, she pulled too hard and caught it with both hands to avoid dumping forks and spoons on the linoleum. *Get hold of yourself before you do something regretfully foolish!* Mentally, she slowed her racing heart to still her sense of being out of her depth.

Long before meeting her husband Steve, she had tried drowning the longing for Taylor in more painting, more people, less time alone. She'd tried the same strategies to lessen her grieving for Steve after his death. Strategies she read about weren't working any better now than before. Pastor Spahn said things take time. Seeing Taylor like this, unexpectedly, opened old wounds better left alone. She felt an urgency to return outdoors, before Greg embarrassed her again.

"You two clear the table when you finish and go get dressed." She balanced a bagel on top of her coffee mug and held the door for Taylor. "Mr. Armstrong and I are taking our coffee outside to talk about our tree . . . down in the yard."

With one low-cut boot resting on the enormous trunk for balance among the maze of branches, Suzanne listened while Taylor explained what needed to be done. They sipped coffee. He ate his bagel with gusto while she nibbled hers. When their eyes met, something the size of a tennis ball formed in her throat. No amount of hot coffee washed it down.

A Utah Highway Patrol cruiser pulled in next to Taylor's truck. *I should have known Doug would show up about now. When Dierdre arrives, it will get even more muddled around here.* Suzanne waved a hello and took a scalding swallow of coffee.

Taylor turned, his eyes so clear blue she could see the sunlight pass through them. *Still the bluest blue there ever was.* Her heart fluttered with thoughts of when she'd last studied those eyes closer than she stood now.

"Hi, Doug." Suzanne planted both boots on the ground, feeling protective of Taylor and unsure of why. She poured the last of her coffee into the grass.

"Storm make that big baby go over?" Doug asked, picking his way among the leafy tangle to join them. He looked at Suzanne to make the introductions.

"Doug Jensen, meet an old college friend of mine, Taylor Armstrong. Taylor, Doug and my husband Steve were partners over in Davis County."

The two men looked each other over while they shook hands. Doug, lean and good looking, stood close to the same height as Taylor's six-two. Suzanne had recently decided Doug's new and very sparse, blond mustache was probably his macho attempt at an Alan Jackson country-music-star look—probably just for her benefit. Even though Doug was a sweet guy, she just couldn't imagine climbing into bed with him for a lifetime or otherwise. Lately, she sensed that's exactly what he had in mind, and she didn't know how to handle his advances. Being kind and distant didn't seem to deliver the message she intended to cool him off. She intended to ask her twin for advice, which would no doubt come out predictably practical and blunt.

"Just thought I'd swing by on my way in and see how you made it through the storm." Doug rocked back on the heels of his black shoes with his thumbs hooked in the wide leather belt that strapped on his holstered gun. "I remember from our fishing trips my little buddy Greg doesn't like thunder storms one frappin' bit. You must've all been plenty scared when this old cottonwood went over. Why didn't you call me, Suzanne?"

"The phone was out like the electricity. Besides, I didn't want to disturb you when you've been dealing with gang vandalism at all hours lately. Why don't you go in and check on Greg yourself? He's gobbling up the last of the cereal along with that book on insects you brought him. Coffee's fresh. You know where the mugs are."

"I'll do that, and let's plan this little item together." Doug handed her an envelope with a fancy cowboy-boot sticker on the flap. His hand lingered on hers. She withdrew it and stuffed the envelope into her pocket. Puzzlement furrowed Doug's eyebrows. He seemed reluctant to leave her alone with Taylor and didn't pull the porch door all the way closed behind him.

"Maybe he's the guy to tell about this deliberate felling of your tree," Taylor said, interrupting her thoughts. "I mean, if he and your husband were partners in law enforcement and all."

"You're probably right. Mind showing him the saw marks when he comes out?"

"Sort of man-to-man?" He smiled and consulted his watch.

"Something like that, yes."

"Okay. Excuse me while I call in and report. Need to pick up messages about other storm damage, too."

THE WIND REMEMBERS

Suzanne heard a familiar engine noise and walked down to the mailbox. The postal delivery van came to a stop.

"Good morning, Al," she said.

"Morning, Suzanne. Sure a shame you lost that fine old cottonwood. Just about the biggest old pioneer-era tree left on this bench." He handed her a stack of mail and started to pull away. A horn blared. Tires squealed. A battered truck roared by, spitting stones. Suzanne was spattered with an arc of mud. Al was barely able to whip his van onto the narrow shoulder of the road in time to avoid the irrigation ditch swirling with storm run-off. Al shook his head, waved at her, and drove away after the jerk in the truck.

Suzanne looked down at splotches like a row of black coral beads across both legs of her best white jeans. "Oh, damn!" She headed back up the drive to the house.

Taylor leaned against his truck, phone to his ear, taking notes. Suzanne passed him slowly and sat down on the porch step. She set her empty mug on top of the envelopes and picked up the package addressed to herself in her own handwriting. Slitting it open, she pulled out her painting samples wrapped in plastic and bound with rubber bands. Tucked within the bands a paper slip fluttered in the breeze. Her heart sank.

My third greeting-card rejection. This certainly isn't my day. She knew she should go inside to finish her mail, change clothes and treat the mud spots before Dierdre had something to gloat over. But Suzanne didn't want to watch Greg's budding friendship with Doug because it filled her with guilt. Some nights she lay awake praying for patience, for the right words to regain her stepson's love, for an easing to the growing resentment she felt toward Doug for getting the love from Greg she wanted for herself. *God must be sick of listening to me ask for help.*

With her fingernails she slit open a strange business envelope and unfolded crisp, expensive paper. Curious, she skimmed the typed words. The full impact of the letter didn't hit her all at once. With growing dread she read it again more carefully:

The Wind Remembers

Dear Mrs. Steven (Suzanne) Price;

On behalf of Rehma Price, we extend our regrets on the death of your husband, Steven. This letter reminds you that at the time of their divorce, the court did not award sole custody of their children, Gregory Steven and Mitzi Ann Price to your late husband. It is appropriate that they be returned to their natural mother, Rehma Price. A suitable six-month period of mourning has been observed.

Should you be unable to return both children to their mother within thirty (30) days, a court date will be secured. The courtesy of an immediate reply at the letterhead address is requested.

Frank Simmons
Attorney at Law

Suzanne leaped to her feet. Her breath came in gasps. *This is just too much!* She fought back tears. The letter shook in her hands. She crushed the fancy parchment and threw it away from her.

"No, no, NO! It's just not possible!" she cried aloud, stamping her foot in fury.

Taylor hurried toward her. Doug whipped open the door and joined her on the step. Suzanne looked from one man to the other. Taylor stuffed his phone in a jacket pocket and reached an open hand toward her, his blue eyes wide with concern. She was sorely tempted to grasp his fingers, and looked imploringly for support just as Doug took her shoulders in both hands, attempting to pull her into an embrace.

Suzanne twisted away from him. *Oh, no you don't buster!* She snatched the paper from the porch. Picking up the mug and the mail, she stumbled to the door and slammed and locked it behind her. She hung Steve's jacket on its peg and bowed her head into its folds, whispering, "What am I going to do now, God? I promised Steve I'd care for our kids, see they get a proper education, help them grow up strong and happy."

The Wind Remembers

Her shoulders shook. Defeated, she gave way to sobs.

Mitzi appeared at her side and put her arms around Suzanne's legs. Her hands patted and patted. Suzanne's crying subsided. She reached down and stroked her fingers through Mitzi's hair until she felt calm and quiet enough to face her. Bending, she kissed both palms of the sweet hands and gave her little girl the bravest smile she could muster.

When she stood up, Greg looked into her eyes, his face a hostile indictment. Turning, he ran and banged through the swinging door at the far end of the kitchen. Suzanne had no idea how long he'd been watching her cry, perhaps hearing her anguished prayer about his father. She knew better than to call her son back or to follow him. The invisible wall between them went up another row of icy bricks.

CHAPTER TWO

RATTLED

Taylor Armstrong

~Saturday the 14th of June

Taylor Armstrong stood waiting, deciding what he would do. He stared at the door Suzanne had slammed and locked behind her.

"What kicked her switch?" Doug asked, stepping down from the porch to join him in the driveway.

"Something she took out of an envelope. Maybe the one you gave her?" Taylor let the implication hang there and waited for Doug Jensen's reaction. It was slow in coming.

"Not likely *my* envelope." Doug pulled at his trimmed mustache with a thumb and a forefinger. "I've never seen Suzanne come unglued like that."

"She'll get over it; she always does," said Taylor, not eager for Doug to see how it also rattled him to see her so upset.

Doug's brows furrowed and his eyes bored into Taylor's.

"You've seen her take on like that before?"

"Once or twice, sure. It was a long time ago."

By the look on Doug's face, Taylor could tell the patrolman wasn't buying it. For some reason, he found himself enjoying the other man's discomfort.

"You two must have been a lot more than casual friends," said Doug.

"I never said we were *casual* friends. Susie just said we were college friends." *A very controlling guy,* Taylor thought. *Whatever he imagines she and I were to each other is festering in him like a toothache. Is the jealousy for his friend Steve or for himself?*

"Suzanne asked me to show you something before I take this cottonwood away."

He turned, motioning with a tilt of his head for Doug to follow. "This tree going over was no storm-caused fluke. It was weakened by a chain-saw cut, with sawdust evidence removed. Damn good thing it fell away from the house. Could have gone over any time, crushing whatever was in its path. Thank God Susie and her kids weren't hurt."

"You're putting me on," said Doug, at Taylor's heels. They hunkered down by the stump and observed the saw marks. Swirling black and white lines chewed into the growth rings of the massive cottonwood's trunk.

"Well, I'll be damned!" Doug traced the blade marks, sniffed his fingers, looked up—frankly puzzled—at Taylor. "Fresh."

"Bingo."

"Shit! You're the tree expert; what do you make of it?"

"I told you what I make of it. You're the cop. You figure out who did it. My guess is somebody wants to scare hell out of this little family. What I don't fathom is why. I asked Susie who had it in for her husband, especially now that I know his cop background."

"So, what did Suzanne say?"

"She blew off the whole idea, but I could tell it scared

her, probably like it was supposed to." Taylor's pager pulsed and he rose to his feet. "Excuse me a minute. Why don't you file a police report on this vandalism? I'll certify as an expert witness. Somebody out there has a dangerous sense of humor . . . or worse."

Taylor palmed his cell phone and talked briefly to his nephew Randy back at the office, while he made pencil notes on a street map and jotted down some names and addresses. From his truck cab, he watched Officer Jensen continue to study the stump. His neat chocolate-brown uniform with short sleeves bulged with lean muscles. Apparently he got a regular workout. Taylor clicked the phone off and called out the window to him.

"I'll be back in a couple of hours to start cutting the main branches into smaller stuff. By tomorrow, after I work on the trunk, I'll have removed the signs of that chain saw—unless you tell me to do otherwise. Wouldn't want to cross purposes with the law."

Doug pulled at his mustache, circling the trunk. "I'll bring our photographer and shoot these saw marks. We'll hunt down the bastards that did this, you can bet on it."

"Let's hope dropping this tree is the only nasty thing somebody had in mind," said Taylor. He smiled, hoping it looked genuine, since he had no reason not to like the cop, even if he couldn't figure out his more than casual interest in Susie. *Maybe she's divorced from Mr. Price and this guy is the reason. What's it to me anyway?* Still, it rankled him, and the feeling didn't go away.

Doug walked briskly around huge tree limbs to Taylor's driver's-side window.

"I don't like the looks of this, not one f-ing bit. I'll write the report up this morning with you and me as witnesses. I'll have it for you to sign later when I bring the lab photographer. You going to be around about 4:30 or 5:00?" A pair of deep furrows above Doug's straight, Nordic nose emphasized his concern. "Whoever did this is likely to drop by to see the results of his dirty work. We'll be keeping a close eye on Steve's property for him."

"I figure you're doing a good job of that already," Taylor said, grinning. He switched on the ignition and spoke above the rat-a-tat idle of the diesel engine.

"You have some kind of problem with that?" Jensen's voice was gruff, a ploy Taylor guessed he probably used to cover his emotions in hostile situations.

"Where is Steve anyway?" Taylor asked, ignoring the defensive tone in Doug's question. As a child, he'd learned to divert attention from what he didn't want to answer by simply asking another question. It usually worked, giving him more time to come up with an answer he felt more confident he could live with if he had to.

"If you don't already know where Steve is, then you're not a very good old friend of Suzanne's after all." The cop's face relaxed and broke into a grin.

Taylor let it pass. He lifted his hand in farewell, threw his truck into reverse and backed slowly out of the driveway. He knew one thing for sure, Doug wasn't going to make anything easy when it had something to do with Susie Ingram, or Price, as he'd learned her name was now. He knew he was leaving with more unanswered questions than when he drove in and got the surprise of his life on her doorstep.

Well, he had to admit it was the *second* surprise of his life when it came to Suzanne. *Her breaking up with me for no apparent reason blew me away.* Now he had to figure out what, if anything, he wanted to do about getting involved with her—or at least her problems—again. *Is she still married? Is she separated or divorced? Had she never married and had kids with a borrowed name? No, Susie wasn't the live-together type. It just hadn't seemed right to ask and put her on the spot. Why does it matter to me if my questions make her uncomfortable or not?*

The money he thought he'd earn on Old Post Road was a bust. He'd have to put Griff on overtime and hire Randy to pick up and load brush in order to make any major bucks this week. They'd want to know why he was taking on a charity job in the middle of their first big break. He puzzled for a minute on how he'd handle it. *I'll tell them I owed an old friend. Just an unexpected opportunity to pay back an old debt.* He laughed at the irony of who owed whom, but figured that story was as good as any for covering his ass with his men.

There was time to clear the medical center parking lot and bid two or three more jobs before returning to Suzanne's to witness Doug's report. Later, he might have time to start carving up the cottonwood, a mammoth mother. For now he needed to stop at a gas station, then try to make up for the income he'd lost in the last hour.

Exiting off of Old Post Road onto the highway, Taylor watched a red-tail hawk rising high over Francis peak. Patches of snow stood out like irregular daubs of correction fluid on a crumpled green document. He loved this rough, northern Utah mountain country, felt grateful to be back after so many years away. His Pops had called and offered him the opportunity to come back and take over the tree-trimming business in "God's country" since his back and his heart were too unpredictable for him to carry on alone. It had only taken a moment for Taylor to make up his mind. He'd imagined in perfect detail the scene passing by.

Across Great Salt Lake to the west, Antelope Island and the Oquirrah mountains rose crisply against a rare, clear sky. A harrier hawk swooped along the fields, rose, and pumped its wings and took up roost on the uppermost crag of a diseased poplar. Though it was chilly, Taylor kept the window rolled down. He loved the smell of fresh rain, and it took a good blowing storm like last night's to clear the polluted air out of the valley. He remembered his sixth-grade teacher telling him the Ute Indians called it the "valley of smoke" for the way the ring of mountains trapped moisture off the lake, even before smog.

He'd left Utah when the car emissions got so bad the air turned brown, especially where it mixed with pollutants from the oil refineries and the Geneva steel mill. Pops swore the trees had grown susceptible to more diseases with all the pollution. Taylor agreed that was a good reason to take his forestry skills elsewhere. Well, there had been a woman reason, too, but until an hour ago he'd gotten over her. The way his heart had beat faster at seeing Suzanne after years without her and the wrench of seeing her cry, he had to admit she might be the reason he couldn't find a woman to replace her. *Whatever.* He'd come back seasoned and fresh. Utah was home, always would be. He'd had to be away long enough to find that out about himself.

Taylor's sweeping gaze noted tree branches and debris littering the roads, fields and lawns along the highway. Tumbleweed and shreds of plastic impaled on fences and tree branches, hung victim-evidence of last night's gale-force winds. He scribbled notes of possible jobs, elated at the windfall of storm business. The golf course had standing water and branch-strewn fairways; seagulls on the greens gorged on drowned earthworms. Apple, cherry and apricot orchards in Fruit Heights had taken a beating. There'd be golf course and orchard-trimming business for weeks. Taylor's adrenaline pumped on dollar signs.

A train with four engines raced him north beside the old Rt. 89 highway. Even at the 3,500-foot altitude and hauling a half-mile long string of loaded coal cars it made good time. The train and his truck were just about keeping up with Taylor's pulse running on the memory of seeing Suzanne again and his enthusiasm for cramming in as much business as he could, after a slow winter and threatening overhead bills. He pulled into the gas pumps at a Flying J. Swinging down easily from the cab, he waited for the dude cowboy in the rodeo shirt to cap his tank and move his ancient, muddy truck. The very one he'd seen earlier on the road at Suzanne's.

When the man hopped awkwardly from his running board to the ground, Taylor noticed he had a bad leg. His silver belt buckle was big enough to use for a saddle, though as tight as his dirty jeans were, he didn't need a belt to hold them up.

The Wind Remembers

Sidestepping puddles in peeling rattlesnake boots, his limp gave him a strangely graceful, rolling gate.

Following him inside the convenience store to the counter, Taylor lifted the Plexiglas lid on the sweet-roll case. With tongs and a square of waxed paper, he selected a sticky bear claw. He tried to catch the eye of the little redhead at the cash register. Her pregnancy had only recently begun to show, and she'd told him just last week how excited she was about her first baby. The space in front of the counter was tight, with not more than a man's stride to where the door swung in from the outside. He was nearer than he wanted to be to the limping dude who, up close, reeked of cheap hero cologne poorly masking ripe body sweat. The redhead was busy with the cowboy, whose tattooed arm brushed her hip slowly on the pretense of reaching past her swollen belly for a can of chewing tobacco. Taylor's neck hair bristled at the cocky man's boldness. He could tell by the look on her face Red liked it even less than he did.

She rapped her knuckles sharply across his outstretched wrist. "Stay on your side of the counter, Bo. Plenty of chew in the display rack."

The cowboy withdrew his arm, grinning like a kid caught with his hand in the cookie jar.

"Cute doesn't impress me before I've finished my hot chocolate," she added, leaning away from him behind the cash register. Her forced-warm manner was professional polite but her voice had an edge to it Taylor would've taken seriously if he were standing in the guy's once-fancy boots.

The cowboy's handsome face broke into a smile. It would have been stunning if his teeth were clean. He put up both hands in surrender, as if she held a gun on him.

"Aw, Honey, be easy on me. I didn't pull my manners on with my boots. You know how some days I'm a real gentleman."

Taylor was mildly amused, but the undercurrent of tension between them nagged him. He didn't feel good about walking out and leaving a pretty woman alone with the smart ass.

If he's been this bold in front of me, what will he do with no one around to stick up for her?

Uneasy, Taylor gave Red a wink, rolled his eyes and turned back to the pumps. On his way out, he kicked the door prop so it would stay open. He wanted to be sure she made out okay. There was something about the cowboy Taylor didn't trust, like the star of a western movie gone bad. He was too phony, too smooth, too cocky, and crude beyond belief.

Munching a couple of toes off his bear claw, Taylor faced the open door while he prepped the gas pump. He adjusted the waxed paper around the pastry to keep it free of gas and dirt. He hated eating on the run without time to wash up. But he knew he'd better put something besides Suzanne's bagel down in there with all the coffee. As usual, he convinced himself the vitamins in the apple chunks offset the cholesterol. Releasing the nozzle on some diesel fuel, he thrust the metal nose into his gas tank. He'd always liked the smell of gasoline vapors but diesel was less pleasant, even mixed with fresh rain smells. Taylor rubbed a bug spot off his side mirror with the elbow of his jacket. In the mirror's reflection, he caught more of the drama of the cowboy and the redhead.

The dude handed her some bills and tipped his dirty gray Stetson in an exaggerated movie-star gesture Taylor recalled from old Ronald Reagan westerns—and about half as wonderful. She counted change into his heavily ringed fingers. They closed intimately on hers and moved up her arm. She yanked her hand away. Coins scattered, spinning in all directions.

Taylor felt his protective instincts rise to an angry pitch. Ramming the diesel nozzle back in the pump holder, he strode to the door. Hearing him, the dude spun on the boot heel of his good leg.

"Little Bitch," he cursed over his shoulder, bumping into Taylor stepping in through the doorway.

"Give the lady an apology and a hand with your mess," Taylor demanded.

The cowboy put both hands against Taylor's chest and shoved hard. They stumbled into the counter. A chewing gum rack went over, spilling its colorful packages among the coins on the floor.

Taylor gripped the man's wrists to stop a double punch, amazed at the punk's strength.

"I don't apologize to nobody, 'specially women," the cowboy growled. He tried again for a punch, but held captive in Taylor's grip, he caught his balance with difficulty.

"You need someone to rearrange your thinking, or your pretty face," gritted Taylor. "Better yet, why don't you just get on your way and leave this lady alone."

It wasn't a question but a command. Taylor hadn't had the urge to punch anybody out for a long time, but the eagerness to mash the cowboy in the mouth was overwhelming. He reminded himself he was building a reputation for stability in his old hometown; he couldn't risk a fight. Red was embarrassed but okay. He'd let it drop for his Pop's and his business' sake. The other man's powerful hard-muscled biceps strained the sleeves of his dingy rodeo shirt. The wildness in his eyes was more animal than human. He attempted to wrench free. Taylor released his grip and stepped aside, his jaw twitching, his own gaze blazing.

"Smart move, you high and mighty son of a bitch," the cowboy spat at him. He lurched out the door and splashed his way through the puddles, limping across the gravel lot to his pickup, muttering curses to himself.

Taylor watched Bo rip open the mud-spattered door and hike himself up and inside. The engine and the radio roared jointly into action. He slammed his door shut and spat tobacco juice out his open window, driving out onto the highway spinning a flurry of gravel and mud. A pair of hunting rifles in the gun rack of his cab window framed his hunched shoulders and his immense, barking dog.

Taylor's breath came out in a long hiss. His chest heaved with the effort to release his pent-up anger in reasonable control. *Cowboy Bo is a hothead just aching for a fight. Not worth the trouble I almost got into*, he thought, turning back to help Red. The bad smell of the man lingered, churning Taylor's hurried snack to a queasy mass in the pit of his stomach. The redhead was on her knees picking up coins and packages of gum. Tears quivered along her lashes.

"I see Stud Hollywood gets pissed when he doesn't get his way," Taylor said, righting the gum-display rack and giving Red a hand to her feet.

"Thanks." She dropped the coins into the cash drawer and straightened the rack where it belonged. "Bo has a short fuse."

"That's not all he has. How about an ego you need to feed with a steam shovel?"

Red relaxed, smiling back at him. He handed her his gas card and watched her hot-pink acrylic nails flash through the business of creating the copies. He could tell by her flushed face she was embarrassed. He cleaned his hands on paper napkins and checked his watch. *Running tight for time.*

"You handled the Hollywood cowboy like you were getting paid by 20th Century Fox," Taylor said, borrowing a pen from the can on the counter.

"Comes with the territory when you deal with some rodeo retreads like Bo. Most of the cowboys who come in here behave like gentlemen."

"Was he any good in his day?" Taylor scribbled his signature.

"A legend in his own mind, as my Daddy would say." She smiled more easily. "No brew this morning?"

"No, thanks. I'm wired enough already on what I've had. Big day for Armstrong Tree Service after that storm. Going to make some sizable bucks this week."

"Spend some of 'em here." She fluttered her nails in good-bye and flashed him an awkward smile. Over her shoulder she added, "Thanks. I'm real glad you were here."

Nodding, he kicked the door prop back into place on his way out. Once in the truck, he turned on his radio for the news. A few of hours of light had probably given the media time to stir up more storm-damage excitement. Taylor planned to cash in on it and blow his dad's mind with his business success his first year.

Suzanne Price

~ Saturday the 14th of June

Suzanne dabbed the cold water from her eyes with a hand towel, calming herself, alternately trying to think and trying not to choke on the threat from Rehma and her attorney, Frank Whatever. *There is no way I'm giving up these children!*

She passed the family room where Greg sat with the insect book in front of the dead TV, clicking his fingernails together in that irritating, repetitive way he insisted was insect music. Sometimes she wished Steve had never given him the idea of a signal between them when they went off fishing together. If one of them got a bite and didn't want to scare the fish off by hollering, they clicked fingernails. She stepped in and touched his shoulder. He jerked away.

Her hand dropped. "Greg, how does your room look for Aunt Dierdre's visit?"

He sat with his eyes glued to the book, his face hostile.

"Gregory?"

Slouching deeper into his dad's big recliner, he turned his back, propping the book higher between them. His thumbnail flicked the nail on his middle finger in the incessant mini-racket that was pushing her to the breaking point.

"Gregory Price, answer me . . . please." She kept her rising voice kind but firm.

"Why should I? You locked my best friend outside. Doug was gonna plan a fishing trip with me. You're mean. Everything bad is always *your* fault!"

"Let's not argue, Greg. Something came up. I'm sorry about Doug, but I need time to figure out what to do. When you finish that page, go straighten your room. I'll be back to check."

The Wind Remembers

"Why? I never get allowance like my friends when I clean it up anyway. My room's cool the way it is. Nobody has to see it. They can just stay out—except for Doug. He thinks all my bugs and stuff are really cool. Not like some people I know."

There was no point in arguing with him and she wasn't about to explain her stress. He was way too young to understand. These days she was picking her battles carefully. The attorney's letter had been painful enough after her tree going over, let alone the shock of discovering it had been done on purpose. *But who did it?* And there was the surprise of finding Taylor Armstrong on her doorstep after so many years. *How could that be? Why now?* And Doug bringing that dance invitation. *I don't want to go dancing with him! Being in his arms all night will only make people think I'm letting him replace Steve. That is one thing I am absolutely certain about.*

Not feeling up to handling any more conflict, she moved away from Greg and down the hall.

Mitzi's voice drew her to the doorway of the living room. She'd posed a row of stuffed animals, with Bear Lovins in the middle, on the couch and sat pretend-reading *Peter Rabbit* in a dramatic voice.

Suzanne retreated to her room and closed the door. After changing her jeans, and putting the stained pair to soak in the tub down the hall, she returned to the bedroom and one by one polished the framed keepsake photos on the nightstand. Remembering all the good times usually had a steadying effect on her. She rubbed the glass protecting her and Steve feeding each other wedding cake. Today she felt only emptiness. It seemed like a century ago, another lifetime. It was as if some couple she had never known smiled happily at her with frosting faces.

She swabbed at the nightstand and replaced the picture in its hallowed spot. Lifting a snapshot of Steve, Greg, and herself on a camping trip, her fingers traced the smiles on all their lips. She caressed them with the towel to erase her fingerprints. Returning the frame to its place, she grasped one of Steve in his uniform receiving a plaque for heroism from the chief. She'd been so proud of him. The plaque still hung above the big TV in the family room. He'd asked to see it the week he died, when he was too weak to leave their bed. She'd held it for his inspection. Tears had formed at the corners of his eyes, which he'd closed and waved her away.

The last frame was a hinged pair of candids: Mitzi riding on Steve's shoulders to the table for her first birthday cake, and Steve showing Greg how to bait a fish hook. The pictures brought no comfort or renewed purpose at all. Her rising anger surprised her. *Has all this pain and love and sacrifice been for nothing? Are these children, all I have left of a good family life with Steve, to be ripped from me and given to his pathetic ex-wife? Is Rehma the focus of my anger? No . . . something else—the argument!*

That was it. The first and last nasty argument she and Steve ever had. She'd felt terribly guilty about fighting with a dying man. It had been ugly and brutal between them. Now she realized full well how important it had been for her to win, but she'd lost. *I'm angry with Steve—and myself!*

She sank down on the bed. Their bed. Why hadn't she continued to press him earlier while he was still strong enough to consider why she might need formal custody of his children to care for them without him. She was the parent left with the responsibilities for his children. *He should have made it easier for me. Now . . . well, now it's going to get really hard.*

Suzanne recalled how Steve simply couldn't believe Rehma would ever want the burden of two children she'd never cared enough about to stay off drugs and other men in the first place. Near the end, he hadn't had the energy to put to a concern he couldn't relate to. He was out of reserves, down to just the strength to let go of life. She'd relented, promising to take care of the children no matter what. She'd stroked his bony forehead, the dear face that had aged ten years in as many weeks and had become serenely childlike. She'd kissed him gently and turned out the light.

The Wind Remembers

The next morning, Janet, the hospice nurse, arrived to refresh his morphine drip and assist with his bath. They'd gone in and laid out everything required for his comfort. She spoke to him softly. His kind eyes had sought hers, all love and forgiveness for the bitter words of the night before. She remembered kissing his fingers and tucking them under the blanket, saying she loved him and something about fixing some coffee and helping the children get ready for school. She'd whispered she'd be right back. When Suzane returned, Steve had lapsed into a coma. She stood spilling a thin stream of coffee onto the carpet until Janet took the pot from her hand and led her to a chair. What followed had been two quiet days and nights of waiting until he drew his last breath in her arms. Her guilt at arguing with him haunted her all those hours and even now.

After Steve's death, Pastor Spahn said when a spouse is dying and important issues are unfinished, fights happen more often than one might think. They are sometimes a way to release all the pain of losing each other. Steve died three mornings after that terrible argument. But now the very security she'd argued for, a formal piece of paper giving her custody over his children was not available to protect Gregory and Mitzi, to protect herself from the loss of what was left of her family. *It looks like I'll have to fight to keep my promise to Steve.* She had nothing but her love for Mitzi and Greg to back up that promise, not even a job to pay for going to court for them nor a legal will.

The anger that surfaced moments ago dissolved. She must find a way, money or no money, to fight the court system that wanted to return the children to their birth mother. *It might be different if Rehma had a good Christian life to offer her children, but she's restless, wild, without direction. What can she offer them now?* Suzanne struggled with where she should begin.

She opened the bureau drawer where she'd crammed Steve's personal papers, his filled note pads and his saved news clippings about cases he'd worked. She'd put off sorting through them. Sometimes, when she missed him the most, she opened the drawer just to look at his familiar handwriting. One day soon she'd force herself to see if there was anything important, then toss the rest. She took out the folder of forms she'd brought home from their safety deposit box. It seemed silly to pay $60 a year for a safe-keeping place outside their home, when she had so little money. She searched each folder pocket until she came to Steve and Rehma's divorce decree. Rereading it, the document verified the attorney's letter of that morning. It was true. Suzanne had no legal right to keep her promise to Steve or to herself. *The children can legally be taken from me in thirty days! Oh, Lord. What am I going to do?*

Putting the decree back, she fought to stay focused on practicalities and pulled out the insurance agreement for the house. Wind damage was covered, but there was nothing about malicious vandalism. Maybe she wouldn't mention to the insurance agent that the tree had been deliberately sawed to make it fall. Her conscience recoiled from the dishonesty, and yet . . . *what to do? Taylor said it would take at least three truckloads to haul it away. It's going to be expensive.*

What if he only trims the wood into manageable pieces and I sell it myself? There wouldn't be a hauling fee then.

But Suzanne knew she didn't have the tools or the experience to split all that green wood herself. *Why does everything have to be so difficult?*

The tree problem must be solved quickly so she could get on to the pressing needs of keeping the children and finding a job to cover expenses and prepare for a court fight. Perhaps she could dip into the children's bonds made out in both her's and Steve's names, the one thing she could be grateful he'd done to ease turning them into cash if anything happened to him in the line of duty. The $50,000 in bonds were stored at the bottom of Steve's locked metal hand-gun box under the basement stairs with his golf clubs. Would it really be so bad to use a portion of the education fund for an attorney of her own to fight Rehma in court? Was it even right for her to fight for the kids or was she just trying to keep her word to a dying husband? She would've promised anything to ease Steve's misery. Still, she was desperate. *I could borrow from those just until I have a job, then pay it back. That would take care of some legal advice and the tree removal.*

She decided to tell Taylor she could pay quickly for his services and rid herself of one stress-building situation while she figured out how to solve keeping the children.

Pastor Spahn would help. She picked up the phone and punched in the numbers she knew by heart. The church answering machine said he'd be away at conference board in Denver, Colorado all week. Suzanne hung up in despair. Perhaps some other answer to her prayers would come about. They always seemed to come from such surprising places. *I must have more faith.*

Her mind stewed on her challenges while she replaced the papers in Steve's drawer, changed the sheets and straightened the room. Shoving the clothes in her closet to one side, she made room for Dee's things. There would be lots of them.

Dierdre, would she be of any help? Suzanne doubted it. When Janet made calls for her the day Steve died, Dee insisted she couldn't arrange to come and be with her—no explanation. Suzanne knew how her twin hated funerals and sadness, but she hated to put herself out for someone else just as much. No, Dierdre would be of no actual help in this custody fight, but for certain she'd have plenty of advice about what Suzanne should do. *Maybe to save an argument, I won't tell her about any of my problems. I don't think I could survive one of her holier-than-thou lectures. If she believed in Jesus she might be more compassionate and less self-righteous.* Suzanne straightened the comforter. *Who am I kidding? I wish I'd never made plans with Dee to be at the Sun Tunnels on the solstice.* Time was all she had and little of it for a custody fight with Rehma. Dierdre would want to play and have fun. Suzanne would be short on patience and money. Her mind returned to the children. What if she packed up the kids and took them somewhere like she'd never received the letter. *Could I pull it off?*

The Wind Remembers

But the police would find her and take them away, then charge her with kidnapping. She'd heard enough stories from Steve and Doug to tell her how fruitless such a plan would be without enough money to leave the country, which was rarely successful even for those who took the risk.

Rehma never called or visited while Steve was bedridden at the end. She'd never wanted to be bothered with Gregory and Mitzi before. *Why now?* Suzanne's turmoil felt physically overwhelming. She sat back down on the bed and closed her eyes.

Lord, she prayed, *this custody problem is as big as cancer. I have to fight it and this time I have to win. Show me what to do. You know I promised Steve I'd bring up his kids and see they have a college education. Please give me the grace and wisdom to do what's right to keep us together as a family. Thank you for all the strength you've given me so far. Forgive my lack of faith. I've lost Steve. I can't bear to lose Gregory and Mitzi, too. Amen.*

She lay back on the comforter and opened her eyes. *There will be a way. I must never stop believing.*

Tap, tap. The door handle turned and Mitzi peeked in. She tapped her knuckles once more on the doorframe. "Mommy, are you crying again?"

"No, honey. I . . . I was just resting."

Suzanne sat up and opened her arms. Mitzi ran into them.

"Do you want a bear hug, Mommy? A real grizzar?"

"Oh, just a regular bear today, until I get my strength up."

They embraced, giggling, and squeezed.

"Time for your bath, young lady, so you'll be fancy for Aunt Dierdre."

Mitzi shook her head so hard her curls tumbled into her blue eyes.

"Not right now."

"Well why not, sweetheart? You love bath time with your rubber toys."

"'Cause you and me and Bear Lovins better check on

The Wind Remembers

Gregory. He's been in my room doing some trouble on my new mural you made."

"What?"

Suzanne ran down the hall and into Mitzi's empty room. Greg had been doing some trouble all right. Paint cans she'd closed last night when the storm came up and the lights flickered, were now open. Insect parts floated on little round seas of red, green and blue. Where the garden on the wall blossomed, splotches of wet red paint suspended dead crickets and ants on half a dozen dripping flowers.

"Gregory Price!" Suzanne shouted. "Get your little buns in here *this minute!*"

"Is my pretty mural all ruined like our tree, Mommy?"

"No, Mitzi, I can fix your mural. But not 'til after I fix your brother."

CHAPTER THREE

FAMILIAR GROUND

Dierdre Ingram

~Saturday the 14th of June

Coming back to Utah was always hell on her skin. Dierdre felt the dryness even in the jetway when she deplaned at Salt Lake International. The assault of desert air gave her the urge to unzip her bags and slather on moisturizer. Better yet, at Suzanne's she'd break open her Vita Bath and indulge in warm bubbles up to her chin. She shifted her shoulder bag and imagined soaking for at least one restorative hour in her sister's deep, claw-footed tub in the old farmhouse. Suzanne had once accused her of spending her entire visit in that tub. Dierdre loved the way the stained-glass window spilled colors on mounds of scented bubbles. If she could get there within the next couple of hours—before the children's bath time—there would still be enough light left for the full effect.

The Wind Remembers

Lord, she was even thinking like arty Suzanne, whom she hoped would be prompt. It was hours since she'd left New York, and more since Florida on a red-eye after midnight, and a miserable layover in Chicago after a fierce storm rerouted her flight. Dierdre imagined scenarios of how she'd put the children's questions off with promises of presents until she could soak herself into a vacation frame of mind. She had reservations about whether coming was a good idea for herself or for Suzanne.

"Paging Dierdre Ingram to a white courtesy telephone," the concourse speaker voice droned.

What on earth would anyone want to page me for? She threaded her way through the crowd and picked up a phone. Listened, said her name, listened to the recorded message and hung up in disgust.

"I don't believe it!"

"Problem Darlin'?" The man in the open pay-phone booth next to her appeared amused. He wore the cap and uniform of an airline pilot.

"My ride can't meet me. I'm on my own."

Dierdre consulted her watch, figured the time difference, puzzled over the sudden change of plans—so unlike Suzanne. She acted as if she were ignoring the pilot, but noticed he replaced the receiver in its holder. Lowering her head so her hair swung down over her cheek, she rummaged through her handbag.

The pilot removed his topcoat and pocketed change. He picked up Dierdre's overnight bag and his own.

"You look like a woman who could use a cocktail and a shoulder."

"A cocktail perhaps, but I don't do sob scenes—even on shoulders as inviting as yours."

He smiled at her.

She warmed to the game.

"My treat then. Let's head for the Crown Room Lounge," he steered her by the elbow. "We'll get away from the crowd."

Pretty smooth, she thought, inhaling expensive musk. *The best thing that's happened since leaving La Guardia on a morning from hell.* With effort she kept up with him, clicking along in Capezio stilettos too high to be practical, but sexy enough to attract the sort of male help she was used to receiving.

"Am I going too fast for you?" he asked.

"I imagine you've gone too fast for a lot of helpless women." She laughed, softly, deliberately.

He chuckled. "I doubt you're so helpless there'd be anything about me you couldn't handle . . . effectively."

He opened the door of the private lounge. She looked up at unusual gray eyes with sun-creased smile lines spreading out in little fans. She imagined fingering them delicately in bed after a glass of champagne or a cigarette. He flashed his membership card to the host and led the way to a table by the window. Dierdre noticed he'd taken the private table with a wall on one side and an imposing potted fichus on the other. He'd done this before. She didn't mind in the least.

Seating herself, she crossed her long legs for his benefit, watching without speaking while his gray eyes traveled from the split in her skirt to her ankles and back again. She wondered if he'd introduce himself first or expect she'd notice Capt. E. Nelson on his lapel name bar and cut straight to the topic of drinks. She bet on the drinks.

"What's your pleasure?" he asked.

"Are we talking about drinks?"

His right eyebrow rose to the brim of his cap, which he removed and dropped casually on top of his coat in the extra chair. He ran his fingers through the kind of thick hair she'd like to play in. His smile reached his eyes and he nodded.

"Then I'll have Crown Royal on the rocks, squeeze of lime."

Dierdre watched him retreat to the bar. She liked the way he moved, trim and lean, carrying his shoulders straight but easy in the crisp black uniform with the gold-braid trim. She liked a man in uniform—or out of uniform—if he were the right sort of man. The trick was finding a safe one. The sort she could enjoy without entanglements. Eventually she'd snare a nice rich man with no children of school age. But until then . . .

Captain Nelson returned with a glass in each hand and set one down in front of her. He lingered for a moment studying her before seating himself in the opposite chair. He extended his legs so the crease of his pants brushed the length of her calf. She waited, tingling with the sensual pleasure of crisp fabric kissing silk and skin. It occurred to her that Suzanne not being here to meet her might have opened new doors for fun before she'd have to be good around Miss Perfectly Correct for ten iffy days.

"Eric Nelson to your rescue." He lifted his glass in mock salute.

"Dierdre Ingram, grateful to be rescued." She felt the iced whiskey travel straight to the pit of her stomach and start a fire.

"I'm deadheaded here with three hours to kill before they fly me to Honolulu. How about you, Dierdre? Lovely name, Darlin'." His tone flowed over her easily along with his eyes.

"I'm on my way to Farr. I'll order a shuttle or a taxi. At the moment I'm not up to fighting the baggage crowd for my clubs. Thanks for the drink."

"My pleasure. But Darlin', nobody who's anybody goes to Farr, at least not for golf. Skiing of course, but golf? Nah. And you definitely look like a somebody."

His smile was warm, promising. Dierdre was on familiar ground. She slowed things down a little. There was enough time to take the game at any speed she wanted; She felt her power as intoxicating as the whiskey. Sipping slowly, knowing he watched, she looked through and beyond the window. A cloud paused high up on the mountain peak across the network of runways. In an analogy, she toyed with the idea of which one of them would be the mountain and which one the cloud. She waited until the puff of white moved on and turned her head to meet his intent gaze.

"My twin sister lives in Farr."

"Hard to imagine another woman like you."

The Wind Remembers

"Actually, though we're twins, that's where the resemblance ends. We're not identical—*totally* different." They both sipped; their eyes locked.

"What are your plans, staying long?" He re-crossed his legs.

"I was going to travel yesterday, but I'm a little superstitious about Friday the 13th. So, I'll be in Utah about ten days, just for the solstice. We've been planning to visit the Sun Tunnels in the desert."

Dierdre adjusted her necklace so his eyes could follow the crystal heart into the opening of her silk blouse where it disappeared between her full breasts. He kept his eyes on hers, surprising her with his control. He would make it last; she was sure of that . . . what a delicious thought.

"Sun Tunnels?" he asked. "Some new attraction at Lagoon Amusement Park?"

She laughed, more freely this time, watching her effect on him. He approved, and moved his leg against hers once more.

"New York sculptor Nancy Holt designed concrete tunnels in the desert. Four times a year the light bursts through them at dawn on the equinoxes and solstices," she explained, wanting her name-dropping to impress him.

"This sculptor a friend of yours?"

"No, I heard about her at a Manhattan gallery opening. I was intrigued with the way she camped out in the early '70s and studied the positions of the cliffs and the stars. She figured out precisely where the tunnels had to be placed for the light-burst effect. Nancy wanted them to work like Stonehenge. The Utah site where she purchased more than 40 acres is the best on the planet. Suzanne and I made a pact to be there at dawn on the twenty-first of June. First visit for both of us."

"You don't look like the type who'd crawl around in the desert with sand and scorpions. Hard on silk stockings and delicate lingerie."

He laughed and took a slow swig of his Manhattan. He seemed to undress her with his eyes, taking his own good time.

The Wind Remembers

Dierdre relaxed into the accustomed territory of this man-woman game; the only game she liked better than golf. She just wasn't sure how much longer she could hang onto the looks it took to play it at this risky level.

Returning the conversation to his earlier question, she said, "I don't have three hours. I want to get to Farr. It's been a long trying day. I'll need about a quart of moisturizer all over my body to keep from aging ten years in ten days."

"Like a ride? I could pick up a rental, buzz you there, and still make my flight. We'd have time to make some plans. I often have layovers in New York. You could show me around."

"You're more than kind, Eric, but . . . I wouldn't want to confuse my niece and nephew or—upset your wife."

Dierdre gestured to the white line she'd been eyeing on Eric's tanned ring finger, where she assumed a wedding band was worn most of the time.

"My wife's in San Francisco. We have . . . an understanding."

"I'm sure you do."

Dierdre had few no-no rules, but 'no married men' was rule number one. She never allowed herself to actually climb into bed with even the most desirable of legally committed men. Eric was attractive and exciting, but not so exciting she'd risk messy social or wife complications. She set her empty glass down on its paper napkin.

"I have a room near here," he said, pulling out cigarettes, offering her one.

"No thanks, I have my own."

"Your own room?" Grinning, he lit up.

"Cigarettes."

She took her time with the flat, flowered package, pulling out one thin cigarette. She knew he watched her long fiery-red nails, probably imagining them moving enticingly on his skin. The game was nearly over, but she liked making him wait to find that out.

"I don't have trysts with married men." She turned and faced him, triumphant at landing the first blow of the finish.

"A crying shame," he said.

She watched him prepare to launch his seduction with one final attempt and wondered what the last ace to his game would be. She took another long drag and played it out, giving him room on her mental stage to complete his performance. It was better than sitting in the audience of a Broadway show. Her twin had never understood this kind of drama, never approved. So much for dear Suzanne and her boring little life.

"You seem to be a woman of the world," Eric exhaled the words with his smoke. "We could meet occasionally most anywhere there's a major airport. Could be exciting—just between us—or we could add my wife. She's game."

Well, I'll be damned! Now there's a fresh approach. She had to give him credit. *I underestimated his ace.* She struggled to think of a sassy comeback. Leaving him with the last word was unthinkable. Mentally, she watched him spread his hand face up, every card on the table, shocking her into an awareness of just how far he would go, probably had gone before. He had stacked his chips, said what he wanted. She liked his brassy way of going for it. She let him think she was weighing his proposition.

Dierdre stubbed out her cigarette and focused on the way the lipstick-stained filter merged with the ashes of his cigarette in the glass tray between their drinks. She looked out the window. The mountains remained unmoved. She liked the full-circle analogy, as though the magnificent backdrop of their stage play had a part in the final curtain scene. She the cloud that floated away, and he the mountain of rock stuck in his own mud. It was so satisfying. She looked over at him through her long dark lashes. Smiling with energy, she sat forward.

"What if we fell in love?" She played her own trump.

"We're too smart and experienced for that," Eric said.

She knew he would. "I meant your wife and I."

His unguarded surprised face, for the moment he allowed it, was her victory.

"It might have been fun, even at that," she said, rising abruptly, not wanting to give him time to recover.

"No doubt in my mind," he said. Keeping his eyes on her, he dashed out his butt next to her filter tip and rose.

"Thanks again for the drink, Eric."

"Watch your lingerie in those tunnels, Dierdre, and chuck the spike heels for your own safety."

It's been sport for us both, she thought. "I'm sure I'll be just fine. I don't dress like this all the time."

"That's what I was hoping to discover, Darlin'."

"I know."

They shook hands. A truce of sorts. They were parting as respectful adversaries, a twist to the game she hadn't expected. He carried their bags to the bar, where he ordered another drink, giving her time to gather her carry-on and her handbag.

She chose not to say good-bye and kept her last words to him as a mental souvenir, backing away, facing him.

He touched his cap brim in farewell and picked up his fresh drink. She smiled tentatively and turned, retreating from him in a slow sensual walk learned on the fashion runway, imagining his eyes on her. At the doorway she paused to shift her carry-on to open the door and looked back at him—expectant.

Eric had carried his drink to the table of a blonde stewardess. He sat down and whispered something to her. They laughed together. Their hands touched. Dierdre felt like kicking herself in the tush, but decided not to allow herself to feel foolish. After all, she'd come out one drink ahead of the game and had a brief flirtation before the ordeal of baggage claim and the hour-long ride north to Farr. There'd always be another man.

For the first time since answering her page, she asked herself why Suzanne—ever the punctual twin—had stood her up. Dierdre hoped it was nothing serious. She'd had enough of serious on her last trip to Farr. This time she wanted to have fun and relax, maybe mend some fences with her sis. She owed her. She'd begin with a sumptuous bath, probably by candlelight now that her arrival would be much later than planned. Suzanne would expect her to sit up talking until all hours, but she didn't feel like it.

Besides, Dierdre didn't want to get their visit off to a bad start by telling her sister to get on with her life, which she inevitably did during their weekly phone catch-ups. She doubted Suzanne had put the painful past behind her since their most recent conversation in the last few days. The nagging doubt about this visit being far less depressing than the last scratched again at the door of Dierdre's mind. Things with Suzanne hadn't been relaxing or fun in a long time. Dierdre wondered if she'd made a mistake coming back to her hometown and proposing they camp-out for the solstice. Waiting in the chilly darkness for dawn to break through the Sun Tunnels with two cranky kids and one down-in-the-mouth sister could spell disaster.

Suddenly, Dierdre wished she'd never suggested the solstice camping idea in the first place. But, since she'd bragged to everyone on the cruise-ship staff about going into the desert to visit the site of those intriguing Sun Tunnels, she'd have to go ahead and see it through. Her closest spirit-seeking girlfriends would be eager for a solstice report.

Besides, only God Himself knew how her sister could change her worried mind and come up positive after praying about whatever it was that troubled her. It was a spiritual gift she envied but was unlikely to ever admit to her twin. Dierdre smiled to herself as she balanced her overnight bag on the rail of the moving walkway.

God would be the one to know what her sister needed, all right. For sure as hell, devout Suzanne would have talked it all over with Him in infinite detail.

Chapter Four

Felon, The Wind

Johnny Carlisle

~Saturday the 14th of June

"Would you like us to bring you another cocktail, Johnny?"

Carlisle looked up at the old man, thirty some years his senior. Seemed like everyone in St. Petersburg was Johnny's senior. Much as he loved the Florida sun, the sight of old people gave him the sick feeling he was one of them way before his time. Old like his father and many of the feeble, wasted bodies of the white-tops in his physical therapy class.

"Yeah, Mr. Levenson, I could use another whiskey."

Johnny handed his empty mug to the nice old Jew from Queens, a retired shoe salesman. In St. Pete you learned everybody's historical highlights in the first five minutes after an introduction. Hearing old people ramble on about who they *used* to be had struck Johnny years ago like pre-game highlights in pro sports. The first time he brought Ginny south for spring holidays, it'd been a welcome, warm vacation when Utah was still getting fresh snow. His dad bought them airline tickets to surprise his mother for her sixtieth birthday. He remembered arranging the falcon tending and hunting to be handled by his great Uncle Vince, who'd let him apprentice in falconry when he was fourteen. Now Vince, like just about everything else that had mattered in his life, was gone too. Back then, Ginny'd never been east of the Mississippi. She was excited about heading for the beach, the surf, the sand, and the sun. In three days, she was too sun-fried to wear a bra. They'd laughed about it for years—the good years.

He watched Levenson and his wife retreat with the mug. *Damn mug.* He despised having to order his liquor in a mug so he could hold it without dropping it.

His dad suggested, "Nobody will pay you no mind, Son. Your pride gets in the way of your sense." Johnny admitted it helped to have a handle to wedge his fingers in. He hadn't dropped a drink here at the American Legion yet.

He saw other Korean War vets like himself, but older, entering the dance hall with their wives. They commented on his physical improvements a couple of weeks ago, while swapping war stories when everyone was driven inside by a sudden squall. These were all good people. Most of the men brought women or came to find them. Widows were eager for companionship, and Vet Post management never turned them away.

His thoughts returned to his Ginny, sunny-disposition, affectionate, self-centered Ginny, the kind of woman who needed a man to lean on who would fuss over her and take her places. When Johnny was laid up in the hospital for weeks, fighting for his life, it'd been too much for her. He shook his head to clear his mind. He shouldn't think about Ginny or their boys. It always gave him the urge to run after them, only he knew he'd never run after anyone again. But he'd begun to believe he could take his time and see justice done by going after one vile bastard, even if it took him the rest of his life. His mind sometimes couldn't stay on track for long, but it always came back to what'd been taken from him and how it'd been done. Mean, low, senseless and brutal. Like being back in Korea, only then he'd been psyched to expect ambush and no mercy. He'd never expected it in the safety of his own falcon mews.

"Here you go, Johnny. Me and the Mrs. are going inside for bingo. You have everything you need?"

Carlisle looked up at Levenson who stood with his neat, white boat shoes planted firmly on the pier, one of them bulging from a hammer toe, his face wizened and his extended fingers crippled with arthritis like his humped spine. He gave Johnny time to take the chilled cocktail with both hands. His tiny, wrinkled and tanned wife remained a little way off.

"Guess this mug springs a leak now and again," Johnny said, laughing awkwardly. "Liquor level drops awful fast on me sometimes."

He took the mug and dipped his head in thanks. It wasn't that he didn't know better than to skip the audible pleasantries of "thank you" and "good-bye," it was just that he was sick of thanking strangers for their help. Sick of needing anyone's help. Sick of being trapped in a half-man's body. That's how he thought of his awkward legs and fingers, his often-muddled mind. It didn't serve him well if he messed up his meds.

Carlisle sat back in the deck chair and watched the old folks drift inside the Legion Hall to join the bingo action and share stories over another chicken barbecue, put on by the Ladies Auxiliary. His dad was in there somewhere like the others, schmoozing old broads for a dance by plying them with large quantities of cheap booze. He'd tired of listening to their syrupy brand of beachcomber bull crap, often delivered through slipping false teeth. Johnny hated seeing his dad flirt at his age, yet he envied him, too. Envied him plenty for an eighty-one-year-old body that still danced and played shuffleboard and often held a grateful woman.

Johnny's mom wouldn't have minded that her husband could still have a good time. He remembered she was fond of telling her bridge girls, her old-lady friends, "Denver Carlisle's always been a good and faithful husband." She'd told Johnny from her hospital bed, "You tell your dad to find another wife—and make it snappy. He can't cook his way out of a paper bag." That had been eight years ago. A lifetime ago. Recently, he'd been going to therapy in the same hospital where she died. Now his dad did most of the cooking.

Johnny Carlisle was sick of being taken care of. He wanted to do things for himself. Even though he was getting better, his dad still insisted on doing most everything for him. They'd had a row about it yesterday and made up by coming here together. Thank God he and his dad always loved one another enough to forgive. His dad was worth forgiving. Some people weren't.

The sun moved to the west, glinting the purpling harbor water with ripples of burnt orange. The tide had turned. Johnny looked forward to the evening here at his favorite spot in St. Pete. A vet, he could afford the discounted drinks, and the members bragged this was the best American Legion Post in the nation. "Nobody else's got a pier on a harbor. You stick with us, Johnny. If those fellows in the post across the bay was smart, they'd haul ass over here and put in with us. 'Course we wouldn't be bringin' 'em on without a hefty fee." There had been laughing and clinking glasses all around. The bartender had handed him his first whiskey straight up in a beer mug with the frosty handle dried off.

He winced at the humiliating memory, making him feel old, ancient and feeble, or maybe little, childish, like a baby. For the first time in his recovery, he hadn't dribbled his drink. He never had to ask for a mug after that, no matter who tended bar. When he ordered his whiskey it came in a dry-handled mug out of respect. Everyone passed the word. Vets did that sort of thing for each other. It moved him to tears then. Weeping still came too easily.

A salty breeze blew sea smells across the water and riffled the fronds of the palmettos and palm trees shading the thatched cabana. Colored lights strung around the patio bar bobbled speckle patterns in the expanse of harbor. He propped his tanned legs on the bottom rung of the pier rail and watched the scene between his scarred knees. Happy voices and laughter at the outdoor bar made him feel almost like he was part of a family again. His favorite place and time. He would miss it.

Gulls and pelicans swooped for fish in the frothing wakes of fishing boats coming in after a day's work and show-off speed-boat drivers whirled wakes that slapped the pilings. Only a couple of shrimpers came in past this pier, squawking gulls swarming them like eager bees to blossoms. Then the sign he'd been watching for: dark fins cutting the water about three-hundred yards out where the current was strongest. Dolphins coming in to feed on the mullion and other small fish running with the tide. Carlisle gripped the mug and sat forward, straining to see every nuance of movement, squinting to catch sight of where each dolphin would surface next.

Untamed, beautiful, graceful, free. The dolphins arched through the current, over and under, as though an invisible hand pulled them by a string beneath the water. They broke the surface, dived below, frolicked among the waves, the last rays of sun breaking golden light across their smooth, wet backs and tails. The dolphins, the wild birds; he envied them all.

Johnny Carlisle was ripped by this time. Four-whiskies mellow, he wished himself floating free of his impaired body, out onto the water, walking like Jesus. He imagined startling the fishermen and the boaters who would drop what they were doing to watch him dance across the waves to join the dolphins. Or maybe he'd just float right up into the air with the pelicans and gulls, the way he used to dream of joining his falcons while they soared on thermals above him—out of sight—watching for prey. Then they'd return when his pointer flushed game birds, or he released homers for them to pursue in training and trials. Thinking of his falcons, his prize gyrfalcon Felon, and his favorite well-seasoned pointer, filled him with an indescribable pain worse than anything he'd endured since waking from a coma to the face of a kind police officer, the stranger who befriended him.

He poured the rest of the whiskey down in one long gulp, trying to erase the flood of anguish that threatened to make him cry on the pier in front of everyone. The memory of his falcons and his hound's light coat splattered with blood that night a few months ago came to Johnny's mind in 3D Technicolor, with Dolby-like sound.

He recalled feeling the contentment of a successful training session with Felon, talking about her to his younger birds while he returned the last hen to set the newest clutch of peregrine eggs. The mood was broken by the sharp yip and moan of his hound outside. Opening the door of the mew to the night sky, seeing her bloody body sprawled on the step, he felt the first bone-crunching blow break through his collarbone and his shoulder joint, leaving his right arm dangling useless at his side.

He remembered stumbling backward, struggling to clear his head to think of danger—survival—but the blows kept coming. Blood oozed into his eyes and blotted out the possibility of recognizing his attacker. Lately, he'd remembered that below the snarling ski-masked face, he'd grabbed at something large and shiny on the man's clothes. Then the pain and the noise had filled his mind while he fought to stay conscious.

Last evening, while watching television he'd seen what'd escaped his mind for so long. Putting it together with the outfit on the jerk in the bar earlier that same long-ago evening, this time he'd be able to tell the officer who his attacker'd been. He could describe him for sure now. All he needed was help in finding the dirty-low-down thug, for surely someone would know his name. His heart beat almost as fast as it'd pounded in his chest that terrifying night.

Again he replayed it, heard the cracking sounds of splintering wood and breaking bones, the last he remembered as he tried to fight the intruder brandishing what the cop surmised was a tire iron. The memory of that night and those to follow were the epitome of Johnny's suffering—the source of his determination to find the man who'd left him for dead; killed his pointer, with a single vicious blow to her skull; destroyed his mew and his marriage—and stolen Felon.

The gyrfalcon he'd bred in captivity and taken to view her first Sky Trial meet was the bird he loved most, and she'd trusted him. Carlisle weighed her regularly on his brass scales and hunted with her on Uncle Vince's ranch, faithfully exercising her to keep her in peak hunting condition. He received as a loving reward her animated dancing and throat sounds, and always felt the honor of her trust when she returned to his glove.

More innocent than Ginny and the boys who'd made their choices, Felon had few, being totally dependent upon Johnny. He was always available to teach an apprentice falconer or two to pass on the joys of the ancient, artful sport of falconry. It'd been as satisfying an obsession as Johnny's commitment to falcon breeding and training. Years earlier, it helped preserve the endangered raptors, and he valued teaching his sons how to take the hawks hunting for their necessary wild prey.

He bit his tongue until he tasted blood mixed with whiskey, wondering if his boys ever missed the birds and their dad. It seemed no amount of booze and time washed away the pain of his losses. They were joys he could never share again. Falconry took a sensitive mind keen on reading the birds. It took physical speed and flexibility as well as strength and timely commitment. He'd been encouraged that physical therapy could restore his quick reaction skills with raptors. But it hadn't taken him long to learn no matter how much of his body strength he restored, his mind didn't always work right. His dad argued that was bullshit. Still, Johnny felt he'd lost it, lost who he was as a falconer and a man. What Ginny called his hobby had been a consuming passion equal to his pride in his family—both over. Recalling the reality of his life now nearly crushed his spirit.

Ginny'd told him she'd felt second to his birds for fifteen years, and being second to his needs for physical tending and his consuming desire for revenge was more than she could live with. Johnny believed it was the companionship and the great sex she really missed. Hell, he missed it too. He wasn't surprised when she told him she was leaving and wanted a quick divorce. Said she was sorry, but she and the boys had to get on with their lives. She found a new man in a hurry and moved with the boys to Hawaii. So much for shared custody. His heart finished breaking then, sapped his strength for a while, and ever since he seemed easily brought to tears. Another humiliation he laid at the door of his assailant.

Why the bastard had destroyed the mew and many of the other birds, and taken only one falcon, had puzzled Johnny until today. No true falconer would endanger *any* hawk. His dad wondered if Johnny's would-be murderer really had another motive besides theft. Johnny couldn't imagine one at first, but the idea nagged him and now it all fit. He'd thought about it day and night until it came to him, at first in fuzzy pieces. He worked on it every waking minute; the puzzle began to come together.

Unlike other nights, when he sat there until his dad came to find him by the pier railing, Johnny wiped away tears with the backs of his broken hands, tightened his grip on his cane, and struggled to his feet. The struggle had become easier, more controllable every day. The therapy was working on his muscles. He'd given up the walker, progressed to two canes, and now required only one. His body was enviable to many at the beach, where even the younger tourists eyed him appreciatively. Tanned, powerful, the healing going beyond his doctor's wildest hopes for him, pinned together with metal parts as he was, his strength—if not his speed—was impressive because of his incredible determination.

Johnny Carlisle knew that though he was regaining some of his old physical prowess, there would be no healing of his heart until justice was done. Maybe not even then. That's why he'd withdrawn his money and closed his bank account, bought a plane ticket to Utah and secured a special-needs rental car to be waiting for him at Salt Lake International Airport.

Tonight, he'd tell his dad after they were back at the mobile-home park. He'd insist on driving them there. That was it! Carlisle felt sure he could drive after sobering up on some coffee. Then his dad would take his going easier, knowing on the other end his son could rent a car and manage by himself.

Yeah, he owed his old man for giving him a place to live when he'd lost everything—a safe place to heal. He at least owed him the explanation he wanted to go put things right by working with the policemen to track the low life who brought him down. For his pride, for his boys, and yes, even for Ginny, though she was another man's woman now, and soon to be married.

He would never rest until he knew what happened to Felon—"The Wind"—his gyrfalcon. The man who either took his bird for himself, sold her, or—as he most feared—she'd refused to eat and died of hunger and desertion by Johnny. He, the falconer she'd imprinted on, had bred and trained her. Wherever she was, if she still lived, he needed to know she was healthy and content. He wanted to caress her feathers and talk to her—reassure her of his love. It was the least he could do for her. Johnny didn't suppose he'd be needing a plane ticket back. From the beating he'd survived, he knew the criminal mind he was up against. What gave him hope of justice was maybe now he'd figured out why he'd been attacked and why Felon was the only hawk stolen.

He'd buy a gun when he got there. Find a way. That's why he'd bought a one-way ticket. His dad didn't need to know that part of his plans. Nobody else would give a damn anyway, except maybe the skinny bald cop. He was a good man, kind and genuine. He'd told Johnny he'd keep his notes in case he ever remembered enough to help the police find the evil man that left him for dead. Johnny'd believed him. Now a couple of things had come to him. It was time to take the cop up on his offer.

When Johnny asked the bartender for his strongest black coffee, he let a rare smile play across his scarred face. Hot sloshing mug in one hand, cane in the other, he went to find Denver Carlisle and insist on having the car keys.

The Wind Remembers

Bo Rodman

~ Saturday the 14th of June

Only because he needed him, Bo Rodman listened hard to Frank Simmons.

"Raptors usually let domestic chicken meat lay," Frank continued. "Doesn't taste wild." He handed Bo a bag.

Bo peeked into the bag stuffed with fur and feathers. "What's this crap for?"

"Well, if this bird's going to live until you find her owner, give her a little roughage every day or she won't be able to cast a healthy pellet. Can't expect a bird of prey to live on people food. She's got to eat raw, wild meat—fur, feathers, and all. Gut birds for her, to limit disease transfer if you want, but give them to her whole."

Bo shrugged. "If you say so. I wanna fly her in Sky Trials for a good purse before I bother finding out who she belongs to." Bo patted the thin wallet in his back pocket, imagining how it would feel when it was nice and fat. Cash would give him freedom to come and go, do as he pleased.

The look Frank gave him was like Bo'd lost a screw. *He's pissin' me off.* With effort, he held his temper because he needed Frank's raptor experience and the important connections he had in the falcon trade. Bo needed to sell the hawk for big money.

Frank hefted the falcon out of Bo's truck. "You haven't the patience for training *any* falcon to fly in competition, let alone a lost hybrid. You couldn't register her to compete in Sky Trials anyway."

Bo stubbed a boot heel in the dust. "What d'yuh mean . . . exactly?"

"You'd need the legal papers to back her up. Besides, it's the powerful males that compete in Sky Trials. Guess you didn't know about that either." Frank grinned, seeming to get a real kick out of showing Bo up.

If it's the big males that win, then trainin' her sure as hell ain't worth the bother. Bo scrambled to think, desperate to pry from Frank ways to make the bird pay for his risk to steal her.

Frank smirked at him, looped the lure cord over his free arm to change his launching position for the gyrfalcon. "She's no breed falcon either, Bo."

Bo sucked air like a dying man. He faced Frank square on, keeping well out of the hawk's reach.

Frank broke into a laugh. "You've got a lot to learn about caring for this young chamber-bred eyas. She's been properly sterilized, according to government requirements for licensed breeders of hybrids."

Bo had no idea what half that gibberish meant, except for one word—*sterilized.*

"Go on!" he sputtered, wiping spittle with the back of his hand across his hanging jaw. "You mean no breedin' her with one of your falcons—or some rich Arab's?"

Frank's smile creased his face wider, making Bo want to smear it off with a fist.

His heart pounded with fury. *This falcon's sterile! I risked prison to steal this damn bird, all for nothin'. Can't sell her for the tens of thousands Frank told me Middle Eastern towel heads pay for a breedin' falcon?*

"What the hell!" He spat, grinding one flexing fist into his pocket, gripping Tracker's leash tighter in the other.

"She's no ordinary gyr-peregrine hybrid," Frank went on, "but a superb specimen, largest of all the falcons. Some breeding expert artificially inseminated a female to cross-breed this beauty from an Arctic gyr and a peregrine falcon. Quite an achievement."

Bo's barely contained fury approached panic. His mind whirled, struggled to take in all that he was learning way too late.

"Where you keeping this gyr?" Frank pressed, getting ready to whirl the lure.

"Up that sheep camp, top of Old Post Road." Bo breathed hard, fighting for cool.

"Be careful or ole Makris will be kicking you off his property. I hear in his eighties he doesn't run sheep on that mountain spread any more, but he's one territorial Greek with a hell of a temper. Still knows how to use a shot gun and hasn't got much else to do but drink ouzo and patrol his fence lines."

Bo watched Frank saunter off with the restless, hungry gyrfalcon on his glove, striding way out into the clearing. *He coos to her like she was some lover woman or a baby child.* He deeply resented Frank's ease with the bird, especially because Bo didn't dare turn his back on the hawk's sharp talons and beak, anymore than he would have on a Brahma bull in his rodeo days.

I've got a gut full of you, fancy Frank. His pulse ticked with resentment, thundered against his ribcage, pounded in his skull.

I don't want her perchin' on my glove anyway. Picturing her razor-sharp beak that near his face made Bo shiver.

Gives me the willies when she lifts her wings and stares them big ol' dark eyes followin' me like her head can swing all the way round. I'd as soon face a mean-assed bull.

While Frank worked with the gyr, Bo played back why he'd thought he knew enough about captive hawks to handle this one. Finding out he was dead wrong shocked him like a cattle prod. His swelling anger nearly choked him.

When we was kids, didn't I help Carly feed the broke-winged Harris we found in his pa's barn? Carly made it look easy; throw it a rat and change its water. Carly's pa showed us the wing bones wasn't broke, just feathers. While we held the hawk still, he cut the bad feathers, leavin' good stubs in the body. He took little chunks o' carbon from his fishin'-tackle box and imp'd the two feather pieces together, then glued 'em to match up. Us boys kept him fed and watered. Soon, the Harris was flyin' again, bringin' down barn swallows off the hog-pen roof.

Bo's rangy hunting dog whined at his side, interrupting his thoughts.

"Stay, Tracker." *Now, sure as shit, this bird is nothin' but a hassle.*

He thought about her thick, white droppings at the base of her perch, so awful to clean up he no longer bothered. In the heat, she wanted a bath, and unless hooded, her screeching attracted attention he couldn't afford to explain, *'specially to old man Makris and his shotgun.* He wiped his neck sweat and under his hat brim with his bandana. *Shit. I'm in a world a hurt. I'm gonna hafta be real careful, more'n I thought.*

Stroking Tracker's head absently, Bo whispered his secrets, entrusting them to his only true friend. "Lucky I didn't get ripped open throwin' a feed sack over that damn bird in Carlisle's shed. Never shoulda bothered. Have to unload her for whatever I can get now, just to be rid of her. Rehma's enough trouble messin' with my life. I ain't puttin' up with a useless bitch bird, too. Have to be careful. Leg band's licensed to Carlisle. Don't want the cops trackin' me down for no murder."

Bo watched Frank and the gyrfalcon circle with the bird's creance clip-anchored to Frank's glove, "in case he lost his grip," he'd said, and how he was "close to letting her fly free to chase a homing pigeon bred for his own hawks. But the gyr had molted key flight feathers, so he couldn't let her off yet on the chance she'd bolt and die in the wild, not knowing how to fend for herself 'cause she'd bonded to a human handler."

Bo hadn't told Frank he knew all about who that human was—never would—and neither would Johnny Carlisle. *He won't never be telling nobody nothin'. I made damn sure o' that!*

CHAPTER FIVE

CHARMED

Taylor Armstrong

~ Saturday the 14th of June

The mobile phone pulsed in his pocket. Taylor Armstrong switched off the searing hum of the chain saw and removed gloves and earplugs. He
scanned the number he'd missed, and punched speed-dial for his office.

"Armstrong Tree Service, Randy speaking."

"You sound mighty professional for a raw recruit."

"Taylor?"

"You expected Madonna with a tree problem? What's up?"

"Phone's ringing off the wall after this storm!"

"Good. Sounds like coins in the cash box. Could pay off this new truck sooner than I hoped. You get Griff busy in the other truck?"

"He's up in Morgan pulling a sycamore off a Corvette. Says the dude had a cow about his sports car. Didn't seem to register the damage to his dad's new horse barn."

"Some people's kids, huh?" Taylor stretched and felt rumbles of hunger. "I'm going for lunch and a gas-up. Before I forget, call the Becker farm on Rt. 89. Bid for $500 to clear their north-pasture access road. I passed it on the way to the McKane building. Chinese elm went over, roots and all, ripped out twenty feet of fence. His cattle will be stopping traffic if they come over the hill and find the break before he does. Get the jump on the competition; handle that one yourself. Keep the commission."

"Thanks, Uncle Taylor!"

"You bet."

"How'd it go on Old Post Road? That Mrs. Price carried on about her cottonwood going over like her dog got hit."

"Yeah, I stopped up there first, figuring by the bench address it was up in the fancy homes and starter castles, but . . . it's an old farmhouse. Not a real moneymaker there. I'm going to grab a sandwich. Keep me posted."

Taylor signed off and packed his gear in the truck. He stacked the last of the trimmed box-elder branches at the curb for the street crew, clearing the medical center's parking lot for business. He was pleased with himself for the cool way he handled the bit about the Price place with Randy. His hunger getting the best of him, his mental calculator ticked off the bucks he'd earned since first light. When he'd climbed behind the wheel that morning he'd known physical comforts would take a backseat to money for the next forty-eight hours.

The drive-up fast-food lanes were all long lines that would cost him too dearly in wasted time. He drove back up the bench to Suzanne Price's place, and though hungry as a bear, he parked in the drive and unpacked equipment. In less than half an hour he'd made considerable progress with the branches of the old cottonwood, working toward the garage. He took a break, switched off his chain saw and engaged the safety. Taylor eased the machine to the ground. His shoulders ached from hours of cutting and lifting. Stuffing his earplugs in a pocket, he sopped sweat with his bandanna where trickles ran down behind his ears.

The Wind Remembers

He checked his watch. Still time to haul what he'd cut up away from the front of Suzanne's garage before he'd need to leave and join Randy and Griff at the William's orchard. The three of them could get in three, maybe four more hours before it got too dark to work safely. Good thing it was nearly the longest day of the year. Every daylight hour spelled money, since the storm. There'd be plenty of fees coming in from trimming and chemically treating the wind-damaged fruit trees, perhaps even enough to make up for the money he was probably losing on the Price job.

Price—the name didn't sit right.

Suzanne's driveway was nearly clear now. The new winch accomplished the heaviest lifting and pulling. Taylor knew he couldn't have managed a clearing of this magnitude alone. If a man could love a vehicle, he freely admitted his passion for his dream truck to anyone who'd listen over a cold beer. "She's a honey. Her engine hums, the winch is worth the salary of two more men, I can write a portion of her off on my business taxes, and she never talks back."

He'd defended her expense to his dad, too. He recalled Pop's reaction: "Can't imagine you wanting a *white* truck, *if* you're planning to get any serious work done. Sissy color if you ask me—'course you didn't ask me." Pop would come around when the money rolled in. Or maybe he wouldn't. You could never tell. Taylor had disappointed him before, wouldn't be anything new. But they always worked things out.

He finished stowing the pulaski behind the driver's seat in the king cab and shut the door, admiring the company logo, updated with a silhouette of two hands cradling a tree, and brown-twig lettering he'd copied from a horticulture magazine. It was one more thing his father had judged a silly waste of money. But it was the nineties. Taylor insisted positioning was important to be taken seriously as a professional by the clientele he was after. They'd let it drop out of respect and love for each other.

Carrying a length of rope with steel clips on the ends, he headed to the last sizable limb to be dragged out of the driveway without the aid of the winch. Once done, he'd have only twenty minutes or so worth of small stuff to clear. Then Suzanne would have access to her truck and he could get on to a money job. She'd just have to understand he'd need to come back and do a little at a time until the trimming, loading, and hauling away was finished. She and her mystery husband, or her boyfriend Doug, could stack the smaller stuff. He lifted his hand in greeting to Suzanne's boy, busy collecting bugs in a jar from the growing woodpile beside the garage. Though the child's eyes met his own, there was no word or returned wave. *Strangely withdrawn for a boy his age*, he thought. Suzanne's back door slammed.

Taylor looked up to see Mitzi carrying her teddy bear and a jacket. He double-looped the rope around the heavy end of the limb and clipped one end back on itself.

"Me and Bear Lovins comed to watch. Mommy said, 'No bahvring Mister Armfrong when his saw is going and no getting in his way.'"

Mitzi's wide blue eyes were serious, her child's voice attempting to sound like Suzanne's. Taylor was charmed. He tugged on the rope, pulling it snug to the bark with the heel of his boot. "It's chilly out here after the rain, Mitzi. You'd better put your jacket on. Bear Lovins already has a fur coat. Need some help?"

"No, you watch me. I can do it all by myself." Taylor let go of the rope and accepted the bear. She spread her jacket out upside-down on the ground in front of her. He decided not to mention the rain-damp grass. The jacket seemed to be an old one anyway. Squatting, Mitzi thrust her hands deep into the sleeves and pulled the jacket on over her head so it came out right side up for zipping. She whirled around proudly and looked expectantly up at him, her small even baby teeth like pearls in her smile. Taylor marveled at her ingenuity and was amused at her delight in herself. She waited for the sort of praise he figured she was used to. He didn't want to disappoint her.

"Where'd you learn to put your jacket on upside down and make it come out right?"

The Wind Remembers

"My Mommy showed me." She beamed. "Only me and Leesha know how at our preschool."

"That shows you're growing up when you can dress yourself." Taylor bent to the task of moving the big limb out from in front of the garage. "If you two sit on that fat log," he indicated with his head, "you can watch me clear the driveway for your mother. Then you won't be where you, or Bear Lovins, could get hurt."

Mitzi scootched onto the log, dragged her bear up next to her, and twisted his head so his glass eyes could watch Taylor.

"We're ready!" she called, like a show was about to begin. Taylor laughed. *Cute kid, no doubt about it.* He hauled on the limb, walking it sideways for the best leverage. Its leafy top branches scraped along what was left of the metal garage door, making disagreeable screeches like fingernails on a chalkboard.

"Mister Armfrong, stop!"

"The noise will be over in a second, honey. Just cover your ears." Taylor continued to drag the limb free of the door.

"No, no, stop! " Her voice was urgent, squeaky. He turned to see her scrambling on her hands and knees among the leafy branches.

"Look!" she cried, rising with her thumbs in the air, each crowned with half of a robin's blue eggshell.

"Baby birds got all broken, too," she said. She handed the delicate shells to him and dropped back to her knees, pulling out a ragged nest. Its base had survived, but the sides were destroyed.

"Oooh," she whispered. "This egg's still pretty."

"Sure enough," said Taylor. He tucked the broken shells into her jacket pocket and pulled out his bandanna, fluffing it loosely into a ball. "Now I know why that mother robin's been buzzing this tree. She knew her nest of eggs was somewhere in those leaves." He squatted on his heels next to her.

"Hold your hands together like a bowl, Mitzi."

The Wind Remembers

She cupped her hands with her fingers like flower petals in a circle pointing to the sky. Taylor nested the egg carefully on its bandanna cushion in her hands.

"Close your fingers gently," he said, putting one of his hands over both of her little ones. "Sit right here for a moment." He lifted Mitzi, egg and all, onto a log. "I'll get something we'll need from my truck."

He brought back his battered, stainless-steel thermos, warm from sitting in the sunny heat of his truck cab. He drained it in the gravel as he returned. Mitzi, still as a statue, cupped the little egg in its handkerchief nest.

"Okay, Punkin. Time to put the baby to bed."

Mitzi giggled and stretched her hands toward him.

Taylor's big fingers gently lifted the cushioned egg and slid it into the opening of his empty thermos. "We have to keep it warm," he whispered, blowing his breath in with the egg before carefully re-threading the stopper.

"We could put it in the microwabe."

"That would cook the baby bird. We just want it to stay warm enough to hatch. My dad breeds doves and falcons. Maybe he'll help with your robin egg in his incubator."

"I wish *my* daddy could see this pretty blue egg. He used to hold me up to peek in bird nests."

"Well, Punkin, maybe if we take good care of it he can see it when he gets back."

Mitzi shook her curls fiercely. "My daddy's not coming back, 'cause he died."

Taylor was dumbfounded, ashamed at assuming she had a daddy somewhere. He looked at Mitzy bleakly, expecting . . . he wasn't sure what. He only knew how wretched and foolish he felt for not thinking there could be a tragic reason for Suzanne and these children to have no one to lean on with this tree trouble. He bent close, searching his mind for something to say to protect her sweet innocence from any more pain than he imagined she'd already experienced.

"I'm sorry, Mitzi. I didn't know. How did it happen?"

He studied her face. She appeared to be comfortable with talking about her daddy's death.

"My daddy had cancer really really bad. He's in heaven with my Grammie and Jesus, so he's not all by himself. Mommy says not to worry, 'cause he doesn't hurt or be sick *anymore*."

Taylor's urge to speak choked on Mitzi's depth of trust. His chest tightened with the effort to not let on how moved he was. The respect and gratitude he felt toward Suzanne for having convinced her daughter of the safety and comfort for her daddy in heaven filled him with a sweetness he'd not felt since his own childhood. He remembered his mother comforting him with similar words at the passing of his favorite grandmother. He'd believed because he wanted to. Mitzi believed with the unquestioned trust of the very young. He didn't wonder how Gregory was taking the loss of his father. *Mitzi's brother has trouble sharing smiles and cereal. He definitely hasn't bought into the "heaven with Grammie and Jesus" business or prefers Daddy to be with him instead of wherever heaven is. Suzanne has her hands full, and she'd been too proud to even mention it to me. Same old tough-it-out Susie.*

He could also imagine she was getting pressure from Doug and wondered if a relationship with him was something she wanted or not. The sparks he'd observed had been on Doug's side, but then Suzanne could be unfathomable.

Mitzi retrieved Bear Lovins. Taylor watched the child return to him. *Damn.* She seemed so vulnerable, so sweet, blissfully unaware of any implications for her own future that losing her daddy probably meant.

"I want to s'prise Mommy with my egg. She loves secrets and s'prises. I'll show her the braked shells in my pocket and she'll think all the eggs are gone to pieces. When this one busts into a baby robin, she'll be *really* s'prised!" Mitzi tapped the thermos importantly with two little fingers.

The Wind Remembers

Taylor bent to her level. "Is it okay to leave it with my Pops? He has an incubator for wild eggs. If anybody knows how to keep this egg warm for hatching, he does."

"Will you bring the baby back when it's borned and make it a secret wif me, Mister Armfrong?"

"You bet I will, Mitzi, if it hasn't been too cold for too long. The egg was protected by the nest and the leaves. It may still have a live baby inside. Only nature and time will tell, but we can try." Taylor zipped his finger across his lips and put the pretend key into his pocket.

Mitzi zipped her finger across Bear Lovin's stitched mouth, then across her own. She put her pretend key in her jacket pocket and giggled with her lips pressed together. Taylor returned to his truck with Mitzi at his heels. She watched on tiptoe while he placed his thermos on the passenger seat and buckled the seat belt through the handle. She smiled, nodding her approval, and helped close the truck door. He ruffled her curls and pointed to her vantage-point seat on the log, then to the porch. She giggled and waved good-bye. Taylor returned the wave and watched her run up the back steps. At the top, she waved Bear Lovin's arm for him and tapped it to her lips, then let herself into the house.

Taylor returned to moving the limb and picked up his pace, his stomach growling his discomforting hunger. *I figured Suzanne might be divorced, but didn't imagine at her age she'd gone through the loss of a husband because of anything as devastating as cancer. So, if her letter wasn't from a separated or divorced spouse, what made her blow a fuse this morning?* He puzzled on that for a while.

Perhaps Dierdre was canceling her visit at the last minute—a very Dierdre thing to do. He remembered well Suzanne's fiery, self-centered and impulsive twin. Neither woman was easy to forget.

He was just testing the stability of the garage door when Suzanne came out to join him, carrying a fat whole-wheat sandwich, bulging with sprouts and cheese in a zip-lock bag. In her other hand was a mug of what smelled deliciously like fresh hot coffee. He stopped shoving up on the bottom of the door with his arms over his head and looked down at her. For a split second, he read something familiar and warm in her eyes. *Or did I imagine it?*

"Taylor, I was really rude this morning over something that had nothing to do with you. I'm terribly sorry. I brought you some fresh coffee and a snack. You've worked so hard, you must be starving."

"Thanks, I *am* hungry. I could use some more adrenaline and something to cushion the caffeine. Things happen. Forget this morning. No harm done."

He wanted to offer help if she needed it, but it was too soon. There was a lot of muddy water under their bridge. He was wise enough to read the signs of plenty of fresh mud around the Price place, too. He shoved the door up as far as it would go. It hung there jammed against the twisted metal of the track. He bent a sprung piece to the side and pushed it into a position where the door wouldn't release without tools.

She waited. He took the mug, enjoying the touch of her fingers when she pulled them from the handle and held the sandwich until his hands were free. He lifted the mug for a steamy sip and looked at her over the rim. So pretty, fresh, her eyes warm with an expression of new depth since they'd been in love years ago. Suzanne had grown up. Old feelings stirred. He squelched them with a scalding swallow.

"I'm afraid your door is history. Wish I had time to take it down and replace it for you, but at least you can get at your truck. Is there still time for you to pick up your sister, or did she have to postpone?"

"We don't have to worry about it, Taylor. Here's Dee's cab now."

The taxi pulled in behind Taylor's truck and stopped. The driver got out and opened the back door before moving on to the trunk. A long slim leg ending in red spike heels appeared first, then Dierdre's dark hair. She stood up, looking drop-dead gorgeous in a tailored red suit, with a white, silky blouse cut very low over full-melon breasts. *A man would have to be blind to miss the impact of a woman like her.*

Taylor smiled appreciatively, watching the sisters greet each other with a hug. The cabby leaned a traveling golf bag against the taxi door while he made change. When it started to slide, Suzanne reached for it. Taylor went to her aid.

"Here, let me get that." He lifted the expensive golf bag and caught Dierdre's eye. Raising the mug in a gesture of hello, he turned with the clubs and started for the steps.

"Taylor! Taylor Armstrong? What on earth are *you* doing here, you handsome hunk of manhood?"

She rushed forward for a hug, smashing firm breasts against his sweaty shirt. *Store-bought,* he thought. He imagined the surgeon's scalpel and several palm-sized silicon implants they show on PBS documentaries. But the effect was voluptuous. Dierdre was a knock out. *Sure of herself as always, but mature and clear about what she wants. I figure she's gotten plenty of what she's advertising for, too. Wonder if she ever attracts a little more than she bargained for.*

"Just performing my duty." He backed away toward his truck, nodding in her direction. Glancing at Suzanne, she seemed to look uncomfortable, or perhaps he imagined it. The taxi pulled away, leaving the women with several bags in the driveway. Mitzi came out the backdoor as Taylor supported the golf bag against the porch rail, drained the mug, and set it to the side.

"My Aunt Dreedra's here, Mister Armfrong!"

"She sure is, Punkin. I've got to be going." He whispered, "I'll take you-know-what to you-know-who."

Mitzi stood on the top step and reached to his lips. He bent toward her. She zipped them shut and put the imaginary key into his hand. Then she hurried down the steps, jacket and curls flying.

"Aunt Dreedra, did you bring me a s'prise?"

The Wind Remembers

Taylor looked hard at Suzanne, willing her to meet his eyes with her own. She did and flushed, pausing next to him with a suitcase of Dierdre's in each hand.

"We'll settle up later," he said. "I've got to get out to the William's orchard and make some mon . . . keep another commitment before dark. Thanks for the sandwich." He patted a jacket pocket.

"I've located our insurance policy, and," she whispered. "I'll be able to see you're paid promptly when you give me your bill. Our adjuster will probably process the paper work next week."

As he got in his truck to back away, he wasn't sure if the surge of pleasure lifting his spirits was all because he hadn't been wasting his money-making time after all or if it had something to do with Suzanne's big brown eyes, lovely as ever. Now that he knew she was widowed, he assumed she was available. There was also the way Dierdre sidled past him close enough for a second whiff of her sensational perfume, when she said, "Don't be a stranger, Taylor. I'll be visiting for ten more days." He turned the key and pressed the accelerator.

Mitzi dragged a wheeled bag half her size up the driveway and stopped to wave good-bye. Taylor honked and waved at his new little friend and drove off with his senses reeling. His elation about Suzanne being a single woman grew steadily. He couldn't deny experiencing Dierdre at close range after all these years was giving his hormones a charge, too. A flag went up in his head that had caution written all over it with the names of both women. Though each twin was desirable and elusive, one of them was direct and exciting while the other was sweet, deep and harder to figure out.

When it came to Suzanne and his re-stirred attraction, he was wise enough to know the living guy always loses because his faults are obvious while the dead man's faults are long forgotten. *Who could compete with that? No time to be a fool*, he told himself. There was still the matter of what made Suzanne blow up over her morning mail, and who had deliberately staged that giant cottonwood to fall. The Price household held a veritable rat's nest of problems. Taylor had enough of his own to make him cautious.

Bo Rodman

~ Saturday the 14th of June

Bo mumbled on under his breath, caressing Tracker's head, chewing and spitting while he watched Frank and the gyr. "I aint goin' back to no pen over a damn bird and a fool what got in my way."

He knew deep in his healing-botched bones Pretty Boy Bo wouldn't be left alone again on the cellblock. "There's meaner cons than me in the pen," he muttered. Tracker whined like he understood. Bo, comforted by his dog, talked on. The sound of his voice was companionship.

"We've hung onto that hawk thinkin' we'd get at least that $3,000 out of Frank he talked about in the Shootin' Star that night—brag jaw-jackin' and nothin' more." He spat tobacco juice with a vengeance.

Pinching a fresh wad of chew from the tin in his hand, he stuffed it inside his smiling cheek, feeling smart for coming up with a better plan. Frank danced out in the clearing with the bird and the feathered lure. Tracker kept going to point, but Bo held him back while spitting streams of tobacco juice into the powdery dirt between his boots.

The gyrfalcon beat her wings and flew in a circle on the far end of her tether, while Frank kept her away from the enticing lure to push her exercise limit and reawaken her hunting hunger. Bo hadn't known hawks dropped their feathers every year. She looked shabby now.

Bo envied Frank's skill with the bird and his knowledge of her habits, watched as he reached in his hawking bag for a piece of raw grouse breast and rewarded the gyr for her trust and work. Frank talked to her softly while she ripped at the meat with her powerful beak, hooking and swallowing a bloody shred at a time. Bo was jealous of Frank's ease on his feet for turning quickly, he moved toward them with a glove on, fearful of getting hawk bitten or scratched. The gyr mantled over the breast meat, arching her wings and screeching at him.

Frank waved him away, roaring, "You damn fool! Don't approach her with that glove on while she's eating! She thinks you want her to rise to the glove and leave her food. You're misprinting her in your ignorance! At the rate you're *un*doing her fine training, she'll be a retraining nightmare *if* she can even be brought around."

Bo retreated. *Damn him. He treats me like I'm a fool.*

The gyr settled her feathers and looked away, disinterested in the meat. Frank, muttering his disgust, returned with her and opened the truck tailgate with his free arm. He placed one of his hand-fashioned leather hoods over the falcon's head, bracing it on quickly, expertly with his teeth. He stroked her speckled breast feathers with the back of his fingers to calm her and cooed sounds of comfort. Delivering the bird to its makeshift perch on a block of wood topped with Astroturf, he clipped her jesses' swivel to the cord on the post.

"She's not happy in this truck, Bo. Makes her nervous. Get her back in your sheep-camp shanty," Frank said. "You need to do the right thing by her before she gets depressed or sick. The way you keep her it's a wonder she hasn't died already. Her eyes are starting to lack healthy luster from inactivity. Fortunately, she's a hybrid, naturally less active than a pure peregrine. Watch her. If her bottom eyelids come up and she starts fluffing her feathers, she'll be in a dangerously low condition." He looked Bo right in the eye. "Just give me time to find her owner with that leg-band number."

The Wind Remembers

Frank had already told Bo he wouldn't take on a bird he knew nothing about, especially with a leg band. Kept repeating how he wouldn't jeopardize his own falconer and breeder's license over what was probably a stolen bird put out to go wild.

"Nah, Frank," Bo countered, "I can't afford to just hand her over when I can git some money for her. Course we could split it. You're the only one she'll eat for. Why don't cha take her and see she's cared for proper? Just 'til I find some other expert like yourself who's got enough money to take her off my, . . . *our* hands and make the trouble worthwhile—for both of us, 'course."

"She knows you don't give a damn about her. Gyrs are exceptionally smart. You mishandle hooding her properly—she'll *always* remember. You're not in harmony with her needs." Frank's knuckles stroked the hawk's speckled chest feathers.

"Her needs, my ass. Whatcha call me takin' care o' her?"

"She doesn't trust you. Get her back where she belongs or to somebody who'll do right by her. Let me call some falconer friends out of state. We'll have to be careful."

"Well, get on it, Frank. I got better things to do than baby-sit somebody's charmin' fussy- assed falcon. Get me some money for my trouble."

The falcon's yellow-orange talons gripped and released the post. She shifted her weight from foot to foot and settled down so still she seemed part of the perch. Frank helped Bo close the creaking tailgate and let down the mud-spattered back window. The broken, tinted side windows were duct-taped open to give the bird air. Bo twisted the handle, latching the tailgate into place. The men went around opposite sides of the cab and opened the doors to let the hot air escape before climbing in.

"You don't work with birds so you don't know how to read them. We falconers have our own individual styles. She knows I won't hurt her. I'm close to a breakthrough, but scared of being caught by a Bureau of Land Management raptor man wondering how I came to have a such a fine hybrid falcon—with no explanation but yours, such as it is."

"You worry too dang much." Bo spit a wad of spent tobacco into the weeds. "Nobody gives a hoot about that bird. I bet not even BLM fellas would give a shit."

"Well, you can bet the breeder who lost her does." Frank rolled his shirtsleeves up to his sweaty elbows. "Maybe there's a reward for her. That would get her off your greedy hands with money in your fist."

Bo pulled a cooler from behind the driver's seat and handed Frank a cold one. He stood scratching Tracker's ears then scooted him into the truck between himself and Frank. Tracker lapped after the cold sweat on the bottle; Bo knuckled his bony brow with his ring fingers.

"Good Boy, Papa Bo's big fella," his voice was gentle. The dog settled between them resting his black muzzle on his dusty paws. His tail flopped rhythmically against Bo's good leg.

"Hold up a minute, Bo." Frank unbuttoned and pulled off his outer shirt. "Let me soak this in the ice melt of your cooler."

"What the hell for?" Irritated, Bo held the lid open and watched Frank sop up ice water with his shirt.

"Open the camper shell and let me wrap this around the gyr's post."

"What now?" Bo grumbled, but he did as he was told, got out again, and reopened the tailgate. Frank lifted the hooded bird long enough to drape the perch with the wet shirt. "The cooling action of the air moving over the wet cloth will keep her feet and body more comfortable in this heat. You ought to keep a spray bottle to moisten her beak."

They re-secured the tailgate and climbed back in the cab.

"If you didn't have a little on my past, Bo, I would've turned you in for keeping a falcon you don't know how to take care of. It's a moral crime, not just illegal."

Frank shifted in his seat and went on. "She's magnificent, or at least was or could be. I'm helping you with her because I can't abide seeing a raptor neglected or mistreated. It's not because I give a damn about you, Bo. Get that straight right now!"

The Wind Remembers

Tracker whined, but relaxed beneath Bo's steady caress.

"Yeah, well Mr. Attorney, you just remember that I *do* know enough to cause you some trouble if you get any fancy ideas 'bout rattin' me out. I could've let her die in that trap she caught her jesses in, or let her go free. She'd have probably either way. Said so yourself. Good thing Tracker and me come along out huntin' when we did."

Bo swigged hard on his beer, on his guard to keep his made-up story the same every time he laid it on Frank, who he knew could outsmart him. He closed the lid on the cooler. Like the refrigerator in Rehma's kitchen, it was full of cold beer, deer scraps, and rodents for the falcon.

Rehma was revolted by the falcon's food. At first it turned him on to hear her freak at the sight of a plastic bag of dead rats. Now, nothing about her turned him on. He was as eager to shed himself of Rehma as he was the gyr. He'd fed her the line about a falconer's bird coming before his woman. She could take him or leave him, he'd said, knowing he had her right where he wanted her. She'd stayed. Now he'd marry her for his own reasons.

He looked over at Frank in his fancy shirt and expensive jeans. His lawyer ways of talkin', and Hunnie keepin' him fed and bred in style on their upper-valley ranch. Frank didn't know how good he had it. *Who are you tuh keep remindin' me 'bout the law bein' on the side of this damn bird?* Bo slurped his beer and drove toward the paved road that led back to Farr.

He'd been a rodeo star, by hell. Nobody better forget he was somebody. People treated Bo Rodman with respect or he straightened 'em out *real* quick—sometimes forever, like with Carlisle. Always had, always would.

Bo mulled over how pissed he was with Carlisle for being in his mews that night months ago. *Didn't I wait 'til after midnight to enter that shed in secret?*

Surprised to find him with his hawks, he'd no choice but to waste him. He'd punished Carlisle not just for being there, but for insulting him earlier at the Shooting Star—and for Carlisle's woman insulting him the worst. Bo was well-armed, disguised in a mask, taking a man by surprise. He'd die before he went back to prison crippled and vulnerable.

So maybe I shouldn't ta patted her little booty. Carlisle made a big deal out of nothin'. She wasn't all that great anyway. But Johnny'd been possessive, punched him in the mouth right there in the bar in front of everybody, like he was some common low life. *He deserved everythin' I give him in that shed. If I'd pulled off the theft the way I wanted to, I'd have a ransom payment from Johnny Carlisle himself for the return of his gyrfalcon!* Raging regret made Bo's blood run hot.

Between swigs, Frank said, "You know, Bo, I don't buy that story of yours. Falcons get their prey clean, pick it right out of the brush or the sky. They don't raid traps for grub unless they're injured or too weak to fly, or have molted too many flight feathers. She hadn't lost that many when you say you found her. There are enough holes in your story to make Swiss cheese. Something about the way you got this gyrfalcon you're not telling me? Maybe something to do with that breeder Carlisle a while back?"

Bo guzzled his beer. His mind grappled with what to say this time.

"I don't know nothin' about Carlisle and his birds, 'cept what I read in the paper and cop talk I heard at the Pump. You just find me some oil-rich falcon'r who wants her, and I'll let you pass her on by fall when her feathers grows back and she's pretty again . . . to a good home for a healthy cut of my take." He laughed mid-guzzle. "That way we'll both be rid of waiting on her like she's a damn princess. 'Course, if you find someone to take her off my hands and put cash in 'em for the favor right now, while she ain't so pretty perfect with some feathers gone, I'd be mighty obliged."

Bo forced a hearty laugh and flashed Frank a smile put on for the occasion, the way he used to smile when he had more occasion.

The Wind Remembers

Heading down hill, he dropped into low gear, spat out the window, and tossed the empty bottle into the sagebrush. Its weight carried it through snapping dry branches until it clinked to a landing and cracked the sparkling black, living crust—undisturbed for hundreds of years—into jagged shapes that burped fine red dust.

CHAPTER SIX

Secret Schemes

Doug Jensen

~ Saturday the 14th of June

Doug Jensen kicked back in his recliner with another icy beer. The foam up to the rim of the giant insulated mug, a birthday gift from Suzanne, Greg, and Mitzi. He switched channels absently while commercials ran back-to-back between innings, his mind not on baseball but on Suzanne. *Time to press my advantage while I still have one.*

Seeing her today with another man—probably an old boyfriend—shook him. He had the odd sensation his timing was off. His plans were slipping through his fingers. Doug looked around the room listing items in his mind to offer Suzanne. *It's me she's going to marry.*

He'd been working up to the right moment to ask her, had looked at rings, planned to press for a serious relationship with her at the dance fundraiser for Greg's ball team next week. He'd imagined she'd open the invitation, and they'd make plans for their first date. *She stuffed my invitation in her pocket without even looking at it. It's not like her to be rude. Whatever came in her mail this morning is in my way. Or is it Armstrong? Is Tree Man the reason she was cooler than usual?*

His timing seemed perfect, until he'd driven to her house this morning. He hadn't expected anyone but the children to be there—for sure not another man. But then he could hardly believe the downed tree either and the horror when he realized how close it came to hurting Suzanne and the kids. The deliberate slashing of her tree had him puzzled and worried. *Could it be part of the gang vandalism the department's working on? Nah, too sophisticated. The cover up wasn't something a bunch of lazy kids out for a good time would bother pulling off. Tagger gangs want recognition. Whoever perped the cut and cleaned up the evidence didn't want to be found out.* He sipped, stewing on it. *Somebody could have put the kids up to it—that's possible.*

The tree business wasn't his immediate problem, at least he didn't think so, except by drawing Suzanne's old boyfriend into the picture. She hadn't explained the reason for her blow up, or acknowledged his invitation to the country-dance, even when he went back with the lab photographer. While he made out his report on the vandalism, he'd tried to get a private word with her.

When the paperwork was finished and Taylor's truck pulled away for the afternoon, Suzanne made an excuse of helping her sister settle in. He'd return to the station to turn in the paperwork. As was his habit after his shift, he'd lifted weights at the Iron Pump for half an hour, taken a steam and a hot shower, followed by a needling cold one, then called her to see if he could stop by on his way home. *She put me off again. Claimed they were heading out to the store before cooking dinner. Ticked me off!*

Doug'd returned to the locker room, changed back into his wet sweats and punched the bag for a quarter of an hour longer to cool his temper. He hadn't bothered to shower again or change. Not stopping by to see her, as he always did since Steve was gone, left him feeling . . . unfinished somehow.

In the station parking lot, he'd passed the Last Tangle adjacent to the Pump and waved to Rehma just closing up. Dicey. He'd never gotten a handle on why Steve ever married her his first time around. She wasn't the only blonde with a wow figure. Her flirting ways with other men bugged his old partner. Finding her drunk with another man finally finished him, he'd confided. Steve'd been clear she wasn't going to raise his kids. That was as much as he'd say, never ran her down to anybody.

Doug licked foam off his mustache. His eyes traveled over the den, his father's pride. He'd let Suzanne change everything in the house, the way he'd heard women do, but not this room. A pair of mounted elk heads with impressive antler racks framed the north window. In the corner, a grouse drooped from the jaws of a red fox, and a pronghorn antelope stared from above the mantel—all needing dusting since he'd forgotten twice to pay his mom's old cleaning lady and she'd quit on him. Two worn rifles were racked in a custom-built case. His dad's name was carved in the pine above the brass latch. The hunting collection, with his mother's reluctant acceptance, filled every room in the house except her kitchen. For years, even their bedroom had a neat row of Ned's most important guns locked in a case he'd built. A rarity in Utah as an only child, Doug inherited the family's old three-story polygamist home with two entrances. His dad sold the farmland to a developer and used the profits to buy the St. George condo for a winter retreat. Now, his father gone and Mom living in the condo for the curative warmth of the southern Utah sun, *I have the family place all to myself.*

The transformation of his dad's rich, loamy fields into a subdivision complete with cul-de-sacs was now blade-skating hangouts for squealing kids and their barking dogs. All the streets dead-ended into his back yard. *I might as well be down working out at the Pump to the pounding of hard rock for all the quiet I won't get tonight.*

The Wind Remembers

Doug thought of the room above him. Steve and Suzanne stopped by at his mother's invitation two Christmas's ago. Suzanne mentioned north light as perfect for a painting studio. He added that room to the mental list for his marriage speech. *Suzanne is practical, not emotional. I mustn't forget.*

All that remained of the once thirty-acre property was the rolling front lawn with its cantankerous sprinkling system and the over-grown garden out back, bordered with a few fruit trees in need of pruning and a collapsing grape arbor.

His mother had burst into tears when she visited and saw "all her years of backbreaking work gone to rack and ruin in the last two winters." Doug tried to make amends, but outdoor work didn't suit him. He'd given up the trimming and weeding, even paid the neighbor boy to mow the lawn and to run his snow blower. The boy's slovenly mother grew tomatoes in a sunny patch against his fence; she shared the red fruit with him from fingers encrusted with black dirt under her badly manicured nails. Her food-spattered clothing made him shudder. Her tomatoes generally went bad in his refrigerator. *Suzanne loves gardening. She'll put the gardens back into shape.*

He lapped at the beer and put the game on mute. The one thing he and his dad had agreed upon—beyond hunting and the value of the family property—was if you knew your baseball, you didn't need to hear the commentators run on at the mouth about stuff that had nothing to do with what was happening on the field. Doug often watched baseball without the sound. His eyes swam with fatigue, from the effort of sorting out his life, and the accumulated effects of five beers in a couple of hours on an empty stomach—after two hard workouts. He sat musing in his dank sweats about Suzanne, afraid to take action for fear he'd make a wrong move.

Things were happening too fast, or not fast enough to suit him; he wasn't sure which. His life was out of his control and he didn't like the feeling. *I'll be sure of myself before going by Suzanne's place next time. I've got to have a plan, and soon.*

He was hungry, not so much for food as for a woman.

The Wind Remembers

Alcohol loosened up his inhibitions, pressed him for release of desires he hadn't exercised in months. He was horny. Beer commercials with bikini-clad women whetted his sexual appetites even more. *I'm tired of holding myself in check to impress her. From the minute I first saw Suzanne on Steve's arm at that barbecue, she's been on my mind.* Though he'd had several girl friends, they never played into anything serious. They were too easy. *I like a little challenge, and I want a lady.*

He wasn't sorry Steve entrusted his family to his old partner. He'd loved Steve like the brother he never had. His eyes swept the wall of photos above the TV that included he and Steve. *We shared everything since we were kids. Pulled pranks, cut school, double-dated, went into the police academy together, fished and hunted, and talked about our first truck sex.*

Losing Steve was a void in Doug's life. He wanted to be his best friend's replacement with Suzanne, deserved it. *Steve made me promise to take care of his family, make sure Greg didn't grow up to be a wimp without a man around. He probably figured I'd marry Suzanne. Steve was all heart. Even if I died in a shoot-out with a perp, I'd never want another man to have my woman. I'd expect her to pine away for me like Mom still grieves for Dad. Except Suzanne's way too young.*

He'd kept his promise to Steve and been there for Suzanne and the boy for months, from the time Steve became too weak to wrestle and carry Greg on his shoulders and take him fishing. *I invested my time; now I want payment. She'll be mine or no one else's. For sure not Tree Man's!*

He snapped the TV set off, made for the kitchen, put a bag of popcorn in the microwave, nuked it for two-point-five, and opened the steaming contents on his way up the curved staircase to the master bedroom. He'd consumed half of it before he had his shower water running.

Sitting around wishing I had Suzanne nailed down isn't going to make it happen. His police training kicked into automatic. He'd take action. While the water warmed, one dry hand fed popcorn steadily into his mouth. His head began to clear. *She's been putting me off.* Needing sex added to his urgent sense of speeding up the course of Suzanne's hearing him out and saying yes.

Tonight, I'll insist she go to the dance with me. Steve's been gone more than six months. Time for us to go out and have some fun, let ourselves fall in love. Start dating. Everybody at the station and half the friends we know expect it.

And soon, very soon, he wanted to bring her here and make love to her on his parents' imposing four-poster. He'd show her how good it could be for them if she belonged to him, here in this great old house full of antiques she'd admired.

The probability that Taylor still found Suzanne as attractive and desirable as he did struck him square in the gut. He'd seen the way Taylor looked at her, while trying not to be obvious. Noticed the same thing from Suzanne. *She blushed, acted giddy trying to be cool, like nothing was going on between the two of them when I walked up. Like nothing ever had. I know better.*

He sensed something different in the way she'd introduced him, almost as if she felt sorry for him and Tree Man was Mr. Wonderful. *Or am I making it all up and torturing myself for nothing, just because I want her so bad?*

Doug couldn't be sure, but while he scrubbed the popcorn from his hands and soaped his lean hard-muscled body, he knew deep down he was running out of time. He had trouble being around her without wanting to force her mouth open in a tongue kiss that would leave him throbbing with desire. *She's attractive, sweet, talented, everything I want—except maybe passionate. She's shy with me.*

He liked a woman with some fire. *She'll learn with me bringing her along. Hell, she's bound to be hornier than I am after all the time she's gone without, even before Steve passed on.*

He meant to be the one to reawaken her, satisfy her needs, and his own. But first he must get her to take his feelings for her seriously. *I've waited long enough for Suzanne to get* over Steve. He was beginning to resent her for his pent-up needs and he didn't want to. *She's a good woman.*

He toweled off and shaved, slid the silver ring that matched one Steve was buried with onto his right pinkie, splashed Stetson across his face, and patted a towel at his mustache.

I want to go all the way to home base with her—all the way. I've spent months of boring afternoons mounting bugs with Greg to win him over. Mitzi was easy to win over. He hadn't spent any time at all with her; she loved everybody.

I'll invite her for a drive alone, override all of her excuses, take her in my arms and give her a tender kiss; not too much too fast, just enough to turn her on a little. I'll make her want me the way I want her. Her sister can take care of the kids; that's what relatives are for.

Doug slammed out of the house feeling high and full of fire, ready to put his plan into action. The sensation was the same as what he liked best about police work—a sense of adventure and power, walking into the unknown with his own agenda.

He drove carefully, knowing he'd had a few. *Can't screw up now. Embarrassing Suzanne with a suspension from the force for a DUI wouldn't cut it with her.*

Keeping one eye on his speedometer, Doug forced himself to take his time while imagining his mouth on hers, her body in his arms.

Dierdre Ingram

~ Saturday the 14th of June

When she opened the door to Suzanne's bedroom, Dierdre's eyes fell on the crudely wrapped box. Shiny aluminum foil secured with uneven bits of tape, a few scraps of red ribbon, and a tattered bow. *One or both of the children have given me a welcome gift*, Dierdre thought. She dropped her Estee Lauder bag onto the yellow coverlet and picked up the package. It felt so light. She shook it vigorously. No discernible noise or shifting weight clues as to contents. A flap of paper taped under the ribbon read: 'THIS IS FUR FUN!!!' Dierdre smiled to herself and relaxed on the bed. *How sweet!*

With the box in her lap, she slid the ribbon off and undid the tape. She removed the lid and gently pulled back the wrinkled white tissue paper. A tarantula the size of a golf ball skittered away into a corner of the box.

"Oh, my HELL!" Dierdre threw the box against the drawers of the dressing table. Tissue paper and spider tumbled out onto the throw rug. The tarantula moved like hairy liquid into the shadows under the vanity, crossed the wood floor, stopped in a corner and waited. Its reddish antennae quivered. Hairy mandibles pawed the air.

Dierdre drew her legs up on the bed and yelled, "Gregory Price, come here this minute!"

Gregory appeared in the doorway, his face amused.

Shuddering with revulsion and mounting fury she sputtered, "Why . . . why did you play such a mean trick on me? What have I *ever* done to deserve this hideous surprise for a welcome gift? Don't you dare deny it either or I'll spank you for sure!"

"You're not my *real* aunt, so you can't touch me. What makes you think I did it anyway? What about Mitzi? She probably did it. Nobody ever blames her for nothing."

"That's a cheap out, young man. There was a note. Mitzi can't print many letters yet. She doesn't like spiders and mister, neither do I. So fess up!"

"So what if I did do it? Murphy won't hurt you." His fingernails made clicking sounds in his pants pockets. "It wasn't for you anyway."

"That's not a very likely story, Greg." Dierdre shook with the abhorrence of things with too many legs, especially hairy ones. She motioned for him to come closer. Unable to leave the safety of the bed, she kept her eyes on the tarantula cowering in the corner. Not being able to recover it gave her the primal urge to move to a hotel.

"Apologize, Greg. Then capture that thing, and get it out of here."

"You can't make me." At her unrelenting glare, his defiant look faded. "Aw, I made the joke for Suzanne, but you opened it first. You probably broke all of Murphy's legs. I might even have to put him to sleep with chloroform."

"Oh, break my heart! It would suit me just fine if you put the little monster out of . . . never mind. If you don't tell me why you would do this to your mother or to anyone else for that matter, I'll smash the creepy thing myself. I used to play softball, and I doubt I've lost my pitching arm. These high heels . . ." She rose to her knees and reached to remove a shoe.

Gregory hurried into the corner and cupped his hand over the lump of tarantula. He lifted the box from the floor and released the spider into its walled rectangle. Murphy scurried from corner to corner, flexing furry mandibles in a way Dierdre found disgusting and menacing. She retreated back on the bed and drew her feet up beside her, in case the horrid creature escaped again.

"That was not a joke, Greg. Jokes are supposed to be funny. It wouldn't have been amusing to your mother either."

"She's *not* my mother! Rehma's my mother."

"Well, Rehma's not the one who takes care of you is she, so you'd better be good to Suzanne."

"Why? She's not good to me. She likes prissy Mitzi the best. I hate Suzanne, even if she is your sister." He put the lid back on the shirt box with both hands. But he didn't leave.

Dierdre hadn't expected such vehemence from a boy who'd always been ready to laugh and give hugs. Something was terribly wrong. She moved off the bed and reached a hand toward Greg, tortured into caution at the thought of being near the box again.

"Please, Honey. You can tell me. Why would you plan to scare Suzanne? Why do you dislike her *that* much?" She couldn't bring herself to say *hate*.

"It's all her fault my dad died. And now I don't have a dad . . . forever!"

Dierdre watched his eyes cloud up and rain tears that blurred his freckles. The tipsy box shook in his fists. Dierdre kept her eyes on it.

"Gregory, your daddy died of cancer. The doctors couldn't save his life. My sister couldn't save him either, though she wanted to with all her heart. Suzanne loved your daddy very much."

"No!" He stomped his foot. "She didn't or she wouldn't have picked a big fight with him the night before he went to sleep and never woke up. I heard her hollering at him. He was too sick to fight back." Greg's shoulders slumped. "He'd have got better if she'd left him alone." His quivering chin jutted defiantly. "Now he'll never be the one to take me camping and fishing again. All she thinks about is doing neat stuff with Mitzi. I hate her. I *hate* her!"

"Greg, have you told her how you feel . . . and why?"

Dierdre reached for him, missed. He turned and bumped the box of spider into the doorframe on his way out. He recovered Murphy and hurried on. She followed him into the hall in time to see him slam his bedroom door shut. His KEEP OUT sign swung back and forth on its thumbtack. She knocked and waited.

"Go away," Gregory sobbed.

Dierdre hesitated, torn between wanting to comfort him and to respect his privacy. *At least he admitted what's eating him up. I can help Suzanne deal with his feelings.*

For the first time in many years, Dierdre put herself in someone else's shoes. Just the way they fit, not necessarily the way she imagined that person ought to feel. *Susie and Greg deserve to be happy.* She retraced her steps and closed Suzanne's door. *It's time for my sis to put Steve behind her and find Greg a new dad to do things with, regardless of what the church might think of a short mourning period. Susie's young; she's wallowed*

The Wind Remembers

long enough. I might as well be the one to tell her. Nobody else will risk hurting her feelings. She's too nice for her own good.

Stepping out of her heels, Dierdre paced back and forth in front of the closet doors. She remembered a visit to this room when Suzanne sat up with Steve all night. The frightening smell of medicine and disinfectant had made her wonder what death would smell like. She'd been reluctant but resolute in leaving Suzanne alone to carry on by herself with Steve and the kids.

It was something Dierdre could not—would not—have been able to do. Two years of it, the rallying and the relapses, until there was nothing more to hope for but the pain-free sleep of death. Suzanne faced it all, and Dierdre hadn't even come for the funeral. She'd made job excuses, but she knew Suzanne understood she couldn't face a funeral after their mother's. *Hell*, she thought, *why am I such a coward?* She came to a stop at the window and looked out into the back yard.

In the fading light, Suzanne cleared light tree debris, dragging it to a loose stack at the back of the orchard. Mitzi helped by bringing little sticks and clusters of cottonwood leaves. A stray calico, perhaps belonging to neighbors far down the road, pounced along behind her. *I want them to be happy.*

She also wanted to have fun and relax. It irritated her that her twin hadn't gotten her life back under comfortable control. *What is her problem? Decide and do it!*

Dierdre stepped away from the window and pulled the curtains, doubting a restorative bath could have its usual effect. Still, she needed to calm her nerves after the spider scare. It was too much to make the trip from Florida and New York in one damn day and not even worth attempting if flying on Friday the 13th didn't spook her so much. She undressed, slipped on the silky welcome of her wrap, grabbed her overnight case and the fat bath towel Suzanne left out for her, and hurried down the hall to the bathroom. With the tub water gushing, she poured in a couple caps of Vita Bath, enjoying the way the scented steam permeated the room with the luxurious ambiance she adored. She lit a votive candle from her night case and set it in the soap dish.

Lowering herself into the water, Dierdre watched for the little sparkles of light from the stained-glass window at the end of the tub to glisten on the bubbles mounding to her chin. The window-glass shapes glowed like faded jewels. The effect was more romantic than she thought ceiling light would be. Twisting her hair on top of her head with a butterfly clip, she settled back, closing her eyes. Captain Nelson at the airport came to mind. The playing of their flirtation game, and how he'd so quickly gone on to his next conquest surprised and annoyed her, but overall she thought she'd handled herself well. The delight in attracting a man and toying with him was one of her basic pleasures in life. And then there was the surprise of hugging Taylor after all these years.

Gorgeous, an absolutely gorgeous man. She'd always been attracted to him, even in high school and in college when he was Suzanne's steady. But now . . . now he was a man who didn't have his name on her sister's dance card. She sponged her face, softening her make-up, remembering Taylor's great-looking ass in his soft jeans. Every part of him looked firm and toned. With his easy confidence, which had always been there but was now so mature, she imagined dancing with him the way she'd wanted to at their senior cotillion when she'd been someone else's pregnant fiancée. The jerk. Dierdre splashed soapy water to erase the image of that night after the dance when she'd told Kevin they'd need to move up their wedding date. He'd freaked.

Men. You dare not trust them with your heart. They want one thing and one thing only. Well she had learned to give it— and get it for herself—without getting burned again. She thought of Taylor and how he wasn't Suzanne's steady now. *I hope he isn't married. I might just have the intimacy with him I used to imagine.* Remembering how hard his body felt when she hugged him in the driveway made her warm all over. *Even sweaty he smelled fresh and outdoorsy and male.* She could tell he liked her appearance, found her glamorous and sexy. Men always gave themselves away in their eyes. She'd seen his beautiful blue ones move to her breasts, her legs. She craved that admiration from a man and worked hard for it.

Dierdre mused about the possibility of getting Suzanne to allow Taylor to come along on their camping trip to the Sun Tunnels. It would be exciting to sit around the campfire, or crawl into a sleeping bag with him. Besides, the tarantula made her positive she didn't like the thought of being out in the dark wilderness without a competent man to take care of the nasty stuff.

It would probably be cruel to be too forward with Taylor in front of Suzanne. I never understood what happened to make them breakup. They seemed so in love.

If the choice of pursuing Taylor for herself came in the way of she and Susie, well her sister would win out. Her twin and the kids were all the family she had left. Besides, Taylor was not the sort of man to not have a steady woman or a wife of his own. Still . . . the attraction had pulsed in their hug and it stood, pursued to another level or not.

She dawdled in the tub until the flickering candle became the only source of bathroom light. Moments ago, Dierdre had heard the backdoor shut. Now the sounds of Suzanne and Mitzi clattering dishes and talking in the kitchen drifted to her. She'd been so touched by Greg's vulnerable admission, reminding her of times in her own childhood when she'd resented Suzanne for goodness and sweetness the way Greg resented Mitzi. *Poor darling.* The look of pain in his eyes was too familiar. Dierdre soothed her body with bath gel on her sponge and thought of how to help Greg deal with his feelings so he could get on with being a happy little boy again. Life was too damn short to worry about anything—even death—for long. *I'll convince him of that before I leave.*

The doorbell rang, followed by footsteps and muffled voices. The low resonance of a man's voice. *Who, I wonder?* Gregory's door opened and his sneakers squeaked on the hall hardwood going toward the living room. Dierdre let the water out and stood to reach for a towel.

The Wind Remembers

There was a knock at the door.

"Just a minute already! Let me towel off and you can have the bathroom."

The door opened. Suzanne peeked her head in. Dierdre stood naked in the slippery tub, arm's length from the bath towel on the old chair. She was relieved it was Susie, but intensely disliked having her privacy interrupted.

"Doug Jensen just arrived. Says there's something urgent to discuss and wants me to take a drive with him—just a short one. Will you watch the kids for me a little while?"

"Hell no!" She gestured for the bath towel. "Look Susie, it's been a long day and it's *our* night. I just arrived, remember? I need some rest, not to play mama. Tell him to make it another night. He's here year round."

Suzanne looked lost in thought, not rescuing Dierdre with the towel. "You're right, of course. I can't imagine anything he needs to tell me that can't wait a day or two. I'll invite him to come for dinner some evening while you're here. Don't come out like that, or we'll never get rid of him."

Dierdre caught her eye. They smiled at each other.

"Ditch the dude, Baby Cakes. Your twin's in town. It's girl-talk time."

Suzanne nodded, her face perplexed. She closed the door.

Dierdre toweled dry and thought of how convenient it might be since sister Susie already had a man of her own on the line to try Taylor on for size. Suddenly, the front door slammed so hard the house shook. Gregory ran muttering down the hall to his room. His door slammed, too.

"What the hell's going on around here?!" Dierdre cursed aloud to herself. "Lord a mighty, why did I come back to my hometown thinking I could *relax?*"

She snapped her night case shut and did a quick revision on her usual assessment that Suzanne led a boring little life. She hoped the makings of a substantial nightcap were hiding in a cabinet somewhere.

Chapter Seven

Wings of Promise

Suzanne Price

~ Sunday the 15th of June

Parking at the end of the church lot, Suzanne heard the click releases of each seat belt. Greg's seemed to let go a stream of his whining along with it.

"Why'd you park so far from the door? It's hot already and we have to walk a long ways now. It's dumb. The seats will be burning hot when we get back." He trailed behind Suzanne and Mitzi. "Why didn't you park up here closer in the shade? Geez."

"Do you see the elderly people getting out of those cars by the chapel door?" She touched his shoulder. "They have trouble walking, Gregory."

She tried to keep her voice kind, just giving information. She could tell something deeper was bothering him. Perhaps he'd tell her soon, before he marred something else she'd painted or before another tarantula-type episode sent Dee packing. Though that might be a blessing in disguise.

"So-o-o!" He scuffed the toes of his best shoes against the pavement. "So what's *old* people got to do with where *we* park?"

"Mommy means they're like Daddy. When he couldn't walk bery good we parked closer and closer . . . 'til he died."

Greg's pouting face paled. He opened his mouth to say something but didn't.

Suzanne patted him affectionately on the shoulder. "Since the three of us can walk easily, I leave the closest parking spaces for those who have trouble."

"Oh." He looked up at her and quickly away. Catching sight of Alex and his family getting out of their van, he asked: "Can I catch up with Alex?"

"Okay, meet us in fellowship hall after your class." Looking down at Mitzi's eager smile, she let go of her hand. "Do you want to join Leesha, too?"

Both children ran ahead to join their friends. She waved hello to Diane and Les who waited for her in the dappled shade of a sycamore.

"Your twin sleeping in this morning?" Diane's pastel dress filmed about her stocky legs in the warm breeze. Les looked handsome in a summer suit, his tie a splash of maroon against his light blue shirt. She envied their happy couple-ness. Nodding, she dropped her eyes so they wouldn't read them and pity her.

Making her voice bright, she said, "Beauty-sleep deprived and jet-lag exhausted. Couldn't have budged Dee if I'd tried, which I didn't. Thanks for waiting. I wonder what our guest pastor will have to say this morning."

Les ushered the women in ahead of him. "Pastor Spahn due back this week?" He followed them, took Diane by the arm. "Sunday after next," the women chimed. They took their bulletins of the service from the usher and entered the sanctuary. Suzanne led the way up the aisle to a seat in one of the middle pews, grateful she didn't have to sit alone. It felt difficult enough to remember sitting in services with her own husband. Worse were weeks without him when Pastor Spahn came to the house because Steve didn't feel strong enough to attend. After his death, it had been even harder not having him at home waiting for her to return and eager to hear all about the service and their friends.

The organist set a worshipful mood while they took their places, nodding and smiling to familiar faces. In the bell tower, a resounding peal of notes rang out to signal Methodist services beginning in this primarily Mormon neighborhood. This little ritual had gone on for a hundred years right in this spot. To Suzanne the church was as secure a comfort to her as the mountains holding the valley in, but then she used to think her cottonwood was forever too. Maybe physical things were never forever or even for a lifetime. Only commitments to spiritual things like family really counted.

Life had become puzzling to Suzanne. *Knowing what's right isn't always clear.* She decided to put all of that out of her mind until she could pray about it and to concentrate on gleaning whatever strength she could from the church service. While the prelude continued, she looked around the vaulted room and thought of the day she and Steve were married. It seemed like a lifetime ago. It was easier to recall his memorial service. He hadn't wanted a viewing, only a graveside service for his family and fellow officers. But she'd needed a memorial celebration here in their church, so powerful for her, and had arranged for friends and family to gather with her and the children.

She wondered if others also treasured the church, with its lofty domed ceiling, held in place by carved beams as thick and long as tree trunks and supported by two-story walls each three feet thick. Faced with brick on the outside, plastered on the inside, and pierced by the majestic stained-glass windows she loved, glowing in Arts and Crafts Period colors of violets, oranges, and greens. She'd often thought how handy it would have been to have photos of them for color-theory class in college. The symbolic image of the crown and lilies on the empty cross reminded her the risen Christ triumphed over his crucifixion, forgave the faithfuls' sins, and remained available to them all. She liked knowing she didn't have to be perfect to have a good life now and after her own death.

The music stopped, the announcements began, and she drank in the serenity enhanced by the wavering candle flames and the sweet scent of fresh roses and baby's breath on the altar. Voices, including her own, lifted in the first hymn, "I Come to the Garden Alone," one of her favorites because her mother had loved it. Call to worship and the opening prayer were given, and she joined in the ebb and flow of the service, comforted by her spiritual family. This was the one time each week when she could count on uninterrupted peace.

The lay leader read from the scriptures, Romans 4:16.

"That is why it depends on faith, in order that the promise may rest on grace."

Suzanne thought the reading seemed meant just for her, internalized the promise, shoring herself up against what was without logic to her. *Rehma wants her children back. Why? Why now?*

"In hope he believed against hope, that he should become the father..."

She wondered if God was gender-bound or not. Should she have any less hope of becoming the *mother*? *Can my promise to Steve be kept as well as God's promise to Abraham? I believe God is fair and wise.*

Smiling to herself, she imagined Steve telling her she could pray for any doggone thing she wanted as long as it included him and his kids. She could almost hear his voice, its warmth and teasing tone, full of love for her.

The white-haired minister walked to the podium to ask for prayers to be offered for particular members in need and celebrations of answered prayer requests to be given. Suzanne's bowed head buzzed with the urgency of her prayers:

Dear Lord, my heart is so full of desire to be a good mother to our children. Please help me keep my promise to their father. Gregory and Mitzi need your love and mine. Show me what to do and help me know your plan for us. Thank you for helping us so far. Amen

Oh, and Lord, please help me be kind to Dee. I don't understand her, but I love her very much.

The tithing offering was taken while the choir sang an anthem about commitment, service, and trust—all reminding her of her purpose. The organ and the voices reached a crescendo that seemed to shake the windows. Then all was quiet while the robed singers returned to their places and took up their hymnals for the closing benediction:

May the Lord bless and keep you,
May the Lord make his face to shine upon you,
And give you peace. Amen

It was over. Feeling put back together again, she returned her hymnal to its bracket on the back of the pew ahead and followed Diane and Les, already deep in conversation with friends, out to the fellowship hall. The smell of coffee and the hum of conversation promised the only social life she'd enjoyed for over a year. She shook hands with the old pastor who seemed pleased with his performance, smiled into his kind eyes and moved on.

"Suzanne, how lovely you look with your hair up like that, like a young girl."

The voice was chirpy, warm, the hand on her arm, brown and wrinkled. A worn wedding ring slipped loosely on one knobby finger.

"Maud, how kind of you. By your suntan I imagine your famous rose bed is already flourishing."

"My best are on the altar today in honor of my dear Herbert. I never get over missing him, especially the week of our anniversary. Oh my! Me fussing on after being without him for ten years and you so new at being without your man."

Her watery gray eyes loomed large and troubled behind wire-rimmed glasses. Her fingers traveled nervously back and forth across Suzanne's sleeve.

"Don't give it another thought, Maud. You're one of the

few who can even imagine I have to struggle to move forward. Many think 'it's high time that young Suzanne Price found a new man,'" she imitated some imaginary well-meaning soul. They laughed.

Put at her ease, Maud relaxed. "Let's get a Danish and coffee, shall we?"

"My sister's visiting, so I'm afraid I'll need to return home as soon as I collect the children. Speaking of the little angels . . ."

"Look at my picture I made, Mommy!" Mitzi, all smiles, shoved her Sunday school art paper before them.

Maud pointed a shaky finger at a purple blob circled with stripes of yellow cut paper. Most edges showed hiccups of white paste that would take the afternoon to dry. Hopefully, they could get home without smears all over the car seat.

"Tell me about this . . ." her fingernail tapped at the purple shape.

"Flowers wake up from baby seeds, just like we'll wake up in heaven when we die and go to be wif Jesus."

"Well, now," Maud mused, "that's a comforting thought for an old lady like me. Aren't you just the smartest child."

"Going to be wif Jesus isn't just for old-lady people. My Daddy's a flower in heaven, and he wasn't no old lady at all."

Mitzi smiled with genuine sweetness. Looking into each other's eyes, neither woman could find fault. Suzanne hoped Maud wasn't offended about being called an old lady.

"Out of the mouths of babes," Maud said. "The next time Pastor Spahn has to be away, we ought to have the little ones guest in the pulpit." With a farewell wiggle of her fingers, she moved off toward the coffee urn.

"Have you seen Gregory?" Suzanne asked, steering Mitzi toward the exit. Her daughter stopped still.

"No, I haven't *seed* our Gregory, and I haven't had snack yet. I need my juice and cookies."

"Okay, but just one cookie. We're leaving early today to be with your Aunt. Sit at this table after you get your snack. I'll

The Wind Remembers

go find your brother, and we'll join you here."

"Gregory's chasing wif Alex in the yard," Mitzi said, quickly hopping to her place in the children's snack line.

"Wait a minute there, missy, I thought you just said you hadn't seen your brother."

"I didn't *see* Gregory, I jus' heard him hollering down the hall and running outside."

Suzanne rolled her eyes. They came to rest on Diane.

"Poured you a cup, too." She was handed a small mug of black coffee. "Gave her a logical question and expected a complete answer the first round, did you?"

"Just when I think my little girl has told me all of what's going on in her head, she surprises me." Suzanne slid the strap of her shoulder bag higher, and accepted the mug in both hands. The crowd chattered on around them. They moved to the outer wall to avoid the jostle of traffic.

"She is a fascinating child, and so's that rascal Greg. I confiscated our sons' ties before they went whooping off to see Mike's fresh litter of alley-cat babies. Born on Friday the 13th, I'm told."

"Not again. Tell me they're not black as a witch's cat!"

Diane gestured for Les to make his way in their direction. "No, two white and three gray. Go figure."

Suzanne sipped and chuckled. "I wonder if other church custodians rescue stray mother cats that seem to know precisely where to enter the storage shed to have their illicit mixture of kittens."

Diane nodded. "Many a needy Farr child has gone to summer camp on the wings of Mike's kittens, no matter how many mama cats he takes to be spayed once they've weaned their little angels."

"Our boys had better not be planning on bringing kittens home when this batch is
ready." Suzanne added, looking out the fellowship-hall doorway, "I assume they've had their share of cookies."

"And punch too," said Diane, "by the look of their shirts

and faces. Do feel free to drop the children by to play while your sister's here. You two need a little time to talk like grownups." She sipped and asked, "Are you still planning to go to that sculpture place in the desert next week?"

Suzanne felt ambiguous but admitted, "That's the plan. Dee's committed, a real crystal-carrying New Ager. She wouldn't miss celebrating the solstice. Her way of 'being in touch with the universe', she says. God to her is 'a being too sacred to name.' I only found that out last week on the phone. She reminded me that it was well accepted as an Old Testament belief. I'm not sure I understand it where Dee is concerned."

"That's because you and God are on such moment-to-moment terms. Now do leave the kids with us. Two more is no trouble over night. They'll have fun and will keep mine from being bored and driving me crazy."

"You're a sweetheart, Diane. I may bring them by for an afternoon or two, but I wouldn't feel right burdening you overnight."

"Nonsense, they'll drive you nuts trapped in the car for hours, asking, 'Are we there yet?' Plan on it. They'll all have a great time."

"Diane, something's come up that I could use your level-headed advice about . . ."

Les motioned to them with their children in tow.

"Can it wait? Les looks frazzled." Diane set her empty cup on the used-cup tray.

"Of course. We'll talk about it some other time. Thanks, for your generous offer." Suzanne drifted back to Mitzi, disappointed but trusting the time wasn't right to talk about Rehma with her friend.

"I'm ready to visit the cem'tery, Mommy. Me and Leesha already cleaned up our crumbs and drips."

"And you did a great job. Now, let's go find your brother."

They drove out of the church lot with the windows rolled down to let the heat escape.

The Wind Remembers

"I don't want to visit Dad's grave today."

Greg had said the words so softly that at first Suzanne wasn't sure she'd heard him correctly.

"Oh?" Seated quietly between her and Mitzi, he stared straight ahead out the front window.

"If Gregory doesn't want to visit the cem'tery can we stop for ice cream?"

Suzanne scrambled for how to respond to her son, always the one who seemed to need a Sunday graveside visit the most to leave a flower, a bug in a bottle, a tightly folded handwritten letter in a taped-shut envelope painstakingly labeled 'To My DAD.' "Did you want to hurry home to Aunt Dierdre instead, Greg?"

"No. Dad isn't listening to me anymore. I don't want to go visit the cem . . . I just don't want to, that's all."

"God's listening, Gregory, even if you don't think he and your father are paying attention."

"Maybe he is. Maybe he isn't."

"You can talk and write letters to them any time you want to feel close."

Suzanne turned toward home, driving on past the wrought-iron gate of the cemetery for the first time since Steve's memorial service.

"What did you want your Dad to listen about, Greg? Maybe it's something you and I could talk about—you know, like we used to."

"Just something, something about Doug and me, and . . . you. Never mind."

He reached forward and turned on the radio, punching SEEK over and over to find a station to fit his mood, settling on rock. It was too loud. Suzanne said nothing.

If Doug's put marriage and daddy ideas into his head I'll be furious. Just in case, I must set him straight and soon.

Mitzi spoke up above the radio babble, "I'd still like to eat ice cream. I only had two cookies, Mommy. I've got lots of room left." She wiggled in her seat belt and looked at Suzanne around her brother.

"Maybe later with Aunt Dierdre, Princess. We all need something nourishing in our tummies first."

She glanced at Greg. His expression was distant, troubled. The sense of comfort and direction she'd felt during the church service threatened to evaporate. With determined effort she resolved to hang onto her promise—and God's.

She wondered if somehow Steve noticed his family went on without him for the first time. *Steve, Greg's troubled about something. He'll want to write to you again and visit. Just not today. He hasn't stopped loving and missing you.*

Taylor Armstrong

~ Sunday the 15th of June

Climbing down from his truck with thermos in hand, Taylor felt the breeze prickle his unshaven face. He strode briskly up the drive to join his dad at the mews and the weathering grounds where he could always be found on Sunday mornings. Pops would be noting the conditions for thermals, as ledge upon ledge of sandstone and granite on the east face of the Wasatch absorbed the sun's energy. Taylor had learned to tell time each season the way Pops taught him by watching the light creep up and down the peaks from dawn to sunset. It had become so automatic he didn't have to check his wristwatch to know it was coming up on nine.

He loved these June mornings in contrast to the winter inversions. The foggy smog often shrouded the mountains and hugged the valley in a murky embrace for days on end, driving even the skiers and snow boarders above the Salt Lake valley to enjoy the higher slopes and bowls, while they worked on their trendy raccoon-eyed tans. At this time of year, it wasn't necessary to take the falcons above five to seven thousand feet to

The Wind Remembers

hawk for high 'waiting on' in a sunny-sky area, for stooping exercise where visibility of them was clear.

This morning held a welcome clarity in storm-blown-clean air, and the sun gave every surface sparkle. Speck would sense it too and be eager with a good edge to his hunger. Pops would have fasted him to inspire a sharp determination to stoop to his prey. Taylor looked forward to a hawking experience that was only occasional now that he'd grown up and left home and rare since taking over the family tree business.

He moved in shadow along the tall pyracantha hedge. It still bore some of last season's shriveled red fruit and its formidable thorns between fresh bright green shoots. The lethal hedge protected a double row of wooden mews from prying eyes and any human predator with harm to Speck in mind. "Since bored teenagers are turning to vandalism and destroying for the hell of it these days, it's best to make it harder for 'em," Pops had said last fall when Taylor had come to severely trim the hedge back as usual. They'd decided to leave it the height of the mew roofs and trim only the side growth. It would be tough to drive a tank through that thorny hedge now. Taylor had lost many sweaty battles trying to trim it without getting pricked through his leather work gloves.

Patting his back pocket, he made sure he'd remembered to bring a sharp pair of pruners along and caught the sound of the old man clucking to the doves and homing pigeons, the splash of watering pans being refilled, and the warbling coo of the birds. Pops raised pigeons and doves for decoys and for Speck's food. When weather was bad or hunting was poor, thawed frozen lab rats and mice from the university were picked up by the public nature centers with raptor populations of their own as well as by serious falconers. Jake Armstrong's commitment to the mundane daily rituals of feeding and cleaning up after the birds dependent upon his care endeared him to Taylor, and brought a flood of memories. Falconry and the out-of-doors were solid bonds between them. "We're stewards of the land and wildlife," Pops often reminded him, "as endangered a breed as these falcons."

.

THE WIND REMEMBERS

When they disagreed about all else, the love and honor between father and son for the wild and captive-bred falcons was akin to what they felt for each other—however gruffly they expressed it. His mother never quite understood, but she endured without begrudging the hours her men spent hawking and caring for the birds.

At eight years old, the dawn following his full-immersion baptism at the hand of his father by the authority of the Melchizedek Priesthood, he was welcomed into The Church of Jesus Christ of Latter-day Saints, a responsible young Mormon man. As a tribute to that passage, Pops had taken him across the desert in the sod truck to his first Sky Trials. Resting between them on a bar perch were two falcons; a 'tiercel' peregrine, the word for male—unhooded and experienced at flying in competition; the other Taylor's leather-hooded immature tiercel, Speck.

They'd driven beyond any settlements or farms, with only the expanse of ancient Lake Bonneville's flat, dry salt bed holding them in against the mountains. The mature falcon had missed nothing out the windshield, and Taylor had watched the sheen of Great Salt Lake glisten to the west, all the while listening to Pop's explanation for the remote location of the Sky Trials.

"We need an unobstructed view of our birds with a minimum of brush that can hold distracting prey during the timed trials." Pops, a protectionist falconer, had added something about how they "could see trouble from intruders a long way off in a rooster tail of warning dust, should any unwelcome animal-rights activist have a mind to crash the competition 'party'." With Speck hooded on his glove, Taylor had hurried along to keep up with Pops who carried his own bird and hawking bag, and took him from Jeep, to truck, to camper among his falconer friends—to be introduced like a man. The proud boy's eyes had stared with wonder at so many different tethered falcons and hawks of various sizes, and the men of many ages and their women who had gathered to fly the birds in timed competition. He hadn't understood that day that there was money involved.

A few, like his dad, were long-standing members of the North American Falconer's Association, NAFA. Others had taken the sport up through word-of-mouth introduction and simply learned from someone patient enough to teach a novice—until and if they acquired their own birds to register. Crates of live pigeon quarry rested quietly in the shade beneath camper chassis or tarps, protected from heat and the eyes of hungry raptors that had been fasted for their launching turns at the pigeons' release.

Stressed by travel, the falcons would require rest and probably bathing before the trials began. The decoys, or at least the three or four percent of them that would be either innocently slaughtered or pardonably sacrificed to sustain the endangered falcons—according to which side of the animal rights and protection issues you stood on—were mercifully unaware of being quarry themselves. So Taylor had hoped at that tender age.

Even earlier when he watched Pops slip falcons to wait on high for the flush of wild game or the release of pigeons, Taylor had remarked to his dad that the birds "looked like little specks in the sky." Pops had suggested then that Taylor name his fledgling, Speck, since he had made the observation, and it seemed so apt to the waiting on of 'long-wing' raptors. Speck it'd become.

Taylor removed Speck's hood that day after the qualifying preliminary flights at the Sky Trials to let him watch the first-draw falcon rise and wait. At the throw of the homing pigeon, the falcon plummeted in more than a two-hundred-mile-per-hour stoop, talons outstretched to strike the frantic, flapping homer that tried vainly to evade it. The falcon struck the pigeon squarely in the chest, stunning it. Taylor's eyes had followed the successful falcon's flight to the ground. Still clutching its prey, it had swiftly bitten with its double-notched beak at the homer's neck to finish the kill, and began pluming tufts of feathers from its breast.

Another dove zig-zagged through the sky, dove for safety under a parked camper, but was pursued by a big male gyrfalcon that finished the job of nailing his prey. While it ripped into the fleshy breast muscles and fed on its reward, Pops discussed the details of the 5-category 20 points-each system in judging the trials. Ever one to use the proper Sky Trial lingo with Taylor, he explained the competition awards system, though there was plenty of talk of changing it these days. Twenty points for Mounting, the pitch the bird reaches divided by the time from cast off of the hawk to serving the quarry, determined in feet per minute. Position to be measured at 1-minute intervals and determined by the angle of the bird's position above the horizon, using an inclinometer. Pitch referred to the height the falcon reaches when served the pigeon prey. Stoop was measured in pitch and technical aspects, according to how aggressively the hawk cut through to its quarry. Pursuit points were earned as the falcon made additional threatening passes or was successful in catching the pigeon and earning the entire 20 points.

Pops consulted his own stop watch while he observed the height of the hawk's waiting on, the speed of its stoop, the economy of wing beats and direction of flight in its pursuit, how clean and swift its attack and kill, how much time it took and so on. No second chances. The falcon must reach a minimum pitch determined by the judges before a pigeon would be served.

"Why is that?" Taylor had asked.

"So the pigeon has a fair getaway opportunity," his Dad had explained, chuckling. "It adds to the excitement and difficulty of the pursuit."

Speck was Pop's last falcon, since after his heart attack he had bequeathed his breeding birds to the World Center for Birds of Prey on the Snake River in Idaho. The director was a personal friend and breeder whom he knew would treat his birds well. Being more committed to the welfare of his falcons than to his pride, Pops knew he would not breed another falcon to raise for a lifetime perhaps short on future. It would be cruel to train a bird to assist him in the hunt and then not stick around to see it through a long and healthy life span that could last twenty to thirty years. The semen-collecting vials and inseminating paraphernalia had gone to Idaho with his last breeding pair. His breeding hat, however, was too precious a keepsake. It still hung on its peg in the barn. Speck was his joy, someone to fuss over and take pride in, a hunting buddy who was always eager to get out of his mews and weathering grounds and go.

Taylor had figured out early Pops orchestrated his primary hawking to Sunday mornings for the wild prey imperative to his falcons' survival and for some personal reasons, too. If he was a little late to sacrament meeting at the ward house or even missed it altogether, that was between he and Heavenly Father Himself. Besides, Pops had always generously shared his love and knowledge of raptors with the Boy Scout troops in his stake. The brothers and sisters among the faithful members of The Church took for granted his unique calling to perpetuate the species of one of the Lord's awesome, fearsome, and endangered creatures. Nor had Pops ever brooked any argument over the years from his wife, nor any well-meaning Mormon bishop, on the subject of which came first, the Sabbath or his falcons. In Pop's mind they were one and the same. He deemed his personal calling as holy as Noah's.

Taylor enjoyed a special connection with Pops and his birds, underscored by the fact that all five of his siblings were girls. None of them had been encouraged to take up falconry, though they'd argued that many women were avid falconers. That discouragement for the girls was by mutual agreement of his mother and Pops, who were both unabashedly sexist about falconry and captive breeding. Taylor's decision to stay out of state after finishing college had nearly broken Pop's heart for the five and a half years he'd hawked without his son. But he'd forgiven Taylor when he returned to assist, then to take over the tree-trimming business little more than a year and a half ago.

With the family orchards and sod businesses managed jointly and profitably by two of Taylor's sisters and their husbands, and Taylor managing the tree and shrub trimming business, it was a good time in Pop's life. Old Jake Armstrong had nothing much to worry about now except taking his heart medicine, working off his wife's hearty farm cooking, "fussing with Speck" as Taylor heard his mother put it, and puttering in the garden. He also enjoyed constructing wooden toys for his sixteen grandchildren and three great-grandchildren and managing whatever bird-egg incubation project he had going with Bee Hive youngsters from the wards in his Mormon stake on their Activity Days. He didn't mind if the girls helped tend quail or chicken eggs for hatching, but falcons were men's work in his not-so-humble opinion. Taylor was just waiting for one of his adorable granddaughters to beg for a falcon of her own. He'd see then how long Pop's gender bias held out against a little heart twisting.

Jake Armstrong emerged from the nearest mew that served as a pigeon cote and set a lumpy hawking bag of live homing pigeons at his feet. He flipped the latch back into place and rammed a twig through the loop of the clasp. Inside, the remaining birds fluttered from perch to perch, conversing in coos about who would feed first on the seed mix scattered for them. Squinting into the sun outside the shaded mews, he lifted the hawking bag and abruptly halted mid-step.

"My hell, Taylor, you trying to give me another heart attack? How long you been out here quiet as a mouse?"

"Sorry, Pops, I hit the bed like a ton of bricks last night. Didn't open my eyes until after it was time for you to be in the barns this morning. Figured I'd just find you here and tag along."

"No harm done. What's up, son? You've never been one much for social calls." Jake whapped Taylor affectionately on the shoulder. "I see you brought your own thermos of coffee. Afraid your mother will serve you some of her cereal-brew?"

They laughed and proceeded on toward Speck's mew at the end of the row.

"Nah, a little . . uh . . . neighbor girl found a robin's egg in a nest after the storm. I wondered if you had your incubators warm for hatching. Told her I'd check with you. She wants to surprise her mother."

"That what you've got in the thermos?"

Taylor nodded. His dad turned away from the mews and moved off in the direction of the barn. Over his shoulder he said, "Can't find a woman your own age yet, I see." He chuckled at his own joke and ducked into the cool barn where he collected leather gloves and a feathered lure. "Or is it her mother you've set your sights on?"

"Pops, if it's too much trouble . . ."

"Didn't say nothing about incubating an egg being too much trouble. Don't get your dander in an uproar."

He opened a room at the back of the barn, pulled a cord, and flooded the space with light. Taylor followed him to a waist-high bench along the south wall where an incubator warmed a long box lidded with fine-mesh screen, a Plexiglas lid drilled with holes over all. Inside, speckled, gray brown to bluish quail eggs no bigger than a walnut waited to be turned regularly by Pop's blunt-tipped fingers.

"Looks like your latest scout troop project is well underway."

Taylor unscrewed the stopper on his thermos and slid the bandanna lump into his hand. Jake lifted layers of lids and switched on a bulb to activate another warming area at the end of the row of quail eggs. He took the delicate blue robin egg, held it to a bulb for a moment, seemed satisfied that all was well with its developing embryo, and gently placed it in the box a safe distance from the warming bulb. Replacing the lid, he smiled at Taylor and gave the box a motherly pat.

"Nature will have to take it from here. I'll call you if we get a bird."

"Thanks. Call me even if we don't. I'll have to have a good story for the little cutie anyway about why it didn't hatch."

Taylor carried the battered army-issue binoculars he'd lifted from their wooden peg and the hawking bag as he had done since his boyhood. He left the empty thermos with its handle looped over that peg so he'd be sure to pick it up on their return. It wasn't as if he felt he could afford to give up time from storm-damage tree removal today, even if it was Sunday. *I want the old pro's opinion about the reason anyone might have for tampering with Suzanne's tree the way it's been done.*

He planned to bring it up carefully so that Pops would never know he was talking about Susie's place. He also didn't want his dad to ask to see the felled tree with his own eyes. He'd try to get some ideas without causing confusion about Suzanne. By this afternoon, her tree would be mostly firewood and no cause for his dad to go snooping at her place. It had always been easier to pick his old man's brain when he was busy with his birds. He felt determined to leave old, moldy rocks unturned.

The welcoming shrill whistlings of Speck signaled he'd heard and now spied Pops through the slats of his mew. He fluttered from level to level on his white-spattered, padded shelf arrangement of Astroturf-covered perches against the back wall, bobbing his head from side to side to get a better view of his visitors. Enormous dark eyes and the yellowish cere of his beak added to his wild appearance. His flexing talons moved in a mesmerizing rhythm that became more animated when the steel lock was opened and threaded out of its loops on the latch. From his tarsi, the leg area above his talons, Speck's permanent leather jesses, knotted with tiny bells, trailed and jingled as they were designed to do in case the bird became lost. The bells could be a danger though in calling attention to the bird for larger wild predators, like mountain lions. Being at the top of the food chain was of no help to an injured or entangled raptor. Taylor was fond of the romantic nod to traditional old-world tracking systems his father preferred, over what he termed "new fangled telemeters with radio pick-ups like something out of *Star Wars*. If you bond with your bird proper and train it well, it won't bolt on you."

Speck roused his feathers erect, shook himself, and allowed his feathers to slowly settle tightly back into place. He chuckered to Jake, his neck swiveling so his marble stare could scrutinize Taylor curiously, bells tinkling softly with every move.

"Hush, hush. Don't you remember me, Speck?" Taylor extended a gloved hand and waited. The peregrine pecked at the

The Wind Remembers

glove, but flew to Jake's wrist before swiveling his head near full-circle and considering Taylor over his shoulder. The white flecked-with-brown feathers of his throat and crop area, just above his sternum, made subtle movements of excitement.

"You're just as beautiful as ever, aren't you, boy?"

Speck rode Jake's gloved wrist until his talons were even with Taylor's gloved hand, then he stepped across and latched neatly onto the hand that had grown to fill a man's glove since they had begun training together in Taylor's boyhood. The tiercel peregrine ducked his head repeatedly and made a series of cries that brought a swallow to Taylor's Adam's apple.

"Still gets to you, that trusting by a hawk, doesn't it?" Jake nodded to his son, caught his eye, looked away, and cleared his throat. "Got to get in here with the hose and make the place decent again. Been too cold and rainy for a while to get at it. Makes my arthritis kick up to beat all if I don't wait until it's warm enough to get through the whole annual process in one stretch. Has to be warm enough to dry the mew out completely for Speck, too. Old age ain't for sissies."

Jake chuckled and scuffed through the gravel floor material, crushing several of Speck's castings of pigeon feathers, rat hair and bones, examining the neat pellets, indigestible remains of recent meals, for any signs of poor health in his bird. Then he gathered a couple of molted feathers and tucked them in his pocket. Taylor passed through the door and stood waiting outside. Jake closed the mew gate and clipped a cord to Speck's jesses. Taylor transferred the peregrine to Jake, who whistled sharply. An answering whoof came from the direction of the orchard. Speck's head turned to the sound. Moments later, a setter with a graying muzzle padded into view at the turn in the hedge. Radar sniffed the pant legs of both men and accepted their affection with enthusiasm, then ran on ahead to check out the path through the orchard he knew they would follow with the tiercel.

Taylor fell in behind his dad and inhaled remembered scents, along with new ones as they passed among the cherry trees, their crowns full of robins, crows, and long-tailed scolding magpies. Beyond the orchard, he caught sight of Radar's tail plume waving. His nose sniffed tufts of sagebrush for whatever had passed by in the night; his hackles rose occasionally at the scent of a raccoon or a deer. There had been more than a few deer earlier this morning or last evening, for their split-hoofed, sharp-pointed tracks and mounds of coffee-bean-like droppings were in evidence. Mule deer frequented this path back and forth from the oak brush on the distant bench to the stream that flowed noisily this morning with snowmelt.

The icy water that had left the higher elevations the previous afternoon rushed in a foaming froth over the boulder-strewn stream bed along the path they followed. In another week or two, the snow above would be gone and the stream would dry to a gully, until the fall rains came. The countryside was mostly hunted out of the big bucks that used to come this low. Taylor missed the childhood excitement of finding their sizable tracks or spying an impressive five-to seven-point rack held motionless among the low branches of shrub oak when he passed by within a few yards.

Now, encroaching housing developments had gobbled up most of the farm and wild grazing land. "Damn Californians," his dad was fond of saying. "They raped their own beautiful state, now they got to come here and ruin ours. Hell, we pipe them our water, what more do they want?" Taylor smiled at the back of his dad's head as he watched the endearing old man and the peregrine and thought about such staunchly held, biased opinions he absorbed as a boy along with Pop's hard-work ethic and honest values.

Jake's thinning snow crop of hair fluttered about his weathered ears and furrowed neck like a silvery halo in the sunshine. The natural moisture in Jake's skin had long ago been sucked away. The flesh had toughened to leather in the relentless Utah sun and high-desert air, the way the knee-high weeds would be parched to brittleness by August. While no longer powerful enough to fell a mature tree single-handedly, Taylor admired his dad's broad, strong shoulders that still filled out a flannel shirt like a younger man in his prime. In spite of his heart repair, or perhaps because of it, this morning his dad's gloved hand held his gallant peregrine falcon steady without apparent weariness. Taylor wasn't sure who he felt was the prouder of the two old birds, but his heart surged with warm feeling for them both.

"Won't be doing much flying this morning. Speck's dropped two more flight feathers, but he'll enjoy being out of the mew for a break in the boredom." Jake spoke over his shoulder.

"Don't kid me, Pops, you just like having him along as a defendable excuse for a good walk in trade for sacrament meeting, even if he can't 'wait on' for his molting."

The remark went unanswered. His dad angled his body in Taylor's direction, while they descended the sloping path and crossed the stream on a stepping bridge of water-worn boulders. There wasn't room for them to walk two abreast, particularly with the falcon and the swift current. They reached the meadow of an old sheep camp area, now overgrown with yellow-blooming dyer's woad. Not a native plant, it was introduced in pioneer times to be crushed for its fabric-dying qualities and became the scourge of the Intermountain West. Cattle avoided it, sheep wouldn't eat it and it spread like wildfire. Only things good about it were the way it held the soil from eroding into the wind and its beautiful yellow flowers that reminded him of fields of mustard in the Midwest. They reminded him of Suzanne, too, because she enjoyed painting fields of both yellow-flowering plants. *Suzanne. . . .* Her big brown eyes followed him in his mind.

Pops motioned to Taylor to let Radar have a go at scaring up some small game for Speck before he resorted to the live prey in the bag. He snapped his fingers at his side and Radar loped off, his sniffing purposeful, tracking faint prints of small birds, snakes, rabbits, lizards and mice.

Speck rustled his wings and followed Radar's movements with intense interest in his immense eyes. Pops raised his arm and stretched it out in front of him for a firm perch. Radar flushed a jackrabbit that bounded away through the woad and sage, showering blossoms and pungent fragrance in its wake. Speck's powerful wings pumped, and he rose in the air in pursuit. Pops whistled and Radar dropped out of the chase and loped back. The tiercel's dark shadow flew after the zigzagging rabbit, flowing over the ground in pursuit as if the shadow itself were a live thing. The momentary distraction of a panic-stricken mouse caused Speck to lose his edge on the rabbit. Both escaped. Pops allowed him a few more seconds of searching on his own, then called:

"Whup, Whup, Whup, Ooooh," and raised his arm in command for Speck to return to his glove.

He settled onto Pop's gloved hand and accepted a limp, thawed mouse in reward, decapitating it neatly and consuming its chest in a few shreddy bites. A trickle of bright blood dribbled from his beak to be captured on the snowy hind parts of the lab rodent whose lifeless, straggling tail attracted Radar's sniffing interest.

"Well, Speck," Pops asked, "did a little taste of mouse pique your interest in another try with old Radar?" Out of habit, his knotty-jointed fingers laced the leather jesses between his gloved knuckles, while he chatted amiably with his feathered pal.

Speck chuckered at him.

Taylor observed, "Guess he's still good and hungry after that meager ounce or two of hors d'oeuvres."

Pops repeated the flushing command to Radar who romped away for his part in the feeding activities. In a moment he flushed a ruffed grouse and her brood of babies. Taylor and Pops laughed as Speck took flight again, low and determined over the fleeing birds, startling more that had been well hidden. Soon the clearing fluttered with grouse seeking shelter from Speck, whose extended talons gripped a young bird, hop-dragged it to a clear place, broke its neck neatly with a bite of his horny beak, picked feathers from its little neck and breast, and consumed the paltry amount of meat quickly.

"He's having a heck of a time bringing down anything

sizable with his missing feathers," commented Taylor.

"Better let him go for one of the girls from the bag," Pops said. "He's been fasting for a while and can't produce new feathers without plenty of protein."

Taylor pulled on his gloves and unzipping the bag, slid his hand inside, grasped a pigeon and brought her out into the sunlight. Her pink-rimmed eyes blinked rapidly. She looked around to get her bearings, nipping at Taylor's glove.

"Whup, Whup," Pops called.

Speck looked up from the scanty remains of the grouse and raised his wings, lifting himself into the air with extra effort. He gained enough height to make a reasonable 'stoop' at the quarry.

"Now!" Pops commanded.

Taylor served the homer who flew out from his throw superbly, caught sight of the on-coming peregrine too late, and turned to change direction. Speck's outstretched talons thwucked into the frantic pigeon's body. The blow took them both to the ground. Speck dispatched the stunned bird mercifully with a single bite to the neck. Pops removed his glove, tossed it to Taylor and approached Speck where he sat with tight feathers, diligently plucking feathers that plumed in the air and drifted around him in the gentle breeze. Speck waited for his handler to 'make in,' making throating inviting sounds toward Pops.

Taylor watched his dad kneel and converse. The tiersel chuckered his invitation to share his kill. Pops congratulated his falcon on the capture and kill, produced a knife and slit the pigeon's breast. He extracted the heart and held it out for Speck to enjoy, choosing not to claim the remaining game as hunters of old would have done. Jake left it for his fasted falcon to feast upon. Speck tore into the rich breast muscles of the pigeon carcass. Pops returned to Taylor.

"You haven't lost your serving touch, Son. Nice work to make it easy for Speck today. His best feathers are in my pocket."

Taylor took the opportunity to pursue his purpose in

coming, while the tiercel feasted on his breakfast, and Radar sat patiently between them sniffing the breeze.

"I've got something on my mind to talk over with you."

"Didn't figure it for a social call, Son. What's up?"

"I'm trying to come up with a plausible reason some weirdo might have for prepping a tree to fall on residential property, right next to the dwelling of a young family. We're talking where somebody could've been killed when it went over."

"What kind of tree?"

"An old cottonwood. What's the type got to do with it?"

"Not much but size, just curious. Missed the house?"

"Yeah, scraped down the board siding and did some garage damage, but fortunately didn't hurt anyone. Of course the owner's mighty upset to lose the old beauty. She had a special fondness for it." Taylor swallowed on the *she*.

"A woman like that can't be all bad." His dad chuckled.

Taylor caught it for a remark to be enjoyed just between them. It wasn't the sort of word play to be tossed about in front of his mother, who even in her late sixties was testy on the topic of women in general and other women in particular. She was a one-man woman and expected reciprocity. They'd joked privately about how she'd have never cut it as a plural wife back in pioneer times. She had enough struggle competing with Pop's falcons.

"What do you make of it, Pops? Why would anyone want to do that right in a neighborhood? Well, it's sort of in a neighborhood. Sits a little ways off by itself at the top of the bench, about where the road paving ends and it goes to gravel on up the logging roads and the old sheep camps."

"You've ruled out anybody with a personal grudge?" Pops put his glove back on.

They watched Speck finishing his meal while he turned the pigeon's remains over and around in the wedge of his talons. Using his beak in jerky peck-and-pull movements, his bells jingled in a rising breeze. Radar sniffed the air and twitched his ears, sensing the falcon was nearly finished and becoming eager himself to return to the stream for a drink.

"Nothing's ruled out so far, just wondered if you'd heard anything going on in the last few years that I might not know about around here. We're too far from Oregon for tree spikers making a save-the-owls statement," Taylor joked. "But I might be overlooking something."

"Ooooh, Whup, whup," the old man called to Speck, raising his right arm skyward twice in succession. He held forth his gloved left forearm for a perch and allowed the falcon to regain his glove. They left what remained of the grouse and the pigeon for scavenging crows and magpies. Speck settled his feathers in contentment with a sated appetite.

The men returned along the path single file. Taylor knew his dad was mulling over the problem he'd presented, and he gave him time without interruption to consider the options. They reached the gate to the garden behind the mews. Even from there, Taylor could hear the doves cooing and fluttering in the back half of the barn. Bells tingling, the falcon rustled his wings impatiently on Pop's arm.

"Speck hears his next meal," his dad remarked. "Or so he hopes."

Taylor latched the gate after them and hiked the hawking bag higher on his shoulder, patting the pigeons on the outside of the bag. "You two will be back in there with your friends in a minute to compare notes and plan your strategy for outwitting old Speck another day."

"You know, there is something that might have a bearing on that tree felling."

His dad delivered the tiercel to his perch in the weathering area. He poured fresh water in the falcon's shaded bath pan and spoke over his shoulder.

"At city council meeting, we listened to a petition by a big contractor who's having plenty of opposition to a bunch of pricey high-rise condos he wants to build up on the bench. Which bench area did you say this tree went over on?"

"I didn't." Taylor's interest picked up. He set the hawking bag of pigeons down just outside the cote door where they'd be less temptation for Speck and waited for Pops. He stowed the binoculars and took his thermos down from its peg.

"Top of Old Post Road."

He chewed at his lip, brushed weed prickers from his jeans and held his breath, ready to defend the lack of need for his dad to go look at the felled-tree situation himself.

"That's right. You did mention the sheep camps. Not many of them left around here. Matter of fact, above Old Post Road is within a road or two of where that guy showed us the blue prints prepared for plotting out the proposed-condo property."

Jake closed the mew gate and rammed the steel combination lock through the loop of metal that served as a latch, then clicked it shut with his thumb and gave the numbers an extra spin. Taylor carried the pigeons back to their enclosure and released them to join the others. He followed his dad to the barn.

"You mean, maybe the tree cutting's got something to do with somebody wanting more of that property up there?"

"Well, think about it, Son. It's still the Old West out here. Somebody wants something, they try to buy it, get turned down, they figure out a way to take it."

"I don't follow you all the way."

They entered the cool darkness of the barn, casting their long shadows from the doorway onto the straw-scattered floor. The horse stalls stood empty now, but the smells he loved of hay and old wood enveloped them. Pops opened the dovecote door, and Taylor ducked inside with him to return the pigeons in the bag and help fill their flat, ceramic seed and water bowls.

Jake clucked at them and told them how much fancier their fanned white tails looked than those of the pigeons. He looked over at Taylor.

"As I recall, it was clear at the meeting nobody but real estate people and bankers were a damn bit interested in another subdivision of any kind on the bench. Dealing with the earthquake fault line and the water rights, not to mention erosion and forest-fire hazards are expensive inevitabilities."

They closed the door and went outside beneath the overhang of the roof to wash up in the deep cast-iron sink that had commanded that spot since the erecting of the barn.

"What I'm saying is, there's got to be easements and widened and paved roads up there at the top of the bench before heavy equipment and materials can be brought in to do the condo building. Many of the homeowners on those roads have been approached to sell their places, but nobody up there wants to sacrifice an easement or sell, according to all we heard at that meeting. The condo thing has been real hush-hush to keep the property prices from going sky high. Some of the town's wealthiest and most influential stand to profit, and they've got the legal pull to keep us quiet."

"So bring me all the way along, Pops. I'm still missing something."

Taylor rubbed his scruffy chin and thought it through again, coming up empty. Some of mom's coffee was in order if he could talk her out of her malt brew. His brain was foggy from lying awake last night mulling about Susie.

"The only way that self-serving son of a gun is going to get his big and profitable condo project pouring money into his greedy pockets is to find a way to get about a half dozen properties on a couple of roads condemned by the county. Then he'll come in and buy them up for a song."

Finally Taylor felt his mind come alive. It made the leap.

"So, either destroy it for habitation, or scare people into selling, right?"

"Now you've got it. Just a thought, but if it's up along that blueprint area, I'd be expecting possible hostilities." His dad wiped his neck with the back of his hand; the exertion of the morning perhaps a bit more than he'd bargained for, but the pleasure all worth it. He smiled. "I'd be mighty careful getting involved, if I were you. No sense biting the hand that feeds your business."

The Wind Remembers

"Thanks Pops, perhaps you're onto something. It was great to go out with you, Speck and old Radar again. Been too long."

They walked shoulder to shoulder out of the north wind toward the brick and timber farmhouse now catching sunlight with its neat pine-tree nursery rows planted to the south.

"Don't be mouthing it around town about this condo business, Taylor. It's speculation on my part. The council agreed to give the proposal two weeks' consideration before we bring it all before the public. Would've been public if any citizens had been in attendance like they're welcome. Just turned out to be a private session because only the council members showed up. Even the newspaper reporter with our beat was off on a more impressive event of some kind. I don't want it known I'm the one who alerted the citizens before we decide if this goes public. I'm sort of fond of sitting on that council. Gives me a kitchen pass a couple nights a month with a respectable place to go, if you know what I mean." He laughed heartily and squeezed Taylor's shoulder.

"I guess I can hold it a day or two, Pops, but if it becomes police business, I make no promises. Except I will say it was a rumor, if I'm pressed."

"Good enough. Let's get a mug of your mother's cereal brew and a muffin, unless she's experimenting with that damned hazelnut crap she brought home last week. Sissy drink if you ask me. Some kind of fake *cappuccino* she says she got from your Aunt Lotty. 'Give it back to Lotty,' I told her."

"Give Mom a break, Pops. She's got to have a little fun around a tough old fart like you."

"Oh, listen to the Romeo give his old man woman advice! You're not very good at keeping a woman happy so far as I can see. Never could figure you letting that sweet Suzanne get away. She's probably married to some man with truck loads of money and living in a fancy house back East somewhere, do doubt producing a brood of brown-eyed younguns." Whack, Jake slapped him on the back.

"Can't imagine why an old Latter-day Saint like you would want me taking up with a Methodist gentile anyway. Of course unlike my sisters you and Mom do stretch your Church limits from Postum to coffee for me now and again."

"Small vices can be forgiven. But a man of any persuasive powers, including the power of the priesthood, should have no trouble with a woman whose heart is in the right place already. You just have to work harder to convert her."

"Suzanne is . . . *was* the sort of woman with a strong mind of her own. Converting her to anything never was likely. That's one of the things I liked most about her."

"Well, she was my favorite of all the girls you ever brought around. I'd have settled for my grandchildren being sealed to the two of you 'for time and all eternity'. Just speaking for myself."

"You usually do, Pops." Taylor laughed.

He had heard it all before. He rummaged in the cupboard for his favorite mug and smiled in congratulations to himself for what he hadn't said about women—or at least one woman in particular. A plate of fresh homemade muffins on the table drove all women but his mother from his immediate attention. He slathered on a layer of sweet honey butter and thought he could find her for a hug by the roaring of the ancient Hoover coming from the living room. His mother frowned on laboring on the Sabbath, so the home teachers or some hungry missionaries must be expected after sacrament meeting or she wouldn't be vacuuming before hurrying off to Church. The instant Postum smelled ordinary, not sweetly hazelnut, and passable now that Taylor had a handle on Suzanne's trouble and a peaceable morning put in with Pops. He filled his mug, smiled at his dad whose mouth bulged with a muffin, and went to say good morning to his mother. He'd ask to 'borrow' a couple of her muffins, as he had since childhood. She was one woman who'd give him the enthusiastic answer he wanted about nearly whatever he had in mind.

CHAPTER EIGHT

Unsettling Circumstances

Suzanne Price

~ Sunday the 15th of June

As soon as they had driven into the yard from church, Suzanne was surprised to see Dee waiting for them on the back step. She stubbed out her cigarette in the zinnia garden, much to Suzanne's dismay, and insisted on selecting and paying for a restaurant Sunday brunch. Which was fine except she didn't want to allow Suzanne time with the kids to freshen up or change into casual clothes. *When Dee's ready to do something, everybody better get on board or get out of the way.*

After a drive up a nearby canyon, Suzanne and the children entered the '30's era restaurant behind Dierdre. Neither twin had been to the Heritage Lodge since coming home from college on Thanksgiving break to be with their mother. The entry ramp for disabled patrons was new; the weathered clapboards looked the same. Aromas from the brunch buffet smelled delicious, and Suzanne felt the moisture gather in her mouth. The vintage ambiance of the interior, antique porcelain platters above the fireplace and cut glass containers sparkling on the tables were lovely. Suzanne hadn't been in a nice restaurant in well over a year.

"Wow, this place is cool!" Greg exclaimed, fussing with the tie she'd urged him to put on again, hoping to obscure the juice stains on his shirt front that made him resemble the 'before' image in a detergent commercial.

"Ooh, Aunt Dreedra, can I have some of those big fat starberries?"

"Mitzi, you may have whatever you want. I'm picking up the check, so let's all enjoy ourselves."

Suzanne was aware they'd suddenly become the center of attention. Heads at table after table turned their way, all eyes eventually settling on Dierdre in her lime-green linen dress belted with shiny copper, coordinated with matching earrings and a stack of clinking bracelets up one slim, tan arm. Brazilian leather sandals showed off her shapely bare ankles completed her knock-out ensemble. Her copper toenail polish hadn't even hit local cosmetic counters yet. The khaki-dressed canyon crowd in hiking shoes and the sedate church-going families in their Sunday best were more than curious about her twin, but Dee feigned being oblivious. Dierdre chose chairs by the lace-curtained window at a table draped in a white cloth, where a bud vase of daisies and roses beckoned.

"I want to sit where I can see everything," said Greg.

"I want to sit by Aunt Dreedra." Mitzi changed places with Gregory and flounced her skirts into her chair, waiting with a look of anticipation, her hands folding and unfolding in her lap.

Suzanne remained standing. "Dee, I'll be right back. Why don't you come with me, Mitzi?"

"I want to stay here and watch, okay, Mommy?"

Suzanne relented. "I'm going to wash my hands and

freshen my face. It's been a long morning since we left for church." She moved away without waiting for Dee's okay. "I'll bring you wet towels for your hands, kids."

She retreated to the ladies' room and waited her turn at a stall, then smiled at the pregnant young woman who guided a little girl ahead of her to the towel dispenser. How Suzanne had wanted babies of her own, but she'd miscarried the only child she and Steve had been able to conceive before his cancer was detected. They'd never talked about it again during his chemo treatments. She'd never mentioned it to Dee. Having Steve's children had been enough to sustain her during her fresh grief. Her own babies would have been lovely . . . if only . . . Her thoughts returned to her most pressing problem. Rehma wanting Gregory and Mitzi back.

Just for today I'm putting Rehma and her wants out of my mind. Today, with Dee in town, I'll enjoy my family—all the family I have.

Suzanne tweaked her hair, washed her hands and returned to the table with two moist towelettes. The table was empty. Dee and the kids were going through the buffet line. Greg smiled and laughed. She breathed more easily and joined them, leaving the damp towelettes on her charger plate. Suzanne was unaware of how many admiring eyes turned to watch her pass by.

Following brunch, they took a leisurely drive over Trapper's Loop to digest the sumptuous food and enjoy the breath-taking views and progress on the new ski lift being installed for the 2002 Olympic Giant Slalom course. Later, Mitzi and Greg begged for a stop by the river at an ice cream stand. Somehow more than five hours flew by. Suzanne was relieved to pull into the driveway at home. She felt a special pleasure at the sight of Taylor loading tree limbs into his shiny new truck.

"That's a fine figure of a man," quipped Dee.

"He always has been," Suzanne said. *You have no idea.*

Mitzi squirmed in her seat. "I like him fine, too. Mister Armfrong sure works hard. He's my new bestist friend."

"Don't release that belt, Miss Wiggles, until I've parked the car and turned off the engine, remember?" *I wonder why Mitzi's taken to Taylor so quickly.*

Greg released his seat belt with a startling snap and sat forward. "Are you still gonna play catch with me, Aunt Dierdre, like you promised?"

"You bet. A promise is a promise. You find the ball and mitts, and I'll change into my shorts."

Suzanne drove into the open garage, parked, and they all got out. The children ran inside to change clothes, while she and Dierdre walked toward the back porch at a speed more appropriate to high-heeled sandals. Taylor waved and kept to his work; Suzanne hoped there'd be time for a moment with Him. She entered the back door and was nearly knocked down by Gregory.

"I listened to the beeping messages," he panted. "We missed Doug. And my mother says she's taking us camping!" His eyes widened with excitement.

Dierdre stepped close while Suzanne pressed the replay message button on the answering machine. She whispered, "What's that, something about the long-lost Rehma?"

Doug's voice came on first.

"Suzanne, sorry last evening didn't work out. When you're back from church, call me right away so we can get together this afternoon. It's important."

She pressed erase. "Well, afternoon's about over, so whatever he thinks is so important will have to wait. I'm bushed." Her heart hammered as she waited through the time announcement for the second message. *Lord, help me handle whatever Rehma's message says without losing it like I did over her attorney's letter.*

"This is it," blurted Greg, jumping up and down. "Here comes my *mother's* voice!"

"Suzanne, by now you know I'm taking my kids back. I've planned a camping trip with them. I'll tell you when to have 'em ready."

Suzanne's shoulders slumped like someone had poked a hole in her air balloon. *The cat's out of the bag with Dee. Rehma has upped the ante without talking anything over with me. How could she? Why?* Stunned to silence, Suzanne punched erase on the phone recorder, wishing she could disappear Rehma in a poof as easily.

Greg looked from one to the other of the twins, his face alight with smiles. "See, didn't I tell you my mom wants to take me camping? Wow! Suzanne, does she mean she wants me and Mitzi to go back to live with her?"

"Mommy," Mitzi tugged at Suzanne's skirt hem. "You told me I can't go nowhere wif strangers. I don't understand about Rehma."

Suzanne's twin took over. "Neither do we, Sweetheart. Sounds like there's a lot to figure out that's all news to me." Dee arched her eyebrows in a question above the children's heads.

Suzanne closed her eyes and took a shuddery breath. *I've had enough of character building, Lord. You better take over. I don't think I have the ammunition or the wisdom for this fight. It's going to get nasty.*

~ Monday the 16th of June

Suzanne slipped from Mitzi's bed, pulled on her robe, and tucked her journal into a pocket. She often sorted things out on paper, an old habit she inherited from her mother. Tiptoeing across the linoleum, she switched on the hanging lamp above the kitchen table.

When Reverend Spahn had suggested she might find comfort for her grieving heart in a journal, she'd laughed, explaining the pages of volume number three were about used up. He'd reminded her she had children to help fill her days, and her painting and drawing to fill her nights, reminding her of responsibilities and skills many others of his pastorate didn't have. He'd urged her to rely more on prayer, friends, and reading scriptures for comfort, assuring her she'd heal, even love again. He'd waited quietly until, uncomfortable, she broke the silence, asking if he thought she was feeling sorry for herself. He'd smiled and nodded, encouraging her to live by faith without answers to all of her questions and fears. He asked if they might pray together. Her hands in his and their heads bowed, Suzanne had listened to his deep, sure voice leading her into a place of exquisite peace. She missed his comfort and looked forward to his return from conference.

Until then, she'd stand on her own and deal with the threat to her family. Greg's painting tantrum, attempting to ruin Mitzi's mural, she knew was really aimed at her. Until Dee told her Greg had overheard her argument with Steve, she hadn't been sure why he was so angry with her. He punished her for losing his father.

Reverend Spahn had told her, "Greg observed how you loved Steve, even when he threw up all over the bedclothes and lost his hair with chemotherapy. He had to notice you loved his dad when he couldn't take you dancing any more or help around the house, or go to work, or near the end, even get out of bed. Deep down, Gregory knows you won't give up on him either. But he's going to test you because he's testing himself. His grief is too big and too confusing for a little boy."

Reverend Spahn had concluded at the door, "You must have patient faith, Suzanne. Gregory will realize he loves you, needs you. Things take time, especially with children. He wants others to hurt as much as he does, so they'll understand the pain he feels. He's so caught up in his own pain he can't imagine yours."

That insight had given Suzanne grace to endure many painful confrontations with Greg without losing her love for him or her tested patience. But lately he was becoming unbearable. Something in him was coming to a head like an angry canker. She felt a growing panic that she must discover what it was soon, or somehow he might unwittingly play them all into Rehma's plan to force Suzanne to give up the children. She struggled to convince herself to have greater faith. *A little faith isn't going to be enough. It never has been. God and I are going to have to work overtime to keep this little family together.*

She journaled intensely, sorting through each problem thoughtfully. Seeing her words on paper restored a sense of control. Her anxiety eased. *I'll find my own attorney. If the children have to earn scholarships to attend college, so be it. The education fund will save this family first. I'll replenish it when I find a good job.*

The coffee maker sputtered to a finish. Suzanne paused to fill a mug, re-opened her journal and began a list of problems on the left and possible solutions on the right. She included Dierdre, and to her amusement discovered she'd listed her twin in both columns. *Well, that's real.*

Not much had changed over the course of their lives. Dee had taught her a great deal about life's realities, often long before she was ready, and definitely with mixed results. How to stuff a bra to get just the right curve in a sweater. The best lipstick and mascara techniques to make sure you were noticed without alarming Mom. The way to get out of making their bed or going to church—stomachaches and menstrual cramps worked for a while. Then Mom had started tracking their periods. The faking was obvious. Grounding for two weeks had cured them. But it was Dee who found youth group on Sunday evening to be a great way to meet boys from other schools. Summer camp was even better, except Dierdre was the twin the counselors searched for after curfew and found in the horse barn or the woods with a friend. Suzanne covered for her sister in the letters home to their mother. She was terrified that if Mom got wind of what was going on with Dee, neither of them would be allowed to return to camp the next year.

The Wind Remembers

Suzanne now admitted to herself how desperately she wanted to confide in Dierdre, ever the practical and adventurous one. Her risk-taker twin could cut to the core of any situation and extract only what she wanted with little apparent regard for those she left bleeding in her wake.

With her hand forced after the phone message Gregory discovered, Rehma's attorney letter wasn't secret any longer. Suzanne had put off explanations to Dee yesterday, but hoped for some truly practical advice that might point out something she'd missed while lying awake most of the night trying to figure out what to do. And praying for guidance. She spent a lot of the night doing that.

Usually Suzanne worried that if she took Dee's advice then someone would get hurt. Now she didn't care if it hurt Rehma to lose custody of Gregory and Mitzi. She couldn't imagine why Rehma wanted them when she was only too eager to part with them nearly three years ago. *I can be tough because the kids will be better off with me than with her, even though I haven't found a job yet.*

It comforted Suzanne when she and Dee talked about things on the phone, even when they didn't understand or agree with one another because there were times she learned something important from her analytic twin.

But, she reminded herself, *Dee wasn't here for me when Steve died. Can I count on her now?*

Suzanne set her mug down hard. Coffee slopped onto her sleeve. She grabbed a napkin and bled the brown liquid from her terry cuff. The swinging door opened. She looked up.

"Is there any get-up-and-go brew left, or have you been quaffing that stuff all night?" Dierdre entered, smoothing her dark hair with long red nails. Her eyes were puffy. She looked out of sorts.

"If there isn't enough, we'll make more. Mugs are on..."

"I know where you keep things. You're as predictable as clockwork. Mom should have named you Timex."

"What gets you out of bed before you've had your

beauty-*sweet* sleep?" Disappointed to be interrupted, Suzanne closed her journal and tucked it back in her robe pocket. She'd wanted to sort out her encounter Saturday night with Doug and her feelings at seeing Taylor again before confiding in Dee. Writing about both men and Rehma's attorney letter would have to wait. She refreshed her coffee and returned to the table.

Dierdre joined her. "I couldn't sleep for dreaming of tarantulas and scorpions. What on earth are you going to do about Greg?"

The challenge again. The gift box Dierdre said was meant for her and her failure with Greg hung between them like a blade ready to stab Suzanne squarely in the heart. *Sis, why can't you just be a friend?* Her desire to confide about the letter and ask advice retreated. Suzanne felt foolish for even imagining she'd wanted her sister to come, to talk, to share fun, and to help her heal. *It's time I take better care of myself with Dee ... starting now!*

She challenged, "Dee, f you can't stand the thought of a tarantula or a scorpion, why did you suggest we go to the desert for the solstice? Sleeping on the ground could invite the little creatures to spend the night in your sleeping bag. Did you ever think of that?" *Finally! I've the courage to change the subject.*

Dierdre poured a sweetener packet into her coffee. "Yes, I have thought of that. Though I admire your spunk, it's a little uncharacteristic of you to switch subjects on me—but a welcome change."

Suzanne had often sparred words with Steve to keep him interested in living and help him understand her need to assure custody of the children, yet away from thoughts that depressed him. She'd learned a lot in two years about the give and take of conversation between herself and a man who had great wit, compassion, and ethical strength. Their lovemaking had grown by spoken paragraphs having little to do with sex and everything to do with intimacy.

She realized she and her twin were rather equally matched at word play. *This is new for me and great! I'm not such a wus after all.*

Suzanne straightened in her chair and let the silence grow, not being the one—for the *first* time—to rescue the situation by filling the void with words, just to erase the uncomfortable, silent weight of what wasn't being said.

Dierdre put down her mug and pulled out a pack of cigarettes. She removed one and put it between her lips, but didn't offer to light it.

"Jesus, I hate that I can't smoke here."

"You can't curse like that here either; Steve and I don't . . . didn't . . . talk like that around the children."

"Oh, don't get your panties in a wad, Susie. I'd hardly talk like that in front of the children. I'm not that insensitive."

"Perhaps."

"Well, that was a nice thing to say." Her nails tapped the cigarette case. "Can we leave the children with some of your church friends and go to the Sun Tunnels, just the two of us?"

"Ordinarily, I would have said yes, Dee, but I wouldn't feel good about leaving them behind. I'm not sure I think it's a good idea to go camping right now after all."

"You made a deal, Susie. So like it or not, we're going. I'm paying the tab and I say we're going. You were all for it two months ago. Now that's settled. Let's plan a golf game. You promised to do that, too, if I'd bring my clubs."

Suzanne felt her cheeks flame. She hated being financially indebted to anyone for *any* reason. Feeling like she'd been slapped, she swallowed hard, refusing to cry. She let out a long breath . . . slowly. Her eyes met Dierdre's angry stare.

"Dee, could we ever have a conversation that doesn't come down to money or who's to blame or who owes whom?" Suzanne twirled her mug slowly in both hands against the table, forcing herself to stay calm and powerful while she avoided slopping more coffee on herself. She kept her eyes on Dee who looked away, apparently not used to Suzanne's direct strength and sureness.

Dee's voice was acid. "Well, if it's not money, what's it

about? You don't have a job or a lover to eat up your time while I'm here, so what's your problem?"

The remark about not having a job when she wanted and needed one desperately stung Suzanne into silence. Lest she say something she'd regret, she closed her eyes for a long moment and prayed for patience and grace to say the right things.

"Or maybe you *do* have a lover. Did you pick up where you left off with Taylor Armstrong, without telling me during one of our recent chats? That must be it! I can't imagine why I didn't think of it before. The man's gorgeous, let's face it."

"Dierdre, grow up!" Suzanne scraped her chair back and splashed the rest of her coffee into the sink. She rinsed her mug and forced her anger down the drain with it, regretting the emotion that sent a bitter coffee taste into the back of her mouth. Refilling the mug with water, she drank it slowly until calm washed over her. Suzanne turned to face her twin.

"I think you owe me an apology, Dee."

"Oh, come on Suzanne, we both know how long it's been since you and Steve got it on. You can't blame yourself if you've been sleeping with Taylor."

"Dee . . . before we say anything more that we'll both regret, I'm going to my room to pick out something to wear. I haven't seen Taylor for years, until yesterday. I have other reasons for being reluctant to do our camping trip as planned. If you were kinder to me I would have told you what they are."

"My, my, you have been practicing your assertiveness training. I never imagined you'd take better care of yourself with me after all these years. There's hope for you yet, Susie. Perhaps you've been reading those self-help books I've been sending you."

"Oh, you *are* too much! Must you own a piece of everyone's accomplishments as though they couldn't possibly have occurred without your special brand of support? Which, I might add, we both know has its *considerable* limitations!" Suzanne whirled and left the kitchen, the swinging door flapping behind her.

THE WIND REMEMBERS

She practically ran down the hall and yanked open her bedroom door, Steve's bedroom door, their bedroom. Her only place of private solace in the house. She was all the way to the closet before the change hit her. She spun around to the dresser, surveyed the nightstand and bureau in a quick assessment. Dierdre came in behind her. Their eyes met in the mirror.

"What . . . *where* did you put my . . . Steve's . . . where *is he*? What have you done with all of our pictures—*my things*—Dee?" Her voice cracked. Their eyes locked. Dierdre's seemed cold, superior to her. Suzanne's fury spilled out in a raised voice. "Tell me! You are a guest in our home. What right did you have to remove my family pictures without asking me?"

"Relax, Susie. They're safely packed under the bed with the dust bunnies. It's time for you to get on with your life and stop mooning over a man who's dead and buried, gone forever. He can't hold you, or comfort you, or pay your bills, or help you with his kids. *Get over him.*"

Suzanne was speechless. All the fury drained out of her. She felt nothing but pity for her glamorous twin. *Or do I pity myself for letting her do this to me all my life?*

Dierdre sat back against the dresser; her hips in the mirror reflecting round moons in emerald-green lingerie. She lit her cigarette and let the smoke curl around her head, exhaling slowly from her nose and mouth. "I was going to break that idea to you gently, dear, but I've blurted it out badly, haven't I?"

Suzanne stepped toward her and removed the cigarette from Dierdre's fingers as though she were a child. "Yes, you have."

Feeling deeply sad, she smashed the ashes into the lid of one of Dierdre's expensive makeup boxes. "I keep thinking you're capable of feeling what other people feel, but you're not. When you leave, I'll do as I like with my pictures of Steve and our family. Perhaps—if you choose to visit us in the future—you'd be more comfortable staying in a luxurious hotel, since you can afford the tab."

She turned and pulled the door closed behind her.

The Wind Remembers

Dierdre opened it and stepped into the hall after her.

"Susie, I'm *so sorry*. I didn't mean to hurt your feelings. I just want us to have fun and relax. I came to be with you, not to stay in a hotel. Of course the children can go along to the Sun Tunnels."

"Now who's changing the subject? You bet they can go, *if* we go, Dee. I'll get my clothes when you've had a chance to air my room."

Suzanne walked away to the bathroom, closed herself inside, and with shaking hands, turned on the shower taps. She cried into the sound of the running water, letting it stream over the wedding ring she somehow had not been able to take off and bury with Steve, or put away in her jewelry drawer. Why did it seem she'd been abandoned to every whim of fate?

I don't believe in fate. Things happen the way God planned them. Why am I having so much trouble believing that?

She wondered if Dee's words had cut deeply because so many of them were true.

~Monday the 16th of June

Between washing and drying loads of laundry in the basement, Suzanne painted shadow details on the last watercolor in a series for a calendar competition.

Happy children chased a puppy across her cold-press paper among apple trees in spring blossom. Focusing on her artwork and the mundane busywork of the laundry released the tension of the earlier argument with Dee.

The door at the top of the stairs opened. Dierdre called down, "How about that golf game? I'll help with the laundry when we get back. Can't we leave the kids with someone and get in a round?" She bounded down the stairs and gathered up a stack of fresh, warm towels.

The Wind Remembers

Suzanne could tell Dee was trying to make amends with a breezy mood as though nothing ugly had happened between them. Apologizing for her outrageous behavior had always been foreign to her.

"I've only one load to go." Suzanne's own mood was mixed, reluctant to leave and waste the day on the golf course, and fearful of the burden of entertaining Dierdre at the house. However, it did feel good to stick up for her self for a change. She rinsed her fan brush and stuck it, bristles up to dry in a jar.

"Give me a few minutes while I clean Steve's club heads and grips. Diane offered to have the kids play with Leesha and Alex while you're here."

She tugged a golf bag out from under the cellar stairwell and pulled off the plastic protector. Dierdre, mounting the stairs two at a time, called over her shoulder, "Skip cleaning Steve's clubs. They're not sized for you anyway. We'll rent some ladies clubs. I've called for a tee time. River View says we can walk on if we'll play with whatever twosome is up."

Out of habit, Suzanne yanked the combination lock on the cellar door leading outside to make sure it was secure. She climbed the stairs with her golf shoes upside down on a basket of warm sheets and underwear. *Maybe I do need to get out of the house. There hasn't been time or money for anything but necessary errands in a long time.* She opened the bedroom closet with a free hand and unfolded a step stool.

The phone rang.

"Dee, will you get that? Tell whoever it is I'll just be a minute." Atop the step stool, she stacked the sheets on the shelf and climbed down. Mitzi appeared at the door.

"Aunt Dreedra says you better answer the phone 'cause it's important and she doesn't want to take a message."

"Okay, Honey." Suzanne picked up the bedroom extension, "Hello?"

"You know it's Rehma. You got my lawyer's letter. What you gonna do about it?"

Suzanne, caught off-guard, wasn't ready to talk to

Rehma or anyone, except Reverend Spahn, about custody of the children. Stunned, knowing Dierdre was still on the line, she struggled with what to say.

"I'm, I'm thinking about it, but I know that's not what Steve wanted. It's not what I want either."

"Well, Steve's not around anymore, Sweetie. I am. I want what's mine. The kids and everything that goes with 'em!"

"What do you mean, *everything that goes with them*?" Suzanne heard the click of the kitchen phone being put back on the receiver.

"Can I go play with Leesha today, Mommy?" Mitzi interrupted, looking expectantly up at Suzanne.

"This isn't Leesha's mother," she whispered aside.

"Stop stalling. I want Greg and Mitzi. I want them soon like the letter said. My lawyer says there's not a thing you can do about it. You're no blood relation to my kids. I want them for the weekend, so Thursday after work I'll be by to pick 'em up. Time they got used to me." Rehma sounded nervous. Suzanne could tell she was smoking, sucking air and exhaling between rushed words.

"That won't be convenient, Rehma. I need more time . . . to prepare the children. Why don't you let me meet you somewhere, so we can talk . . . about *your plans*?"

Dierdre walked into the bedroom, motioning to the phone, mouthing "*the* Rehma?"

Suzanne nodded.

"Like I said, Sweetie," Rehma snapped, "I'll pick them up after I close the shop on Thursday. Pack their stuff for the weekend." Rehma hung up.

Suzanne held the phone and looked at Mitzi and Dee. Her heart pounded in her ears. Since the cat was out of the bag, she made a decision to talk things over with Dee away from the kids.

"I'll call Diane so Mitzi and Gregory can play there while we golf." She pressed the number buttons and waited, frustrated that Rehma had given her no opportunity to buy off or compromise. Diane agreed the kids could be dropped off for the afternoon.

Mitzi ran off, calling, "I'll get Bear Lovins and my backpack ready, since we get to go play at Leesha's. Gregore-e-e-e-e."

Suzanne brushed her hair in the mirror, bracing herself for Dierdre's questions.

"So what's with Rehma and a lawyer?"

"We'll talk about it after we deliver the kids to Diane." Suzanne gathered her visor, sunglasses, and Blazer keys. "Let's go. Bring your clubs."

***

After they waved good-bye to Diane, the four kids, and a bevy of romping pets, Suzanne pulled away and took the turn-off for the River View Golf Course.

"Okay, Susie, spill it." Dierdre's voice was kind but insistent.

Suzanne, quiet for a moment, weighed how much to say and how to say it.

"Suze," Dierdre continued, "I was rude this morning. Removing your pictures without asking was . . . presumptuous. You're right about a lot of things, but you're *not* right about how much I can feel what other people feel. I can see you're in trouble. I want to help."

"Dee, I don't know who can help me." Suzanne turned up the golf-course lane and found a shady parking spot behind the clubhouse.

"Is Rehma trying to take her kids back?"

"That's her plan, though why she wants them now, when she couldn't wait to get rid of them before, is beyond me. She never so much as telephoned when she learned Steve was terminal, let alone offered to take the kids once in a while or to visit Steve. I haven't seen or heard from her since she sobbed through his memorial service."

"She probably knew Steve didn't want the kids around

her. Has she gotten herself a lawyer we know?"

"Frank Simmons, no one I've ever heard of. He has a local address, but no partnership names on the letterhead." Suzanne got out and went around to the rear of the Blazer. Dierdre followed. "Dee, I'm scared to death. I promised Steve I'd raise Gregory and Mitzi as my own. I intend to. They're all I have. I love them."

"You need a lawyer too, then."

Opening the trunk, Dierdre tugged at her clubs, lifting them to the pavement. She adjusted the fluffy green head covers and shouldered the tailored leather bag.

Suzanne shut the trunk. "Sis, my golf game is rusty. Don't nag me if I don't play well. I couldn't handle any more stress right now. I took a few lessons from Steve, but that was long ago. My mind isn't going to be on the game."

"What are sisters for?" Dierdre paid for rental clubs, soft drinks, and a new glove for Suzanne.

"I wish you hadn't done that. I don't play often enough for you to buy me a new glove."

"I'd agree with you Susie, *if* you had an *old* glove. *No* glove is a no *no*. You're going to hit twice as many balls as I do. Sore hands are miserable. If it bothers you so much, tuck it in my bag when we finish. Our hands are the same size."

"Thanks, I'll do that."

They strapped bags of clubs onto the back of an electric cart, stored soft drinks up front, and climbed in. The sun was high; the air hot. Their luck came for a 12:10 tee time. Play was slow, everyone out for a beautiful afternoon. Suzanne looked the other players over. She took them for retired or rich and jobless on a Monday during business hours. She envied them for what she imagined to be lives with fewer problems than her own, then chided herself for judging others and wallowing in self-pity, a fault she was embarrassed to own.

At the first tee box, Dierdre led off, sailing her pink ball nearly out of sight. Suzanne—intimidated—squared up, swung through, and dribbled her ball down the hill. It came to rest behind a shrub.

"No biggy, Susie. You lifted your head. Keep it down next time. Golf is a concentration game."

"I warned you that concentration wouldn't be easy for me today," Suzanne said.

Dierdre drove the cart down the hill to Suzanne's ball and parked. "Take it out and toss it on better grass in the fairway." Suzanne did as she was told, resenting how she had to be given a break to keep play moving for everyone else.

At an overcrowded hole, they sat fourth cart back, waiting their turn. Sipping colas, using tees, they cleaned moist black loam from their cleats. Groundskeepers pruned broken branches and bagged debris along the out-of-bound edges of the fairways. Suzanne thought of the windstorm and her destroyed cottonwood. She felt the pain of its loss and that it was purposeful like a brick of grief and fear in her chest.

She looked at Dierdre, picture perfect in her designer golf outfit, everything color-coordinated, her makeup flawless, not a hair out of place. *Can Dee get past being concerned to the last detail about herself, enough to care if I tell her about my problems? Guess I don't have much more to lose. She might offer some of her analytical insight.*

"Dee, did I mention that someone cut our cottonwood on purpose?"

"You're kidding. You're *not* kidding? Susie, that's really scary! Are you sure? What does Doug think about it?"

"I didn't want to believe it and neither did Doug, but Taylor showed us the chain-saw marks. Doug says I must be careful. He's having the night-shift patrol car go by several times between midnight and seven a.m. I think it's probably some teenagers. There's been a lot of gang stuff going on in Farr in the past few months."

Dierdre turned to face her. Setting the cola back in its carrier, she waved the elderly couple they were paired with to go ahead and took off her sunglasses.

Suzanne felt relieved to finally be taken seriously.

THE WIND REMEMBERS

"Susie, you don't really think it's a prank do you? The tree was huge. It must have taken a lot of work to cut it. Somebody had to hear or see what went on and maybe even who did it. When were you gone long enough for someone to use a chain saw on your tree and not get caught?"

Suzanne smiled, recalling Doug asked the same thing. "Sunday is about the only time I'm gone longer than an hour of grocery shopping. We go to church and generally out to lunch afterward, then stop at the cemetery to visit Steve on the way home. We're gone two and a half or three hours. Depends on how much Mitzi has to eat and how much patience Greg has for not being the center of attention every minute. Though I did have a movie coupon we used last Thursday for the Disney matinee."

"Would that be enough time to make the cut Taylor showed you?" Dierdre started up the cart and moved into next-on-deck position.

"I would guess so. Watching Taylor, he can cut through huge pieces pretty fast. It would take a very strong man to fell a tree of that size."

"There, you see Susie, you said *the man* would have to be strong. I don't think you believe it was done by a bunch of kids."

Suzanne had to agree.

They were up. Dierdre drove her ball more than two hundred yards. Suzanne's turn. She forced herself to concentrate. Steve had told her she had great form and had given her a simple system to follow. She squared her driver face to the ball and stepped back, brought the club up slowly in an arc until her chin touched her left shoulder. Then she swung down through the ball until her chin met her right shoulder, before she lifted her head, and looked after the ball. It had gone straight a hundred yards or more.

"Way to go, Suzanne!" Dierdre slapped her hand in a high five as they stepped into the cart. "Now you're cooking. Whatever you did, do it again in the fairway." She pulled their golf cart to a stop. "Take out your four iron and hit the hell out of it, same swing as a minute ago."

The Wind Remembers

Suzanne addressed the ball. The slant of the hill put the ball higher than her feet. It felt awkward on her practice swing. "Now what do I do?"

"Grip further down on the club to shorten the shaft in your swing. That's it. Now swing as usual." Dierdre smoked a cigarette while she coached.

Suzanne took off her sunglasses and thrust them in her pocket. She lined up, shortened her shaft length by moving her hands down the grip and swung through—right shoulder, left shoulder—before looking up. The ball arched through the air, popped and rolled to the edge of the green. Her success lifted her spirits.

"I wish you could give me *life* instructions to follow that worked that well." She rammed her four-iron back in the rental bag and climbed into the cart.

"Perhaps I can. You have to come clean with all of your problems though and be clear about what you've decided you want out of life. Then I'd know how to help."

Dierdre switched the lever under her long tan legs into reverse, backed the cart around a sand trap, switched the lever back to forward, and drove up the cart path, parking even with the green.

Suzanne carried the putter over to her ball, thinking, *Dee always makes everything seem so black and white. Life does this; you do this or that about it. No waffling, just make a decision and do it. Is that all there is to it?* Not concentrating on her game, she struck her ball too softly. It rolled off course and ended up further from the hole than before she'd putted it.

"She who hesitates is lost," sang Dierdre. "Hit the little sucker. Don't be short. Better to overrun the cup by a little than to be short."

"You mean just go for it," Suzanne said. It occurred to her the way she played golf was too much like the way she played her life. She couldn't seem to just solve things between herself and Greg. Couldn't tell Doug she liked his friendship but that was all. Had no idea what to do about the deliberate cutting

145

of her cottonwood, except to wait for Doug to find out who did it—if he could—and worst of all, she hesitated about Rehma and fighting her for custody of the children. Suzanne had to admit, *hesitate is the name of my game off the golf course as well as on.*

Dierdre's ball rolled decisively into the cup. Suzanne replanted the flag, determined to make some choices for action Dee-style to solve her problems. The afternoon progressed comfortably between them.

"Par," Dierdre called, picking her cigarette up from the grass where she'd dropped it to putt. She gripped it between her lips while she tucked her putter back into her bag. "It's easier work to play up here in the thin air of these mountains. Sea level doesn't spoil a person for distance, and I do love these sweet greens. Don't miss the Bermuda grass one bit. Did you see my little ball roll right into the cup?"

"It was a terrific putt all right, Dee. This next hole's our ninth and last for me. Could we talk a little afterward, I mean before we pick up the children?"

"If you're not up to eighteen holes, sure, you know me, Susie. Girl talk is right up there with sex and golf. Well, actually first, when it's you and me." Dierdre laughed and stomped her cigarette out in the grass. "Let's leave the cart here and walk to the tee box. Bring your driving weapon."

Suzanne caught up with her. They hit their drives, finished out, and returned the cart to the clubhouse garage, clattering their cleats across the cobbles to the entrance. Inside they ordered sandwiches and iced tea. Dierdre changed her mind and had a beer, settling into the booth across from her twin.

"Okay, Suzanne, cover the high points for me. Stay focused on the results you want. We'll worry about *how* to get them after I understand."

"I have to win custody of Greg and Mitzi. That's number one. I have to find a job, because though the house is paid for, regular expenses have to be met. An attorney will cost me, that's third. That'll do for starters."

"Aren't you leaving out a few other high points?" Dierdre

nibbled a vegetarian sandwich and sipped her beer. Her eyes never left Suzanne's. She swallowed, smiled, and waited.

"Like what?"

"Oh, how about Doug, Taylor, Greg, Rehma?"

"Gregory and Rehma I can relate to, but I can't see what you're getting at about either of the men." Suzanne washed a bite of BLT down with iced tea. She put the sandwich back on its paper plate, her appetite gone. She was in uncomfortable territory. The only thing good about the timing was that the kids weren't around to listen in. Her sister's penetrating questions were as direct as she remembered their mother's had been.

"Susie, the reason you're so vulnerable is because you're not the children's birth or legal mother and you're single, without an impressive-salary job."

"You think I don't know all that? That's why I have to *find* a job! That's also why I'd rather not waste a couple of days going to the desert for a campout." As usual, Suzanne felt Dierdre didn't give her any credit for having two brain cells to rub together.

"You have to find a job for a lot of reasons, but you don't have to keep Steve's kids unless you want to. Or maybe you could let Greg go, since he's being such a pain in the ass, and just fight for Mitzi. Let's carry this stuff to the porch. I need a cigarette."

Suzanne felt her mouth drop open. She closed it with a sip of tea and swallowed. "I'm keeping them both. Rehma can't get her own act together . . ." She followed her twin to the porch, "let alone take her children on."

"Who died and made *you* God?" Dierdre lit up.

"I can't believe you'd say that to *me*, Dee!" Suzanne felt her cheeks flush. The incensed feelings of the morning returned.

"Think about it." Dierdre exhaled. "Rehma does have legal rights. She may never have exercised them before, but she has them. Maybe she *is* getting her life together. It happens. You, on the other hand, aren't getting *yours* together—that's the point. Why don't you get married and offer two parents to the court?

Then you'd be more likely to have the upper hand."

"But, there isn't anyone I'd want to marry." Suzanne ignored the part about not getting her own life together and wiped her mouth, ducking to the side to avoid Dierdre's next burst of exhaled cigarette smoke. She crumpled her napkin viciously, preparing herself to endure whatever her sister said next without popping her in the nose.

"Doug would marry you at the drop of a hat, justice of the peace tomorrow or elope with you if you wanted. From what you've said recently on the phone, I gather he's already panting at your back door with every shift change. You could divorce him later if it didn't work out, but at least you'd have won custody of Steve's children." Dierdre smoothed her hair and tucked her sunglasses on top of her headband.

"It never enters my mind to use people the way you do." Suzanne toyed with her napkin.

"It's not like Doug wouldn't enjoy having you, even if it were only for a while." Dierdre pushed her plate away and freshened her lipstick in her compact mirror.

"Let's go." Suzanne stood. "We don't think enough alike to have a conversation I can be comfortable with."

"So marry Taylor. I never understood why you dumped him, but if he's not currently taken I bet you could get him back. If I were you, I'd sure go for that option. Maybe you wouldn't even want to divorce him later. Of course he may not be interested in a ready-made family. That's why Doug's a stronger bet."

The topic of Taylor and her past choices sent Suzanne's frustration over the edge. Her pulse thundering in her throat, she left the porch bench, dumped her lunch and trash in the bin, and headed for the Blazer. After opening the trunk, she sat on the tailgate to change shoes. Dierdre arrived nursing a fresh cigarette. She slung her clubs into the trunk and sat down next to Suzanne to remove her own golf shoes and change into exquisite Feragamo sandals.

"Sorry I ticked you off. Why are you so touchy about

Taylor? I always thought you really loved each other."

"I loved him. I have no idea if he loved me or not. He never said one way or the other." Suzanne peeled off her socks. "You're the one who made me change my mind about waiting to hope I'd hear 'I love you' from him."

"*Me?!*" Dierdre looked incredulous. Her Ferragamos swung from her fingers by their straps, frozen in the air between them as if sculpted in marble.

"When you got pregnant and told your fiancé about it, he told you the wedding was off unless you got rid of the baby. I wasn't even engaged, but Taylor and I were close to going to bed together. If he had gotten me pregnant and told me he couldn't deal with a baby, I couldn't have done what you did. I'd have kept our child and supported it somehow. I wasn't willing to risk my promise to myself and to Mom to finish my degree. I said good-bye to Taylor, hoping he'd say he loved me and beg me to change my mind, maybe even propose that we get married before we finished college. But he didn't. He just said, 'If that's the way you feel, I'll be on my way.' Love obviously wasn't what he felt for me."

"So you're blaming me for dumping my fiancé and getting an abortion instead of strapping myself with a conceited boob for a husband and a helpless child I'd have no idea how to care for? I kept my promise to Mom too, you know. You aren't the only twin who's a university graduate. If you've been blaming *me* all these years for losing Taylor, get over it. You made your choices and I made mine."

"I'm not blaming you, Dee. I'm just saying Taylor and I burned our bridges a long time ago. He's not a marriage candidate for me. Nobody is. When I get a job I can handle things myself; everything will be just fine."

"In the meantime, you better get one impressive attorney or you'll be the one borrowing the kids for the weekend, *if and when* Rehma says you can."

Suzanne drove the rest of the way to Diane's in troubled silence. Dierdre smoked out her passenger window, not attempting to continue a conversation. They picked up the children and went the last block home with Mitzi jabbering about the cats and gerbils at Leesha's house.

"Did you have fun with Alex and his new dog, Greg?" Suzanne glanced in the rear-view mirror to catch his response.

"Yeah, I guess."

"Great," said Suzanne, pulling into the driveway. "Okay, everybody, when we get inside, all parties to the basement to carry up the folded laundry, then we'll start dinner."

"Oh, do we have to?" Gregory's face clouded. He slammed the truck door.

"I'll play cards with the first one finished," Dierdre challenged.

"It'll be me," squealed Mitzi.

Suzanne detected the attempt at enthusiasm in her sister's voice, and appreciated the gesture of Dee putting herself out on someone else's account. She watched her twin take the hands of both children and go on ahead to the back porch. They waited for Suzanne to unlock the door, then everyone descended to the basement. Suzanne put her golf shoes back in the pocket of Steve's bag and stowed it under the stairs. She gave instructions to the children about their various stacks of clean clothes, while Dierdre hooked hangers of sweet-smelling T-shirts through her fingers.

At the washer, Suzanne opened the lid to drop in the last load of darks. The rat floated in a slow circle, its dead eyes wide and glistening. She screamed, "A dead rat!" and kept on screaming until Dierdre dropped her T-shirt hangers on the folding table, rushed to her side, and closed the washer lid.

"Gregory, why do you want to scare me, so much?!" Suzanne looked at him, her tone accusatory. Her heart hammered against her rib cage like it was trying to get out.

"I didn't do nothing. You always think bad stuff is because of me. I've been gone all day, just like you." He wrenched himself away from her and ran up the stairs.

"You're right, Greg. I'm sorry," she called after him.

The Wind Remembers

He slammed the door.

Mitzi ran up after him. "Gregory, Mommy said she's sorry. She's just uh-scared of rats."

"Already the little peacemaker." Deeply frightened and sad about accusing Greg, Suzanne looked around the laundry-room-studio space. The cellar door to the outside stood ajar.

"I made sure that door was locked before we left," she wheezed, nearly paralyzed with alarm. A cold fear settled around her hammering heart, reminding her of the feeling when Steve was slipping away and she felt helpless to stop it.

"Someone has it in for you, Suzanne. I think you'd better call Doug." Dierdre put an arm around her waist. Suzanne hadn't been able to lean on anyone but Reverend Spahn in a long time. The love she felt for her twin deepened in that moment. She recalled the best of their childhood experiences, feeling them come back to nourish her at this terrifying time.

Together they mounted the three steps to the underside of the old double cellar door where coal was once delivered. They examined the combination lock. Its swing arm had been cut in two. Dierdre helped Suzanne run a wire coat hanger through the latch on the inside and twist it to hold the door shut. On their way upstairs to make the phone call, Dierdre touched her shoulder.

"Are you sure there's nothing else you're keeping from me? I'm really frightened for you."

"That's two of us. I'm glad you're here. I guess we better check for what might be missing." She opened the canning cabinet, and took out Steve's gun case. The lock securing both guns and savings bonds was still in place. She breathed a sigh of relief and replaced the case and closed the cabinet doors.

Dee's warm smile comforted her. At the top of the stairs she heard the familiar diesel-rattle of Taylor's truck in the drive. Through the back-door window, saw him coming to the house. She wanted with all her heart to run into his arms and ask him to help her protect the kids. She reassured herself pride would keep her from ever doing anything so foolish, but it didn't make the wishing any less powerful.

Brushing her longings aside, Suzanne went to the phone and dialed Doug's pager number while Dierdre let Taylor inside. Listening to the beeps, she tried to imagine who was doing things to scare her and why. She wondered if something worse was going on than the threat of fighting Rehma in court. Only moments ago Suzanne had begun to believe the felling of the cottonwood wasn't some idle prank. Some evil person was actually trying to frighten her. Would he—or them—hurt, or perhaps even try to murder her family? What had seemed inconceivable yesterday seemed entirely possible now. When she hung up the wall phone, Taylor's look of concern when he listened to her sister's explanation, met her own eyes across the kitchen table.

Rat

~Monday the 16th of June

Rat's thumbs shifted his bike into a lower gear. He crossed the bridge heading east up the bench and rolled into view of the Price place, taking plenty of time to check it out. He smiled to himself. The big cottonwood had toppled sooner than planned, probably done by the high storm winds. *All the better*, he told himself, gathering details. A lot of the big stuff was stripped of leafy branches and cut in lengths already. A muscled guy loaded trunk chunks into a trailer using big grippers mounted on a fancy truck. The stack of brush out back would make a good bonfire. He made a mental note.

Wow, who's the babe in short shorts playing catch with the kid? Rat wondered. *Sure ain't old lady Price. She's pretty enough but not a turn-on like this broad. What a pair of tits; like to examine those up close and personal!*

He'd keep this new woman to himself, maybe slip back after dark for a look-see in windows at the back of the house. He'd done it before, and it had been well worth the wait a couple of times. But this mama would be worth the extra trouble of keeping busy elsewhere until bedtime, if she stayed the night. He sure hoped she'd be hanging around.

The white walls of the garage interested him with the tree's overhanging branches no longer in the way. He might return with a plan to make himself a little better known with the brothers. For now, he'd go up and hang out waiting for Sky, while Big Blue worked on him. If they'd come over the ridge to the sheep camp by the old lumber road, they might not know the tree had gone over. Rat pumped his stout legs and heaved with the effort of stroking beyond where the pavement turned to gravel, on his way up the bench to the Blue Tattoo's hideout. His thin blue jacket flapped like crows wings behind him. He hoped he'd be first with the tree news. It always paid to have plenty of news for Big Blue. Rat took pride in having the best news first among the brothers.

Overcoming his deep disappointment that Big Blue already knew about the Price tree going over, Rat shoved the open bottle of Blue Nun into the towering sixteen-year old's hand.

"Here, Sky, drink the rest of this before you go back in there. Don't let on it's hurting you this time or Big Blue will really go for the pain."

"I can't do any wine. Dad smells it on me, he'll kick my ass."

"Getting your ass kicked ain't half as bad as what Big Blue can do to you with his needles. For sure when he's been sniffing. The wine will cut the pain. Besides, Blue-brand booze is lucky for Blue Tattoo members. Have some cinnamon gum to kill the wine smell."

He thrust a couple of wrapped sticks into Sky's hand.

"Thanks, Rat. I owe you—for gettin' me in, too."

"There's no owing between Tattoo brothers. It's good

you're finally in."

"We'll see," said Sky. He swigged the wine down and passed the bottle back. Rat looked for signs of how his friend was taking the first stage of his initiation. Noted the long, thin fingers that fumbled with the silver gum wrappers, crushed them into tiny balls, and dropped them one at a time into the dirt. Sky's thoughts appeared to be somewhere else beyond them both.

"Don't leave any signs around that we've been here or you won't have to wait for your dad to kick your ass. Big Blue will do it personally." Rat picked up the balled gum wrappers and stuffed them in the pocket of his jacket. He looked up at the new brother and motioned for him to stick out his right arm.

Rat's chubby thumb traced gently over the fresh red welts. The blood speckles were clotting well at the needle marks. The blue dye stains roughly outlined the shape of a sword and the beginning of a bird's wing on Sky's forearm. It smelled powerfully of rubbing alcohol.

"He's getting better at it. Yours is going to look real good in about three weeks. Better than mine, but mine's a couple years old. Had it since I was fourteen."

"Guess I'm glad he practiced on somebody else first," Sky said, chewing hard on the gum and wiping the back of his other hand across the thin line of his mouth.

Rat saw Big Blue at the door of the larger of the two metal sheep-camp wagons—gang headquarters. His stocky shoulders filled the narrow doorway, all muscle from clearing ranch-land brush on his grandpa's place up Farr canyon. Rat let go of Sky's arm and stepped back.

"Hey, Sky, you ready to have me put the words on the sword and finish that eagle with about a hundred needle pricks? Or, are you gonna be a cry baby, Sky Baby? Hey, that's really good. Sky Baby, I like that."

Rat was glad he'd had a few swigs of the wine himself. Watching Big Blue high on crack always gave him the urge to oink down about three double-cheese burgers, just to quiet the knots in his stomach. He hated Big Blue for filling him up with fear like that. At the same time, he admired him for his power over all the brothers.

Big Blue was impatient to get started again. Rat could tell by the way he slapped the needle, a wooden-handled frog sticker, rhythmically across his dirty open palm. He had too big a smile on his face. A bad sign. Rat felt sorry for Sky. Their leader really got off on taunting all of them. Someday Rat'd make the bully pay and pay plenty for all the insults. He pictured himself to be more important in the gang before long. He wanted to be equal in strength and power to Big Blue and a lot less mean. When all the brothers were turning their money and drugs over to him, he'd be able to afford a car. Used or not it would be four wheels and less work than peddling his bike.

For now he contented himself with being the mouth and ears for the Blue Tattoo. Rat was smart enough to know Big Blue needed him. On his way home, he planned to start showing him just how valuable he already was, and have a little fun while he was at it. Rat used the gang as much as the brothers were using him. He adjusted his backpack and watched Sky duck inside the tilting doorway of Makris' old sheep-camp wagon. Its wheels groaned at Sky and Big Blue's weight. The door creaked shut behind them. Even muffled, Rat could hear when Blue pumped the volume on the boom box up a notch.

Rat dragged his dirt bike out from under the oily tarp, where it had been hidden with the others all afternoon during the strategy meeting. Big Blue always dared any of the brothers, on threat of being cut up, to be careless about leaving somebody reason for turning them in for trespassing on old man Makris's vacant sheep-camp property. Rat replaced the tarp and scuffed up the dirt to get rid of their tracks.

He hurried his bike upstream under cover of the thick growth of tamarisk and the natural wall of pink granite boulders that funneled spring snowmelt down to the valley below the bench. Rat dismounted and lifted his bike through the break in the pole-and barbed-wire fence, startling a magpie off its nest, a clot of twigs in the branches of a sickly tree. The bird shrieked at him from a nearby branch, cocking its long black-barred tail and fluttering at him. Rat took extra time to suck in his belly to squeeze through without getting his clothes or his flesh hung up in the rusty wire.

Once clear, he scrambled back on his bike and followed the path through the shrub oak for fifty yards or so to where it opened out onto the unpaved bench-end of Old Post Road. He crossed the two-lane road and biked up the incline on the other side, staying out of sight along the upper ridge. He came out where the pavement started again along the stream gushing down the rocks by Farr's orchard. He crossed back over at the angled culvert that jutted out from under the road, where snowmelt emptied into the river.

He'd lost time when Sky got scared and needed a break to get through the first stage of his tattooing. Now Rat needed not only time but light to get a jump on the other brothers. With any luck, the way would be clear for him to earn a piece of Tangie, if he could work for at least twenty minutes. He'd picked out the biggest target he could find within three miles of the sheep camp to claim for new gang territory. It would be tricky to pull off because it was right near the road and afforded him no protection from being seen, but he'd been having fantasies about Tangie every night. He didn't fool himself she'd be as good a lay as the broad he'd watched in the green nightie at the Price place last night, but she was good enough for him. Besides, she was Big Blue's personal property. That made her worth plenty of risk.

This time it would be done Rat's way. Big Blue was too busy with Sky at the sheep camp to give the orders now. Just the way Rat liked it best, on his own. *Someday I'll lead my own group of brothers, maybe even take over the Blue Tattoo.*

How, he wasn't sure, but he had time to work on that. His powerful thighs pedaled west on Old Post Road. It was easier going downhill on the pavement, but he was pouring sweat when he headed in the direction of the sun glinting off the valley-wide expanse of Great Salt Lake. He could taste his body salt mixed with wine. His thirst was overwhelming; there'd be time to sneak one of his mom's beers later. He pulled off onto the gravel shoulder about a quarter mile from the house where the giant cottonwood had gone over. He hid the bike in the thick cattail weeds near the weed-choked irrigation ditch, and went the rest of the way on foot. Practicing the required movements in his mind, he was ready when he came up through the flowerbed on the backside of the garage. The roar of a chain saw starting up and screaming into green wood assaulted his ears. He peeked around the garage. The big workman's back was to him.

Rat retraced his steps to a wide, clear place where the back wall of the garage was exposed between tall cedar shrubs. He slid the backpack to the ground and unzipped the top compartment. He'd have to hurry; the light was fading fast. He didn't want to be making noise if the tree cutter turned off his saw and heard what he was up to.

A police cruiser whipped into the driveway.

"Shit!" Rat ducked deeper into the brush and threw himself flat in the scratchy weeds. The saw whined through raw wood, speeded up to a shrill shriek until the chunk fell away, then the motor turned off. He heard men's voices.

"Shit, double shit!" He was trapped in broad daylight by a cop within throwing distance. The perspiration that poured from his body was the cold sweat of fear.

Chapter Nine

Coming Together Coming Apart

Suzanne Price

~ Monday the 16th of June

Suzanne sipped from the wine glass Dee left for her with the admonition: "I'll rally the kid troops to help me cook while you relax in a bubbly blur; *always* works for me to take out the kinks. If you're smart, you won't get out 'til you're called for dinner."

Suzanne laughed to herself, toying bath bubbles with glistening toes. *Cooking for Dee probably means a delivered pizza with Greg and Mitzi opening the box.* A relaxing tub was a rare treat she wasn't about to refuse—especially after the disturbing events of the week.

Fading sunlight sifted through stained-glass panes on the west wall, reflecting a peculiar blue swirling on the translucent orbs around her.

What is it about that particular blue? She imagined paint pigments she'd use to replicate it. *Cobalt's too intense,*

The Wind Remembers

ultramarine perhaps with a touch of vermillion and lots of water to soften the tint? Yes, but what does it remind me of? Sipping for a lazy while, she thought about her favorite blues in nature.

It's the blue of wild chicory flowers!

Suzanne swallowed deeply, set the half-full glass on the tile floor and slid into the bubbles up to her chin. She closed her eyes and for the first time in many years, allowed herself to slip through a door in her mind that held back old hurts—and older joys that were not about Steve.

What could it hurt to think about the past? Everything lately has blown what's left of my mind anyway.

Nudging open that long-locked door, she ventured back years before her marriage and remembered how the spring air on campus had blown fresh with scents of lilacs and newly mowed grass. At eighteen she'd been so young, so naïve.

Descending the steps of the art building, she'd inhaled those dizzying perfumes while searching for a view to paint a required sketch for her university scholarship-renewal portfolio. She'd paused before a massive elm, walked around it, found a promising angle where light stuttered through its branches in golden patches on the green lawn.

Unloading her paints, she'd sat Indian-fashion on the grass and unscrewed the lid on a pint jar of water. Using a fat sable brush, she bathed the dried blobs in her palette box with enough dribbles to soften them. Later, in mid-stroke of a blue wash, a lavender shadow appeared across her Arches paper block. Momentarily confused, she'd realized someone stood behind her, blocking her light. Her brush stopped. She sopped the puddle with a tiny sea sponge before the blobbed sky dried irreparably in the breeze.

"Sorry to disturb you," he'd said. "I'm glad someone's paying tribute to this fine old elm before it's history. The forestry department's marked all the blighted elms on campus for removal this summer. I'll be helping with that for my senior project."

The Wind Remembers

His voice was a deep baritone, easy, kind, and genuine. Suzanne remembered her first heart-stopping look into amazing chicory-blue eyes fringed with blond lashes. Sunburned skin stretched over strong cheekbones and a cleft chin. His smile was direct and engaging. She'd wondered even then, *Is it safe to trust a man as handsome and charming as he is?*

That part hasn't changed, she thought, opening her eyes and reaching outside along the tub for her wine glass. *The warm water and wine are softening my mind as well as my mood. When did I begin to fall in love with Taylor?*

She filled her mouth, held the wine around her tongue, and breathed in and out slowly, savoring taste, a little wooze, a lot of unexpected tenderness.

Can I remember the special times, too, not just the painful way we ended? She rested the glass on her tummy amid the bubbles, held it by the stem, and waded deeper into those early memories.

Other students had passed by chatting, consulting their pagers and hurrying to classes in nearby buildings. "Hello," she'd ventured, eyes on her painting, feeling not too pleased to be interrupted.

"Mind if I watch?" He'd seated himself with his long legs folded knees-to-sky, his sun-brown hands clasped loosely above his loafers. "I promise not to talk while you concentrate."

"If you can keep that promise, you're welcome to watch. You'll be bored soon enough." Susanne remembered he wore no socks. *Like Einstein and probably a lot less brainy*, she'd thought at the time. It made her laugh now. She'd soon discovered he was very smart and an independent thinker. *That smart independence intrigued me and perhaps was why I broke off with him.*

True to his word, he'd waited nearly an hour until she finished painting, poured out her gray water into the grass, and recapped the empty jar. While she gathered her supplies, planning a tactful escape, he held the wet watercolor block flat as she instructed so the colors wouldn't run before they could dry.

"That tree will never look as lively as you've painted it. When do you sign your name?"

"When it's dry enough," she'd said, zipping her bag shut.

He'd laughed then, a laugh she'd warmed to from that moment. "What *is* your mysterious-artist name? You didn't sign your painting. I'm Taylor, Taylor Armstrong. Graduated three years ahead of you in Farr, Utah."

"Oh, I don't remember you, sorry. Suzanne Ingram." She'd shouldered her bag and taken the paper block back, awkwardly shaking his hand with just the tips of her fingers underneath it.

"I think your sister's an OSU cheerleader here like she was in high school, right?"

Suzanne remembered how her heart had sunk somewhere below her knees. "Of course," she'd whispered, half turning away. "You've probably dated her."

"No." He'd grinned and steered her down the sidewalk by the elbow. "But I'd very much like to date her sister."

At her bewilderment, he'd laughed heartily while she stumbled along in shock.

Ah, I didn't just begin to fall in love, I absolutely crashed. And he knew it.

Exquisite shards of more tucked-away memories pierced her heart. She didn't dare return there—yet—if ever.

Suzanne smiled to herself, unhooked a lufa from its cord on a faucet, and soaped it to a bubbly froth. Scrubbing vigorously she realized with surprise that remembering the beginning of their romance had been more pleasure than pain.

Taylor and I share a love of trees that brought us together. Now a tree I've painted over and over has brought us together again because I need him to cut it up and get rid of it. Did I end things between us before they could grow into a lasting love—with marriage and children of my own? Not children of someone else's that I have to fight for in court? She sighed. *No matter now. I wouldn't have missed my precious years with Steve or his kids.*

It was twilight. Bath water gone cold, the bubbles sagged and evaporated. Suzanne pulled the tub stopper and watched the faded bubbles pop and disappear before she stood and rinsed under a hot shower. After toweling off, she switched on the lights, drained the wine in one gulp and brushed her damp hair.

Somewhere down the hall on the way to her room, the thought occurred, *it would be nice to be in love again.* It scared her more than a little. She pushed the idea aside and went to dress for whatever Dee had "cooked."

Taylor Armstrong

~ Monday the 16th of June

Taylor kicked another log out of his way. One more ten-foot branch to cut up and load for Suzanne, then he'd be finished for the day. He'd put her job off until last, knowing he wasn't eager to finish it and run out of reasons to see her. It would be dark in less than half an hour. He set his spinning blade against the bark and let the weight of the saw carry it down through the green wood. It shrieked against the resistance of the resin-filled wood fiber, sending up the particular smell of cottonwood. The piece cracked off at the bottom of its own weight. He rolled it with his heel to make room for the next one.

Moving up the trunk-thick limb, his stomach growled in time to the rhythm of his cutting strokes. He'd worked up a hunger this week, covering Suzanne's tree job and all the other tree-removal jobs underway between himself, Griff, and Randy. Business was great after the storm. Pops was impressed. Taylor avoided mentioning he was doing a job for Suzanne. When the romance ended, Pop'd said Taylor was too damn proud for his own good, and she was too fine a woman to let go so easily, especially without giving him a reason and him too stubborn to ask for one.

The Wind Remembers

Taylor was worried about her, attracted to her, afraid of complicating his life with her, and generally wondering what in hell to do about his feelings on all points where Suzanne was concerned. This thing with the tree, and now the dead rat floating in her washer, culminating in the break-in to do it, made him anxious. Whoever was doing these numbers on her had a sinister mind. He couldn't shake the feeling of wanting to fix it, take care of her, yet he wanted to peel out of the driveway and never come back to get hurt again. *I wonder what I'll do about her, if anything*. A movement caught his eye. He glanced up. Doug Jensen stood waiting. He signaled over the racket for Taylor to finish the cut he was on and stop.

Taylor kicked the length free and switched off the motor. He set the saw down, pulled off his gloves, and removed his earplugs. He hadn't heard Doug's cruiser pull in the drive.

"What's up, now?" He looked hard at Jensen, trying to read him.

"The lab officer just finished the results of his investigation in the basement. He said whoever cut the lock and opened the washer lid to drop in the rat wore gloves. No prints. The pisser is, a crowbar was used to break in. Why would the guy bother to cut the lock when he was already inside?"

Taylor stood straight and stretched, every muscle tired from pushing himself. "He's a weirdo all right. I don't like it. How's Suzanne taking the whole thing?"

"She's spooked now, for sure. Being brave for the kids, so she's not saying much in front of them. Got a couple questions for you; just take a minute." Jensen dug in a pocket of his uniform and came up with a pad and pen.

"Sure. Shoot. I'm hungry and beat for today anyway."

"About this tree, how long do you figure it took to make that big cut at the bottom of the trunk and clean up the sawdust?"

"Depends on if there were two men or only one." Taylor clipped the safety on his saw and stuffed his gloves into his back pocket.

"Spec it out for me both ways." Doug flipped open the small notepad and started writing.

Taylor leaned against the garage and wiped his face and neck with a bandanna. "One guy would need an hour or more; two guys could have done it in twenty minutes. Either way, we're talking experienced. The burrs on the bark where the saw roughed it up were brushed off behind the root weeds, so the cut would be even less obvious unless you walked right up close and parted the tall grass to look. Smell would be strong though for an hour or two."

Doug noted that. "What's your guess, one or two men?" He chewed on his mustache.

"My guess is one man did the cut. Doesn't mean somebody else didn't do clean-up detail, though." Taylor was curious to know why Jensen was asking some of the same questions he'd answered the first day, but he thought Doug probably had his reasons or was checking to see if his expert's story would change.

"Why one man for the cut?"

"The type of saw used, by the direction of the blade marks, is a one-operator machine. The cut's angled too. Whoever did it doesn't know how to keep it level on the side away from him or isn't strong enough. It's an art of leverage that takes experience."

Doug looked at him and got hard-nosed. "But you said the cutter *was* experienced."

"With a saw yes, with tree cutting professionally, no. But he's seen enough somewhere to know how far to cut to weaken the tree without having it go over until he was well out of the way."

"The break-in was done with a crowbar and a heavy-duty metal cutter afterward, quick and sloppy. He sure wanted to scare her with that goddamn rat. Can't figure what he's up to."

"Any chance somebody's got an old score to settle with her late husband and is just now taking it out on Suzanne?" Taylor had been giving it some thought. "I've probably watched too many late-night movies where the jailbird gets out and goes after the cop who put him away—or his family."

"Possible, I guess, but I think I'd have a lead just knowing what Steve handled the last few years. We talked over our important cases. Seems you figured out he's . . . dead."

Taylor stepped away from the garage and picked up the saw, seeing Dierdre coming toward them from the house. "I've got a quick question for you, Doug. Any chance these two incidents are unrelated? I mean, done by two different men for two different reasons?"

"Shit!" Jensen rammed the pad back in his pocket. "Naw, doesn't figure. Both tactics were meant to scare her. I can't figure *one* man who'd have it in for Suzanne, let alone two."

Taylor wasn't satisfied with Jensen's kiss-off answer to what seemed to him to be an idea worth exploring, but he turned his attention to Dierdre who joined them. That had never been hard to do. She was just as good to look at as ever—maybe better.

"I've sent Suzanne to the tub with my favorite Vita Bath and a glass of wine to take out the kinks. I want a moment alone with you two."

Taylor wondered what she was up to. With Dierdre you could never tell but there would have to be something in it for her. From past experience he was sure of that.

"I've made some of my supremo spaghetti, chilled the wine, prepared an incredible Caesar salad to toss at the last moment, and the kids are setting the table to include you both. You can't disappoint them."

Taylor shook his head in protest and started to turn back to his truck to put the saw and his pulaski away. She stopped him with a hand on his chest.

"Don't either of you men tell me you're not starved. Besides, we twins could use some light conversation after the disturbing events of the day." Taylor, feeling awkward, looked at Doug to decide what to do. Dierdre's mood seemed to change. She turned off the flirting.

"Actually gentlemen, I have an ulterior motive. I'm only going to be here a few more days, and I'm terrified something worse is going to happen. I have to know Susie will be in good hands after I go back to my job."

There's the part I was waiting for, thought Taylor. *She's lowering her own stress about her sister by laying family responsibility on someone else. She hasn't changed.*

"You can count on me to take care of her," Doug said. He stood up taller than a moment ago, all macho—looking at Dierdre, or looking her over, Taylor observed.

"I think there's something more you need to know about the pressure Suzanne is under right now. She wouldn't want me to tell you, but this whole thing is too big for her to handle alone." Dierdre ran her red nails through her dark hair and moistened her fiery lips with her tongue. "Rehma still has legal custody. She's gotten herself a lawyer to take the children away from Suzanne."

"You're *shittin'* me!" Doug looked shocked.

"Excuse me," Taylor was surprised. "You mean Greg and Mitzi aren't Suzanne's own kids?" *Ah, the blue eyes instead of brown like hers.*

"You really have been out of touch for a long time with your *dear* college friend Suzanne, haven't you, old boy?"

Doug's voice had a triumphant edge that sounded to Taylor like high-school locker-room jabs between guys trying to move on the same girl. If it hadn't been about Suzanne, he would have dismissed it as childish. It was obvious the other man saw him as competition. He wondered if that was why Dierdre had included him in this conversation, or if there was some other reason not yet clear. He propped his chain saw on-safety against a log and waited to find out.

Dierdre ignored Doug's sarcasm and continued. "My point is guys, do you think Rehma would put someone up to these fearful things to make Suzanne so jumpy she might be too muddled to get an attorney of her own and fight for custody in court?"

"I don't even know the woman, why have me to dinner?" Taylor wanted to know Dierdre's motive and decided blunt was best. *She has to react somehow, maybe it will be with the truth.*

"Suzanne is very proud, Taylor. Even if she wanted your help with this mess, she'd never ask *you* in a million years. Personally, I think she needs all the help she can get. Also, the more objective the input, the more likely we are to stumble onto the reason these things are happening. No offense to you, of course, Doug." She gave the officer a disarming smile and touched his arm in a lingering stroke. Taylor noticed Doug ate it up, but only until he realized how she'd opened the door for the competition to move in on territory he'd staked for himself. Doug pulled his arm away.

"If I can't handle your sister's safety by myself, there are plenty of Steve's buddies on the force who'll lend a hand. No need to involve Taylor in something that's none of his affair. Right, Armstrong?"

Taylor took the conversation's turn in stride. If Jensen wanted a man-to-man adversarial role between them, so be it. Though he still hadn't decided how far he wanted to become involved in Suzanne's problems, he preferred making his own decisions.

"It seems to me, Jensen, Suzanne might be the better one to decide if it's any of my affair or not. She wouldn't take kindly to any of us making her plans for her. She and I being old friends and all."

Doug turned back to Dierdre, while he pulled absently at his mustache. "How long has she known about Rehma going for the kids? God, Steve would roll over in his grave if they aren't brought up by Suzanne."

Dierdre glanced up at the house, probably noticing as Taylor did, that a light had gone on in what he thought was likely to be Suzanne's room.

"Look," Dierdre went on more urgently. "I'm simply making the point that Rehma's a factor in the picture that you don't know about. For whatever reason, now after all this time, she wants her children back. Suzanne's frantic. I'm worried she'll be too upset to think her way out of this without getting burned and badly. Consider that Rehma might be behind this harassment, that's all I'm asking."

"Rehma's all show, little brain, and no backbone," said Doug. "She's sure as hell not playing with enough marbles to figure out a scheme as scary as this one."

"So, does she have a loony boyfriend who is?" Taylor asked.

"That might be a thought if her current live-in weren't a drifter with a lazy lifestyle. He works part time and mooches off Rehma. The nut that's perping these stunts is one twisted son-of-a-bitch who's got to work hard to pull this stuff off. Besides, he may be odd but I don't think the guy's a fool. He knows Suzanne has police officer friends."

"Just because he lives with Rehma he knows her ex-husband's wife has cops for friends?" said Taylor. "How do you figure?"

"The guy works whenever he feels like it as the maintenance man and all-round go-for where most of us guys on the force go to work out. He hears all the talk at the Iron Pump when he's around."

"Does he work out, too?" Dierdre asked. "I mean, you know, does he take advantage of the equipment to stay in shape. Is he strong enough to cut down a tree and crowbar his way into my sister's house?"

"Yeah, but he's a cripple. And like I said, he's lazy. He probably wouldn't pick up a Kleenex to blow his own nose, putting it nicely for a lady."

"Let's go inside, boys. It's getting dark and my supremo sauce will simmer dry in this high-desert atmosphere."

Dierdre linked arms with Doug and pulled on Taylor's sleeve. "Store that chain saw on the porch and come wash for dinner."

He lifted the saw and hefted his pulaski to his shoulder, following along behind the bony ass and the soft curved one. He wondered if Dierdre swung hers just for his benefit, or if she always walked like a siren. No matter, nothing wrong in his mind with checking out the menu, as long as you didn't order anything troublesome and take it home. He stowed his equipment behind the railing and followed them inside.

Suzanne Price

Suzanne entered her kitchen, noisy and crowded with Dierdre, the children—and to her surprise—Doug Jensen and Taylor Armstrong. She shot daggers to her sister, who ignored her. Damp hair, a sweatshirt and jeans, no make up, and no energy for any more unpredictable happenings made Suzanne bristle at Dierdre's impromptu dinner party. *As usual, without consultations between us! Dee's need-to- show-off personality could drive me right over the edge.*

But the edge was off after a relaxing bath and the glass of wine Dee had delivered to the old marble-topped stand by the tub. Suzanne had to admit it was an unusual treat to walk in and find a tempting meal already prepared, surprisingly not even out of a box. She tried to feel no need to impress anyone, but regretfully wished that she'd fussed over her hair and put on mascara and lipstick, noting Dee wore a lavish amount of both, plus one of her Persian perfumes scenting the whole room. She sat down between the children, opposite Taylor who nodded to her and smiled. He raised his shoulders in a gesture indicating he was just as bewildered at his presence as she was at finding him at her table. *What is Dee up to? Even Taylor seems confused.*

"Doug, how soon can we go fishing? Alex's dad says they've been stocking browns at the reservoir." Greg's voice sounded wistful.

"Not for a couple of weeks. We've got softball practice two afternoons next week, remember, Champ? Pass the spaghetti, please."

Suzanne took the pasta dish as it was passed, pulling out enough strings to be gracious for all Dierdre's trouble. She didn't have any appetite, but helped Mitzi with her portion, adding pungent sauce for them both as it came around. She glanced at Taylor. He was ravenous and appeared to be trying hard not to gobble his food. She wondered how often he had a home-cooked meal and who cooked it for him.

"Hey, Doug, I sure like that new insect book you gave me. It's really cool!"

"Greg, let's talk about bugs sometime when we're not eating." *I've had enough of disgusting creatures for one day.*

"Aw, gee. You're no fun. We hardly ever get to talk, and Doug's my best buddy. Aren't you, Doug?"

"You bet. We'll talk about bugs all you want over a soda after practice tomorrow. Dierdre, you make a mean spaghetti sauce. Can't say as I care much for Caesar salad, but for salad it's okay."

"Thank you. Glad I could drag you in for some male company. You two guys are filling a void here."

"What's a boid?" Mitzi asked, smacking her lips and straggling one long loop of spaghetti all the way from her mouth to her plate.

"A void means a lack of something," said Dierdre. "Like when you run out of . . . jelly beans."

Everyone laughed.

With her fork, Suzanne reached toward her daughter's plate. "Let me cut that pasta for you, Mitzi."

Mitzi protested, "I can do it. Bisketti is lots of fun."

"We won't watch," said Dierdre. "Let her eat the way she wants to tonight."

"Sure, baby always gets *her* way." Greg pouting, took a huge bite of garlic bread.

The Wind Remembers

Suzanne sipped at her second glass of wine. Petty problems just weren't big enough to be bothered with for the energy they would take tonight. She'd given up on trying to impress Taylor with what a 'normal' life she led. Her private laundry had all hung out for him today in her washing machine.

Dierdre raised her glass. "A toast to friendship." Everyone clinked glasses, even the children with their milk. "We should also toast my sister's success on the golf course this afternoon. She just missed a par after a regulation drive on number five."

"I didn't know you were a golfer," said Taylor. His genuine surprise delighted Suzanne more than she let on.

"You don't know a lot about her," Doug put in before she could ask if Taylor played.

"There's probably a great deal you don't know about me either, Doug." Suzanne reached for the salad, hoping someone else would change the subject.

"Do you still paint watercolors?" Taylor pressed on, "I asked the other day, but we were interrupted before you answered."

"Mommy paints all the time. You should see my pretty mural. It was real pretty 'til *Gregoreee* stuck bugs on it."

"Mitzi, we agreed not to discuss Greg's misunderstanding or *bugs* at meal time." Suzanne rose from the table and refilled the sauce bowl at the range.

"It wasn't no misunderstanding," Greg said. "I just wanted to put bugs in Mitzi's garden. You can't grow flowers without bugs, 'cause it takes bugs to make flowers in the first place."

"Perhaps I'd already thought of that and hadn't painted them in yet," Suzanne said. "Nevertheless, the bug topic is closed until a time when we're not eating."

"Then let's talk all about rats!" said Mitzi. Her enthusiasm was so innocent the adults laughed.

"See," said Greg. "Everybody thinks it's cute when she says something I get in trouble for. Spoiled baby."

The Wind Remembers

Dierdre put an arm around Greg from her end of the table. Suzanne was grateful they'd put so much behind them today.

"Greg, I saw my sister's sketches for your room's mural. So you don't have to feel left out. Let's talk about the plan for our camping trip to the Sun Tunnels. Aren't you excited to go camping with your Aunt Dierdre? I think we can both talk about that without getting in trouble." She held the bowl for him while he ladled out his own helping of sauce.

Suzanne was enjoying Dierdre's support with her family. She flashed her twin a smile. "I'm still not sure that's wise, Dee," her tone kind, but firm. "Perhaps things should settle down before we go . . . away . . . anywhere."

"Susie, the solstice light bursts through the Sun Tunnels come twice a year. If I can't get you out there in nice warm weather, I'm surely not going to have any more luck dragging you out to a campsite in bitter winter wind. I don't want to go then myself. Back roads would probably be impassable with snow anyway."

"That's another after-dinner topic." Suzanne made her voice sound unequivocal.

Taylor rescued her. "Suzanne, I want to hear more about your painting."

"Okay. As Mitzi said, I paint all the time. I've nearly given up finding work in the area of my first love, but I keep trying to break into the freelance market. I'm getting a watercolor series ready for next year's Arbor Day calendar. It's a competition. The winning artist gets $5,000 and an open-ended contract for the calendar and some note cards. It's a long shot, but my work is getting better all the time. Even if I have to take another sort of job away from home while the children are in school, I'll continue to try to sell my paintings."

Taylor had put down his fork and was giving her his full attention. "Tree subjects still your favorites?"

He had the most wonderful chicory-blue eyes. She nodded assent, surprised and pleased at his interest in her skills and subject tastes as an artist.

"Suzanne, about that little dance invitation I gave you." Doug's interruption irritated her, and she hated being on the spot in front of Taylor. "Don't you think it's time you said yes? Here while I have witnesses. It *is* the biggest fundraising event for Greg's ball team, you know."

"We could talk about that later, too, Doug."

"Well, Dierdre, if you dance half as good as you cook, old Taylor here would probably want to swing you around a little bit. Right?" Doug turned to look at Taylor, whose mouth was full, in the eye. "We should make it a foursome."

Suzanne's fingers squeezed the stem of her glass until her cuticles turned white.

Taylor brought his napkin to his mouth thoughtfully, and took a sip of water before answering. He looked at Suzanne, then at Dierdre.

"When's the dance?"

Doug jumped on it. "Wednesday evening after ball practice. A real country hoe down. Wear your best Western duds. I'll spring for the tickets for you two to join us."

Suzanne's fork wiggled a path through her salad. The control of her life eddied away from her again.

"You okay with that, Suzanne, or would Dierdre and I be imposing on your privacy?" Taylor's tone was serious, but his eyes seemed playful. She was confused, stymied for a comeback.

"I think a dance is just what the doctor ordered around here," said Dierdre. "If you're game, Taylor, then count me in."

"Can I come dancing too?" asked Mitzi.

"It's just for big people, Sweetheart." Suzanne patted her hand.

Greg slurped his milk. "Who'd want to go to a stupid old dance anyway? If it's after practice on Wednesday, Doug can't take me for a soda. The team thinks you coaches should do a bake sale for new-uniform money."

"Bake sales are fine with good cooks around, little buddy, but they don't make enough money for uniforms. It's settled then. Let's meet here, Taylor, and we'll squire the ladies to the ball." Doug smiled broadly at everyone and lifted his glass in a victorious salute.

Dierdre caught Suzanne's eye and recaptured control of the conversation. "Maybe after dinner you'd like to see Suzanne's paintings in her studio downstairs, Taylor."

"But watch out for dead rats!" Mitzi added.

"Mitzi!" Suzanne scolded.

"I'm sorry, Mommy, but I want Mr. Armfrong to see my mural. Specially since you fixed it pretty again. My friend Leesha wants one just like it, but Mommy says she'll paint Gregory's next."

"I'm full, can I be done?" Greg shoved his chair back. "I want to watch TV, unless Doug and I can go to my room to look at my new b . . . collection from the wood pile." He caught himself. Doug shook his head no and pointed to his fresh mound of spaghetti.

Suzanne looked at the pile of untouched salad on her son's plate, recognized it for the un-winnable argument it would touch off, and nodded assent.

"Wash your hands and brush your teeth before you turn on TV. One thirty-minute show, that's it. Then off to bed."

"Okaaaay! Gees, you'd think I have school tomorrow. It's summer, who cares if I stay up late?"

Suzanne gave him what she hoped was a withering look that meant 'hush up.' He took the hint and left without further comment. She turned her attention to Mitzi while the men worked on their seconds. Dierdre poured more wine for the adults.

"Mitzi, it's past your bedtime now. How much more do you want to eat? You're just dawdling with your food." Suzanne smoothed a few curls back into the sunflower barrette.

"I'm all full, 'cept if there's any zert if I eat more bites of bisketti."

Dee spoke up. "Not tonight, Sweetheart. Aunt Dierdre and your mother are always trying to stay trim. Having sweets around is too tempting."

Dierdre sounded so domestic Suzanne couldn't believe it was the same sister who arrived day before yesterday, fought with her this morning, and came to her aid after the break in. Then again, Dee was behaving more like the old sister from their childhood. It was great. Suzanne felt a surge of happiness that in the midst of all this turmoil, what she had needed from her twin for so long, was at last happening.

"I'm going to get my jammies on, Mommy. Me and Bear Lovins are tired today. We played hard at Leesha's house. Mr. Armfrong, you come see my mural before you have to go home."

Suzanne tried to spare him staying longer than necessary. "Maybe some other time, Mitzi, Mr. Armstrong is tired tonight after working so hard for us."

Her sister took over. "Susie, it's time to stop hiding your talent under a bushel. You can give us all a little tour of your mural painting. We'll make it quick."

Dierdre was in an orchestrating mood but Suzanne knew that was Dee's style. The biblical reference to the bushel parable was amusing coming from her agnostic twin. Mitzi kissed her mommy on the cheek. With her napkin Suzanne mopped the sticky spot off and dabbed at her lips. Mitzi left.

"By the way," said Dierdre. "Do either of you guys know anything about a man named Frank Simmons?"

"Dierdre!" Suzanne was stunned that her sister would venture into her personal matters without her permission. *At least she waited until the children were out of the room.* "I'm not ready to discuss . . ."

"They already know about Rehma wanting the kids back. There isn't time to be choosy about your pride. You need all of our help while there *is* time."

"You certainly seem to be in the mood to conduct my affairs." Suzanne gathered up the children's plates and took them to the sink.

Doug, in professional cop mode, came alive behind her. "Dierdre's right, Suzanne. We have to look at all options of who could be perpetrating these incidents."

Turning the water on full blast, she clattered plates for a quick rinse to buy time to get her bearings before returning to the table. *What else is she going to go into tonight?*

Taylor's eyes met hers over his wineglass. She looked away at Doug who was still speaking, not liking the way he could turn his vocabulary, good grammar, and his manners on and off when it suited him. But she knew she needed him now, for safety's sake, even though she resented his friendship with her son and his growing seductive innuendoes with her and tonight with Dierdre. She needed him all right, in spite of the fact he was spending a lot of time with his eyes lost in the front of Dee's deep V-neck tee-shirt. She determined to hold her resentment in check for the sake of her family.

Doug, flushed from the wine, blurted, "Simmons, Frank Simmons? *He's* Rehma's lawyer?"

"So why wouldn't he be a good choice?" Dierdre asked.

"He came here a couple years ago from California to ranch and breed falcons. He's not actually a practicing attorney anymore. I think he lost his license to practice law over some under-the-table dealings that came to light and got him disbarred. He wouldn't be allowed to represent her in court. If she really wants to get the kids, Rehma will need somebody better than him—good enough to win out over a class-act like you, Suzanne."   *Doug is laying it on thick in front of Taylor and Dee.* "Not necessarily," Suzanne countered. "This is Utah. Rehma's the biological mother and the legal custodian of her kids. I'm only their stepmother. Without their father or a job, I'm afraid the law is on her side. I'm just lucky she's single like I am. That's got to be an equalizing factor."

Taylor leaned forward. "Doug, she's right. That's why it doesn't make sense to me why she'd be the likely source of all these attacks against Susie."

Dierdre toyed with a cigarette pack, longing for a smoke as Suzanne well knew. "What I can't understand is why she wants the kids back now, after all these years. Rehma couldn't wait to give them up to Steve and Susie. Something pretty powerful must have changed her mind after all this time." She rose and brought another bottle of wine and the corkscrew to the table.

"What does she do for a living?" Taylor asked.

"She's got a hair salon across from the Iron Pump."

Dierdre tapped the pack against the table. "You told Taylor and I her boyfriend lives off of her, except what he makes as a part-time janitor. So how does she expect to afford two little kids?"

"What else did I miss while I was in the bathtub?" Suzanne was ordinarily not interested in Rehma's lifestyle. It was always troubled with questionable men, alcohol, or drugs, but tonight everything she'd taken too lightly in the past seemed of critical importance. Even to the happiness and safety of her family. "No idea what she's planning. So who's the guy living with her now?"

Doug drained his glass and set it down. "Bo something. Can't recall his last name."

"Is he the broken-down rodeo dude who could use a bath and a haircut, maybe even somebody big and tough enough to teach him some manners?" Taylor was serious.

Suzanne felt a growing sense of alarm.

Doug looked at him like he had a brain and no right to have one. "How do you know Bo?"

Suzanne kept finding herself feeling protective of Taylor. It was beginning to bother her, because she knew Taylor could take care of himself. Still, Doug was rude, and it embarrassed her in her own kitchen. She didn't want Taylor thinking Steve's partner was the best she could do for a choice of friends.

"I ran into a Bo somebody at a Flying J on Saturday. Mean and unpredictable. Then he wheeled by while I was here assessing the tree damage, nearly ran the postal truck off the road, and splattered Susie with mud. Arrogant S.O.B. If he's the one Suzanne's up against, I wouldn't put murder past him. He's one cocky, hot-headed prick. Excuse me, ladies."

"Taylor, don't frighten Suzanne even more than she already is," Dierdre cautioned him.

"I'm a getting little more than weary of everyone speaking for what I think, need, feel or fear I can't handle. If Taylor wants to tell me what I'm in for with Rehma, and the sort of animal who will father my children if she wins in court—because I am going to protest her custody with a lawyer of my own—then more power to him."

She shot a drilling glance in Doug's, then Dee's direction. Feeling Taylor's eyes on her, she addressed him. "I had no idea you even noticed I was spattered by that awful truck. And that dangerous jerk driver is Rehma's boyfriend?!" Suzanne wanted answers tonight. "Back to Frank Simmons, Doug, how does he fit in as Rehma's attorney? Why would she pick someone who isn't a partner in a reputable firm?"

Dierdre poured Doug more wine from the fresh bottle. Suzanne had the distinct impression her sister was loosening information out of him. *Go for it*, she thought, putting aside her habitual ethics.

"Maybe Rehma doesn't think she needs anything more than a formal scare tactic like the letter to get Susie to hand over Greg and Mitzi," Taylor suggested. "Some people put a lot of stock in the clout of lawyer's stationery."

Doug sipped and offered, "Let's face it, Rehma's not too smart. She probably took the first law recommendation from one of her regular nail customers. Or it could have been one of her old stripper friend's experience she relied on." He laughed and pawed a fork through what remained of his spaghetti. "Doesn't make sense," he continued. "Frank keeps to himself pretty much, though he hits a bar up in the valley once in a while. His hawks take most of his time, except for when he helps his wife run her fancy, summer riding-stable program for rich kids."

"How do you know about him, Doug?" Suzanne wanted every scrap of information she could get to arm herself against what had become a terrifying possibility. She had no idea if Rehma and her boyfriend were involved in scaring her or not, but she wasn't taking any chances from here on about being unprepared for a court fight.

"I answered a complaint last summer up at Frank and Hunnie's place. The mother of one of Hunnie's riding students got all up in the bucket about her daughter telling how Frank trains his falcons with live-pigeon decoys. They don't die a very pretty death. The girl's mother's an animal-rights activist. She filed a complaint, but Frank's a licensed captive-breeder. He was perfectly within his rights. Falcons die if they can't cast roughage from live wild prey. She had to eat crow."

"Oh, how very punny of you, Doug," Dierdre quipped, adjusting her shirt for his benefit, or Taylor's, as it seemed to Suzanne.

Taylor interjected, "It isn't just casting mutes from prey that's essential for the health of a falcon. Pops and I always wash rabbit and pigeon meat until it's white and free of fat so the forceful ejection of the mute scrubs the tract and keens the bird down to hunting weight."

Doug had seemed to enjoy being the center of attention in front of Taylor. At the interruption he gave a wry look at them all for sympathy. "So you know something about falcons?"

Suzanne found Doug almost unbearably immature, but she'd never paid more attention to what he was saying. He was smart when it came to being a policeman. "Yes, Doug, he does."

Doug continued, "Frank's okay, just strange in his ways. He's probably pulling some extra cash from Rehma for the use of his name to scare Suzanne into giving up without a legal fight."

"There's another angle that might have a bearing," Taylor put in. "I've heard there's a developer working to build some condos up here on the bench, and he's pressing people hard to sell out at a loss so he has access. Have you been approached by anyone trying to buy you out, Susie? After all, you're the house highest on the bench before the old sheep camps."

"There was someone who came by maybe ten months or a year ago, but I explained to him there was no way we were interested in selling and not to bother us anymore. It was the worst time for Steve, and I simply . . ."

Mitzi appeared in the doorway in her pink bathrobe and rabbit slippers.

"Mommy, me and Bear Lovins are ready for prayers. Can't Mr. Armfrong come and see my mural now?"

Suzanne pushed back her chair and motioned them all to follow. On the way past the den, she peeked in at Greg. He'd fallen asleep with the remote control in his hand; the television droned on. It reminded her warmly of Steve. She stepped in and kissed her son on his forehead while Mitzi led the others to her room. Suzanne pulled an afghan off the couch and covered Greg. Switching off the set, she rejoined the group.

Taylor stood near the bedroom door, his stubbled chin tilted to the ceiling. When she entered, he looked down at her. She met his eyes; he seemed tired but comfortable. She realized in that moment how much she'd missed the nearness of him. Even needing a shower and a shave after a hard day's work brought happy memories of years ago flooding to her mind.

"Susie, this is incredible! Any kid would go nuts to have a room like this. Look at the clouds, the stars, and the birds on the ceiling, and *the trees on every wall*. You've even made each tree species distinctive! I'm impressed! You must love your mural, Mitzi." He ruffled the little girl's curly hair with his fingers.

"Watch this, Mr. Armfrong. I've got a secret s'prise, too." She reached up on tiptoe and flipped the light switch. The room plunged into darkness, but the moon, the stars, the wings of the owl, the moths, and the clouds' silvery shimmers glowed in the dark.

"Wow!" said Taylor. "Fantastic!"

"My Sis is a genius! If you lived in New York or California, Suze, you'd be in such demand you'd have to hire assistants to help carry out your designs." Dierdre came over and gave her a hug.

Suzanne was thrilled with their spontaneous reaction. For a change, she allowed herself to believe it was genuine and perhaps she did have a special talent that would one day be her livelihood. Later she would recall this moment and blame some of her giddiness on the wine, a rare drink for her, and the nearness of Taylor at her elbow.

"What do you think, Doug?" Dierdre asked in the dark, "You're awfully quiet."

Mitzi flipped the lights back on.

"I was just thinking I can see why Greg's jealous of this mural. I thought it would be a painting you'd done maybe on one wall, Suzanne. With the whole room painted up like an outdoor scene of every season—and all the animals and kids playing—it's no wonder why he's been so hard to handle lately."

Dierdre laughed. "Maybe this is why I mistakenly opened the box of tarantula meant for you."

"Can you find me and Greg and Leesha and Alex, Mr. Armfrong?" Mitzi looked up at him adoringly.

Suzanne couldn't imagine why her daughter had taken such a liking to Taylor. Doug had been around for two years, and she'd hardly given him any notice at all. She exchanged looks with Dee that sent the same message between them.

"You show me your friends, Pumpkin. I've found you on every wall already." He moved around the room with her hand in his and stopped where a curly-haired girl and chubby, redheaded Leesha played in a spring puddle. He pointed to a likeness of Mitzi peeking around the side of a hanging shelf, caught in the branches of a cherry tree, and moved on to each wall in turn. There was Mitzi kicking golden aspen leaves, and the last wall pictured her wearing a bright pink snowsuit and dragging Bear Lovins on a red sled dish. Greg slogged along behind, rolling a huge snowball to finish the snowman in front of the fluff-covered house.

"Isn't the entire effect enchanting! Sis is a clever little darling. I'm so proud of you." Dierdre gave her another hug.

"Thanks, Dee. Okay everyone. Show's over. Time to tuck this curly head in bed."

"I'll clean up the kitchen while you do the prayer thing,"

said Dicrdrc. "You big strong men can clear the table while I rinse and fill the dishwasher."

The others filed out comparing notes on what they each thought was special about the full-room mural. Suzanne knelt next to the bed and bowed her head, waiting for Mitzi's ever-original nightly prayer.

"God bless Daddy in heaven, and bless Mommy and Gregory, and Aunt Dreedra and me, and Leesha and Bear Lovins. And bless Mr. Armfrong and our secret with his daddy, Amen."

Mitzi snuggled into her summer blanket while Suzanne tucked her in.

"What secret do you have with Mr. Armstrong and his father?" she asked gently.

"Mommy, the secret's between me and Mr. Armfrong and God—'til we're ready to s'prise you. Don't worry, it's a good s'prise. Not like dead rats, I promise."

"Okay, Honey. Goodnight, I love you until morning and always."

"I love you, too. Goodnight, Mommy."

Suzanne turned the night-light out. Stars glimmered from the ceiling.

"Mommy?"

"Yes?"

"Mr. Armfrong was smart to find all of me, don't cha think?"

"He surely was. Now, watch the sparkles twinkle out and go to sleep."

Suzanne returned to the kitchen, which was almost entirely restored to order. What a wonderful evening it had been in spite of how awkwardly it had come about.

"I must be leaving, Susie, Dierdre." Taylor removed his windbreaker jacket from the chair back where he'd sat for dinner. "It was delicious and nice to sit around family-style for a change. I'll be back tomorrow afternoon."

"Taylor, I'll get a flashlight and walk out with you. I have something to ask." Suzanne grabbed Steve's jacket and when Doug tried to catch her eye, looked away. His disapproval clearly etched in his face, he stared openly after her, looking a little bleary from the five glasses of wine she'd counted. She felt defiant he should presume to define her choices.

On the porch, Taylor picked up the saw and the pulaski and walked next to her in the bobbing beam of the flashlight.

"I hope you'll save me a dance or two Susie, that's the only reason I said yes to Doug's little plan."

"Oh, I . . . well, *yes*. Of course, Taylor. I'd like that very much." In the dark her face warmed. They used to love dancing together. *Being in his arms again would be heaven.* She hadn't been held close by a man in a very long time. However, thinking of him dancing with Dierdre made her wince away from the idea of his arms around her sister. *Her maddening ways.* It wouldn't take Dee long to do her flirtation number on him. She needn't imagine Taylor would remain interested in her once he'd danced with her glamorous twin.

"Taylor, Mitzi says you two have a secret with your father. I know it's probably quite innocent, but I don't think I need any more surprises just now."

"We're hatching a robin egg from the nest that broke when your tree went over. She wants to surprise you. It probably won't work, but Pops has an incubator and I offered to have him bird sit. Okay?"

Their shoulders brushed against one another. Suzanne was relieved. She liked his closeness, his familiar presence, and the scent of his physical maleness.

"Do you smell something funny?" he asked. "Strong, chemical? *I sure do.*"

Inhaling the air around her more deeply, she also smelled something strong and peculiar. "It's like too many permanent marking pens in a closed room."

Suzanne swung the flashlight in arcs along their path.

"Sweep the light to my truck so I can store my gear, then I'll walk you back inside, then I'll get Doug and we'll look around for the cause."

Suzanne cast the light beam on the swing-down panel of his truck.

"God damn son-of-a-bitch!" Taylor's fury unleashed, he dropped the saw and the pulaski in the gravel. Stones flew up against their pant legs.

"Oh, Taylor, I'm *so* sorry!"

Suzanne stood by while he grabbed her flashlight and examined his new white truck, now sprayed with blue paint. 'BLUE TATTOO, BIG BLUE TATTOO' in fat letters covered the tail end and both doors, obliterating the Ben Lomond Tree Service twig-style logo. He hurried her past Doug's cruiser, flashing the beam along its doors. 'BLUE TATTOO, BIG BLUE, BIG BLUE'.

"Holy shit, somebody has brass balls to graffiti a cop's cruiser!"

Suzanne was shocked at Taylor's language but felt he had good reason to be angry. She stumbled up the steps after him. They burst into the kitchen.

"No need to call 911 Jensen, you're already on the scene. We've got to get our vehicles to a paint expert or they'll be permanently ruined, maybe already are. Damn it!"

"What are you talking about, man?"

"Come see for yourself. When I get my hands on the bastards that did this, I'll break their damn necks!" Taylor tossed the words over his shoulder, motioned for Doug to follow, and slammed back out into the night.

Suzanne, shaken and devastated, blurted to Dierdre, "Now I've dragged Taylor into something that wasn't even his to be concerned about. He'll hate me for ruining his brand new truck! What else can go wrong?"

The Wind Remembers

Rat

~ Monday the 16th of June

"How's the tattoo?" Rat checked the view out each side of the phone booth and waited for Sky to come up with an answer. It was hard to hold back on his news.

"Swelling's gone down some. Be okay in a week or so. I'm sure sick of wearing long sleeves in this heat."

"Your dad will have to know one of these days anyway, but he'll go easier on you if it's healed good and the scabs are gone before he sees it."

"How'd you get your old man to let you use the phone?"

"Didn't. I'm down in front of Speedy Wash in the booth. Got to tell you how I'm going to make it with Tangie."

"You're dreaming out your jeans, Rat. Ain't none of us going to earn enough points for Tangie. Big Blue will see to it. He just dangles her in front of us like a carrot, so we'll keep the money coming in for getting high and making him look important."

"Listen up. I'm out of quarters. I did it big, bigger than Blue, I'm telling you. Tagged the whole back side of that garage on Old Post where the tree went over."

"That ain't great enough to get you five minutes with Big Blue's red head. Now down on Main Street'd be different."

Rat rubbed a torn-out page from the phone directory against his paint-stained sleeve. Careless, he hated it when he was careless. Phone cocked to his shoulder, he chewed on a cigarette butt he'd found on the floor.

"What would you say if I told you I tagged a couple of vehicles, shiny *new* ones."

"You're shittin' me sure."

"Nope, I'm telling you, Sky, I can practically taste that chick right now."

The Wind Remembers

He kicked at the pile of dirty Styrofoam chips on the floor of the booth. Rat felt high, higher than he'd ever been on crack or speed. High on himself and what he'd done, risk and all.

"I'm going to have all the points I need for Tangie, maybe even get the brothers to follow *me* now. Big Blue will have to let me have her at least once. He can't afford to go back on his word to all the brothers or he'll piss everybody off. I've got him by the balls this time."

"What you smokin', man?" Sky's voice squeaked like Rat knew it always did when his friend got nervous.

"I'm not on nothing. I tagged a truck and a *cop's cruiser*! Both of them shiny as new dimes. Nobody seen me, neither. I finished and got away in the dark. Wish we could be there in the morning when they see the full effect in broad daylight."

"You crazy?! You're ass is going to be in jail, that's what's gonna happen in daylight. You'll have us *all* in jail. A *cop's* car? What the hell was you thinkin'?"

"That's why I'm calling. Lay low at your dad's or go visit your granddad. I'm going to Mom's place and help her clean up, for an alibi. Probably won't have to worry though. Big Blue will be taking the rap for me."

"Like *hell* he will!" Sky's voice squeaked on the word 'hell' and didn't come back down.

"Trust your Brother Rat. Our big-mouthed leader has been in jail more than once for hassling cops. They'll be looking for him, not us with clean records." Rat kicked the folding door open and turned to hang up. On his stolen watch his time was about gone.

"Bullcrap, Rat. You've given us all up, man. I get hauled in, my dad will never let me come home. I'll have to get a job or live on the street like a bum! Damn it, you never said nothin' about settin' me up to get kicked outta the house if I joined Blue Tattoo!"

"Relax little brother. I tagged everything "Big Blue, Big Blue." The cops will go for him straight out. Don't tell me you wouldn't rather supply your own nose habit. Just think how he enjoyed sticking you and how much you hate him like the rest of us do. You'll see. Now, all the brothers would rather follow me."

The recorded voice requested a quarter. Rat hung up and sidled over to his bike, swung aboard, and rolled down the street, doing a couple of wheelies in the intersection. A car horn honked. He gave the driver the bird and took his time making it to the other side of the street. Ahead, the winking neon of Ruby's Place glowed red in the darkness.

Might as well help her clean up 'cause she'll probably have the cook throw on a burger for me. Maybe two. I'm starving.

He'd call his dad from the diner, beg off coming home tonight and lay low at his mom's for a while. He'd been meaning to make a break with his boozy old man anyway. *Might as well change everything for the better while I'm at it.*

He could see himself at the sheep camp heading up a strategy meeting while Big Blue cooled his mean ass in jail. *He always carries his drugs on him. It'll be a long time before Big Blue gets out. By then it will be too late.*

Rat would be the headman of the Blue Tattoo, and Tangie would be *his* woman. He spit his cigarette butt out ahead of him and ran over it with his front wheel, imagining himself crushing the power out of Big Blue, high on feeling the satisfaction of letting the cops do it for him.

Johnny Carlisle

~ Monday the 16th of June

Johnny Carlisle entered his cheap motel room for the second time that evening, this time with two paper bags and a newspaper. Shoving the door shut with his hip, he dropped the weightier bag on the bed with the *Farr Star,* and plunked the fast-food sack and the room key on the TV set. The fingers of his more agile left hand clipped the chain lock into place, his body and mind weary from airport connections and driving north from Salt Lake City. He hadn't risked much coffee to keep him awake because it went right through him. Stopping along the road made it too easy to set himself up for a mugging. These days he didn't trust anybody.

Upon reaching Farr before noon, he'd checked into the cheapest motel he remembered, stashed his few belongings in the room, and crashed for half an hour of restless sleep. Awake, he'd down his meds and stood in the shower until the hot water turned uncomfortably cool. The steam gave way to clammy tile walls grouted with black mold. For a high-desert climate, that much mold was unusual and spelled poor maintenance to him. His skin crawled at the thought, but he couldn't be too choosy.

Somewhat refreshed, he'd driven up the canyon to find a private gun dealer in a pawnshop he used to know who did some of his best under-the-table business from his ramshackle house. Monday nights most of his nosy Mormon neighbors were busy with 'family home evening.' It had taken Johnny a few wrong turns to remember how to find the place, but he persevered and was rewarded for his patience. Now he looked forward to stretching out on the bed after stoking up on a couple of fish sandwiches and about a ton of fries. He'd clean and load the second-hand gun before he called it a night.

With his quarry at last likely somewhere nearby, Carlisle counted on catching the first good rest he'd had in the months since he'd been left for dead. When he felt ready he'd take his revenge. There was nobody standing in his way for going after his mark. Tomorrow he'd drive into Farr and look up the police officer who'd befriended him. He still had the officer's name and office phone number on a worn paper in his wallet. He didn't want to leave a message. His home phone number must be unlisted because Johnny had searched a column of Prices in the motel directory, no Steves or Stephen Prices. Maybe the cop with the Kojak-style skin head had been transferred; he'd been too young for retirement. Johnny would be careful how he asked for help with finding the rodeo dude he was after, so his intent to kill him wouldn't be obvious, 'til it too late for anyone to stop him.

He owed Price a thank you, too. If it hadn't been for the cop who'd sat by his bed and listened while he struggled with semi-consciousness and the aftermath of a stroke, trying to explain in garbled words what had happened to him, he'd have given up long ago. Back then, he hadn't grasped why his gyrfalcon had been stolen, when he'd survived the attack. He'd done more than survive. He could talk, feed himself, and walk. Hell he'd even driven more than an hour from the airport, then up the canyon, and around town. He was more of a man than he'd given himself credit for. *More of a man than my wife believed, damn her.*

Johnny unwrapped the oily papers from his sandwich sack, replacing the smell of the room's pine disinfectant and stale cigarettes with the deep-fried aroma of hot fish and fries. His mouth watered, and he managed a sandwich to his lips with his crooked right hand, while he undid the snaps of his shirt with his left. It would take more time and practice before he'd choose to eat in a public restaurant, at least until he learned to do the whole business without dripping all over himself. Eating awkwardly alone or with his dad had become routine, but he'd never forget why it was necessary. Never forget who he was after and finally why, even though he didn't know a name.

He stared at the paper bag on the bed while he chewed. Imagined pumping the bullets he would stuff into the handgun's chambers doing their job of boring holes into the son-of-a-bitch at close range. Imagined standing over him, listening to him beg for mercy, watching the blood seep out of him into a pleasing pool Johnny could smell the way he'd smelled and tasted his own blood, while feeling it escape from every part of himself before he lost consciousness. It wouldn't matter if the cops put him away or killed him afterwards. Johnny Carlisle already had a life sentence in a body that only did a fraction of what it once had, what he wished it could do. He'd make the scum pay with his own life, slowly, painfully, the way Johnny paid every day.

The Wind Remembers

Somewhere Felon paid a creature so low his belly should crawl in the dirt, the honor of returning from the hunt to his glove. He thought of how he'd love to wrench that glove off for a souvenir in his own moment of vengeful reward. He puzzled over what he would do with the gyrfalcon if she could be found. He couldn't care for Felon on his own anymore, and without months of wilderness training, the falcon wouldn't be able to go free into the wild and survive. He tried not to think of how painful it would be when he found his own miserable quarry, if Felon had been destroyed. One of the things he must do in a day or two was locate a falconer through old friends, someone who could care for the hawk so it would not perish when he wasted the thief. The innocent bird must not be hurt or lost. Carlisle's quarrel was with his attacker. His regret at being unable to take on the demanding role of a falconer himself for the saving of his hawk added to the cold furry that stirred more intensely to life in him with each passing hour.

Disposing of the fast-food papers, he pressed the TV remote and caught the evening news while he washed up. Some teenager had sprayed graffiti all over a cop's cruiser and some tree expert's new truck. The media announcer said the police had a line on the perpetrator, a small-time gang leader. He'd be caught soon. They flashed a picture of the big surly kid from previous arrests and asked for the public's help in locating him.

Johnny flipped channels to an old Clint Eastwood movie, thinking how the police station would be humming with the latest on some little graffiti punk tomorrow. The cops had better take time to help him find Officer Price and the man he was after. After that, he'd go out to Antelope Island in Great Salt Lake for some target practice. He hadn't shot a pistol in a couple of years and back then he'd been in peak shape. When the time came he didn't want to waste his first two bullets. They might be all there'd be time for.

From his duffel bag he brought out a ragged tee-shirt and a knitting needle he'd taken from his mother's old sewing basket in Florida. Opening the pawnshop bag, he pulled out the Smith and Wesson 38. He'd selected a double-action revolver that could fire as a single or a double. The gun was worn, but well—not badly. Somebody who cared about it had kept it clean and carried it enough to wear it smooth here and there on the grip and along the 2-inch barrel. He held it in his right hand, flipping open the cylinder so as it opened on the left he could use his best hand to fill the chambers with shells and pull back on the trigger. Johnny practiced with imaginary bullets, filling the 5-shot cylinder, closing it soundlessly, squeezing the trigger so the hammer would go back—fire—and let the next shell fall into place.

He'd picked this gun from among the others for the way its moving parts found their places smoothly, quietly, without a crunch or grind. He liked the smooth, crisp break of the trigger. It made no more noise than a dime dropping on a tile floor. Even to get within twenty-five yards of his mean-assed target, he'd have to be as quiet as possible. He might not get a second or third chance to kill him if wounding cost him his surprise. All he wanted for an advantage was to slow down his prey, make him hesitate.

Johnny watched Clint move down the street of a cow town where armed gunmen staked out every roof on Main Street, walking tall and strong, his gun in the open, his confidence solid. It couldn't be like that for Carlisle, he'd have to be secretive. Use the police to get just enough information to relocate his hawk, remind the cops of the menace the guy was to innocent people.

He opened a can of Hoppes #9 gun oil and dribbled it onto a shred of the T-shirt. Using the knitting needle, he rammed it into the gun barrel held between his knees. It was good to hold a revolver again. He liked the orderly mechanics of it, the predictability. For him it was a tool to get a job done. This time instead of putting down a suffering animal at close range to use for bait or food, it would put an end to his own suffering. In the back of his mind Carlisle saved one bullet for himself.

The Wind Remembers

Suzanne Price

~ Monday the 16th of June

Deep-down tired, Suzanne curled her back against the headboard and faced Dierdre stretched across the bed. She hadn't felt like she was on such an emotional roller coaster since the week of Steve's death, his memorial service, and graveside funeral. Then she'd wanted the comfort of family, Dee in particular, and there'd been no family but the children, really only Mitzi. Greg had been angry, hurt, withdrawn—except with Doug. Their closeness still added to her pain and devastating loneliness.

Now she looked gratefully at Dee for being with her on this upsetting night. The old misgivings and anguish at Dierdre not coming to be with her when Steve died didn't seem to matter any more. Pastor Spahn had cautioned her not to lay her grief at her twin's door for a lifetime like some people do. "Everyone deals with death as well as they know how," he'd said.

The twins had comforted one another at their mother's passing a few years earlier, and neither had ever known their father. Their mother never mentioned him. Privately, the girls joked about their 'immaculate' conception, except not knowing who their father was, wasn't really very funny to either of them.

"Dee, you did a great job with dinner tonight. We haven't entertained in this house for . . . well, a couple of years. Thank you for going to all of the trouble."

"I was working on Doug, and I wanted Taylor there because I think you need all the help and protection you can get. I guess you could tell I had a private agenda. Somehow we have to find out who's doing all this stuff and put a stop to it. I haven't given up on wanting to go to the Sun Tunnels as we've planned. I want your mind free to have a good time."

Dierdre ran her nails through her dark hair, pulling it up

in clumps and spinning it like thread through the tips of her fingers until it made a dark halo all around her head on the pillow. The scent of one of her exotic perfumes filled the air. Suzanne felt ordinary by comparison, a lifetime feeling.

"Weren't you working just a little on Taylor as well?" Suzanne pulled the newspaper toward her and slid its rubber band onto her wrist, attempting to keep her voice casual.

"On your behalf I might have made a few overtures." Dierdre smiled and rolled onto her side facing Suzanne. Propped on an elbow her bulging breasts were emphasized.

"Like the deep V-neck shirt?" Suzanne knew she didn't quite keep the judgment out of her voice. She had been stunned when Dee had implants done on an already gorgeous figure.

"Think what you like my dear, but that cleavage was for Doug's benefit. Part of the charade to keep his mind befuddled and his lip loose."

"I believe you were particularly effective, in fact if he hadn't sobered up over the graffiti on his car I was going to make him stay with you tonight. I was afraid he couldn"t walk away from my table, let alone drive home safely." She gave Dee a high five and swatted her with the *Farr Star*.

Dierdre grabbed the newspaper. "Give me a load of what's coming down in my old hometown. Personals and marriages, please. I'll start with those."

Suzanne slid her hips lower onto the bed and let the pillows cushion her shoulders, head, and neck. This was the kind of time she liked best between them. "Read to me. Erase my troubles with somebody else's."

Dierdre folded back a double page, skimmed a nail down the lines and sat up abruptly, startling Suzanne.

"Well, kiss your single-edged blade good-bye, Susie! Rehma's about to marry her hero." She let the paper crumple between her folded legs, gesturing with her arms in supplication. "The gods are not shining on you, Honey. That's for damn sure."

"What's the unlucky groom's full name?" Suzanne rolled up into a sitting position and reached for the paper. "So now she'll be offering the court a set of parents for Greg and Mitzi. You're right, I'm going to have my work cut out for me to keep them. Don't you think her getting married makes it unlikely Rehma is the one behind trying to frighten me though?"

"It's not just Rehma that worries me, Suzanne. Except for a meal ticket, why would any man with even half a mind want to marry a set of problems like her—for life? Think about it, if this Bo Rodman's already been getting it all for free and no commitment, why would he sign on the dotted line now?"

"Rehma's not all bad. I think she's just weak and misguided. Not a good mother choice, but she's nice enough when she's sober. She is attractive in a hard sort of way."

"You, as usual, are too kind. Everybody does everything for a reason. We're not going to bed until we decide how to find out what it is."

"Sorry, Dee, I have to get some rest. My competition pieces are due shipped with a postmark tomorrow. I'll be painting on them all morning. You'll have to fend for entertainment on your own, or just sleep in until afternoon when I get back from shipping my entries and picking up the children from Diane's."

"Maybe you should spend tomorrow finding an attorney and a job. You can't just put dreams in the court's pot and expect the judge to find you more competent as a parent than a reformed stripper-biological mother, whom I need not remind you already *has* custody of our kids. Now add her new husband who has a job at the Iron Pump, just as Doug told us." Dierdre shoved the paper at her, looking at her with love.

Suzanne slid off the bed and stood up, feeling stung. Her fingers gripped the newspaper. The undeniable truth pelted Suzanne's mind with alarm urgency. It was time to do things differently, only she had no idea what to do. She couldn't run away from it any longer. If there was any time left, it was now.

"Help me," she managed. "How should I begin?"

"Attorneys advertise; then move to job's available."

Chapter Ten

Unraveling Tangles

Suzanne Price

~ Tuesday the 17th of June

Suzanne checked her watch often while she completed details on the last two of six watercolors for the Arbor Society Calendar Contest. At ten minutes before nine in the morning, she rinsed and replaced her fine-point sable in the jar, bristles up, and contemplated the quality of what she'd accomplished. It was her best in composition and technique. The paintings were comparable in style to one another, an important criterion. Washes were clean, layer work maintained freshness, and details were not overdone. Her favorite painting featured the cottonwood.

In the submission-form box she lettered its title: "Late Great Friend with Arms that Held the Sky." Her heart still grieved for the majestic old tree. Suzanne savored the moment, pleased and confident she'd make her post-mark deadline with exhibition-quality work. She brought out Steve's camera, set up the auxiliary flash and photographed all six pieces onto slide film. Later in the morning when the paintings were completely dry, she'd package them for mailing in the afternoon. *Thank you, God, I'm going to make it!*

In a great mood, she bounded up stairs and phoned the attorney's office listed in the newspaper. Dee had made the final choice among their attorney options: "This woman opening a new practice is most likely to be young and cutting edge, hungry for clients, and able to see you on short notice." Her twin proved correct on the latter. Suzanne had less than an hour until her appointment. She showered, dressed and dropped the children at Diane's house so Dierdre could sleep in. Parking behind the bank, she took the elevator to the eleventh floor. Bette Edango's shiny, polished-brass nameplate proudly attested to her new law practice.

Answering the door personally, attorney Edango's handshake was firm, her enormous brown eyes direct, and her smile not only genuine, but stunning. Suzanne felt comfortable with her immediately and hoped her surprise at Bette Edango being a Black woman didn't appear obvious. There were few people of color in Farr, particularly professional career women. She felt she should have picked up on the Nigerian surname, since three families in her church had names with similar African spellings.

"Thank you for seeing me so promptly, Ms. Edango. I'm facing a law suit, and I've no experience with this sort of thing."

"Please," the attorney offered a chair, "call me Bette. May I call you Suzanne?" Suzanne nodded. "Good. Did you locate your late husband's divorce decree, living will, and the attorney letter from the children's birth mother?" Her intonation warm, musical.

While Ms. Edango read through the documents, Suzanne studied her elaborate hair-do of meticulous thin braids scooped up high and looped in the back. Soft coils fell along her flawless chocolate cheeks from temple to ear. The effect was exotic and sophisticated. Gold earrings and a hammered bracelet set off the shimmering peacock print blouse and simple navy suit. Suzanne imagined a watercolor portrait.

Ms. Edango looked up. "With your permission, I'd like to photocopy these documents, Suzanne." Her cultured voice had a clipped British accent. *She's probably Nigerian born and perhaps UK educated.* Suzanne was enchanted and if not so bent on getting help would have ventured a few questions to salve her well-pricked curiosity.

"Certainly," she said. "Whatever you think you need."

She buzzed for an assistant. The young man entered. His fiery face and sun-bleached hair gave him a just-off-the-sailboard appearance.

"Curt, we're helping Mrs. Price today." Suzanne and the young man exchanged polite nods. "We'll need two sets of copies." Rising, Ms. Edango handed the paperwork to him.

Suzanne followed them into a sunny corner office. Views of the wide city streets lined with buildings stretched up to the south bench of the Wasatch peaks, Great Salt Lake, and the Oquirrh Mountains to the west. *What a studio this room would make, such light!* She and Ms. Edango sat opposite one another on batik-patterned love seats banked by thriving potted plants.

"How long have your husband's children been your exclusive responsibility?"

"Steve died in January."

"I'm sorry, Suzanne. Such a young man with a young family." Her empathy was apparent in her melodic voice and on her sensitive face. "You assured me on the phone you want to be awarded sole custody of Gregory and Mitzi. I assume your commitment is long-term, regardless of an eventual remarriage."

"Yes, absolutely!" Thoughts of remarriage were the least of Suzanne's worries, though Dee had tried to make her think otherwise yesterday. *Heavens, was it only yesterday? Life is on fast forward.* "I'm frightened of the fact that Utah is a biological-mother-oriented state. I don't even have a job to make things secure for our children."

"Did your husband want you to remain at home caring for the children full-time? Is that why you're unwilling to pursue some sort of joint-custody arrangement with the children's natural mother, to lessen the pressure on yourself?"

Suzanne fingered her handbag nervously. "Steve tried to make sure his highway-patrol pension would make it possible for me to stay at home at least until Mitzi's of school age. Now I'm seeking employment because we underestimated his medical expenses. Frankly, I'm just making it. We do have a $50,000 college fund of savings bonds set up for the children after Steve's parents died in a plane crash, the year Mitzi was born. Steve bought the bonds with his inheritance. I'll be paying your fee out of that money until I have a job, so don't be afraid I expect charity."

"What does the former Mrs. Price offer her children? Does she have a stable and healthy home with stimulating educational opportunities?"

"Well, . . ." Suzanne struggled. *Steve took the children away from Rehma when Mitzi was three months old. He left Rehma to 'do her drug thing with her drug friends,' and divorced her. If I say that it sounds like a crude put down.* "She . . ."

"Suzanne," Bette uncapped a pen above her notepad, "I need you to be specific about her visitations and child support payments if any since the papers confirm she has custody. Tell me about phone calls to the children, cards, gifts, and so forth to the best of your recollection, both during your marriage to their father and since you've been the only parent in the home. We can get specific through canceled checks and other means later. Just give me a picture of what the biological mother has been providing, so we know how to prepare our counter and . . . whether sole or joint custody is reasonable to go for from the court's likely point of view."

"Rehma never did *any* of those things." Suzanne felt bewildered. "That's why her sudden demand for me to turn the children over to her is so puzzling. She never even offered to help with the children when their father was dying, or to comfort them when he passed, even at his memorial service. Her wanting to take them now makes no sense."

Bette capped her pen and sat back. She smiled her stunning smile and spread her arms to embrace the air between them. "I believe *you* are the *real* mother by commitment. Let's start with parental neglect and abandonment and build your case by contrast from there."

On Suzanne's mental sketchpad, the beautiful brown diva sprouted wings.

Dierdre Ingram

~ Tuesday the 17th of June

Last night, she and her twin had agreed that in the morning Suzanne would call for an appointment, job hunt for a couple of hours, and ship her painting entries to postmark this afternoon. Dierdre admired her sister's commitment to her talent against odds, which would have beaten her own perseverance years ago. Susie explained she believed her gifts were God-given and giving up on them would be close to sacrilege.

Dierdre's energies turned to her idea of how to find out more about Rehma's motive for wanting the kids back. It occurred to her while she brushed her teeth before bed. It seemed so simple she wondered why it had taken so long to come to her.

Getting out of the house without saying where she was going had been easier than Dierdre expected. Suzanne had risen before dawn and gone to her basement studio space to paint for the contest until the attorney's office opened at nine. Meanwhile, Dierdre dressed quietly, called for a taxi and went out right after Suzanne's departure with the kids she was dropping off at her friend's home.

Now Dierde paid for the cab a block from Rehma's salon, chipped at the polish on her nails, and deliberately twisted a red, gel nail tip until it sprung free of her natural nail. Ripping it off at an angle, she dropped it to the pavement, adjusted her sunglasses, and hurried around the corner. The shabby Last Tangle sign hung precariously above the sidewalk from one of its two wrought-iron hooks.

Through the glass door, Dierdre observed that Rehma hung up the phone and made busy stocking hair-spray cans at the back of her tiny lavender shop. At the sound of the doorbells jingling on a tasseled rope, she turned. Rehma'd been pretty once, but too much drinking, drugs, and hard living had aged her beyond her years. The place was tacky. Everything needed a good scrubbing with some industrial-strength cleaning products. Stacks of old hair-fashion magazines spilled around the lone hair dryer, an ancient aqua model from the '50s. Dierdre wondered if it worked and was glad her plan didn't include having the little blonde bomber with a soap dish for a brain actually touch her hair. The thought of Andre sobbing over her ruined Sassoon bob made her smile. *He's going to love this little story!*

Rehma came toward her wearing a lavender smock over tight pink stretch pants and open-toed wedgy sandals—all spotted with various colors of hair dye. Dierdre felt a twinge of anxiety about getting a manicure. The smell of stale cigarettes and the sight of ash trays spelled some promised comfort for the nerves she needed to pull this off without being discovered for Suzanne's spying twin. She rummaged in her bag for her menthols so Rehma could lead off.

"You're new here. Need directions or want an appointment? You can see I'm way busy, but maybe I can work you in if you need a trim." Rehma tucked her gum to the side of her teeth while she talked, smiling too broadly for her neglected molars.

Dierdre thrust her hand across the space between them.

"Tore my nail getting out of the cab. Do you think you could repair it and match my polish? I'd want a *perfect* match." She knew Andre's Miami shop mixed polishes to give her a particular, signature shade. Matching it in a place like this would be impossible.

"Oh my hell, honey, I don't know if that red can be matched or not. Bright reds like that are the hardest, even for professionals like me."

She watched Rehma finger through a row of red polish bottles and hesitate at one or two. Shaking the brassy fluff out of her eyes, she deftly switched her gum to the other side of her teeth with the point of her tongue. She flounced onto her rollered stool and gestured for Dierdre to sit in the vinyl-covered chair opposite. Dierdre lowered herself gingerly, narrowly avoiding sharp-edged cigarette burns in the plastic upholstery which could snag her linen slacks.

"I'll have to polish all these over after I replace that tip, so they'll look the same color. What did you say your name was, honey?" Rehma sorted through her nail-tip case and finally selected one with a reasonable match for nail-bed width.

Dierdre lit up a menthol and turned her head to exhale. "Lilly," she took another drag, "My name is Lilly, and yours?"

"You can call me Rehma. Folks here all know me, so I don't bother with a name tag. I'm getting married soon, though. I'll have to wear one then, 'til my clients get used to Rodman."

"Congratulations, Rehma. That's really exciting, a bride-to-be doing my nails. I guess you took off your engagement ring to work with chemicals." Dierdre enjoyed sticking her with the humiliation of no diamond to brag about. She left her the neat excuse to soften the fertile ground of conversation between them.

"Aren't you way smart to think of that now! You're the first customer I've had that understood why I don't wear it without me havin' to say." She blew the tiniest bubble and cracked it at the side of her mouth. 'Course I can tell you're used to fine salons and all, the way you're dressed." Rehma's eyes checked out Dierdre's clothing and jewelry with a practiced glance. "Don't you ever take those sunglasses off, Lilly, honey?"

"Allergies. This high-desert air gives me red eyes. I wouldn't dare expose them to any more light than necessary. Are those adorable little children your niece and nephew? I mean you're so young this is probably your first marriage." Dierdre nodded to a poorly framed photo of Greg and Mitzi taken when Mitzi was six months old. No doubt her heart-of-gold twin had thoughtfully provided it. Dierdre had the very same photo in her Florida condo. She changed hands with her cigarette to free up five more nails to the cotton ball of polish remover, watching expensive red drizzle away into a cheap, lavender plastic cup. *Consider the sacrifice*, she told herself.

"Oh my, no. Those are my very own kids by my first husband. He died of cancer. Now they'll have a new daddy."

"Does your fiancé get along well with them?" She skipped any condolences for Steve, knowing if Rehma acted like she'd been with him through it all she'd end up reaching over and throttling her for such a barefaced lie.

Rehma looked uncomfortable, cracked her gum several times in succession, and scrubbed vigorously at Dierdre's nails with a little lavender brush oozing cold and questionable detergent bubbles.

"He will. They just haven't had much time with each other yet. As a matter of fact, we're going to all have a nice picnic when I get off work this week. Going camping. I usually work Friday and Saturday, but I canceled all my appointments to take this special trip. Sort of to help my fiancé get to know my kids better." She poured nail monomer into a chipped shot glass.

"You don't say. Where do your little darlings spend the day while you work?" Dierdre puffed eagerly waiting for the answer, imagining how this woman's mind worked. Prying for the right entrance, not knowing exactly what she was after, Dierdre was certain she would know more when she left than before she came.

"Well, Lilly, it is Lilly didn't you say? I . . . I leave them with friends when they're not at school. They're much older than that picture. I just keep it here 'cause it's my favorite."

They both became aware of a refrigerator closing somewhere behind the wall with the fading pink-flocked wallpaper. It peeled at the corners to reveal the room had once been a kitchen with yellowed hens and roosters prancing in alternate rows just below the pressed-tin ceiling. That explained the domestic looking sink and hot plate beneath the sagging shelves of discount-brand hair spray and shampoo.

"Is that your children coming home? Kids always head to the fridge first." Dierdre pressed, seeing for some reason Rehma appeared more nervous. "I'd love to see how they look now."

"Oh, no, I didn't hear anything."

Dierdre knew it was a lie because when the refrigerator door had closed somewhere behind the wall, Rehma had jumped, spilling the lavender cup. She sopped at the mess with paper towels, chewing savagely at her gum. While she poured the remaining fluid into the sink, Rehma's sleeve crept up her arm, and Dierdre spied an ugly bruise. Black and blue shapes formed the distinct imprint of someone's grip. Dierdre swallowed and stubbed out her cigarette. She surmised she might already have a lead for Doug, Suzanne, and the attorney about why Suzanne should remain the children's custodial parent. The thought of a mark like that on Susie, let alone Greg or Mitzi sent chills up her spine. She looked upon the woman with sympathy and fear. What was this bottle-blonde foo-foo allowing to happen in her life? A life that drew Suzanne into its ugliness like a creeping sickness. She pressed on.

"Rehma, I know I heard your children in the fridge, couldn't I please meet them?" Dierdre insisted. She wanted to up the tension, get Rehma to say more than she intended.

"Now Lilly, you're way curious over nothing. Probably the neighbors. They're always banging around. No respect for a woman trying to run a business." Obviously too warm in the long-sleeved smock, she blew her hair back from her face without using her wet hands, and sped up her nail activity.

"Is that a locket you're wearing on that lovely chain, Rehma?" Dierdre cooed in her most disarming voice, all innocent sweetness.

Without thinking, Rehma tilted her head to the side and leaned toward her so her collar could fall open for her customer's better view of the cheap necklace. The unicorn trinket lay against a collarbone bruised to match her arm. Dierdre took stock of Rehma's nail progress and decided to go for the jugular.

She cleared her throat and whispered in an intimate tone, "How long has your sweety been beating you, Rehma? I'd think twice about marrying a man like that."

The pink-handled nail file clattered to the floor. They both bent to retrieve it, eyes meeting at knee level below the table arm bridging the distance between them.

"Does he have any other kinky habits that aren't safe to have around your children? If he'll hurt *you*, aren't you afraid of what he'll do to your son and your daughter?"

Rehma snatched the file and sat back up, yanking tissues from a box at her elbow.

"You're way too nosy for bein' a stranger, Lilly whoever-you-are." She refused to look up. Her shaking fingers covered an orange stick with tissue and ran it under one after another of Dierdre's nails, too roughly for Dierdre's comfort.

She toughed it out, knowing she was onto something.

The shower curtain serving as a doorway drape at the back of the shop was thrust aside by a man Dierdre assumed to be Bo Rodman, the fiancé listed, minus the happy couple photo, in the newspaper. Rehma's fingers supporting the palm of Dierdre's hand trembled. Dierdre knew she'd struck home. Grateful for her dark glasses, she examined the man in detail, imagining relating it all to Doug and Suzanne by evening. He did appear to be the man Taylor mentioned having had a run-in with recently.

Tight jeans with a silver rodeo buckle seemed oddly too hot a clothing choice for the summer heat, though Bo wore no shirt. His body was tan and muscled, lean and well formed. Obviously he worked out. Here and there around his ribs, scars stood out white against the brown skin and dark hair of his chest. He smiled. The look was boyish, charming, male, and confident. Cleaned up he'd be a good romp, she was sure of that, but dangerous, into power beyond reason. Rehma's bruises attested to that. Why did he want a wife—a wife with two kids? What could he want? His entrance had cut off her chance to pry for a clue from Rehma.

She puzzled over his reasons as he came toward them. When he moved she saw he had a severe limp, perhaps even a prosthesis, where one of his legs should be. *Hard to tell. Voila, the long jeans in this sweltering place*, she thought. Bo stopped behind Rehma, the impressive bulge in the crotch of his jeans resting on her shoulder. Dierdre was frankly shocked. He slid one hand down over Rehma's smock, fingers coming to rest within reach of her nipple.

"Not now, Bo, I'm working."

Amazed at his forwardness in front of her, Dierdre felt like she'd stumbled onto a C-grade movie, that just turned X-rated. Bo's eyes were on Dierdre when he leaned down to kiss the hair at Rehma's temple. This show was for *her*, not his fiancée. He kept his eyes on Dierdre and laughed. The invitation was clear.

"Miss me, Baby?" Bo turned his face into Rehma's throat. She squirmed away.

"Miss Lilly here broke her nail getting out of a cab. You go on in back for your lunch and let me finish." Rehma appeared embarrassed, uncomfortable. Afraid of him and knew 'Lilly' knew it.

Dierdre had learned what she came for, but she needed just a little more. It would only take a reaction from one or the other of them. She worded it with care.

"I'm so glad your shop was right in the center of town, now I won't look such a fright when I track down a lawyer I'm looking for—Frank Simmons. Do either of you know if his office is near here?"

Bo straightened up. The smile left his face. Rehma looked up at him and back at Dierdre. She lifted the manicured hands and turned on a little hand-held dryer, playing it nervously over the nails she'd just painted an uncultured red from a cheap bottle with dribbles drying on its sides.

"Never heard of him," said Bo. "What would a fancy

chick like you want with a lawyer anyway? You look like you could get your way easy enough without ever threatenin' to go to court about anything." His new smile looked forced, his voice sounded tight.

The perceptible sudden chill in the atmosphere left Dierdre feeling victorious at making them both supremely uncomfortable. She kept her niece and nephew in mind and devised a new twist to the conversation to ante up the tension and provoke fresh revelations, without, she hoped, bringing on more blows for Rehma after she left.

"Oh, I have to serve Simmons papers to appear in court in California on some fraudulent dealings. He's not going to be a bit happy about getting a court order to return by the 23rd of the month, whether he likes it or not. Mr. Simmons may not return here for many years."

The blonde looked terrified. Bo looked pissed. She'd ruffled them all right. Best to get back and have Suzanne warn Doug that anything could happen now.

Dierdre watched their faces while she nudged some bills toward Rehma with her wrist, so as not to smudge her hideous nails. "I see by your poster that nail repairs and manicures are $25. Thank you for working me in between your other appointments on an emergency basis, Rehma. I wish you luck on your coming marriage." She skipped a tip.

Bo stuffed the twenty into his jeans pocket. Rehma, her splotched face terror-stricken, hadn't moved a finger toward the five. The little doorbells tinkled pleasantly against the glass as Dierdre made her escape.

THE WIND REMEMBERS

Suzanne Price

~ Tuesday the 17th of June

Suzanne entered the house by the kitchen door, thinking Dee ought to be awake and nursing a mug of coffee by now, but she wasn't. She called out, "Dee, time to rise and shine. I've great news from the attorney's office."

She dropped her purse and keys on the kitchen table and walked to her bedroom expecting to see her sister dousing herself in perfume or applying a theatrical amount of expensive make-up. The room was empty, the bed made. Odd. Dierdre was the let-me-sleep-in type.

Where could she have gone without a car? It's not like her to hike off through the neighborhood for exercise. She'd rather show off her body at a gym where she can draw an admiring crowd, perhaps snag a dinner date. Last evening she mentioned old school friends she might look up in town today. Perhaps she called someone to chauffeur her around.

Suzanne returned to the kitchen, poured an orange juice, and checked the job offers in the morning paper, wanting a back-up plan if the afternoon's interview didn't pan out.

The phone rang. Expecting Dierdre, she didn't wait to find out who was on the line. "Hi, where are you, Dee?"

"Have the kids ready at five on Thursday." Rehma's blithery voice caught her off guard. "There's a customer at my door. I'll be by after I close the shop to get them for the weekend. Pack their favorite stuff. I'm not used to entertaining kids."

"Rehma, I'm not . . ." The phone clicked and went to a dial tone.

"Well, there is *no way* Greg and Mitzi are going *anywhere* Thursday or any other night with you Miss Barbie Doll Brain. No way! Now I have an attorney, too. You'll have to go to

207

court to take Greg and Mitzi away from me, over my dead body!"

She pressed Pastor Spahn's number and listened through his answering machine directions before leaving her message: "If you're calling for your messages, please return mine—I need your advice and your prayers—this is Suzanne Price with an emergency."

This time she didn't feel guilty for disturbing his vacation. Dierdre had convinced her that helping people was her pastor's life work, not just a nine-to-five job. She glanced up at the clock. Eleven-forty. Less than two hours before the interview at the hospital. With the kids at Diane's for the day, she could package the competition pieces and mail the box downtown before her appointment.

"Thank you, God, for answers to my prayers!" Her heart bubbled with joy. She'd prayed for direction and felt the warm glow of certainty she was on the right track. It might mean blow-drying the paintings before packing, but she could hit the deadline if she made this time count. Walking in faith she called it and fairly danced down the stairs with the combined relief of the attorney's support, Dierdre's encouragement, and the sustaining comfort of prayer and her faith.

She'd been preparing mats and competition entry forms for her paintings for an hour when she heard tires crunching gravel in the driveway. She bounded up the stairs thinking it must be Dierdre coming with one of her friends.

It was Doug. She tried not to appear disappointed and irritated at the interruption. Over his shoulder she saw Taylor hopping down from an old pick-up that had just pulled in at the side of the garage. His new white truck must still be getting its logos cleaned of graffiti or repainted. Doug gave a knocking gesture before her face at the screen door.

"Yoo hoo, anybody home, Pretty Lady?"

"Sorry, Doug, my mind is a million miles away. I'm afraid Greg isn't here now. Did you need something?"

"Yeah, I thought I'd let you know we have our graffiti

expert in custody. Punk we've dealt with before by the name of Big Blue. A big kid, way too big for his britches. Fancies himself a gang leader. Captured him at his little hideout. He's not talking yet. Shouldn't be long before we find out why he's harassing you. With his sorry ass in jail, you won't have to worry about rats in your washer or letters on your garage."

"I hope you're right, Doug, but I'm not so sure a kid or even a gang of them have done all these frightening things. Perhaps Taylor's idea about the scare tactics of the bench developers has something to do with it." She could see by his disappointed expression that Doug wanted her to think he was the hero with everything under control.

"You may have seen more cruisers than usual around here. The men and I have pulled some extra duty to keep your place covered like I promised. Don't worry, we'll get the rest of Big Blue's gang. With him in jail they'll spill the rest of the beans."

"Thanks, I appreciate all of you men looking out for us." She wanted him to leave so she could secure each painting in its mat board and package the stack. It was hard to be polite.

"I'll swing by every shift to check on you, and after work." He pulled at his mustache, smiling at her. "I sure am looking forward to that dance on Wednesday. Figured it would be easier for you to handle a foursome on our first date."

Her mind wiggled away from the obvious intent in his eyes. "It's not really a date is it, Doug? I'm not sure I'd have said yes if it weren't a fundraiser for Greg's team." She didn't unlatch the screen door. His hand dropped away from the knob. His cheerful expression sagged.

"You can't hold me off forever, Suzanne. I've paid my dues of being patient with you. I'm part of your life around here and you know it. Let's get on with our life together. You know I want you for my own. I want to pick up right where my best friend left off. I think you know that's what Steve would have wanted, too."

"Doug, what you want or what Steve wanted and what I

want may not be the same thing. You're a good friend. We couldn't have made it as smoothly without you after Steve died."

She played at a strand of her hair, shifting her weight to the other foot.

"You thinking maybe you'd rather have a go at Mr. Tree Trimmer over there? Is that where it's at?" He looked over at Taylor stacking brush, then back at her. "Did you two have a little fling in the past?"

Suzanne bristled. Said nothing, looked directly into his eyes, unwavering.

His face softened. "We'll talk about it after the dance. I'll show you a good time. You might be surprised how much fun we can have together when we're off without the kids." He smiled his most engaging smile. She'd seen him turn it on for Dierdre and knew it was contrived to get what he wanted. However kind he had been in the past, she had the idea it had perhaps been for his own purposes rather than out of any debt he owed Steve. Dierdre had made her look at that possibility while assuring her if Doug was the man she wanted, she should just get on with it. If he wasn't she should be more direct in disengaging him, *and soon.*

"Okay, Doug. We'll talk after the dance. Thanks for checking on me. I'm fine." She stepped back from the door.

He gave her a brief salute, retreated down the steps facing her, and walked over to Taylor rolling tree rounds away from the spray-painted garage.

Suzanne sighed with relief and went back downstairs to check her last painting. It had dried taut, the paper tight as a drum. She cut through the paper tape with a craft knife. The painting snapped free. She posted it on the wall with pushpins. Stepping back, she compared it to the rest of the series. All six were at last complete with her signature. Her best work was a good sampling of tree species from across America, painted many times until she'd captured just the distinctive characteristics, seasons, and surrounding landscape typical of its native region. She checked her watch. Just time to bathe and dress for her interview before packing the entries. Hospital human resources staff probably expected their employees to be fastidious about their hygiene and appearance. She ran up the basement steps, showered, and was just zipping up the blue linen skirt to her only suit when she heard the front doorbell.

She ran to answer it. Taylor stood at the door looking amused and awkward at the same time. She motioned him in while she did up the sleeve buttons on her blouse.

"My, don't you look professional," he said, stepping inside.

"Oh, Taylor, do I really? I'm rushing to a job interview. I need a regular paycheck. Do you think I look competent enough to work in a hospital office?"

"You'd impress me as a congresswoman running for reelection. Competent, absolutely." His warm voice was encouraging. She basked in it.

"Is there something you need?" she asked.

"You didn't hear me at the back door. Kind of embarrassing to ask, but I'd like a glass of water and the use of your bathroom."

"Of course. I should have offered earlier. How thoughtless of me." She felt foolish for putting him in uncomfortable straights when he was going the extra mile to help her out.

"Help yourself to coffee, the fridge and the bathroom. I've got to run downstairs and pack my contest entries, so I can mail them on my way to the interview. I'm going to hit the deadline after all. Oh, and the attorney this morning was encouraging about my keeping the children legally." She smiled up at him.

"Glad to hear it. Thanks, Susie." He undid the strings on his boots and left them at the door, then padded to the hallway behind her.

"Make yourself at home," she called, on her way through the kitchen to the basement stairs. "Just set the back door lock and pull it shut when you leave," she added.

211

The Wind Remembers

Moments later, she heard the steps squeak under his weight and looked up from securing the paintings into their mats with hinges of transparent tape. He descended the basement stairs in his stocking feet.

"May I see your paintings before they go?" He came to stand next to her at the old slant-topped drawing table he recognized as the one she'd had since high school. The six watercolors spread out before them, each an outdoor day caught in just the right light and mood to express the tree that best suited the climate she'd chosen. The most recent one the cottonwood now destroyed.

"You've gotten quite good, haven't you." He stated the question like a fact. She felt pleased. He'd always been picky. She respected his opinion.

"I haven't seen your work in years, but I think I would have known it anywhere. This one's my favorite." He pointed to the Douglas fir rising in splendor before a background forest of its kind, on a cliff above a tumbling river. Sunlight glinted believably on its upper branches and the surfaces of wet boulders in the water.

"I could have guessed," she said. "It must remind you of that summer in Yellowstone fighting forest fires." She brushed his arm in picking up the painting. Her hand felt electric with tingles. She caught her breath. His fingers closed over hers ever so lightly, almost in a question. Their eyes met. Her heart beat so fast she gasped for breath and let go of the painting. It lay forgotten on her drawing table.

He turned her body to him with his hands on her shoulders. His eyes searched hers, his breath soft and slow. The scent of him was intoxicating. Memories of such moments flooded her mind. He cupped her chin with his thumbs and fingers. She wanted him to kiss her so much that her jaws ached and her mouth watered. He brought his face to hers and almost touched his lips to her mouth. He stopped, pulled back, and looked more deeply into her eyes. "May I?" he whispered.

Suzanne lifted her face to his, closed her eyes, and met

his lips. She waited. Taylor kissed her softly and pulled away again. She opened her eyes. His smile was all invitation and relief. He drew her close against him once more. She felt their hearts beating and her body's desire responding to his. If flesh could melt she felt herself ooze into his space, felt their bodies merge through their clothing. Her heart beat against him. She felt his answering response.

"Suzanne, Suzanne," he mouthed into her hair. She felt their urgent need for each other. Their kisses were open-mouthed greed, their tongues mingling, their breath loud in her ears. He backed her against the washer, lifted her hips, and set her down just above him. He pressed his face into her throat, moved his lips softly down into the opening of her blouse. His fingers kneaded her back, her hips, her thighs. She kissed his hair, laced her fingers into handfuls of it, and drank in the feel, the remembered and new smell of him. Taylor's face returned to hers. They kissed long satisfying kisses that seemed to last forever and not long enough at the same time. Her passion surprised her, absorbed her. His desire for her filled a place in her being that had long been his alone.

She felt the past anguish over Taylor melt away, leaving her with no more questions about whether or not she still loved him. She did, always had, *always* would. But she wanted more than stolen moments like this. She wanted their love to be the way she had wanted it long ago. She'd matured enough to know she would have him no other way. Holding each other, touching, speaking in touches, feeling his pleasure in her, she risked believing he might be able to give her the commitment she'd always wanted. She wished urgently for the specific words "I love you" to issue forth between their kissing tongues.

Long passionate moments surged between them. His words were breath upon her skin, her hair, but none of them the words of love she had longed for years ago and in the end given up believing she would ever hear. She kissed him once more and pulled back, sliding off the washer with his hands at her waist. He stood her before him at arm's length, but did not release her.

213

"Mmnh, Taylor," she mumbled, struggling to straighten her hair, her clothes. "I must not miss my interview." Checking her watch she was startled by how much time had elapsed.

"Oh, no! I haven't time to pack these and mail them before my appointment. They won't go out post marked with today's date! They *have* to or my work will be disqualified."

She was soberly aware that time had not stood still while she let go of her pride over the past and tasted passion between the two of them. Now she faltered. It had been wonderful, but had it been worth not having a chance to have her work considered and perhaps selected for the prize money her family so badly needed? Had it been worth having to choose between keeping the job-interview appointment and calling to postpone it until her paintings were on their way postmarked today?

No! These moments could have waited. Devastated and feeling foolish, she knew she'd literally kissed away her opportunity to win the contest. Torn between desire and wisdom, it was a place she'd been before over the same man. The knowledge overwhelmed her.

He studied the eyes she turned up to him and read their expression of frustrated bewilderment. "I'm sorry, Susie, it's my fault. Tell you what, give me the address and the paintings, drop me at the Fed Ex office, and I'll ship them off while you're getting hired for that new job."

"I couldn't expect you to do that for me, Taylor. Besides, I can't afford Fed Ex. The good old U.S. Post Office is expensive as it is. All I need is today's postmark."

"My treat, I insist. You run upstairs and put yourself back together. I'll cover from here. I'm an old hand at sending important government forestry documents against perilous deadlines. You can count on me."

She broke away then and hurried up the stairs. "Thank you! Oh, Taylor you're an angel. I . . . got carried away." She stood awkwardly at the top landing looking down at him. They were both disheveled and smiling at one another.

The Wind Remembers

"I helped." His grin spread across his tan face. He waved her on and placed clean sheets of newsprint paper between the matted paintings. He reached for the masking tape.

She whirled to leave and ran smack into Dierdre just coming out of the kitchen with hands full of paper towels and a bag of cotton balls.

"What happened to you, Honey? Run into a freight train?" Her twin asked.

"I might return the compliment," Suzanne said, sparkling, and she knew it. "Got to run, I have a job interview you found the ad for in last night's paper. We'll compare notes later. I've wondered where you've been all morning. Hope you had fun."

"You'll want to hear *all* about it." Dierdre busied herself at the sink removing some hideous red nail polish with a reeking drippy cotton ball. The tap water ran like blood to the drain.

Taylor came into the kitchen and laid the stack of hastily wrapped paintings and the previously filled-out entry forms on the table. He interrupted her at the faucet to fill a glass with water and drank it all down in one long guzzle. Dierdre looked from one to the other of them. Suzanne smoothed her hair and straightened her blouse.

"Well now, I know a pair of freight trains have collided when I'm standing right on the platform!" Dierdre smiled and whacked her sister on the rump. "You little vixen. Wouldn't Doug just die?"

Taylor wiped his hand slowly across his mouth. "Yes, and you my dear date for the fundraiser, better let me have a few dances with your sister." He gathered up everything he needed to mail for Suzanne.

"You'll both have to return to hear my good news and my bad news," Dierdre called out the door after them.

"Me first," Suzanne hollered back. "That attorney you suggested was more than encouraging. We'll pick up the kids on our way home and compare notes. I have good news and bad news too. I'm going to need everybody's help come 5 o'clock on Thursday."

"Well, it's about time you were able to ask for help! Just remember, Sis, we'll be busy packing then for the Sun Tunnels."

Suzanne caught Dierdre's words while rolling up her Blazer window for the air conditioning. She backed away. Yes, she was learning to reach out to others for the help she needed. For too long she'd been locked into surviving on her own with only Doug and Pastor Spahn for support. Her twin had noted that for a Christian she certainly turned her back on all the helpers Jesus had been sending her way. Though she doubted Dierdre was a believer herself, she recognized true wisdom when she heard it, and turned the accusation over in her mind for a long time before dropping off to sleep last night.

Looking over at Taylor, she was filled with gratitude, wonder, delight. Could they recapture what they'd once flirted with, a romance ending in marriage, one of those old-fashioned family marriages with two parents and two kids, a home, and happiness? She almost dared to hope—and stopped herself. The words 'I love you,' had still not been spoken. Without them, she would *never* commit herself to anyone.

By the time she pulled onto the main road she was all business. A stolen glance at Taylor revealed his smiling face staring straight ahead at the traffic; his big strong hands cradled her paintings like newborns. She swallowed, reminded herself to keep walking in faith, and signaled for the turn at the hospital.

**

The hospital lobby received its afternoon flood of visitors in chattering lines at the information desk and in groups by the elevators. Suzanne moved in their stream, finding Ms. Halsten's office easily. She adjusted her blouse collar the zillionth time and entered the narrow vestibule.

A pink-uniformed lady with snowy hair looked up and smiled. Her glasses sparkled with tiny rhinestones on their edges, reminding Suzanne of the fairy godmother in Disney's

Cinderella. She imagined a good wish for the success of her interview and stepped forward.

"May I help you, dear?" The woman even sounded like the chubby fairy with the magic wand.

"Yes, I have an appointment at two with Ms. Halsten. I'm a few minutes early. I'll just wait right here."

"Would you be Mrs. Price?"

Suzanne nodded.

"She's expecting you. I dare say if you're as sweet with our terminal patients as you appear, you'll be just what she's looking for, not that it's my place to say."

The Pink Lady pressed a key on the intercom. Suzanne almost expected sparkles to form in the air and regretted leaving her travel sketchbook in the truck. Norman Rockwell and Walt Disney would have propositioned this enchanting woman for a portrait and rushed her immediately to a studio to pose. She wished she could do the same, but suppressed a smile when she imagined showing the woman to her laundry room. Nervous beyond belief, her mind played childish tricks. She told herself to shape up. She had a serious need of a regular paycheck. Pronto.

"Your two o'clock is here Ms. Halsten." The lady's stubby fingers fiddled with a pink-spangled earring matching her volunteer uniform. "Yes, I'll show her right in." She motioned toward the half-door separating the waiting area from her tiny office. "Ms. Halsten says no need for you to wait. She'll see you now."

Suzanne swallowed hard, and prayed silently. *Here we go God, I'm in your hands. You know what I need better than I do.*

A stylish woman of ambiguous age, auburn hair swinging in a sassy cut, rose from a leather armchair to greet her. Her black-trimmed, taupe jacket hung to a calf-length hemline the way only pure silk drapes. Matching shoes and an ivory blouse completed a sophisticated outfit Suzanne found enviably cosmopolitan. With supreme effort, she avoided the pitfall to her confidence of allowing herself to feel frumpy by comparison.

"Mrs. Price, so happy to meet you. I'm Penny Halsten. How thoughtful of you to be a little ahead of time. That's hard to come by with applicants in Utah. Life seems more casual in the West." She offered her hand. The shake was comfortable. They took chairs before the impressive desk that seemed coordinated to Ms. Halsten's burnt-sienna hair.

"You're not from Farr, then?" Suzanne ventured.

"I'm a fairly recent transplant from the Midwest. I love your mountains here; how could I not?" She gestured toward the rocky expanse of bench cliffs that filled the window. The pleasantries put Suzanne at ease. A handsome man in a silver frame smiled at them from a bookshelf.

"Let's get right to the topic at hand, shall we?" Ms. Halsten tucked the long side of her hair behind her gold-studded ear. She flipped open a file and withdrew what Suzanne recognized for the lengthy application form she'd filled out in the morning and left at the main desk on her way to her attorney.

"I see you have personal experience with cancer patients and their treatment." Her voice was kind. "My condolences on your husband's death. I'm glad to see you're ready to return to working away from home. Your thoughtful answers to this standard, boring form impressed me. Frankly, I rescheduled two appointments to meet with you today because I believe you have the wisdom and compassion to work effectively with the dying and their grieving families. Your payment desires are well within our range for this position, and your appearance is professional. You are precisely what I'm looking
for in an hospice liaison." She closed the file and pinned Suzanne with a penetrating look. "Now that I meet you, something about you worries me, however."

Suzanne's soaring confidence plummeted. "I know I don't have professional medical experience Ms. Halsten, but I'm eager to learn." She felt the void of formal medical training like a physical weight on her heart. She needed a job so badly; her children, her life seemed to weigh in the balance of what this woman thought of her. An art degree certainly hadn't helped her get a job yet. Whether she could be trusted with other people's life-and-death moments, and get paid for it, was suddenly of as much critical importance to her as she supposed it probably was to this hospice director.

"Your lack of medical training is not at the heart of my concern. We have needs for a broad variety of talents, personal experience, and formal preparation. May I call you Suzanne? I'd be more comfortable if you called me Penny. Good, now then . . ." She hesitated.

Suzanne's comfort had already gone out the window. She felt ready to follow it.

"I wonder if it's healthy for you to work with the terminally ill," Penny said. "You've just come through a tragic time. I imagine you need to laugh and smile and experience joy in abandon for a change."

That may be a luxury I can't afford, Suzanne thought.

"Rewarding as it is to ease the discomfort of suffering terminal patients and their loved ones," Penny continued, "you know it can be a gut-wrenching experience. Are you really ready to do that all over again? Is this the kind of work you *must* do to feel fulfilled?" Her hair swung to the sides of her cheeks. She leaned into the space between them, her eyes, her voice, her body an intense question pressing for an honest answer. She would miss nothing. Suzanne thought for a long moment before even attempting to respond.

Where are you now, God? How can I be totally honest and convince her I'm the one she should pick for this job? If I lie and get the job, will it be the right thing to do because of the children? These choices are too hard! Why is my life so difficult?. I need a job; I want this one. I learned a lot while helping Steve. I know I can be good for others. It's not fair to make this need for a livelihood a question of what I want for fulfillment. I want to paint! If this hospital job isn't what You want me to do, why lead me to this opportunity?

She felt angry, angry with herself, angry with God. Like the last time she'd been in this hospital. Disney didn't film stories like hers. Some good guy always came flying to the rescue. God was the only good guy she'd ever really counted on, only now Suzanne didn't feel like He, or Jesus, or Holy Spirit were even listening.

Taylor Armstrong

~ Tuesday the 17th of June

Taylor shifted Suzanne's Chevy Blazer from park into drive, watching her enter the hospital as he pulled away. She looked eager to make a good interview impression. He'd wished her luck as he'd slid behind the wheel after she got out and he'd fought the urge to kiss her smiling mouth one more time. His senses still throbbed at every level from the mutual passion of their uninhibited kisses.

Maneuvering through the traffic on automatic pilot, his mind did an instant replay of her response to his desire for her. She wasn't the hesitant girl he'd last held years ago. This time Suzanne was a woman eager for more than a job interview. The intoxicating nearness of her body perfumed his shirt and his skin. He no longer questioned whether he wanted to be involved with her. He accepted that he did, but was irresolute about just how involved he wanted to be in her complicated life. He feared making a fool of himself or reopening old heartaches more than he feared the unexplained danger targeting her family. He knew that friend or more he would help her because in good conscience he could not do otherwise.

Suzanne would want more from him now that she had greater needs for a man, a husband, a father. She wasn't the kind of woman who'd carry on an extended affair in front of her kids. Steve's children. She'd want marriage and perhaps even children of her own. Unless she couldn't have them. He wondered about her, about himself. He wasn't ready for more commitments and responsibilities. Taking over his father's business and trying to make a go of it was about all he wanted to handle. Now even his new truck was getting a refreshing paint job on its logo today. His entanglement in the police investigation to arrest Big Blue for making it necessary was eating up time, too. Why he thought he could add the time and money burden of courting a woman and still make a profit he wasn't sure. He only knew he wanted to see Suzanne more often, hold her, touch her, be touched.

Taylor admitted to himself that he even wanted to be loved by a woman with Suzanne's depth of good feeling and intelligence, her kind of loyalty and passion. He didn't know if he was up to giving back what she would need from him, but he wanted to try if she'd let him into her life again and help him understand what she needed from a man. He knew he might have to risk finding out what had made her dump him years ago.

The feeling of no longer being on the fence about her filled him with a renewed energy for life that he welcomed. He was suddenly aware he'd been searching for a long time, for something more meaningful than making money and being successful. He did want a home and a loving woman to fill it with him. What a surprise. He marveled over it, toying with the wonder of a part of himself he hadn't understood until now. The realization made him feel wise and yet very green.

He drove into the parking lot of the Fed Ex building, a nearly new warehouse facility on the south end of Farr, eased the old Blazer over the speed bumps, and cruised around for a space to park. Eventually finding one at the end of the lot, he gathered Suzanne's painting entries and multiple forms and walked toward the customer entrance. In the storm's wake, broken tree limbs took up several parking places on either side of the trash bins and the warehouse door where trucks were being loaded. Taylor passed two uniformed-delivery drivers on their smoke break and nodded as he went inside.

He laid the stack of Suzanne's art on the counter at the customer's island and pulled out a Fed Ex shipping form from one of the cubbyholes. He debated over using Suzanne's return address or his own. He settled on hers and a cash deal instead of using his own Fed Ex account number. He didn't want to make her upset. She was so proud; he could never tell when she'd feel her independence or competence was being compromised. Since he had no idea why she'd broken off with him in the first place, he didn't care to risk getting dumped again just when she'd expressed some genuine interest in him. He wondered if she'd ever clung to Doug with that kind of enthusiasm. He doubted it. He smiled to himself and felt kind of sorry for the guy, but only for a moment. Doug had a too-sure-of- his-hold-over-Suzanne attitude and treated her with a lack of genuine caring that bothered Taylor. He'd never seen her flirt with him or offer him any encouragement either.

A woman pushing a toddler in a bedraggled stroller banged her way through the automatic plate-glass door and came to share his counter space. The child let go of a sucker and grabbed Taylor's leg with sticky fingers. The woman noticed and looked away, attending to the sheaf of papers in her hands. She forced the thick stack into a letter-size package, wrinkling most of the pages in the process, not appearing to care that they would arrive at their destination in a mess.

Taylor stepped out of reach of the kid's fingers and tilted Suzanne's bubble-wrapped stack into the largest shipping box, added crushed paper, and sealed the end. He affixed the clear-plastic pocket and slipped in the completed form. The toddler's sticky hands explored his leg. The smell of cherry candy filled his nostrils. Could he go through this with kids of someone else's or his own? He struggled with the thought, retreating from the idea of having kids that did disgusting things like this.

"Excuse me, Ma'am? Could you turn your stroller away from me? My pants . . . your child has been eating a sucker." The sucker clung from the toddler's sock.

The woman looked up at him, all innocence. "You must not have little ones of your own to tend." She smiled a crooked smile, crooked only because of the way her unflattering lipstick was applied. It looked like her kid had drawn it on—in a hurry. She lowered her eyes and went on filling out a form, seemingly absorbed in the mystery of her own handwriting. Taylor disengaged himself and looked down at his jeans, now smeared with sticky, red sugar juice. He picked up his package and stood in line at the counter, grateful only one person was ahead of him. He didn't want to make Suzanne wait for him or to have the stroller get within sticky-finger distance again.

Why was it some mothers kept their children clean and shepherded them through the social graces in public, including clean hands, fingernails and faces, while others neglected themselves and their kids? He looked over at the woman's oily tangle of hair straggling in her eyes and thought of Suzanne and her tidy farmhouse, old but clean and orderly like herself. Simple white cotton curtains at her kitchen windows hung from the rods on bright yellow rings that matched the yellow place mats on the table and the blue and yellow mugs that had held his coffee. Well-scrubbed kids and a sparkling kitchen floor made everything cheerful and under control. But he had been mistaken long ago when he had thought everything was under control—his control—when Suzanne said things were over between them. So hell, what did he know? Maybe this rag-tag female with the grubby kid was lightening in bed and a sweetheart to get along with, maybe even a great cook.

The man ahead of him finished and left. Taylor stepped up to the counter and slipped the form out of the pocket on the box. The big man behind the counter appeared friendly and he didn't have a sucker. *Two strokes in his favor.*

"Standard overnight?" he asked.

"Priority, express, insured six-hundred value," Taylor corrected.

"Oh, a really *big* spender!" The clerk chuckled.

"It only costs a few more bucks to get it there insured the fastest way." Taylor peeled off the bills for the extra charge. Much as he usually didn't like parting with his money, particularly on someone else's account, right now it felt damn good.

"Take good care of that baby; she's full of valuables." He handed the box over. The man's big hands closed over both ends, and he held it up to his ear.

"What you sending, the family fortune?" His clean-shaven black skull glistened under the ceiling light, his even white teeth smiled below a neatly trimmed mustache, short on one side where the scar creasing his cheek ended in a sort of exclamation mark.

"Close," said Taylor. "These are the family dreams. Paintings for a contest entry. Put your best whammy on them."

"You bet." The big man knuckled his fingers across the top of the box, put it into a canvas bin on wheels behind him, and gave it an extra pat.

"Are you the manager here?" Taylor asked, counting change back into his wallet. He shifted gears with the conversation to take care of his own needs while he was at it.

"Today I am. The boss is putting siding back up on his house. Going to take him most of the day I expect."

"Storm damage?" Taylor pocketed his wallet.

"No doubt about it," the clerk said. "My wife and I are glad we live in a rental place; all the problems belong to the landlord."

"My business is tree trimming and landscape maintenance. Been doing a lot of storm clean up this week. How about I give you a bid on that mess of limbs in your parking lot? I counted five parking spaces you can't use, and it looks like a hassle for your drivers to skirt the mess by the loading dock." He fished for a business card in the top pocket of his jacket and scribbled $650 on it, then passed it toward the big, black hand shoving the cash drawer shut.

"I don't know what he'll say about it, but I'll see that he gets it. He'll be plenty sick of storm work when he comes back. Who knows, could work in your favor."

"Thanks, I'd appreciate your company's business. Tell your boss for another $100 I'd trim up that double row of boxwoods growing into each lane along the driveway, too." He smiled and left quickly before the child with the sucker, now behind him in line, could add any more sticky prints to decorate his jeans. Little brat had smeared him up but good. He shot the woman and her urchin a crusty and cut out the door to Suzanne's truck.

Ten minutes later, in the men's room of the hospital lobby, he was scrubbing sucker slime off his jeans with wet paper towels. He washed his hands under water as hot as he could stand it, scanning an announcement taped to the wall while he dried them. Printed on bright green paper, the prominent sentence in large type caught his attention.

> **ARTISTS WANTED**: SUBMIT DRAWINGS FOR 3 LOBBY MURALS FOR THE NEW PEDIATRIC WARD ON THE WEST WING. **Only serious and experienced designers need apply. Portfolio/references required. Application materials at the front desk.**

Taylor returned to the lobby, selected a chair near the window, and slid down until the high back cupped the base of his skull. He closed his eyes and imagined Suzanne painting on a ladder here in this hospital, bringing to life a group of healthy children playing outside. Maybe even a few kids on crutches and in wheelchairs, but happy. He wondered if she would hear about the mural painting job or if he should tell her. Somehow he thought better of leading her too directly. She liked making her own decisions. He was sure it would have to be her idea. Perhaps he could think of a way to let her discover the opportunity for herself, apart from entering the men's room. The sign had to be posted elsewhere in the hospital and maybe in the newspaper want ads.

He reviewed the day, allowing the drone of conversations around him to lull him into a reverie of returning to Suzanne's tiny studio space in her basement. She floated to his senses as he'd observed her from the top of the stairs. Her hair pulled back with a clip at the nape of her long, slim neck, bent forward in intense concentration over her drawing board. She hadn't heard him until he stepped down from the top landing. She'd seemed sweet and childlike, so honest and good. *Maybe too good for me.*

He'd often wondered if she'd broken off with him because he'd told her he'd always be working with his hands, with trees, with the land. Though the trees and the land were dear to her heart, she didn't like cutting trees down, not for a minute. He couldn't picture himself, college degree or not, cooped up in a white-collar office somewhere away from the air and the light and the smells and sounds of nature. She'd called him an old romantic and smiled up at him with that look he loved—had loved. Maybe being an artist she'd had a fancier picture of her future and her man than he measured up to. Still, he thought, *She married a cop and lives in the oldest farmhouse up on the bench. Her place isn't fancy. Neither is she. Susie's an enigma all right.*

He mulled for a while. What if church-going was the reason? He'd noticed the same tiny gold cross at her throat she'd worn as long as he'd known her. Though she didn't lay religion on people, his father called it, "Keeping her own quiet counsel. She's a refined Christian woman," he'd said. Yeah, that could be it. It'd been a long time since he'd gone to a church for anything other than his aunt's funeral. Suzanne would never tell him if he weren't good enough for her in a church-going way. That must be it. She knew well enough that he could swear and carry on when they were young, but after the way he'd blown up when his truck was sprayed with graffiti, by now she knew he'd perfected cursing to a fine crude art. She knew he liked to party and dance too. If it'd been about church a long time ago, why hadn't she just come out and asked him to go to services with her? A hard woman to understand, but then, what woman wasn't?

What if she'd asked him? Would he have taken up church-going? There was no way he wanted to become a sheep in a baaing flock of do-gooders, who couldn't think for themselves or make a decision without calling on the bishop or the reverend. He was sure he couldn't swallow that approach to church. Still, Suzanne didn't seem to be the kind that if the pastor said, 'Jump off this cliff to prove your faith!' that she'd push to be first in line. She could think for herself all right. Trouble was, she might not tell him what was going on behind those big brown eyes. That'd always been the trouble, he hadn't figured out how to gage what she was thinking.

He felt a tap on his shoulder and opened his eyes to look up into the very lovely brown eyes he'd been thinking about. They looked troubled.

"As long as you've been gone, I figured you'd already started your new job." By the look on her face he could tell he'd said the dumbest thing possible. It was too late to take it back.

"It's twenty of four; let's hurry home before the next crisis arises," she said, turning toward the entrance. He shook himself alert and caught up, just in time to open the door for her. She was in her own world, wherever that was. He felt like an outsider again as he followed her to the truck. She didn't even ask about her package or thank him for his trouble. Her ingratitude ticked him off. What a sap! He'd have to watch himself in the future. He'd regretted more than once that he didn't take good enough care of himself around beautiful women, especially this one.

Bo Rodman and Rehma Price

~ Tuesday the 17th of June

"So we knowed he ain't no straight shooter from California when we hired him to write the letter. Don't get on my case about Frank bein' made to go back and face the music for something he done in his past. It ain't the end of the world. It don't change *our* plans." Bo pulled open the pop-top of his beer can and straddled a chair.

"*Your* plans," Rehma reminded him.

He leaned toward her, his arms resting on the top rail of the chair back, gesturing with the can to make his point. She was always too dumb to catch it on the first round. His patience was wearing thin. He was plenty pissed about it sounding like Frank Simmons wouldn't be around to help with the Price kids' money or the gyrfalcon anymore, but he wasn't about to let on to Rehma. Time was running out.

She sat sniveling into a tissue, her mascara running black streaks down her sweaty cheeks. What a turn-off. He often wondered what in hell he'd seen in her in the first place. Tits and ass over a few too many Coronas, he guessed. Not the first time he'd disappointed himself about a broad.

"Don't you see, Bo, it's better if we don't try to get the kids. Where would we bring them up in this crummy dump? In this neighborhood? This is no place for them brought up the way they been, what with school, and church, and all. I love them enough to see we can't give 'em what they need. You don't even care. We hardly have money for cigarettes anymore, just your beer, and whatever else you spend it on. How'll we pay for their food and decent school clothes? We don't make that kind of money, now do we?"

"That's enough, bitch! You just don't get it do you? If we play our cards right we'll get the house too. It's a great old place. Don't believe I can pull it off, do you?"

Rehma dabbed at her eyes.

"Answer me, damn you!"

"I just don't know *how* you mean to do it, Bo. I don't understand what you want with that money Steve meant for my kids. I never should have told you about it in the first place. Dumbest thing I ever did."

Bo kicked the chair away from him and grabbed her by the shoulders. Her head fell back. Her eyes bulged wide with fear. He relaxed his grip and smiled.

"That's better, Rehma Baby. Just remember what you got for mouthin' off to me the other night. You keep in mind who's boss around here and everything will go just fine. Otherwise it'll be your face I go for next time—where it shows."

Rehma crumpled against the dresser, crying, watching him. She said no more while he raved on.

"You remember what I say. That money is yours as much as it belongs to your kids. To hell with their edjuh-cation. Let 'em grow up and get jobs like everybody else. Nobody handed me uh edjuh-cation. I've made my own way. Got busted up but good doin' it, too. Those kids'll be all right. You and me, we got plans . . . gettin' married and all. That money and that house will both be ours. You mark my words."

She ventured then, fearful but strong, in a whisper that cut through the heat of the dingy room.

"Bo, I'll go along with you getting your hands on Steve's money once we have the kids, but you ever so much as lay a finger *or a harsh word* on one of my babies and I swear I'll kill you. Some night when you're sleepin' off a toot, I'll slit your throat and leave you bleedin'—sure as shit. Once I have my kids you can take half the money and clear your ass out of my life."

He rifled the can at her. She ducked. It smacked into the mirror, sending glass shards tinkling across the dresser top. He turned and loped out through the shower curtain, hating needing her, hating the sight and sound of her. She wasn't even a good romp anymore. He knew he'd scared her too many times for it to be fun.

Rehma poured a drink while she listened to the bells on the shop door jingle when he slammed out.

"Good riddance you lousy bastard," she said out loud to herself. The angry tone of her voice sounded powerful in the quiet, comforting her in her loneliness. She sat staring at the blank TV set that no longer worked and drank herself into a stupor. It never occurred to her to wonder where Bo was off to. That he was gone was all she needed to lower her panic to a level where the liquor stash she'd discovered in his gun case could take over.

"Let him wonder if he drank it all himself," she muttered, smiling about her meager triumph into what remained of her image cracking in the mirror.

Doug Jensen

~ Tuesday the 17th of June

Doug returned to his desk at the station and checked with the dispatcher for his messages. Janet handed him a couple of pink slips and indicated a man waiting on a bench in the hall.

"Did he say what he wanted? Anything about Big Blue?"

She shook her head. "Asked for Steve, doesn't seem to know he's not on the force anymore."

"From around here?"

"No idea."

"Okay, Janet, thanks." Doug pushed the swinging glass doors open and walked over to the big, muscled man with the cane. Sad looking guy, handsome, maybe early forties. Hard to tell, scarred up some, bad auto accident by the looks of him.

"What's up?" He stuck out his hand. "I'm Officer Jensen. How can I help you?"

"I don't think *you* can do much of anything. I need Steve Price. Last I knew he worked out of this office." The man fumbled, unfolding a worn piece of paper from his wallet. "He was helping me on an attempted murder charge. My murder— only I lived. I want you to catch the fuc. . . worm that did this to me." He corrected himself, gestured toward his arms and legs.

What connection did he have to Steve? Doug thought for a minute about whether to shine the poor guy on or take him down the hall to an interrogation room for privacy where he'd tell him Steve couldn't help him or anyone else anymore. He chose the latter.

Behind closed doors he popped a couple of sodas and handed one to the man who introduced himself as Johnny

The Wind Remembers

Carlisle. Name was familiar, but not ringing any serious bells. It took both of Carlisle's hands to control the drink can to his mouth. He dribbled a little and brushed his chin dry with the back of his good hand.

Doug tried to be extra kind to the big man. "Steve and I were partners for years. I thought I knew all of his cases, the big ones. Attempted murder would be big enough. I just don't remember your face or your name. Help me out with highlights of your case."

"I want to talk to Price. He knows all about it. Took notes by my hospital bed."

"Steve's not here anymore. If he cared about you enough to visit you in the hospital, I know he'd want me to help you if I could. Help me out here, Buddy. Tell me about your case. Did it happen here in the county or somewhere else in Utah?"

"Look, Jensen, you just tell me where Price's working now and I'll find him. He knows the facts of who I'm looking for. I don't remember much." Carlisle tapped his forehead. "I need his notes to help me track the bastard myself. After the coma I had a stroke in recovery; wiped a lot out I used to know. Price has plenty in those notes or in his head if he tossed the papers."

"Steve's never going to be able to help you, Mr. Carlisle. He died of cancer six months ago." Doug laid a hand on the man's arm, watched the news sink in, saw the tears begin. He swallowed hard. *Jesus I hate to see a man cry, especially a big hard-muscled macho man like this.*

"You'll have to count on me, Mr. Carlisle. I know Steve would've helped you if he could. He was more than my partner; he was my best friend all my life. I'll take your case on myself. There'll be records we can check because Steve had to make out reports for his time like the rest of us." He patted the arm, felt the muscles knot and twitch.

Johnny looked up at him, tears streaming unchecked down his scarred face. Doug could see someone had indeed worked him over pretty good. With whatever was left of his mind, it wasn't too likely Johnny Carlisle would give up finding whoever it was that nearly killed him.

"I'll help you man. If the bastard's in Utah, we'll find him. Tell me what you can remember, starting with when and where."

THE WIND REMEMBERS

CHAPTER ELEVEN

DANGEROUS GROUND

Bo Rodman

~ Wednesday the 18th of June

Bo headed straight for the Pump, his hatred for Rehma seething in every tense muscle of his body. There was no time to work out his frustration in the weight room, not with Frank in trouble in a way that'd mess up all Bo's plans. At least he wouldn't have to give him a split of the Price take any more for his letter writing trouble. What Rehma didn't know wouldn't hurt her. He picked up his pay envelope, tore off the end, and blew inside it on his way to the parking lot. Pulling out the check, the few hours he'd bothered to put in on the job were reflected in the skimpy wages.

"Damn bird takes too much of my time. Son of a bitch." He approached his truck. "Not enough money to keep me in cigarettes or beer for long." His hand reached for the door handle. It was then he noticed two men descending the police-station steps across the way. He paused. Tracker sat bolt upright, startled from a snooze. He nuzzled Bo through the open window, was rewarded with an absent-minded rubbing by his master, whose attention was captured by Doug Jensen. Rehma's dead husband's old partner kept pace with a big fellow in dark glasses struggling down the steps one at a time. Seeing another man having a harder time to walk than he did made Bo stop to watch. One hand on the railing, one gripping a cane, the big man kept his head down, sunglasses focused on his feet. When he conquered the last step, he lifted his head.

The sun caught his cheekbone and spilled across his broad brow. Scarred, maybe a rodeo man like himself? Bo puzzled over why the stranger seemed familiar, watched him settle with difficulty into a car with levers at the wheel of the driver's seat, noted from the back the set of the man's broad shoulders and thick neck. . . . Bo froze with his thumb depressing the release button on the handle of his truck door.

"Jeezesust H Christopher, it's Carlisle! . . . *it can't be!*"

But deep in his gut Bo knew for sure it was. Like a hunted thing he shoved Tracker over, slid behind the wheel, hunched down, and pulled his hat low over his face. He closed the door quietly, his eyes never leaving Carlisle who pulled his own door shut, fiddled with the ignition and levers, and drove the car out into the traffic behind Jensen's cruiser. They headed down Main Street out of town. Where were they going together? He wanted to follow and find out, but it wasn't smart with no cover and him probably under suspicion. He wondered why they hadn't come after him at the Tangle or the Pump.

Bo sat stunned for some minutes, unable to think of anything but replaying the shock of knowing he hadn't killed Carlisle. The falconer could breathe, walk, talk, and had no doubt in hell dumped his guts to the cops about Bo Rodman arguing with him at the Shootin' Star and surprising him later with a ski mask on, beating him senseless. Sweat poured down his face. He swabbed at it while Tracker pressed his head into his shoulder and pawed his thigh for attention. Ignored, the big dog settled down to wait.

Carlisle busted up but alive scared hell out of Bo. He'd been so sure he'd done away with the birdman, been confident he'd never be found out about it either. He thought he'd made sure Johnny was dead, bleeding everywhere, didn't seem to be breathing. There was no pulse he could feel through all the blood. Hadn't Carlisle's place gone up for sale? Hadn't he watched the wife and kids moving out, even drove down and watched the new family move in? That'd fixed in his mind the Carlisles was long gone.

The newspapers'd been quiet about it after one short mention, and the cop talk around the Pump had soon been all about Steve Price getting bad sick and dying. No more'd been said of Carlisle, probably because he was no rich bitch or power-hungry politician, just a common blue-color man nobody gave a shit about. The dawning on Bo that he'd been over-confident, like underestimating another bull rider's skill at a rodeo, made his pulse pump to competition level. He had the sensation of being dropped astride a Brahma and somebody pulling the gate before he had his grip on the bull rope.

His anger toward Rehma, and his humiliation over Carlisle surviving his murderous attack, merged into a cold fury that deepened as the full meaning of the mess he was in belched to the surface of his mind.

I ain't goin' back to prison for attempted murder, no fuckin' way!

He did a U-turn, pulled into the bank drive-through and cashed the pitiful check. Whipping out into the traffic, he swung into a shady parking place in front of the Last Tangle. He decided spur-of-the-moment to take Rehma out for some quick grub and talk her into parting with the rest of her take for the week. He knew he'd been too rough on her lately. She was spooked and mad at him. He'd have to work her easy, lay on some sweet talk, bring her around to trusting him enough to get her money for his getaway. She always had a little stash somewhere. With Carlisle alive, buddying up to the cops, there was no way he could stick around to let his plan for marrying her play out to get at the Price woman and her kids' money. He'd come back later for his gear when Rehma was too drunk on her ass to notice or to stop him with a noisy scene that might show his hand to the neighbors. Everything he did had to be on the quiet from now on.

He climbed out of the truck and went around to the back of the camper shell, pulled up the flap, and checked on the gyrfalcon. Her hood and tethered jesses were secure. She hardly ruffled her feathers at the sound of him or at the feel of more fresh air sweeping her perch from the windows. The inside of the shell was hot. He knew she was drowsy from the heat and needed to be pegged out for a bath up at the sheep camp. He dropped the flap in disgust at the bother of her. Unless he could convince Frank to take her on the pretense of just needing a few days to take care of some business, he'd have to waste her or let her go on his way out of Utah.

With Carlisle in town he sure as hell couldn't be caught with the hawk. With Big Blue in jail for screwing up Jensen's cruiser with spray paint, the police knew about his gang using Makris's sheep camp. It wouldn't be safe to hide the falcon up there anymore. He'd heard the cops talk about looking for the rest of the Blue Tattoo gang. Everything in his life was getting too damn messy. A risky plan formed in his mind that sure as hell beat going up for attempted murder and getting his ass stuck back in jail. He had little to lose now.

He went in the shop's front door. Rehma was closing up, tucking something between her boobs. When the doorbells tinkled she looked up startled, a little bird caught off guard. He put on a big smile.

"I just got paid, Baby. Let's go grab a bite and plan our camp-out with your kids." He waved his cash before her eyes and patted her behind. "Don't you look like a magazine 'pitcher'," he gushed.

Rehma turned her back and shoved the cash register drawer shut with a bang.

"Aw, Baby, I know I been a bad boy, mean and low, but I love yuh. It's my nature to act tough. Rodeoin' and all, people expect it. But I'm a soft ole marshmallow inside. You know it, Honey."

She moved away through the plastic shower curtain and beyond it into their apartment. He followed close on her flapping wedgy sandals, hating the cracked black edges of her heels, hating her more because he needed her. He checked his temper and touched her shoulder, willing himself to act gentle.

"I know you're tender hearted and I don't deserve yuh. You deserve better'n me." He danced around trying to hug her.

She wrenched free, looking hot and tired, in no mood for put-on bull. She buffed her nails on her hip, looked at him, looked away, studied her nails while he rambled.

"Tell you what, I know you're bound to be worn out, 'specially after that high-falootin' bitch lawyer's news about Frank, and us fightin' a silly fuss over somethin' we can't help and all. How 'bout I spring for dinner at the cafe and let you relax for the evening to yourself? I promised Blue I'd help him clean his huntin' rifles tonight." He hoped she hadn't heard how his nephew was cooling his heels in jail.

"We'll buy you a new one o' them women's romance magazines you like and a cold bottle a wine to keep you comp'ny 'til your good ole Bo is back home in bed where he belongs." He'd smiled through all of his words the way he used to charm the wanna-be cowgirls at the fairground barns to get into their britches.

Rehma's eyes softened. Her mouth loosened into a giving-in smile. He moved close and ran a hand around her waist, up to her breasts, keeping his touch gentle.

"What do yuh say, Baby? A little din-din with your soon-to-be?"

She brushed his hand aside, took off her smock, and tossed it to a chair.

"Gimme a minute to put on some lipstick." She rummaged in a drawer and cocked her head to apply a purplish red to her lips in what was left of the mirror.

He'd won and he knew it. He slapped her gently on the ass. "How about a little titty for dessert later?" he laughed. She shrugged her shoulders and looked up at him in the mirror with eyes that held something wary he'd never seen in them before.

"You trying to soften me up for something, Bo? You gotta know I'm not trusting you much lately." She applied her lipstick with shaky fingers, smoothed the effect with a pinky, and straightened to face him.

Bo leaned close enough to kiss her throat, smelled whiskey on her breath and her sweaty skin and choked down his fury that she'd raided his stash. He needed money, needed every dime he could lay his hands on. He stayed focused on anything it took to get every dime of it.

"Ain't you hungry, Baby?" he cooed, the way he'd heard Frank coax the gyrfalcon to eat. "We can eat grub or feast on body parts right here in the bedroom," he laughed, his tone a tease, his mind hoping he wouldn't have to go that far now that he held no lust for her. "Let's plan that campin' trip with your kids. Hell, when we're married I'm goin' to be their papa. I gotta get to know them kids so they can show me some respect." He laughed again, trying to read her, floundering in her out-of-the-ordinary stand-offishness.

"Bo, I've been thinking . . . I don't want you around my kids. Your bad temper comes on mean with no warning. That's not good for kids." She didn't look at him but rolled her eyes around the corners of the room like a cornered animal looking for an escape route. "It's not good for *me*."

He hated wimps, hated her, thought of the fancy woman in the shop looking for Frank, thought of Carlisle blabbing to the cops. Bo felt his world narrowing, his options in everybody else's control. Watching her, he felt his anger at his mucked-up plans rise behind his chest, engorge his throat, felt his lips twitch at the sight of the fear in her eyes. He gripped her arms, pulled her to him, and growled a command.

"How 'bout I just clear out now, Sweet Face? You give

me that money," he ripped at her blouse, closed his fingers on the thin roll of bills between the soft flesh of her breasts, wrested it away, and kept her locked in his arms, "and I'll just head on out of your life. We'll just see if you can attract another bee to your honey cunt, which I doubt since you let yerself go so bad."

She tried to pull free. The two of them fell against the dresser, her naked fear arousing no pity in him, but rather a pleasure in his power to make her afraid.

"You've got what you want, so get out," she whispered against him, her voice barely audible.

"You give me one more thing I want and I'll go." He backed her to the wall, one hand to her throat. "Just where do you spose ol' Price kept the money for his kids? Where would his sweet little widow keep that $50,000 you told me about?" He felt Rehma's frantic pulse within his grasp.

"I . . . I don't know, Bo. How would I know a thing like that? Maybe Steve and Suzanne spent it on that house." He squeezed. She fought him, choking out her words, "Steve never . . . talked . . . about that . . . money . . . after he left with the kids."

Tears trickled from the corners of her bulging eyes. "Please . . . Bo." He squeezed harder. Her gasping breaths came in shallow wheezes, her flared nostrils darkened to match her smeared lipstick. Her mouth opened. Her tongue protruded. Sickened at the sight of her, he wanted it over.

"You won't mind if I just help myself to the whole $50,000, now would you, Babe? I got plans and splittin' the take with you would kinda slow me down."

He slugged her in the stomach with his free hand, forcing air from her lungs in a whoosh of whiskey and bile. With both hands he strangled until her struggling stopped. He let her slide to the floor.

The silence of the room pleased him. Only the sound of the clock ticking on the wall above the hot plate interfered with his release of pent-up tension. He opened the fridge and pulled out a beer, popped it open, guzzled it down, and tossed it on the table. The can rolled off and came to rest against one of Rehma's outstretched legs. He stared at her for a moment splayed before him, spent, defeated. He moved a chair and dragged her by her feet into the middle of the rag rug. Rolling her up inside it, dirt eddied into rings on the floor where the rug had been. He stacked her like cordwood near the back door.

Bo shook out pillows and filled the cheap, flowered cases with canned goods, beer, cheese, a bag of dog food, and a plastic tub of the falcon's frozen mice. He grabbed a box of rifle shells and a couple of flannel shirts from under the bed. Resting the bulging cases against the rug roll of Rehma, he added his hunting rifles and the transmitter-receiver Frank loaned him for tracking the falcon.

He went out, drove the truck up the alley to the shop's back door, and loped inside to take his fiancée out for the very last time.

Johnny Carlisle

~ Wednesday the 18th of June

Johnny steered along in the far right lane behind the police car, braking with the hand lever whenever necessary to flow with the traffic, his feelings a mixture of deep sadness over the death of Officer Price and utter frustration at another unfair blow to his well-deserved revenge. At the news, despair had clutched him by the throat and nearly felled him in the police station.

But Price's old partner offered him a shred of hope. Price's widow might know something, if her husband had discussed the case with her before he died. To Johnny's surprise, Officer Jensen seemed eager to get right on that possibility without putting him off for even a few minutes. Up ahead he could see Jensen using a hand-held cell phone, probably telling Mrs. Price they were on their way to her house right now.

The Wind Remembers

***

The two women sat together on the couch while Johnny took the side chair with upholstered arms and eased himself into it. Tired, but allowing a glimmer of hope to carry his energy, he braced himself for information he'd lived for or another grinding disappointment.

"I don't recall Steve talking about your case, Mr. Carlisle," said the one Doug introduced as Price's wife. "But I do remember a couple of evenings when he picked up his medicines in the hospital and said he was going to visit a man who'd been badly beaten. You were the last job-related person he felt bent on helping, even though he was sick with chemo treatments most of the time."

She was kind like her late husband. Johnny liked her. Strange how the cop never mentioned he had cancer. The other woman was pretty too, but with a hard edge, less open, listening to everything like a buzzard waiting for a turn at road kill. Jensen didn't seem able to keep his eyes off of either one of the women for long. *Maybe that's why he was so eager to come here, spur of the moment.*

"Suzanne, you sure Steve didn't say who he suspected of beating Mr. Carlisle here to a bloody pulp?"

"Please, Doug, not such rough talk in front of the children."

"Take a hike, little buddy," Officer Jensen said to the boy hanging out in the doorway to the den. "I'll catch up with you before I leave."

"Oh, sure, just like the last two times you stopped by. Fat chance." The boy left and slammed outside. *Sassy little kid*, Johnny thought, *could use a dad*. Maybe now they could get down to helping him follow the trail to his quarry. But he could hear a younger child's voice singing along with a recording of some kind down the hall, and doubted they'd get very far without another interruption. He hoped he could sustain the energy he needed to get what he'd come for.

"Steve *never* discussed police business with me, Doug. He made every effort to separate his job from his family life and took pride in being able to keep his word." She looked at Johnny, and he felt her goodness and concern, thankfully just short of pity, for the shape he was in. "Mr. Carlisle, I think what you've experienced is a terrible shame. If I knew of a way to help you, believe me I would."

There was a knock at the kitchen door and Price's sister moved to answer it. Everyone seemed to be waiting to see who it was. A man appeared and stepped inside.

"You here again, Armstrong?" Jensen looked and sounded irritated.

Mrs. Price smiled at the newcomer. Johnny could tell she wasn't one bit sorry to see him. "Hello, Taylor," she said. "Something you need?"

The sister sat back down next to her, watching everybody, reminding him of a news reporter posing with a smile that didn't always reach her eyes.

"My truck is back. I can finish moving the last of the wood now that I have a power-operated winch. Just wanted your okay before I crank up the noise." The big man was handsome in the athletic way Johnny remembered being good looking, before all of his broken bones and scars.

"Of course, that's just fine." Suzanne gestured. He felt the stranger's eyes appraise him. "Taylor, let me introduce Johnny Carlisle. He's trying to locate a man who . . . who left him for dead, and he thought perhaps my . . . he thought perhaps Steve had told me who he thought it might be. You'd probably find it interesting that his gyrfalcon was stolen during the attack."

"I don't think this is any of Taylor's business . . ." interrupted Jensen.

"Yes, you're right Suzanne, that does interest me," Taylor shook hands, appearing to sense immediately the one Johnny was most likely to offer, ignoring the rude cop.

The Wind Remembers

"My dad's a breeder," Taylor said, looking him right in the eye. "You know how tight falconers are in the network. I guess you're trying to find your gyr? Maybe Pops's heard something that would help. I'll check if you'll leave word here with Suzanne how to reach you."

Johnny sat up. "Hey, I could use every clue to the b . . . sorry ma'am, . . . guy who did this to me." He didn't want to offend her; she was a real lady.

"Must have been a mean son of a gun. Doesn't seem much like a falconer's personality to me, more like a street punk wanting to maim somebody to feel important, than a man who has the sensitivity and kindness to devote himself to birds of prey." Taylor squatted down eye-level with him.

"That's what I think, too," said Johnny. "I remembered something nagging my memory. I've been counting on Officer Price to help me with a name I've forgotten."

"What is it you've remembered?" asked the widow, leaning forward with interest. "What made you think my Steve could have helped you if he were here?"

"I was watching a rodeo on TV the other night in Florida, they're mighty popular down there, too. This cowboy they interviewed wore this big shiny silver belt buckle, some prize he won at national finals he said."

Johnny's hand gripped his cane. "I remembered telling your husband how I grabbed a buckle like that when I was going down. Last thing I remember because he hit me over the head with a tire iron. Thing is, there was more I remembered just after the buckle part came back to me. The night before the guy surprised me in my mew, my wife and I'd been grabbing a burger at the Shooting Star. I scuffled with a rodeo cowboy over him going beyond flirting with her, but that's all I can remember. There was a time when I think I knew his name. Your husband took notes by my bed. I just hoped he remembered what I told him. I want to find the jerk, real bad."

Johnny sat back, exhausted with the task of remembering and expressing himself to strangers when he'd struggled to make sense of it for so long.

"Remind you of anybody we both know, Doug?" Taylor asked, pointing to his belt buckle.

"Sure does, or at least a little bit it does," the officer answered. "The name Bo Rodman ring any bells for you?"

Johnny turned the name over in his mind. Nothing stirred. He shook his head.

"Suzanne," said the sister. "What about that box of notes and clippings of Steve's in your bureau drawer? Do you think Mr. Carlisle's mystery assailant's name might be among that stuff?" She uncrossed her pretty legs and rose to go. Mrs. Price stopped her with a hand on her arm.

"Good idea. I'll get them."

They all sat waiting. She returned quickly and seated herself with the box on her lap. Sorting through it, she offered Officer Jensen a small flip-style notebook, while examining press clippings and photos. "Here's a little note in the *Farr Star* about you, Mr. Carlisle," she said, handing it to him. "It just says you must have surprised a burglar, that you were on the critical list, but there's no description of a suspect or a name other than your own."

"Well, looks like my buddy Steve did have a good handle on who you thought it was before that stroke," said Jensen, pausing with a finger on a notebook page.

Johnny's heart nearly stopped.

"Says here whoever your cowboy was he was drinking with Frank Simmons, a falcon breeder you were just getting acquainted with. Steve believed you'd put your finger on the motive. He notes here he asked Frank about you and whoever he was drinking with that night, but Simmons claimed he didn't remember the incident."

"Or wouldn't," said Mrs. Price's sister. Johnny couldn't remember her name, but she'd perked right up at the name of Simmons. He wondered why, because the name Frank Simmons no longer meant a thing to him. He couldn't even put a face to it.

"Well, maybe we'll just have to talk to Attorney

Simmons. We can jog his memory and put a little scare into Rodman while we're at it," said Officer Jensen.

He sure seems to want to look awful important in front of these women.

"Doug, I met Bo Rodman this morning myself," said the sister. Things were going too fast for Johnny. He was having trouble keeping up but knew he'd better try. These people were the first steps he'd had in the direction he was determined to go.

"What do you mean you met Rodman?" Mrs. Price asked. "Where *were* you this morning?"

"I went to Rehma's shop and did a little detective work on your behalf. Bo Rodman beats her up, so why not imagine he might try to kill somebody over a falcon? There's no way in the world you want him around Greg and Mitzi, I can tell you that much." She crossed her long legs and looked around at all of them.

They all look surprised as hell, thought Johnny.

"I can't believe you'd do anything so impulsive, Dee." Mrs. Price set the box on the coffee table and faced her. "How could you jeopardize what I'm trying to do with my own attorney, which I remind you was *your* idea? Didn't Rehma recognize you?"

"We've never met, so I wasn't worried. We may be twins, but we look nothing alike."

"You shouldn't have risked it, Dierdre," Taylor said. "He's dangerous."

"So I noticed by Rehma's bruises," the sister looked smug and sexy at the same time.

"I think it's time to fill everyone in on just what you did and didn't say to Rehma and Bo," Officer Jensen said. "I just hope you haven't thrown a wrench in the works for those of us who have to investigate and don't need the danger of him being forewarned."

"Well, you policemen are trained to handle mean people. My sister isn't! So don't you lecture me, Doug Jensen. Somebody had to do something besides drive by in a patrol car to see what else has threatened this family—*after* it happens."

Officer Jensen scowled at her.

Taylor rose and put out his hand. Johnny took it and looked up at him. "Let Suzanne know how to reach you. I'll check to see if my dad and his friends have heard any word of your missing gyr. Sure hope you get your falcon back."

He nodded to everyone else and retreated through the kitchen. Officer Jensen took over again. Johnny felt exhaustion overtaking him. He feared his growing tremors might cause him to spasm dramatically in front of them all. Even though he wanted to hear more about Rodman and what Price's wife's sister had to say, he couldn't risk a seizure.

"It's been a long day for me. I'm overdue on my medication." He handed the policeman and Mrs. Price a couple of the cards he'd picked up from the motel desk. "Just call for me, and they'll put you through to my room," he said. "Or you can leave a message. I'd like to know what happens when you follow up on this guy, just in case he is the one who busted me up. He deserves to be in jail, and I intend to prosecute. I won't rest until I find out what happened to Felon too, if I can. I probably won't be able to care for her by myself any more, but I know falconers who might take her on." With Jensen's help, he struggled to his feet from the soft chair.

"Perhaps Taylor's father could help you find a home for your falcon if it can be recovered," said Mrs. Price. "Felon, what an interesting name. Does it mean criminal?"

"Not to me," said Johnny. "In Gaelic it means *the wind*. When I named her I never thought she'd be taken away from me." His eyes filled with tears.

She patted his arm. "Steve would have wanted me to help you. You keep the clipping and the notebook. I've been meaning to dispose of them anyway. Glad I kept them for you. We'll stay in touch."

His hands were shaking so bad he feared driving, but just walking seemed to help a bit. He was able to pull out of the driveway all right and head for the motel for his meds. He wondered why they suspected Bo Rodman and experienced the clamping gut pain of anxiety that came when things appeared logical to everyone but him.

CHAPTER TWELVE

DANCING ON THE EDGE

Suzanne Price

~ Wednesday the 18th of June

Suzanne put off asking for Dierdre's help until after breakfast. After washing up the dishes, they went through suitcases and closets to locate something suitable to wear to the Western fundraiser that evening. Mitzi sat on the bed with a wooden puzzle, grasping little knobs on each piece. Her lower lip protruded while she concentrated on where to fit the rabbit. Greg, operating a remote-controlled car with his friend Alex, could be seen and heard outside the window in the yard. To Suzanne's delight, the boys set up an obstacle course using tree trimmings to create jumps for the racecar to maneuver. It was the first happiness she'd observed in weeks for her son. She knew the kids would have a great time at their overnight at Diane's.

Dierdre shook loose a flannel shirt and hung it from a closet doorknob. "While we're at it we should plan for the Sun Tunnels. We leave Friday, you know."

Suzanne turned back to the mirror and looked at the outfit Dee had come up with this time. The phone rang. Mitzi scootched off the bed to answer it, spilling puzzle pieces in the shifting bedspread.

"I'll get it, Honey," Suzanne reached for the phone. "You finish your puzzle."

"We'll never finish picking out what to wear at this rate," Dierdre said.

"This outfit will do just fine, Dee." She picked up the receiver. "Hello?"

"Hey, Suzanne! Doug here. Sure looking forward to dancing with you tonight."

Suzanne swallowed. "Yes, it should be lots of fun. Have you warned . . ." She started to say 'Rehma', but stopped herself just in time with Mitzi, all ears, in the room. "You can guess what I'm not free to say, Doug?"

"I drove by Rehma's shop on my way in. Usual interior lights weren't on. Called her from the office. No answer. At the Iron Pump, nobody has seen Bo since he picked up his paycheck yesterday. They'll both turn up today. She's probably sleeping in."

A sinister thought occurred to Suzanne. She shivered involuntarily. "Doug, if Bo *is* the culprit, couldn't it be dangerous for Johnny if he saw you two together yesterday when he thought he was . . . you know, not around anymore?"

Suzanne felt inexplicably cold. Her eyes caught Dierdre's. They both let out an audible breath. Doug was quiet for a long moment too.

"Wear something real pretty for me tonight."

The Wind Remembers

He was early. Suzanne opened the door and stood back while Doug entered. He brushed her cheek with a kiss in passing. The prickle of his mustache lingered like a question mark. *What will he be like tonight?* She closed the door and turned. Cross-legged and resting on the heels of his best boots, he leaned against the kitchen counter, his fingers drumming the Formica. Cowboy hat set at a rakish angle, she thought him as good looking as a lean, country singing star. His grin was engaging. It puzzled her why she had no interest in him beyond being friends. She'd always felt a twinge of discomfort for reasons she'd never put a finger on.

"I wanted to beat Taylor here and have a moment alone with you. You're looking real pretty in that Western get-up tonight, Ma'am. Can't wait to take you in my arms and swing you around the dance floor. You must know I've wanted to for a long time."

She stood by the protective solidity of the refrigerator, as if could keep the situation between them cool. "Doug, please let's not go into private things now. Dee or the kids will walk in any second."

He moved away from the counter and planted himself within inches of her body. "Steve's gone and I'm here for you. The kids and your twin will catch on soon anyway."

The refrigerator halted her retreat. She nearly stopped breathing with the smell of too much sweet after-shave, cigarette breath with gum overtones, and the intense look in his eyes. His fingers caressed her shoulders in little circles. She stiffened.

"It's time for us, Suzanne; we've waited long enough. Steve would want us to go on and be happy . . . as a family."

She knew he was right about Steve. *Too darn bad. I do not love you and I'm liking you less. Why can't I just say that?*

Doug's fingers moved on her collarbone. "You've got to be struggling financially. I admire how you've held off dipping into what my buddy set up for his kid's education."

She wondered how he had guessed or if he had an in at the bank. He bent to kiss her. She turned her face away.

"I can offer you a fine home with that art studio space you like upstairs and all the love and security you could want." His fingers crept below her collarbones. "I love you, Sugar. You know you want to let yourself fall in love with me. The kids want it, too."

She put her hands to his chest and pushed him away. "Doug, have you been filling Greg's head with the idea of you and I getting married?"

His look was surprised. "Hell, no!" He laughed. "But I think it's a damn good idea, don't you?"

"Let's just go to this dance and have fun as a foursome making money for baseball uniforms." She toyed with the fringe on her denim vest, fiddled with her concha belt buckle. *Why did he insist on coming early and making an already awkward night out together, all the more difficult?*

Doug ran his hands down his thighs, removing lint that wasn't there. "We'll have to go alone in my cruiser. Back seat's full of boxes I didn't get time to deliver to the new branch office." She immediately associated the triumphant edge to his voice with Gregory when he thought he'd pulled something over on her.

"That's okay," she smiled, "the four of us can fit in my Blazer."

The swinging door banged open. Mitzi bounced in. "Mommy, me and Bear Lovins is all packed for sleeping overnight at Leesha's house." She dragged a bulging tote bag and clutched her teddy bear. "Ooh, I like your twirly blue skirt." She let go of the tote handles to fluff the folds of Suzanne's flowered, broomstick skirt and finger the filigreed metal tips on her Zodiak boots.

"Me, too," added Doug.

"Are you going to dance wif Mr. Armfrong, too, Mommy?"

Suzanne caught Doug's eye and registered his surprise and irritation. "Oh, we'll *all* be dancing with each other tonight, Sweetheart."

"That's certainly *my* plan," said Dierdre, joining them. Suzanne noted her snug-fitting jeans, the red jacket to her traveling suit and Doug's eyes on the cleavage of the low-necked white T-shirt he'd been unable to resist during her spaghetti dinner. Red nails and crimson spike heels completed her usual stunning, if overstated un-Western appearance.

A knock at the door sent Mitzi scrambling to answer it. "It's Mr. Armfrong!"

Taylor bent at the knees to shake her hand. "How's Miss Curly Locks this evening?" Mitzi giggled and unzipped her lips.

Suzanne warmed to the sound of his voice, while absorbing every detail from his sandy curls and blue eyes to the wide-yoked blue-and white-striped Western shirt that accentuated his impressive shoulders. He wore brushed denim jeans and ostrich skin boots, and looked as if he had gone to some trouble to look terrific. She wished she didn't have to share him with her twin.

"You look mighty Western, Miss Susie." His clear blue eyes traveled quickly up to hers and locked there.

"Thanks," she breathed.

"I'll tell Gregory everybody's here and it's time to go." Mitzi darted between them and pushed with both hands on the swinging door, bonking Greg on his way in.

"Little Brat!" He entered rubbing a fist to his forehead.

"You okay, Sport?" Doug clapped him on the shoulder.

"Yeah, but it hurts. Suzanne's always yelling at me when I run through that door, but she never says anything to Miss Princess. I thought you'd come to my room as soon as you got here, Doug, so I waited. If you were here all the time, it wouldn't matter so much when the little brat's getting her way."

"I'll work on that, Little Buddy."

"Stop calling me little, I'm lots bigger than baby Mitzi."

"Sure, sure." Doug backed himself to the counter next to Dierdre, where Suzanne saw he took quick advantage of an over-her-shoulder view down her twin's shirtfront.

So juvenile, she thought. "How about we all pile in the Blazer and deliver the children to Diane's on the way to the dance?"

Moving quickly to her side, Doug snaked an arm around her shoulders. "Can't seem to get it through the doll's head *we* are going *alone*. You two are on your own."

"I want the children in seat belts, Doug, and your back seat is full of stuff, so the Blazer it is."

He snapped the elastic gathering at the neckline of her peasant blouse. "Like I said, Lady, we're going alone. We'll meet up at the dance."

Suzanne blushed at his familiarity and pulled the blouse back up over her shoulder. "If you're like this all night, I may have to pop you one." She made an effort to laugh, acting flippant while she helped Mitzi collect her things and tried to think of a way to regain control of the car situation. She shot an imploring look at Dee who missed her cue, her eyes on her own reflection in her compact mirror.

Dierdre snapped it shut and dropped it into her bag. "Taylor, I've no intention of being squired to a country-dance ball in a truck with a winch on its tail—not very romantic. I know where Diane lives, so you and I will take the kids in the Blazer, and we'll meet them at the dance."

"Hold it, hold it," Taylor broke in. "Too many chiefs and no negotiations with us Indians." He included Suzanne in his gesture. "No way am I parking my repainted truck here to be spray painted under cover of darkness again." He patted Suzanne on the shoulder as if she were a good old hunting dog, or so it seemed to her.

"Yeah, Taylor's right," said Doug. " Security checks here won't be as frequent tonight with most of the guys on the force at the dance."

Taylor nodded assent and continued, "Dierdre and the kids can take the Blazer to Diane's. I'll follow and then your twin can follow me to my place at Lone Pine Mobile Estates. It's only a couple of miles from here on 89. You'll see the big sign.

We'll drop off my truck and meet up with you two at the dance, so don't push your luck at heading off into the sunset without us."

"I don't see why this has to be so complicated," said Suzanne, picking up her keys, grateful for Taylor's parting remark.

"Because I want you all to myself," said Doug, guiding her behind the others with a firm hand across the middle of her back. He stood waiting beside her on the porch while she flipped on the outside light and used her key to shoot the dead bolt into place.

Taylor backed out of the drive and allowed Dierdre and the kids to take the lead in the Blazer. Doug and Suzanne followed. The three vehicles descended the bench. The blazing sun, nearing its longest day of the year, poised above the peaks on Antelope Island in the distance, before slipping an inch in their windshields, setting Great Salt Lake on fire.

Doug's hand reached across the seat between them and found Suzanne's. She resisted the urge to pull away, hoping to avoid starting the evening off with a confrontation. He squinted ahead at the glittering pavement, glanced at her, and smiled to himself. She felt sorry for him, knowing what he wanted from her she didn't feel, couldn't give. A relationship with less than her whole heart was out of the question.

"Loosen up, Suzanne. You know I'm crazy about you. No need to hold back any more." His mustache curved above his smile.

"You're a nice man, Doug. You've been there for us. I'm grateful . . . Steve would be, too."

He laughed and squeezed her fingers. "I want more than your gratitude." He stroked her knuckles and hummed to the country ballad on the radio. "What do you say to going out afterwards for dinner and a toddy? With the kids staying overnight, we don't have to hurry you home after the dance."

"Perhaps, . . . if all four of us are going." She extracted her hand to smooth her hair. He waited for it, and though she dropped her hand to her lap, he reached further and took it in his own again.

"Sure, all four of us."

She regretted with all her heart that Taylor wasn't the man saying the words of love and intimate implication she so wanted to hear from him and feared she never would. Perhaps he had a serious woman friend, probably did. She imagined being stuck holding Doug off, knowing how much of a friend he was to Greg, or maybe being without any sort of man in her life forever. Would she be content with only the children, a job, and church to fill her life? Perhaps, but the last few months had been almost unbearably lonely.

For a moment she felt angry with herself for not being able to fall in love with Doug. He was devoted to her and good to the children, dependably employed, good looking, easy going—actually, too easy going. He seemed happy to go with the moment. *Still, nothing really wrong with that.* Nevertheless, the only reasons she was willing to endure this evening with him as her date were raising money to fund Greg's team uniforms and the promise of dancing with Taylor. Guilt at using Doug pricked her conscience. She looked down at the hand over hers and knew the most she would ever feel for him was friendship. Tonight, the way he was being so pushy, even friendship was in question.

Her eyes scanned the accumulation of dust and smudges on the dash, the ashtray overflowing with cigarette butts and gum wrappers. *Sometimes it's the little things that make life's decisions difficult,* she thought, then heard a small voice in the back of her mind add, *and little things can make the direction of decisions abundantly clear, if you look at them realistically.*

She rolled down her window to let the stale smell of cigarettes out and the fresh air in. Doug let go of her hand to switch off the air conditioner. Taking a deep breath of air, she relaxed . . . until his hand closed over her fingers once more.

※※※

The Wind Remembers

The county-fairground building buzzed with activity and the cacophony of a country band blasting their test racket on the sound system. Cowboy musicians duct-taped wires out of the way and took their positions on stage. Their boots stomping time, they counted backwards to the downbeat and progressed through an opening medley. At the rear of the hall, first arrivals chatted at concession tables covered in red- and-white-checked, plastic tablecloths. Suzanne spoke to police-officer parents and friends, all the while aching with longing for the sight and sound of Taylor Armstrong. She was in awe of how thinking about him had come to consume so many of her waking hours.

Doug drew her along to show her off like a trophy to his friends on the force. She hadn't experienced that feeling since Larry Lansford took her to the high school prom, on a dare, as she later found out. She didn't like being on parade then, she hated it now.

"About time you two were out and about," said the matronly mother of a dispatcher, always the one who organized the food at police events. She'd taken on those responsibilities before her husband retired from the force years ago. *Is this me in thirty years?* Suzanne wondered. *No man of my own, just filling my hours serving brownies for other couples? I hope not!*

"Yep, finally got her out for a little dosey doe-ing," said Doug. He looked proud as a kid with a new pony.

Then, blessedly, Dee was at her elbow. Suzanne felt the comfort of an ally, or so she'd dared to hope. Taylor smiled. She was painfully aware of her hand in Doug's and how it must look to him.

"Powder room time," she said. "Doug, Taylor, we'll rejoin you two in a minute." She extracted her hand, met Taylor's eyes, and smiled up at him. "Thanks for making us a foursome."

"Believe me, the pleasure's going to be all mine," he included both twins in his sweeping glance and happy grin.

"For heaven's sake, Sis, it's not as though he had to bring the family dog."

"Dee, I didn't mean . . ."

"Oh, I know what you meant. Let's find the ladies room in this cow barn."

Doug's expression was dismal. "We just got here and haven't had anything to drink to make you two run to the potty so soon. What gives?"

Suzanne hurried away with Dee at her heels.

"You in some kind of a rush?"

"I'm uncomfortable with Doug. I mean *really* uncomfortable." She stopped Dee outside the restroom area. "I need a break from him and some advice."

"Already? What about?" Dee rifled through her bag for a pack of cigarettes. "You talk; I'll inhale. Thank goodness you don't make the smoking rules *here*, Susie."

"Somebody does. Remember you're in Utah, Honey." Suzanne pointed to a no-smoking sign and laughed.

"Damn!" Dierdre shoved the flowered box back into her bag. "Well, what kind of sisterly advice do you need?"

"You mean before I eat your cigarettes?" Suzanne stepped closer and whispered, "Doug says he's in love, wants to marry me, and he's coming on scary strong. I don't love him. He's been good to us, and I don't want to hurt his feelings, but I have no desire to marry him." It was out. She felt better.

"Got the hots for Taylor again, do you?" Dierdre said in full voice. Smiling, she folded her arms. "Good!"

Suzanne shushed her and went on in an exasperated whisper, "Taylor has nothing to do with what I don't feel for Doug."

"Maybe, maybe not. But I bet having the hunk around gets some old juices flowing and makes you sure of what you'd rather have."

"What should I do?"

"Tell Doug to cool it. Let him know straight out that you're not in love—at least not with him—and you don't want to marry him." Dierdre's voice was enviably firm.

"Simple as that?"

257

"Simple as that."

Suzanne sagged against the tile wall. "I don't think he'll take 'no' for an answer. I'm not up to justifying my lack of feeling for him, at least not every two minutes."

"What part of 'no' does he have trouble comprehending?"

They burst into hysterics. Dierdre opened the restroom door, saying over her shoulder, "Start by telling him you refuse to hold hands all night like a wet puppy."

"It's that obvious?" Suzanne, mortified, felt the flush crawl up her throat, caught sight of her reflection in the mirror and watched her color deepen. Her eyes locked with Dee's above the chipped-porcelain. The smell of industrial disinfectant permeated the stall-lined room.

Her twin combed her nails through her bob, swishing it to fall back against her cheeks. "You and Doug definitely have everyone buzzing with speculation."

"Oh, no. What must they think of me . . . with Steve just gone?"

"He isn't 'just gone' and they probably are quite happy for you."

Suzanne freshened her lipstick, since she'd been savagely chewing it off, and dropped the applicator into her purse. She closed it with a determined SNAP that made Dee jump. They giggled and returned down the drab concrete and tile hallway.

"So what took you so long?" Doug came to her side as soon as she and Dee reentered the blaring exhibition hall where dancing was well underway. *He's so intense tonight, a totally different approach. What on earth is his problem?*

"Let's get started." He grabbed her hand.

She pulled it free. "We'll walk my sister back to Taylor first. She doesn't know anyone here. We won't be so rude as to leave her standing alone. Have you seen him?"

"You're a big girl aren't you, Dierdre? Bet you can find him all by yourself. Time's a wastin', Sugar!" He pushed his hat back and opened his arms to Suzanne.

"Doug, we have all evening to dance. Please stop grabbing my hand."

Dierdre winked her support, just as Taylor joined them looking yummier to her than an ice cream sundae on a sweltering afternoon. It nearly killed her to watch him accept Dee's hand on his arm. Both of them seemed to be enjoying it.

"Good, tree man is here. Now you and me can get down to some good old-fashioned dry grinding!" Doug swung her into a clutching embrace before she'd had time to recover from his course remark. *Good heavens, is he going to be obnoxious all night?*

She congratulated herself for surviving the first three back-to-back dances with him singing the lyrics of the love songs into her ear, giving special emphasis on the most erotically literal phrases. His breath smelled of whiskey, which it hadn't earlier in the car. Her uneasiness increased.

"I thought they weren't serving liquor tonight," she ventured.

"They aren't. I had a few sips from one of the boy's flasks while you powdered that pretty nose of yours," he breathed into her hair. His hand, stroking her waist, moved lower.

She took her own from his shoulder and replaced his hand at her waist. "You're moving too fast for me, Doug." She leaned away from him and met his eyes so he could see she was serious.

He pulled her close. "I've held off as long as I could. I want you for my girl. Why are you still putting me off?"

"You're a good friend Doug, but I don't love you."

"Love, shit, you're not quite over Steve yet. You gotta give me a chance to show you how good it can be between us."

Taylor called above the din of dancers singing lustily to 'She Thinks My Tractor's Sexy.' "Hey, you two, get into this line dance. 'Boot Scootin' Boogie' is a team sport." Gesturing for them to join a row of dancers, who with few exceptions, looked professionally choreographed, he added, "Dierdre's giving lessons."

"Dee knows how to Western line dance?" Suzanne broke free and went to see for herself. "Where'd my city twin learn to be so country fancy, in high heels, yet. Dee?" She squeezed into line next to her twin and Taylor, watching Dee who beamed, obviously proud of herself for attracting quite a line of followers in the rows of dancers. Her undulating hips did a seductive roll and bump, followed smoothly with a kick turn. Appreciative whoops escaped from laughing men and women in front and behind her.

"Line dancing is a big deal on cruise ships," Dierdre chirped. "As a CD, I'm expected to know how to set the mood and the creativity."

"What's a CD?" asked Taylor, cross-stepping the vine down the floor to her left.

"Cruise Director," she and Dierdre said together, laughing.

Doug pulled Suzanne into line next to him. His voice was loud above the music, "If you want to line dance, you're gonna do it with me."

"You're giving a lot of orders tonight, Doug." She didn't like his domineering tone and whirled her skirt at him, kicking an extra beat for emphasis. She hadn't been dancing since the policeman's ball Christmas before last, when she and Steve had sat out all but the slow dances. This fast line-stepping was fun, and she could watch Taylor on the dance's every turn-and-follow move. Their eyes met several times. They smiled at one another, both returning to the fascination of watching Dierdre basking in the attention her sensuous and confident moves garnered. From the sidelines, men with and without dates gathered to clap and whoop in time with her. Too soon the dance was over. Suzanne dreaded fighting Doug off again.

He put an arm around her. She smelled his sweat and was repulsed by tobacco, alcohol, and cologne in stifling combination. She could hardly wait for the evening to be over and was positive she'd turn down the 'opportunity' to go for 'dinner and a toddy' as a foursome afterwards. If he didn't straighten up and lay off the alcohol, she'd refuse to ride home with him. Turning her attention to Taylor, she took in his graceful, easy hip and shoulder moves, and her heart beat faster than the music. *Will he ever ask me to dance the way he said he would?*

"They'll play one more before they take a break. Let's make it count," said Doug, pulling her close.

"Sorry, buddy. It's time we trade twins." Taylor rescued her by spinning her out of Doug's half hug and into his own arms. She felt a thrill of anticipation and twirled away as he spun her expertly into a sliding two-step. *Thank God*, she thought. *This is worth everything Doug's putting me through tonight.* She glimpsed Doug and Dierdre over Taylor's broad shoulder and felt a rush of relief when they danced away.

Focusing on Taylor's closeness held no contest to any other thought. His hands held hers lightly, and he led her through the steps with gentle pressure at the small of her back, leading with the palm of his upraised hand against hers. They flowed together effortlessly, gliding, turning, stepping. Wordlessly they moved as though no one else in the world mattered, and in truth for her they didn't. She allowed herself to be drawn close and felt the throb of the music underscore how it was the only place she ever wanted to be. What she remembered of dancing with Taylor as a college student made no comparison to the growing ardor she felt for him as a grown woman. The ripple of his body moving against hers, close but not too close, drove her senses wild. *If only I were his date tonight.*

"Listen to the words, Susie," he said, looking right into her eyes. "This is for us."

His meaning thrilled her. She focused on the lyrics of a George Straight ballad, heard snatches of the words and interpreted them to Taylor's implication they were for her from him. Some lines of the words floated away with the intensity of her feelings, others took root and made her swoon with happiness.

The Wind Remembers

Life could never be the same without you,
 Love was never really love without you,
Here beside you is where it's at,
 What do you say to that?

He twirled her away from him, flashed her a smile powerful enough to stop a train or her heart, and drew her close again. She realized she loved Taylor as wildly as a young girl and as deeply as a woman who had known a good and honest love with a man she respected. There would never be anyone else for her but the man who smiled at her now and moved rhythmically to the music. She tried to concentrate on the words streaming from the speakers above them and caught only scraps of phrases as she drank him in.

"You're always in my dreams," he whispered to her before rolling her out at arm's length, "I promise I'll never leave." He brought her against his thudding chest. She felt faint and snuggled against him for support and to fill her need of him. He mouthed the lyrics to her:

What do you say to that?
 My heart knows that this is real at last.

Could he mean every word? She wondered. *Why couldn't he do a Doug thing and just say loving meanings in his own words?* She felt the old nagging torment of fear that he'd never tell her he loved her. *Lord, Taylor, why won't you just say it! Will you always leave me wondering what you feel?* "Do you have... a special woman in your life?" She dared ask.

"That depends on you, Missy." He pulled her close enough to feel their hearts beating against each other.

His scent intoxicated her, made her feel heady with cologne and musky subtleties that were his own body essence. She couldn't get enough and couldn't think of a casual thing to say back to him.

"You appear to be Doug's property tonight."

"It's not what you think. The feelings aren't mutual, I assure you."

He laughed softly and brushed her forehead with a kiss. "Good!" he said, and tilted her head to his shoulder with his own. The song ended. "Thanks, Susie. You brought back a lot of fond memories . . . and gave me some special new ones."

"You, too," she said, reluctant to have it end. It was the most intimate conversation they'd ever had and her happiness felt boundless. Everything about the drab fairground hall seemed beautiful. The lead singer on stage seemed talking just to them when he promised another set in a few minutes after they took a break. Taylor kept a hand on her shoulder as they walked to the concession tables. Doug and Dierdre were surrounded by admirers finding out who Dee was. *Keep him busy, Honey,* she thought. *Better yet, trade me partners*. Taylor spoke easily with an old high-school classmate of his, wife of an officer she knew only by acquaintance. Too soon for her, Doug noticed her and came over. Suzanne sipped a diet cola and stayed close to Taylor.

"How's my girl?" he asked. "That sister of yours is a dazzler. The guys are asking plenty of questions about her."

"I'm not your girl, Doug," she sighed. The drain of maintaining her autonomy against his relentless assumptions about their future as a married couple wearied her.

"We'll see. I've got plans. You wait and see how you feel about me by the end of the evening." His arm slid around her waist, catching Taylor's attention.

"You horning in again, Jensen?" He said jovially, moving between them, setting down his cola. "You left me one dance in the first set. We're just getting reacquainted."

"Yeah," Doug said, "so I've noticed. Well, she's my date, so cool your jets, tree man."

"Oh, for heaven's sakes, Doug, I'm not a piece of boot leather you own and can fight over. We're here together as friends, period. I don't want to be rude but you're presumptions are not the way good friends treat one another."

Doug appeared surprised by her brush off and excused

himself in a huff. They watched him shoulder his way though the milling crowd, his gray Stetson bobbing toward the rear door. *Where's he going now?* She wondered. *I hope it's not for another whiskey.*

Dee rejoined them. "Your drooling entourage is going into withdrawal," joked Taylor.

The three of them laughed like best friends.

"You sisters are the prettiest women here," he said. "Been a long time since the three of us were at the same dance."

"Don't bring back unsavory memories," Dee said, accepting a brimming paper cup, her face clouding. She patted her face with a napkin. The band struck up a swing dance tune that drew much of the crowd onto the floor. The cloud disappeared.

"Dierdre knows I want another dance or two with you, Susie, but we'll wait here together until Doug returns to squire her around." Taylor's openness about having discussed his dance plans about her with her twin was a delightful surprise.

Dierdre grinned and shrugged. She patted Suzanne's arm.

"You two go on and dance before the vulture returns. I'll freshen up in the lady's room or wander outside for a cigarette. I am in dire need of some nicotine."

"You're a doll!" Suzanne hugged her and swung happily into Taylor's dance embrace. They glided to a spot near the door where he could sail her away from him in a twirl and pull her backwards against him, then turn her to his side with an arm across her shoulders and hers across the back of his waist. The sensuous movements of his back and hips made her feel as frenzied as she had in her basement studio.

She spied Doug coming in the door. He saw her and strode toward them.

"Guess you missed my point, Taylor." His voice was rough, possessive. Suzanne was shocked. He reeked of whiskey.

"She's my girl tonight. Better find the glamour twin and leave this dance to me."

"Oh get a grip, Doug." Suzanne's irritation turned to

anger. "For a man who promised me a fun evening, you're ruining it."

Doug tipped his Stetson to them, suddenly grinning sheepishly. "You're right, Suzanne, I'm not being much of a gentlemen. I can wait until the next dance." He stepped back and leaned against the wall to watch, looking uncomfortable. If he weren't behaving like such a pain, she'd have been able to conjure up some pity for him.

Taylor spun her into the crook of his arm and positioned her smoothly at his side. She smiled up at him. His handsome face glistened with perspiration. She sensed her own body moisture from the unaccustomed exertion of the dance and the excitement of being near him. Whenever she risked a glance in Doug's direction, he appeared sullen and as pouty as a child. The dance ended. Everyone clapped and whistled their approval. The next one was a slow waltz. Doug hurried over and asked Suzanne politely for a dance, exaggerating his best manners. Taylor smiled a farewell and turned away. *Probably going to find Dierdre,* she thought.

Feeling Doug pull her closer as the waltz progressed, she could tell he'd connected with more alcohol. It made her not only nervous, but angry. She decided to insist on driving back home with Dierdre and Taylor in her own truck, whether Doug wanted it that way or not.

"You like him, don't you?" He said, slurring 'don't' and 'you' together.

Feeling protective of Taylor and her private feelings about him, she wiggled away enough to breathe. "We're old friends."

"So you've said. Just how close of old friends were you?" He lifted her chin and stared her down.

She dropped her eyes, "That's really no one's business, Doug, certainly not yours. I've been honest with you about my feelings of only friendship toward you."

His jaw tightened. "Never mind," he said, "I'm getting the picture about where your feelings are." He pressed her to him until their hips touched. Instantly aware of the hard bulge in the front of his jeans, she recoiled.

"Let me go, Doug. You're drunk as a skunk." She twisted in his grasp and broke free. Suzanne moved through the dancers in the direction Taylor had gone. Couples in her way had no choice but to let her get by.

Doug caught up with her, gripped her by the shoulders, and turned her toward the door, pushing her ahead of him down the steps and out into the parking lot. Hurrying her in the manner she imagined he'd use with a captured fugitive, away from the lights near the building, he caught both her hands. They struggled. Relentlessly he pulled her along a row of vehicles and pinned her against a van, her hips trapped with his own; his throbbing erection insistent, bruising.

His mustached mouth greedily sucked at her throat, his hands pulled the elastic gathers down over her shoulders. He used his teeth to pull her blouse below her breasts, then with his lips fondled and bit at her through the lace of her bra. Shock, fear, revulsion coursed through her. She fought him, panicking when she found his strength so much greater than her own.

"Stop it, Doug, for God's sake stop it! You're drunk. Please don't, don't," she tried to raise a knee to his groin. He restrained her. She hated his strength and cried out in terror and humiliation. "Oh God, stop him, please somebody help me . . . HELP ME!"

He pressed his wiry-haired mouth against her voice box and squelched any further audible protest. His lips and tongue lapped at her breasts, explored her nipples. She found an ear and bit down until he cursed and raised his head, losing his hat. Her throat freed, she screamed. "HELP!"

Doug clamped a hand over her mouth.

She bit him and screamed "HELP" again.

He slapped her hard. She fell against the van grazing her head on a side mirror. Her head buzzed with the blow. She clutched at a door handle, missed it. Dazed, she slid to the ground and covered her ringing ears with both hands, trying to roll her body into a protective ball with her back to him.

Somewhere rows beyond them in the gravel, she heard someone running. *Please God, please let it be someone to help me.*

Struggling to stay conscious, she came to her knees, felt dizzy and collapsed, fighting nausea and tingling blackness.

"S-sorry," Doug babbled. "Just wanted a little kiss. Want you to feel my love for you. Want to show you how good it will be for us." He stood above her.

She stayed crouched too vulnerable to expose her face or her body to more humiliation and pain. Everything seemed to her to be happening in slow motion, like a bad dream when you try to move out of danger and nothing works. Suspended in time, she wondered how to get away without being hit again, or raped. She thought of the children, of returning to them unscathed physically. Her heart hammered. She forced her head to clear enough to outwit him. With the alcohol he'd become someone she didn't know. Footsteps in the stones nearby gave her hope.

"Suzanne, Suzanne!" *Taylor.*

Is it Taylor calling me? She raised her head, called out, "Taylor I'm . . ."

Doug squatted near and clamped a hand over her mouth.

"Jesus, what have I done?" He pulled her into his arms and lifted her face with his free hand, hushing her, keeping one hand firmly over her lips. "Baby, I'm *so* sorry." He brushed at her tears, smoothed her hair.

She struggled to turn her face away into his palm, to bite him if she could to make him let go, while fighting a blackout.

"Suzanne, where are you?"

It IS Taylor! She whimpered and tried harder to push herself free. The silhouetted shape of a man approached behind Doug. *Taylor!* Grateful, she slumped in relief, pulling at her blouse to cover herself. Her face burned with shame.

"What in hell are you doing, you sorry son of a bitch?!"

Taylor yanked Doug aside, gathered Suzanne up, and lifted her limp body.

"Good Lord, her face is bruised and bleeding! I'll deal with you later, Jensen. If you've hurt her bad, so help me God I'll come back and take you apart with my bare hands! I don't care if you are a pathetic excuse for a cop!"

"Don't know what got into me . . . wouldn't hurt her . . . she'll be all right . . . wouldn't hurt her."

Taylor left him blubbering like a baby in the gravel. He carried Suzanne through a gathering crowd, crooning words of comfort to her.

"I'm a medic," said a man hurrying toward them. Suzanne struggled to make everything come into focus and for her ears to stop ringing.

"Stop, Taylor. Help me stand and walk."

He halted, released her legs and helped her gain her balance. She inhaled the night air deeply and struggled with her blouse to get it back up on her shoulders. Feeling a trickle at her top lip, she touched it gingerly and realized her nose was bleeding and her face was swelling.

"Bring her inside to the light where I can check her over. What the hell happened, she fall down or something?" The medic put an arm around her.

The two men lifted her off her feet through the doorway and set her down inside at a table on a hastily brought folding chair. He checked her pulse and felt her head, discovering a rapidly forming goose egg. Suzanne groaned at the pressure of his probing fingers. Her stomach rolled with nausea at the pain which seemed to be everywhere.

"Well, she's got a doozy of a knot on her temple and there'll be a sizable bruise on that cheek bone by morning, but other than and a bloody nose her vitals are good. Her pretty nose doesn't appear to be broken."

"Thank God," Taylor took the wet napkin he was offered and wiped her face. His touch was tender, his eyes full of concern. "The bastard," he said, under his breath. "I'll press charges with you, Sweetheart."

Dierdre arrived through the stomping dancers, met eyes

with Suzanne and dropped to her side. "My good god, Suze, what happened?"

"Doug. . . Doug. . ." Suzanne couldn't bring herself to say how violated she felt. "We were right about there being a part of 'no' he doesn't understand. . . ." She tried to laugh and choked on it, bursting into tears of relief and embarrassment that streamed down her swollen cheeks. The welt of Doug's slap rose from jawbone to brow. She was appalled at the realization she'd become the pitiful center of a growing group drifting away from the dancing to come and gawk in concern at her.

"Let's get her home, Taylor." Dierdre's hands smoothed Suzanne's hair tenderly.

"Where's Jensen?" someone asked. "She came with him."

"Sobering up," came someone else's answer behind them. "I think he got a little too frisky with his buddy's widow."

"Damn. You don't say."

"Hush, Joe. Mrs. Price is embarrassed." The brownie maker's voice was kind.

"You okay enough to make it to the car, Sis?" Dee hugged her gingerly.

"Why would he treat me like that?" Suzanne said. "He's an animal. I never imagined he could be so brutal. I don't ever want him around me or my children again!"

"Of course not, Susie." Dierdre wrapped Suzanne's shawl around her and held her hand, patting it as if her twin were a bewildered child.

"I want to go home, Dee. Thank heaven Greg and Mitzi won't be there to see me like this."

"It's okay, Honey. It's okay," Dee repeated, shaking her head. "My God, I can't believe Doug would force himself on you, drinking or not. I'm so sorry. We should never have left you alone with him. You tried to tell me how you felt about how he was acting. It's all my fault he hurt you."

Suzanne rose to her feet with all the dignity she could muster, smiled with determination at the concerned and gossiping faces, moved with the support of her sister and grim-faced Taylor back out the door and into the night.

At the row of cars, Doug's buddies were walking him to his truck. His bony shoulders slumped. His eyes downcast to the gravel, his fine Stetson didn't sit rakishly anymore. Suzanne looked away. For the first time, she felt no pity for anyone but herself.

Bo Rodman

~ Wednesday the 18th of June

"Finally somebody's cuttin' me a fuckin' break!" Bo stepped over the doorsill of the Shooting Star onto the boardwalk that fronted Utah's oldest continuously operating saloon. Frank, close on his heels, smoked a thin, black cigar, which he left in his mouth to speak. They stepped on down to street level in the deserted upper Wasatch valley town that served skiers in winter and boaters, water skiers and bikers in summer. Laughter and pool-game talk filtered out into the night.

"The buyer's picky, Bo. He wants top-quality falcons, no foot disease, no evidence of broken beak, damaged feathers, bumblefoot, neglect or abuse." The reddish-amber end of the dark cigar glowed while Frank sucked on it. "She wasn't looking as good as she should the other day. You don't care for her proper. Show her to me now, so I can e-mail my connections that she meets their standards, *if* she does."

He talks like some professor up the college. Last thing I want to do is to get in the back of this truck tonight, with a rug full of woman. Better be dark enough out here; gotta pull it off. Bo yanked up the rear window and kept his flashlight on the hawk, careful to leave the tailgate up and the roll of carpet obscured. "Check her out for yourself."

Frank loosened the traces that held the hood secure to the falcon's head. "Lower the light, give her a chance to accustom her eyes to the dark. Play the light on her feet."

Bo did as he was told, illuminating the perch.

"Her talons still look healthy." Frank examined the bird's wing feathers, her tail . . "Screech . . . Screech," the gyr cried out and shook herself.

"I'm feeling leg and wing joints for signs of injury. Her keel bone is too prominent. She's underweight. I wouldn't hurt you girl. What a beautiful specimen you are." Frank talked around his stogie. "She's spending too long in this camper shell." He retied her hood. "She'll do though."

They closed and latched the rear tailgate window.

Bo turned off his flashlight and chucked his sandwich scraps through the driver's window to Tracker, keeping the bag for later. "So what's he willing to pay for my trouble to deliver her to the Canadian border at that place you circled on the Montana map?"

"I'll give you a $300 advance now on the $1,500. You'll get the remaining $1,200 from the buyer when you deliver in three days; 3:30 A.M. Four o' clock he said will be too late, deals off."

Bo held his hand out for the money, felt three bills, and decided against checking their value by flashlight. He folded and pocketed the money. "What's your cut?"

Frank chuckled, blew smoke, tucked his wallet back into his jeans. "Reasonable," he said. "You wanted me to take this falcon off your hands. I want to see she goes to some falconer who respects her needs and gives her the attention she deserves. That's what I've arranged. The guy's only slightly more than a novice, so he'll be thrilled with her. That's all you need to know. My Coronna's getting warm. If I don't get back in there, Hunnie will be out here looking for me. The less she knows the better. You clear on how to find that Montana farm on the border?"

Bo nodded his head. "I'll find it. Thanks, buddy. By the way, you been run to earth yet by that sexy lawyer from California with a warrant for your arrest on some fraudulent dealings?"

"What the hell are you talking about, Rodman?" Frank's teeth lost their grip on his cigar. He stooped for it in the dust at their feet.

"She came by the Last Tangle lookin' for you. 'Course we never let on we knew you." Bo could tell Frank was nervous by the way he stuffed the stogie back between his teeth with barely a dust brush off and bit it near through.

"I haven't had any California dealings in years. Sounds like mistaken identity to me." He spit to the side. "See you don't screw up this deal of ours or I'll deny I ever saw you and the gyr." Frank climbed the wooden steps that creaked under his weight. He pushed on the swinging door and was swallowed in the noise and smoke of the saloon.

Bo climbed behind the wheel and received lapping kisses from Tracker. "Good ol' boy. You like the taste of burger."

Moonlight broke through the cloud cover.

"Guess we'll hang onto that falcon after all, ole fella. Just when I was gonna waste her tonight." The dog licked his fingers and whined for more. Bo gave him the steak bones to chew on the floor and tossed the empty bag the bar maid'd brought him from the kitchen trash, out the window. The breeze picked it up and tumbled it ghost-like across the parking lot.

He rammed a pinch of chew into his cheek, checked to make sure the three bills were hundreds, turned off the ceiling light in the cab, and threw the truck into reverse.

"Things are looking up for old Bo Rodman, and it's just the beginning. We'll both be eatin' steak before long ol' boy."

His belly full, his spirits high, Bo drove down the winding canyon road and up the bench again toward the Price place to get his hands on Rehma's kids' $50,000 or to force the Price woman to give him the key to the bank box, if she didn't keep that much dough around. He'd go up from her place along the dirt road to the sheep camp. It was time to let the gyr feed and be noisy away from where anybody would hear or give a damn, *if* she would eat. He needed a place to hide the rug too.

While the falcon ate he'd get rid of the other female he'd

no more use for—some place nobody would find her. Then he'd either take the money from the Price house, and the falcon and head for Montana, taking his time for a couple of days, or start out after he made the Price woman get the money out of the bank in the morning. That was a lot of thinking for Bo. His head felt full. Tracker chomped happily on his T-bones.

Rat

~ Wednesday the 18th of June

Rat felt damn lucky he'd heard twigs snapping after sneaking around back to catch some negligee action at the Price place. A few lights were on, but nobody was home. At first he thought he'd biked all the way up the bench for nothing, but finding out he wasn't alone, figured he might as well hang around and learn what somebody else was up to. Dropping behind a pile of cottonwood logs, he avoided being caught in the bobbing beam of what he was surprised to see was Bo's flashlight. He held his breath while a log was rolled under a window and upended. Bo smashed the glass pane with the butt-end of his flashlight, knocked around the edges, and climbed inside.

As soon as his ass was over the sill, Rat high-tailed it in the dark for his bike hidden in the cattails by the irrigation ditch. He struggled with the urge to make a break for it down the bench, but knowing he'd be a sitting duck on his bike in Bo Rodman's headlights for more than a mile to town, he decided to sit it out. Getting forced over by Bo, who had a mean streak ten times wider than his nephew Blue's, made him shrink from having to defend what he was doing up there in the dark so far from home. There were no excuses except the truth.

Now that Rat'd caught the SOB red-handed, Bo would be paranoid, more even than when he and Blue helped him cut into the cottonwood and clean up the mess, before the Price mother he wanted to scare came home. The others got away clean in the truck, but he'd barely had time to take cover behind the lilac bush with his bike when she'd pulled in the drive with her kids. Fortunately, hiding where he wasn't supposed to be was something Rat was good at.

Now, after waiting in the weeds for what felt like an eternity, he heard Bo coming back through the gravel, then the weeds, his muttered curses moving out ahead of him in the still air. His arms were full of stuff he'd taken. He passed by within a few yards, avoiding the soggy ditch banks, and limped up-hill to a grove of trees to his camper truck. Rat breathed a little easier and crouched deeper, muddying his high tops, feeling the suck of the goo on his socks, hating the cloying earth smells he knew would probably never come out of his hot Nikes. Heart hammering, he expected the sweep of the truck lights, prepared for it, and heard the engine and the grind of gears, but was surprised as hell when Bo didn't use his head lights. Instead of driving down toward town, the truck turned up the mountain.

Rat raised himself and parted the cattails, staring after Bo who switched on the lights once he left pavement for gravel road. There was nothing up there but sheep camp and beyond it the national forest. What was Bo up to? Rat's curiosity won out. He followed when he felt it was safe to not be picked up in Bo's rear-view mirrors.

Winded after the up-hill bike ride, Rat warily tracked Bo's truck through the wild brush above the sheep camp, keeping well behind him along the abandoned and overgrown national forest fire-break road. Something big was coming down. He could feel it in his gut. His gut was never wrong.

He'd kept his bike light turned off and now waited in a stand of quaking aspens not twenty-five yards from where Bo's truck rattled to a stop, headlights beaming into the rock shelf a truck's length beyond where he parked in the oak brush.

"Stay, Tracker." Bo shut the cab door. The dog whined with his long ears drooping over the lowered window on the driver's side facing away from Rat.

Rat feared to go closer or the dog would get wind of him. He heard the rasping response of the tailgate release, followed moments later by the cry of a hawk. Bo swore loudly, fiddled with something in his cooler, the shrieking subsided. There was a rustle of something heavy being dragged over the bed liner of the truck. Rat strained his eyes into the dark behind the tailgate, but could see nothing distinct in the deep shadows.

At last, Bo came into the light of his truck beams, body bent with the weight of a rolled-up rug over his shoulder. He staggered forward, angling his body and his burden this way and that, limping through the trees mumbling to himself.

Rat shrank into the shadows, his skin crawling with raised goose flesh and running with the sweat of his biking exertion, nervousness, and prolonged apprehension. His heart hammered in terror at being found out by Bo, who'd as soon beat him to a pulp as look at him. The cowboy was nobody to mess with. *Why did I follow him?*

But he knew why. He was driven to know what others would not. He sucked in his breath slowly, let it out in even streams between his chubby lips, and watched the secretive man between the ominous troops of black tree trunks that conspired with whatever dark business was going on. Rat made it an art to spy on people and was usually well rewarded. He settled into the familiar waiting drill with anticipation, licking his lips.

He'd have something on Blue's uncle now, something F-ing awesome to leverage for power with—maybe even with the cops if he ever needed it. Secrets were power. He'd used their trade potential before.

Bo paused at the rock wall, hurriedly chose a crevice level with his knees and lowered the carpet roll. He wedged it into the space he'd found and shoved it tight with the boot heel of his good leg. Straightening, he gathered rocks and thrust them in along the carpet roll, lodging them wherever they would stay. His voice rose with his efforts.

"God damn son of a bitch! Why didn't you get a hold of those kids and that money a long time ago, you dumb bitch?

Where in hell does she keep that money? The bank? Is she that smart and careful or wuz the whole damn story made up from the start?"

When he finished, the carpet was so well camouflaged someone walking by wouldn't detect it. "That'll do alright." Bo broke a live branch off a shrub oak and turned back into the light.

Rat froze in place, closing his eyes to slits lest their shine betray him. He knew his eyes were not the right size nor space apart to be recognized for anything but human. Spooky as Bo could be, Rat didn't care to be shot for the hell of it. Whipping the underbrush with the branch, Bo roughed up the dirt where he'd walked, backing away from the rock ledge and into his truck lights. His long shadows with their waving arms danced a heathen ritual into the trees, his cursing like a blood-thirsty chant.

"One thing's sure, Baby, I won't be needin' you for nothin' no more, but I got a plan for your kids. It'll only take one, but two's better. What's a little 'kid borrowing' on top uh murder? It ain't nothin' to me no more. I got one chance left for that money, and I'm takin' it. If there never was no money, that little woman'll find some for me to get yer kids back. Sure as hell, she will."

Bo tossed the branch in the weeds and hurried back to the truck. He fiddled with the hawk in the dark, slammed the tailgate shut and backed out the way he'd come. The smell of exhaust fumes drifted through the woods. Then . . . all was quiet.

Rat switched on his key-chain penlight and crept forward. *What did Bo hide in the rock shelf? Did he really knock somebody off and stash a body?*

He reached the rock wall, scanned it with his tiny spot of light, found the rug and felt along it to an open end. He dislodged a few stones and reached his hand inside. At first he was unable to feel anything but rug ribbing, then as he was about to yank the whole thing out to unroll it in the woods, he felt something soft. "What in hell?!"

He drew his hand out quickly, as if he'd touched electric

wire and been shocked. He'd touched skin and human hair. His mouth went dry. His pulse roared in his ears, drowning out the quietness in the woods, pushing aside every thought except grasping hair. *A body for damn sure!* He felt along the bundle of rug to its far end, tugged the flap loose and rolled it back on itself. There in his small light, a shoe sole, a woman's polished toenail. He crammed the rug back into the crevice, skittered back to his bike, and made his way to the road his pulse racing like his hide was on fire.

Far down the bench he could make out the receding twinkle of a pair of taillights, the left one bobbing and rakish. Bo's truck. He coasted after them for town, letting his bike wheels do the work, while his legs and lungs took a breather. Only his heart hammered his horror and the excitement of his pent-up secret.

Johnny Carlisle

~ Wednesday the 18th of June

Johnny lay awake in the motel long after there was nothing left on local TV but shopping channels and infomercials. He flexed his fingers, tired from hours of target practice with the 38. The surge of adrenaline had hit him that afternoon when he could aim and hold a steady site long enough to get two shots off, without losing his balance at the recoil. The excitement left him pumping alertness even after his last dose of painkillers and seizure medication before turning in for the night. He felt ready now, knew he could accomplish his mission.

Come morning, he'd go to the Iron Pump on the pretext of a much-needed workout, not altogether untrue, and find out where he could locate Bo Rodman. He'd tail him until he got him alone and found out what he'd done with Felon. After that, he'd have the pleasure of depositing a handful of bullets into Rodman, slow-like, while the bastard begged for mercy the way he remembered begging, sobbing for his falcon and himself. In repayment—with interest— he sure as hell would give Bo none.

Taylor Armstrong

~ Wednesday the 18th of June

Taylor drove Suzanne's Blazer into a parking space near his mobile home, relieved to see his own truck still boasted an unmarred new paint job and company logo. He'd been paranoid lately and determined after tonight to anticipate trouble a little better. His chest hurt from the effort of holding onto the patience it took to care for Suzanne and get her and her sister back home safely, instead of finding Jensen and beating the living shit out of him. He cut the engine. The silence swallowed them for a moment.

"You two okay?" he ventured into the dark void of sadness and shock.

"I'm feeling much better, Taylor," Suzanne paused. "I hate to be a bother, but could I use your bathroom? I'm so nauseated, I'm not sure I can make it home without being sick."

"Sure, you bet." He helped her slide across and out the driver's side while Dierdre got out on the passenger's side, fumbled with her lighter and managed to get a hesitant cigarette going between trembling fingers.

"I'll wait outside by your door. I'm in desperate need of a smoke."

"I . . . I'll hurry," Suzanne stammered, shaking, even in her shawl.

Taylor feared she might be in shock after the strain of Doug's assault and nothing to eat all evening. *God damn Jensen. No wonder pushy cops get the name 'pig.' I'd like nothing better than to smash your mustache into the nearest hog wallow.*

He opened the aluminum door and held it for her, touched by her brave vulnerability and incredible dignity. How he could have imagined walking away from her in any time of trouble amazed him, because tonight had convinced him he loved her enough to be there for her no matter what. There'd never been a woman he admired, loved, or desired more. Suzanne stepped inside on the throw rug his mother had crocheted for him. He watched, his hand supporting her nearest elbow, while she looked around in the light he switched on for which way the bathroom was.

"To your left, first door," he said softly, catching sight of her swollen face welted worse now in the shape of Jensen's hand. *She'll cry when she looks in that mirror. Hell, I feel like crying myself.*

"Thanks." She moved away on her own down the narrow hall.

He watched the door close, hoped he'd put the toilet seat down, went to the sink and washed his hands. Drying them, he thought of a ginger ale he kept in the refrigerator for his mom's visits, brought it out, popped it, and poured some of it into a jelly glass. He didn't know what else to do but wait for Suzanne's return. The bathroom door opened and she came out, Kleenex to her nose, damp face free of make-up.

"I rinsed my face and used your towel, hope that's okay," she said, looking as betrayed and innocent as a child.

His heart ached. "Susie, I'm so sorry."

He moved to take her in his arms. She stood still in his embrace. "You need some sugar to stave off shock. I've poured you a ginger ale, pretty easy to digest, even on an upset tummy." He heard himself speaking in the tone and words he might have used for Mitzi, wanted to take it back and treat her like a grown woman who'd been brutally wronged. It was too late.

"That was thoughtful of you, Taylor." She took the glass; the contents quivered on the way to her mouth. He watched her sip tentatively with puffy lips, then swallow slowly until the little glass was empty. He moved to refill it.

She shook her head. "I want to go home now." She walked to the door, looked into the tiny living room, hesitated, looked at him and again at the far wall. "Is it really that painting I gave you for Christmas years ago?"

"Yes," his voice was soft. "I've carried it just about all over America. It always makes me think of . . . our good times."

"Oh, Taylor. I'm so much better at painting now. That one's pretty primitive." She looked at him, her eyes shining. "I didn't imagine you'd thought of me anymore."

"I love you, Susie." He stroked her cheek ever so gently with the tips of two fingers. Tears formed at her lids and rolled in streams that bumped over the swollen places before running underneath her chin and down her throat.

"Are you just saying that . . . now . . . because . . . because you feel sorry for me? I couldn't bear it if you pitied me, Taylor. After everything else, I just couldn't bear it." She looked at him with her heart in her eyes, guileless as Mitzi, her world in shreds.

"Oh, Suzanne, don't you know I've always loved you?"

"No, Taylor, I don't know that." She managed a crooked smile and sniffled into the tissue. "That's the first time you've ever told me you loved me. I wanted to hear it."

"I'm sorry. I always thought you knew. . . Is that why?"

She nodded.

"Can we get beyond my stupidity?" He spread his arms toward her and waited, hoping she'd forgive him for all the times he should've told her, years ago when he was too damned young to know what a woman needed.

She lifted her arms while he gathered her against himself like a fragile statue, which gave way to softness. He felt her yield herself to him. The shudders became sobs for the briefest time, until with his hand rubbing her back her tension relaxed. She blew her nose, gently, into the crumple of wet paper in her hand. He supposed it hurt her nose and lifted her face to see if she'd set it to bleeding again. It was fine. He smiled at her. "You are so beautiful, Missy, even now."

"I love you, Taylor, even more than I used to." Her smile wobbled. Fresh tears threatened at the corners of her eyes.

He smiled and nodded his acceptance of their confession of love to each other. "Time to get you home to a safe and warm bed. You and Dee can lead, I'll follow."

"Oh, that's not necessary," she protested, bucking up, which made him chuckle.

"Humor me, Brat." He turned her toward the door and lifted his truck keys off the hook where they hung by the thermostat.

"You remember calling me that?" She laughed into his shoulder.

"I remember *everything*." In moments he'd tucked her into her passenger-side seat belt and chucked the keys at Dierdre already behind the wheel, exhaling the last of her cigarette out the lowered window. "I'll follow," he said, brooking no argument.

"You're coming home with us?" Dierdre asked in surprise.

"Let's just say I'll sleep better if I know you two are all safe and sound. Besides, I'm too wired to wind down for a while. If you weren't so exhausted, Suzanne, I'd insist on a hospital check up and a trip to the police station to file an assault complaint against our fine, upstanding Officer Jensen."

"Then, I'm glad I'm so exhausted. I don't care if I ever see or hear from him again—for *any* reason."

He could see her mood was lifting and the shaking was over, not that he could say the same about her twin.

Ever the cool and collected one, Dierdre appeared more withdrawn and anxious than he'd ever seen her. Glamour floated out the window with her cigarette smoke. "It's all my fault," she whispered to him. "All my fault."

Suzanne Price

~ Wednesday the 18th of June

After Dee unlocked the door, Suzanne entered and knew something was amiss. A pain in her stomach signaled danger. The house was quiet. The landing light she'd left on to the basement stairs illuminated the light switch to the kitchen. She flipped it on before stepping through the doorway. The unexpected mess on the floor took a moment to comprehend. Her sister and Taylor entered behind her, expressing their own shock in gasps and curses of surprise. Cabinet drawers had been emptied onto counters and linoleum. She moved toward the swinging door. Taylor rushed to step in front of her.

"You two stay put!" he whispered fiercely, pushed the door slowly, listened, and glided away from them into the hall, allowing the door to close silently against his hand.

Clutching each other the twins strained to hear his footsteps going cautiously from room to room. In a few moments that seemed to crawl by, he returned. Dee looked as relieved as Suzanne felt.

"Your back bedroom window's been smashed in and drawers in your bedrooms and in the den are overturned like these in the kitchen. Somebody's been here looking for something. Any idea what could be so almighty important?" His voice reflected the anxious look on his face. "I don't think it was a search for drugs or pain killers because the medicine cabinet's okay."

Suzanne hated seeing Taylor worried again. Slumping against the doorframe, her emotions drained away into an emptiness that reminded her of the hours after Steve's death. Her heart felt as if a cold fist squeezed it. She raised a hand and rubbed where it hurt until she could speak because the thought of Greg and Mitzi home with a sitter if she hadn't taken Diane up on her offer of an overnight, gave her the shivers. At that thought, Suzanne didn't know if her imagination was working overtime or if it had just dawned on the truth. The last piece of the puzzle of harassment in her home slid into place.

"The children's money," she said. "Someone's after the children's $50,000. Doug and Rehma are the only ones who know about it."

"Maybe not," Dierdre and Taylor chimed.

The three of them stood looking at one another until he went to the phone. Suzanne listened while Taylor reported the break-in to police headquarters and stipulated that he wanted any officer *other than* Doug Jensen to come immediately. He called Randy; told him to bring his hunting rifle and the dogs and join him for the night.

At Suzanne's suggestion, he explored the basement, returning with the disassembled parts to Steve's scoped hunting rifle and a box of shells. Suzanne sent him back for Steve's handgun case, opened the combination lock and counted the bonds on the kitchen table. "All here," she said. "They didn't find what they were after."

Sinking into a kitchen chair, Suzanne let Dee wrap her in a blanket, tuck it around her knees, and was surprised at her offer to fix a cup of herb tea. Deep-down tired, Suzanne felt a surge of love for her and smiled at the irony of her twin actually boiling water on someone else's behalf for comfort, not to wheedle for something she wanted.

Doug Jensen

~ Wednesday the 18th of June

His buddies gone, Doug came around to sober, stretched out on his den couch. Stomach raw, head throbbing, he hadn't felt so bad since he and Steve, horses spooked by a cougar, had hiked out of the canyon with a body bag, following a two-day search for an armed murderer who'd escaped from county jail.

Only this time every miserable feeling he had, every humiliation he'd experienced tonight and would experience in the days to come, was nobody's fault but his own. He'd be damned lucky if Suzanne or Taylor didn't press charges. He could see his job on the force and reputation as a good cop slip away, his retirement gone, his mother mortified in front of her Church friends, and them aghast at how far her only son had fallen.

His fear a pulsing thing in his chest, Doug's mind reeled with the replay of what he's done to Suzanne and how he'd been found out in front of his friends, in front of tree man. He'd never wanted a woman so bad, never felt more deserving of Suzanne's love, nor more frustrated that she wanted Taylor more than him.

He allowed a glimmer of gratitude Armstrong hadn't knocked him around for roughing up Suzanne. He'd had way too much to drink, nearly two fifths of whiskey, had known it was stupid as he did it, couldn't seem to stop himself. God, he'd blown it, blown it so bad there was no fixing it. He couldn't remember much of how it all happened so fast, but he couldn't stop seeing her dark eyes, wide with fear and confusion, after he slapped her.

I slapped her hard! I could have broken her jaw, maybe even did. Oh, God Almighty, I'm one low son of a bitch.

He couldn't believe he'd hit her, made her cower in fear of him grappling in the gravel, her trying to fight him off. He remembered enjoying being stronger, willing her to let him have his way. Even now, the feel, the smell of her soft breasts and lips filled his brain.

When his gaze came to rest on a picture of he and Steve holding up a fine seven-point buck, taken on their last hunting trip together, Doug reached the pit of his wretched self-loathing. He'd let Steve down in the worst way, chosen his own desires above his promise to his best friend to care for his wife and kids. Knowing how low he'd sunk buckled him. Throbbing head in his hands, he sobbed. At last, he lay back exhausted, awash in the pain of his remorse and his loss of Suzanne, ashamed to the depths of his soul.

The phone rang and went on ringing while he considered the gun cabinet. He heard the click when the phone went to answering machine, listened dully to Janet's voice from the dispatch desk.

"Doug, thought you'd want to know. There's been another break-in at the Price place. Suzanne wanted anybody *but you* to come, must not have wanted to bother you, again. Lopez and Reed have responded. Everybody's okay, nobody home when it happened. G'night."

Sick anew that he wasn't ever going to be Suzanne's knight in shining armor again, Doug kissed everything he'd ever really wanted good-bye, all the way to sorry hell.

Chapter Thirteen

Raining Consequences

Suzanne Price

~ Thursday the 19th of June

Suzanne awoke to the sound of dogs baying and the hum of distant voices beyond the garage, down by the irrigation ditch. She felt tired in a deep place within, hauling herself up over banks of boulders, coming from a far place to consciousness. The tiredness had little to do with the physical and had not been alleviated by a sleeping tablet and seven restorative hours of somewhat sound rest.

The air felt unusually muggy for Farr. *Like the night of the storm*, it occurred to her. Flat light seeped in through the curtains. Only by similar effort to her own, did it awaken in this room. Her breasts and upper arms were tender to the touch. Sitting up, she gingerly fingered the swelling and the soreness in her jaw and was relieved that the puffiness at least had been reduced considerably from the night before. She wished the evening that ended in a nightmare had been only a dream.

Warm thoughts of dancing in Taylor's arms melted as she remembered Doug fondling her, breathing whiskey over her mouth and her eyelids, heard his husky voice, slurred words, and felt his wet mustache, his probing tongue—all too real, too close.

She whipped off the covers and escaped from the bed to leave thoughts of him behind. Crossing the room to the mirror, her worst fears were confirmed. The side of her face bore an ugly bruise that for a few days no amount of make-up would hide. What would she tell the kids? The children . . . she looked at the clock and watched the digital read-out roll to 10:21. She'd told Diane she'd pick up the kids by 10:00 this morning for sure. What would she tell Diane, let alone Greg and Mitzi?

Greg would never believe Doug had gotten drunk and hit her. Hit her? *My god, if we'd been in a more private place, he probably would have raped me. How could he? What was he thinking? He wasn't thinking, at least not about anything but his own immediate crotch.*

She laughed out loud at how her thoughts were running more like Dee's than her usual self. The sound of her wry laughter in the quiet room began to dispel surreal vestiges of the night before. Remembering arriving home to find her house in disarray when Taylor had followed them, thank God, she chose to focus on the support she'd received from him and her twin. The words "I love you," she'd heard from Taylor at last. She was awake, happy, wary, and prepared for anything—or so she hoped.

For a moment she waffled while considering telling Greg and Mitzi some made-up story about her face and why she wasn't going to allow Doug around them any more. *That would only complicate everything. The story would come out all botched and worse in the end.* She settled on telling the truth and living with the consequences. Though she hadn't caused Doug's behavior, she regretted not taking her intuitive misgivings about him more seriously. She should have cut Doug off long ago, had been a fool with no one but herself to blame for letting Greg down. How dare Doug use a friendship with a little boy—who'd lost his daddy—to further his own ends in a relationship? Probably from the beginning, it had all been a sham to get her to himself! His deceitfulness appalled her. Greg would just have to get over Doug. The man was weak and vile. She was glad Steve would never know how far his best friend had fallen.

If Pastor Spahn had been correct, Gregory would feel safe and loved enough to be angry with her. She'd probably bear the brunt of his anger toward Doug and herself. His healing would take time she could give him. Now with an attorney of her own convinced of her ability to win sole custody of both kids, she felt powerful. Where ordinarily a supplicating prayer would have formed, her mind seemed to stretch to a new place of gratitude. Emotional weariness lifted. Released and strengthened with the validation of her instincts about Doug, she'd survive this blow to her naiveté, and so would Greg.

"I'm a little late," she said aloud, "but I am growing up! Thank you, God, for new awareness and the strength of truth. Thank you also for Dee and Taylor. I believe you wanted them both to be with me and the kids during all these bad things."

After her shower, a towel twisted turban-style on her head, she searched for Dierdre and spied her through the kitchen window, talking in the yard with Taylor who stacked wood while they chatted. His nephew, Randy, held rein on a pair of eager hunting dogs nosing at Taylor's pant legs. Young Officer Lopez, back again this morning for a full-light check of footprints and other signs of who'd broken into the house, tucked a notepad into her pocket. Officer Reed, on the car phone, motioned for Lopez. Suzanne felt wonderfully relieved that whatever evidence remained of last night's burglar was in someone else's more capable hands. Carrying a banana back to the bedroom, she peeled and nibbled at it as she went, dressed and dried her hair. She polished off the last of the fruit, brushed her teeth and applied make-up, gave that up, and carried her shoulder bag and keys out to join everyone but the officers, who had departed. The air was unsettling. The dogs sniffed at horrific organic smells, the predictable odors often preceding a storm front drifting in from Great Salt Lake.

Her eyes were on the scudding clouds obscuring the upper peaks of the mountains when she descended the back stairs. Taylor's voice came from the woodpile.

"Well, you look much better after some rest than when we tucked you in last night." He moved to hug her, dropped his arm and stepped back, appearing unsure of how to act toward her. His eyes searched her face.

She looked up at him, "You, on the other hand, look as rugged as a lumber jack who spent the night playing cops and robbers and protecting us damsels from further distress." On tiptoe, she kissed his chin and sealed it with the pressure of two fingers, reading his pleased reaction all the way to her toes.

"At your service, Ma'am," he said, catching her fingers before they left his face. He squeezed them quickly and let them drop.

Dierdre embraced her. "Pretty good camouflage job, Sweetie. Doesn't she look great?"

"She always looks great to me," said Taylor. "Always did."

Randy untangled leashes behind him and added, "Morning, Ms. Price. The dogs are hungry, so if you're all okay, they've finished their tracking; we'll head out for now." The yipping and whining became frantic.

"Wait. Did you and the dogs find anything?" Suzanne wanted the facts, regardless of how disturbing the news.

"They found evidence of two men," said Dee.

Taylor added, "Both sets of foot prints, the cowboy boots and the basketball sneakers are big enough for men. With the size of teenagers now days, who can be sure?"

"Looks like the one wearing treads came by bike," said Randy. "My dogs tracked those sneakers from the broken window and the woodpile to the bike tracks in the muddy ditch bank. Seems more like something a kid would do than a man."

"The boots from your window lead to that stand of scrub

and some truck-tire tracks," said Taylor. "You remember the dogs tracked a scent through the house last night. It matches the one for the boots. No finger prints anywhere, though. We checked the scent of the sneakers to see if there were any traces inside the house, but the dogs couldn't find it, meaning only the man in Western boots came in."

Dierdre bounced with excitement. "So, Sweet Cheeks, you and I and the kids are going camping! We are all out of reasons to stick around this spooky place." Dee's exultant tone made Suzanne laugh.

"If I didn't know better, I'd think you staged this elaborate hoax yourself, just to get me to go on this infernal solstice trip with you. It's past time to pick up Greg and Mitzi, so I'll catch you two later." The breeze had become a wind that snatched the last of her words away and flung them down the mountain. Sprinkles began.

"Infernal, my foot," Dierdre said, shaking her hair out of her eyes and removing the keys from Suzanne's fingers. "I'm going after the kids, taking them to McDonald's for something they don't need while I break all the latest news to them. Then we're coming back here to help you pack. We'll leave first thing in the morning."

Suzanne thought of arguing to be the one to explain her bruised face to the children, then left it alone. "Lean a little," Dierdre had told her last night. "This time I'm here. I'm up to it now. Honest, Sis. Let me help you." Her reassuring words had been a comfort. Along with Taylor, Randy and his dogs, and the officers, Doug was nearly driven from her mind enough to sleep.

"You'll tell them *for* me?" Suzanne was aghast. Dee always avoided the difficulties if there was another way out. *What's come over her?*

"I've practiced what I'll say, and you know Greg would never buy into *you* being the one telling him about Doug. I'll be kind, but I'll be firm about Doug not being welcome here anymore."

"Well, the break-in does sound like a good excuse to get

out of Dodge tomorrow," agreed Taylor. "I'll hang around here tonight, so you two can get an extra good night's rest, then I've got to get some major pruning work accomplished while you all play in the desert."

"Oh, Taylor, I'm sure staying here again tonight is not…"

"Oh, yes it is necessary," her twin finished for her. "We are NOT going to be alone here with the kids tonight. I just asked him to stay and he already agreed."

"Okay, you two. I know when I'm out-numbered." The leaking clouds suddenly dumped their load in fat raindrops. The smell of ozone and lake stink filled the heavy air. Lightening danced along the lake water, across the valley floor and up on the ridges of the east bench where it crouched waiting beneath the cloudbank. Here and there spidery lightening arched and flashed. Thunder rumbled.

"Make it three," interjected Randy, already running. "I'm bringing my hounds back tonight, too. They hear anything, they'll go nuts before Taylor can lift a rifle barrel." He scooted the wagging animals into their holding pens in the back of his pick-up and covered them with a tarp. "Later," he waved, ducking behind the wheel. The rain pelted his windshield obliterating him from view. Dierdre hurried into the garage. Taylor grabbed Suzanne by the hand and rushed her up the stairs to take refuge in the house.

In the kitchen, Suzanne put the kettle on for a cup of herbal tea. She didn't think her stomach could comfortably manage coffee. Taylor finished washing up in the bathroom, returned to the kitchen and rinsed out the cup he'd used earlier.

"I thought I'd be out on a job and home and cleaned up before you'd see me all scruffy again, now with the rain . . ." He let it trail off.

"You look good to me, Taylor," she said, winking, "always did."

They laughed. He turned and their eyes locked, drawing them together like their essences were magnetic. Their arms went around one another. Their eyes, their smiles tender. He spoke first. She sponged up his words as they came from his mouth, turning them over in her mind, getting used to them, and tucking them away to be retrieved and savored again later—as often as she wanted.

"Suzanne, I love you so much. Do you think, do you want . . . would you give me a chance to make you a really good husband? I know I can't make up for what you and Steve had, but I . . ."

"Shhhhh," she cut him off. "What I had with Steve was good, and I will never forget him. What I had with you began when we were young and awkward and naive about what love is really all about." She reached up and ran her fingers through the damp curls at his temple, smoothed them, took her time explaining. "What we can have in the future is entirely up to us, entirely new, and it will have its challenges."

She felt such a wellspring of tenderness for him, of love that gushed from a door within her long held against a tide of feeling that nearly swept her from his arms into a place of its own. But she held it there for time enough to say what she should have said years ago, instead of good-bye.

"I wanted you to say those love words seven years ago when I felt I needed to protect myself from you, from us, from me becoming pregnant and not finishing college. I loved you, but I didn't know if you loved me, didn't know if we had a secure future together. But I also didn't know then that *nobody's* future is secure. It's how you deal with the insecurities that makes a good love, a solid marriage. Since you finally got around to loving me and being able to say so, if you are asking me to marry you," she smiled up at him, confident, full of sweetness and joy, "Yes, Taylor Armstrong. If you can take on a woman with two children and all the problems that come with us, there's no one else on the planet I'd rather spend my life with."

He took her face in his hands ever so gently and bent his mouth to hers. She felt the rasp of his beard and the soft hunger in his lips. "Thank God," he whispered. "I couldn't bear to lose you again. Oh, Susie, I love you. I didn't know how much I cared years ago until you were gone. I was such a fool to not ask for an explanation and for not begging you to reconsider."

"Glad you didn't throw your life away on some other lucky woman," she teased. "Are you willing to do the church thing? I could never be happy if we can't find a way to work out being a Christian family."

"Does it have to be Methodist?" he asked.

"Does it have to be Mormon?"

"You know I hardly ever go to church, but we can work something out." He looked at her earnestly. "Your faith means a lot to you, doesn't it." It wasn't a question.

"Yes, Taylor. I don't want to attend church alone with the children. I've been doing that since Steve was too ill to go with me. Marriage to me includes the spiritual aspects of being two people in love. Much as I want to marry you, that is what I need, what parents need to give to their children, even when they aren't the biological parents."

He kissed her, "Do you want children of our own?" One hand rubbed her back, moved up to her neck and massaged gently.

"Oh, Taylor, that would be lovely wouldn't it? Babies of our own?"

He kissed her in answer, a full tongue-exploring kiss that tingled through their bodies. She felt the swell of his ardor against her lower belly and unlike her response to Doug, felt an answering passion in her own body, felt the ache in her nipples, her thighs, her most private parts. She didn't care that his beard was rough, didn't care that they would have challenges about church and children, where to live and how. Just wanted him with a desire that left her panting and unwilling to lose him again for any reason.

The phone rang.

Startled, they pulled apart. Not letting go, he walked her backwards within reach of the wall phone, both of them grinning like teens caught mid-necking party by a shocked parent.

"Hello?"

The Wind Remembers

He stroked her hair. Teased her with his tongue to her other ear.

"Oh, Ms. Halsten, how nice to hear from you." She pushed him away enough to concentrate. "Yes, I suppose so, it's not a really good time, but if you're that close by . . . yes, do come on then. Last house at the top of the hill." She hung up the phone. "It's the woman who interviewed me at the hospital, says she's nearby visiting with an hospice patient's family and wondered if we could talk about hospital job opportunities. Isn't that a bit strange to you?"

"Right now, my whole life is strange to me." He stepped back and looked around. "How about I straighten up this kitchen counter, then take all the blankets and pillows Randy used out of the living room. You put yourself back together. Last time I saw you looking this delicious, I was on a mission to Fed Ex." He kissed her throat and let go.

In moments, Ms. Halsten's car, a black, late model BMW, drove up as far as possible near the back steps. Once she switched off her wiper blades, they could see her through the glass preparing to launch an umbrella out into the downpour. Taylor ran out into the rain and helped her to the porch overhang. He took her umbrella and freed her to enter the house with Suzanne.

"Taylor is here to help." Suzanne ushered her in. "The house was broken into last night. You'll have to forgive our disarray." She saw Ms. Halsten's practiced medical eye studying her face and knew what topic was up next.

"You were here and tangled with the intruder?" Her tone was deeply concerned.

"No, but I was assaulted by a drunken . . . cowboy at a fundraiser for my son's ball team last night. It has not been the best twenty-four hours. Please, come into the living room."

Taylor followed them, gesturing to her behind Ms. Halsten's back. "If you ladies will excuse me, I'm going to go install the window glass replacement I picked up this morning." He escaped to the bedroom where she heard the door close on the racket he'd create.

"Suzanne, . . ."

"May I offer you a cup of . . ."

They both began.

Ms. Halsten dropped her handbag to the sofa. "No, no thank you, I came by to talk with you in a less professional atmosphere where you can be as frank as I was with you at the hospital."

They sat down and Suzanne watched her guest's eyes take in the room. With a stranger's eye, Suzanne noticed the worn corner of the sofa, one of Greg's sneakers under the footstool she'd missed in the clean-up rush, and a crumpled tissue that hadn't made it into the wastebasket. *What is she here to say? Why not just send one of those form rejection letters to add to my growing collection.*

"Suzanne, I believe I was not only unprofessional, but presumptuous to a fault to have cautioned you about hospice work after the loss of your husband . . . perhaps even illegal."

"Ms. Halsten . . ."

"Call me Penny, please." She sat forward. "I'd like to put you on my staff, hold the liaison position open for a few months while you get your feet wet to see if it's for you, then if you're comfortable, promote you to the position you applied for. What do you say?"

The phone rang. The bedroom door opened. "You want me to get that for you, Suzanne?" called Taylor.

It rang again. "No, I'll ask whoever it is to call back later." She ran and picked up the receiver in the kitchen. "Hello?"

"Suzanne, I want to apologize." *Doug! Of all the people on earth to call me now.* "This is not a good time Officer Jensen . . ." she began, speaking louder than necessary in a noncommittal tone from the hall, saw Taylor enter the living room and guide Penny to Mitzi's bedroom. *What is he doing? The beds haven't even been made. He's losing me this job before I even have a chance to beg for and accept it!*

295

Doug's voice was contrite, urgent. "Suzanne, speak to me, please. There are no words to tell you how sorry I am. I'm begging your forgiveness."

"Doug, you showed me what kind of man you really are." She had to get rid of him and find out what Taylor was doing with Ms. Halsten. Feeling frantic, she nearly hung up, but faltered at being so rude.

He's crying! She could hear it in his voice. "That was liquor, not me. I'm not like that. Give me a chance to make it right with you, Suzanne. Never would I ever lay a hand on you again."

"We won't need you to visit again, Doug. Forgiveness is between you and God and your bishop. I want to heal my face and my shock and forget what you did to me. Don't come around or call Gregory. Just leave us alone."

"Is Taylor there?" Doug's voice became professional.

Like turning the faucet from hot to cold. "That's none of your concern," she said.

"This is business about his truck. If he's there, put him on."

She laid the receiver on the counter and went for Taylor, finding him and Ms. Halsten discussing Mitzi's mural.

Taylor was saying. "You should see it in the dark when it glows with black lighting!"

Suzanne interrupted, "Taylor, D . . . Officer Jensen would like to talk to you, something about the spray painting of your truck."

"Oh, sure. Excuse me." He hurried off, but only after flashing her an impudent 'cat with canary' grin.

Ms. Halsten said, "I'm afraid I have to withdraw the offer I just made you in the living room."

Suzanne's heart sank, but she held her eyes steady on Ms. Halsten's, fought for composure and won. *Well God, what are you up to this time?*

"This is the most amazing mural work I have *ever* seen, and I've visited many hospitals and galleries." She smiled and touched Suzanne on the shoulder.

"It would be a crime to give you a position with the terminally ill. They would benefit greatly from your experience and compassion, but would join me in wishing you to continue with your gift, your talent for painting." She steered Suzanne back to a chair in the living room.

Taylor's voice could be heard behind the closed swinging door in the kitchen. She wanted to go in there and give him a healthy piece of her mind for interfering, and perhaps a hug and a thank you—when she could let herself believe what she was hearing. *What influence can Penny have to help me find a job that includes my painting?*

"Making money from my art isn't likely to support two kids." Please, reconsider."

"But I simply can't, Suzanne. You must take the directorship of our hospital mural project into your capable hands. The three immense murals must be completed before the grand opening and dedication of the new pediatric wing this time next year."

Penny sat back, smiles playing about her lips, watching Suzanne take it in. "Your friend, . . . brother? Whoever Taylor is, told me he read our sign in the men's room, urging artists to submit portfolios for the mural project. He's been trying to find a way to tell you to go for it without being pushy. Discussed it with your twin just this morning."

Suzanne's mind reeled. *A chance to paint—for money!* It was too much to believe. She checked her enthusiasm. "A one-year's job project is not the sort of long-term security I need for my family, even though it's a fantastic opportunity."

"Nevertheless, I insist you take this on. I'll help you work into something else later. Who knows, perhaps the Artistic Director of PR will run off to Guatemala with her hairdresser. Life can be serendipitous. We need creative people on permanent staff."

Suzanne laughed. "What will it pay, Penny?"

Taylor crept down the hall without a glance in her

direction; she knew he listened.

"Thirty-seven thousand dollars with hospital and dental benefits and all equipment, supplies, and support volunteers included."

The bedroom door shut on a triumphant note.

Dierdre Ingram

~ Thursday the 19th of June

"So what did Suzanne do to make Doug mad enough to hit her?" Greg sucked air through his straw and blew bubbles into his soda. He stared intently at Dierdre, a bit too smug and dispassionate for her liking.

"You want the truth, or do you want me to pretty it up for you?"

He didn't answer. She went on. "Since you don't seem to believe that your buddy Doug could have turned out to be a big poop, we can leave it. Or if you think you're old enough for the truth, I'm prepared to give it to you." She knew her nephew's protective barrier was thick. *Best to get it over with. How I hate being this brutal. If there are some of my guardian angels in the vicinity, Greg and I could use a lot of support about now.*

She fingered the crystal heart at her throat, looked through the play-area doors, and waved at Mitzi, still small enough to fit under the height requirement, gleefully wading through a colorful sea of plastic balls with other children her size and age. Dierdre hoped McDonald's could keep her niece busy while she kept her word to Suzanne about Greg.

Greg slurped and stared her down before dropping his eyes to his tray. "Sure, I'm big enough for the truth. How do I know you're not making stuff up just because your sister told you to?" He drew circles in his ketchup puddle with a limp French fry, not looking at her. Under the table his other hand clicked fingernails rhythmically.

"I guess you'll have to trust me, Gregory. When you see Suzanne's face you'll know we didn't make this up to hurt your feelings." Her iced tea was insipid. She pushed it away, waiting for his decision.

"Why can't I ask Doug about it myself?"

"Because your mother and I don't want him around anymore. I told you that."

"Yeah, you told me." His voice was flat, a whisper.

"I'm really sorry. He's been your grown-up friend since your dad died. This has to be very hard news for you to accept. I just didn't want you to see Suzanne's bruised face and not know how it happened and why Doug isn't welcome to call or come over anymore. I don't think it's necessary to tell your little sister all the details about it just now, do you? Perhaps we can say your mother bonked it somehow."

"Why did he do it? Besides being drunk, I mean." He put the dripping fry in his mouth, but he didn't chew.

"Doug wanted Suzanne to kiss him and . . . more. He tried to pull her clothes off, and when she wouldn't let him he hit her so hard she fell to the ground in the parking lot. Taylor heard her crying for help, found them, and carried your mom to safety."

"He probably just wanted to marry her."

"Yes, he probably did, Honey. But that's not the way to show love to someone. That's the way to scare the wits out of them and hurt them seriously."

"Can we go now?" He stood up, smashed all of his fries into a wad with the sandwich papers, and carried the tray to the trash bin.

"Okay, you bet. How about we go home and pack for tomorrow's camping trip?"

Without a word, Greg rammed his tray into the waste slot, shoved the mess inside, and stacked the tray atop the others.

Dierdre retrieved Mitzi and followed him to the Blazer.

Head down, Greg scuffed through the rainy parking lot, lost in thought, wiping savagely at his sniffling nose.

Her heart ached for the little guy. *Damn you, Doug Jensen, damn you all the way to bloody hell!*

Suzanne Price

~ Thursday the 19th of June

Taylor had just polished the new window clean after puttying over the glazier points when Suzanne touched him on the shoulder.

"That Johnny Carlisle just drove in. Could you go talk to him? He makes me a little uncomfortable. I don't think it's how sorry I feel for him. I'm just jumpy today."

"You've got every right to be jumpy, Sweetheart." He kissed her gently on the unbruised cheek. "I'm finished with this anyway."

"Thanks on all counts. What would I do without you?" She hugged him, heard the bell and let go.

"Waste away, no doubt about it."

She smacked him on the rump. "I love you, you know."

"Yes," he grinned, "and it's making me nuts."

Suzanne brought them lemonade in the living room in time to hear Johnny say, "I talked to a man down at that gym on the main drag, you know, the one where the police officer said that Bo fellow works part time."

"The Iron Pump. Go on," said Taylor, accepting a frosty glass and the caress of her fingers.

"He said one time he ran into Bo outside a bar." His words came out slowly, but he seemed far more agitated than he had on the first visit. "While these guys were talking, a big kid with spiky hair, earrings, and tattoos everywhere came up to bum some money from him. Called him Uncle Bo."

They waited while he grappled for his train of thought.

"Seems Bo told him to make his own bread or get it out of his red-head broad up at the sheep camp. Sorry, Ma'am, that's the way I heard it. The man said the only sheep camp he knew about close by was the one on the bench up above this place." Johnny sipped his drink with both hands, then set it down with great care on the coffee table. "You know anything about this kid? Not sure I want to check him out alone if he's a street tough."

Suzanne exchanged glances with Taylor. *I wonder if he's the one who did all these terrible things to scare us.*

Johnny went on, seeming to struggle to say all he'd come to say before he lost his thread of thought. "I want to find out what happened to my falcon and find a good home for her. I don't care about this Bo, except to see justice done and get my Felon back."

The back door banged open. Greg ran down the hall, stopping for a moment to look in at them. His eyes went to Suzanne's face. His chin quivered. She put out an arm. He hesitated, moved closer, stopped just out of her reach. She dropped her arm. He came and leaned against her. She touched his shoulder and smiled.

Taylor broke the awkwardness, "Hi, Gregory. I'm thinking of taking Mr. Carlisle over to my Pop's place to see his falcon mews. Too rainy to do much else. Think you might like to tag along? We'd like your company."

"Mr. Armfrong!" Mitzi squealed, running up to his knees. "Can I come, too?" She unzipped his lips and pretended to pocket a key. "We could see about our s'prise."

"Sure, you two can both join us. Pops has a big barn with plenty of room to run around inside out of the rain."

"Is that okay with you, Suzanne?" Greg asked her.

"It's fine." She hugged him. For the first time since Steve's death, he didn't pull away. *I thought he'd hate me over losing Doug and he doesn't!*

"I'll follow in my car," said Johnny. "If I get too tired, I can always head back to my motel without you changing your plans."

"The rain has already changed my plans today," said

Taylor. "Whatever you say, though. Okay, you scramblers, let's dodge rain drops all the way to my truck."

"Taylor?"

"Yes, Greg?"

"Does your Pops have a dog?"

"He sure does."

"Goody!" piped Mitzi. "I'll leave Bear Lovins at home, so he won't get his feelings hurt when I pet the dog."

Dierdre came in from the garage, greeted Johnny, and went to put an arm around Suzanne's shoulder. "All promises accounted for," she whispered.

Suzanne breathed deeply and let it out in a whoosh of relief. She and Dee watched the men and the kids leave through the back door.

"Doug called," Suzanne said over her shoulder on her way back to the living room.

"You're kidding! Brass balls. What is he, a man without a brain as well as no heart?" Dee flopped on the couch and drew up her bare feet. She'd left her wet sandals by the back door. "Catch me up."

"Do we have to start with Doug?"

"There's more? I don't need to hear about you and Taylor, I can read high second-chakra-energy vibes in the atmosphere." She giggled.

"I've got a job." Suzanne sat beside Dee, scootching her over with a bouncy hip. "Designing and painting murals. Can you believe it?"

"Hah!" Dierdre grabbed her shoulders, shook her like a rag doll, and lay back. "That's fantastic. How did Taylor get you to go for it?"

"He didn't." She was delighted with the totally puzzled look on Dee's face and had the fun of explaining all about Penny's visit. Then Dierdre told her how Greg had taken the bad news about Doug. Later, as they tugged out blankets and pillows and made up the hide-a-bed sofa in the den for Taylor, Suzanne filled Dee in on what he'd told her of the conversation he'd had with Doug.

"The kid that spray painted the cruiser and the truck has been caught. Well the description of this Big Blue smart aleck fits this nephew of Bo Rodman's that Johnny was just telling us about, and guess what? He's been hanging out at the sheep camp at the top of this road!"

They changed fresh pillowcases for Randy in the living room. "I bet he's the one who came here on the bike," said Dierdre. "Probably looking for quick drug money."

"Good guess. He had cocaine in his jacket pocket. Now that he's in juvenile detention on vandalizing and drug charges," said Suzanne, "I'll sleep a little better tonight. But I'm not going to urge Taylor to go home."

"Well, I do wonder why," Dee said, with a lilt to her voice. "We've got the men's sleeping quarters under control, now let's pack camping gear and study a map. I'm so excited to finally visit these Sun Tunnels on the solstice like I've wanted to for years I can hardly stand it."

Taylor Armstrong

~ Thursday the 19th of June

"Come this way, Johnny. Pops will be feeding pigeons and Speck about now. No taking him out in the rain to fly for his breakfast this morning, footing on the stream rocks is too slippery for Pops."

Taylor, with Mitzi by the hand and Greg kicking along behind them humming to himself, led the way through the barn. He switched on a row of lights that flooded from the rafters, dispelling the gloom. "Pops can walk this place in the dark, but the rest of us might need to see where we're going, for safety's sake. Keep a sharp eye for cats and mice, Mitzi."

At the sound of Taylor's voice, Radar woofed and came

bounding, soon sniffing and wagging his hellos. Taylor noted that Johnny seemed as happy to pet a dog and receive lapping kisses as he and the kids were.

"That you, Son?"

"We're coming, Pops."

There was hand shaking all around. "Don't get many rainy-day visitors. Happy to meet you. Johnny you say? Taylor said on the phone that you're a falconer." He laughed. "Guess on these car phones you probably heard him tell me that."

"I drove my own car, handicapped vehicle, you know, so I didn't hear your conversation."

"You look mighty familiar." Jake's plaid flannel shirt sleeves rolled up on impressive forearms, he lifted Mitzi to a shelf where new kittens meowed at their mother's belly.

"Mr. Armfrong, there's baby kittens in this box!"

"Let me see," said Greg, hiking himself up next to her to look. Taylor boosted him and held him loosely.

"That's one smart momma cat," said Jake. "Found her up in there making a nest away from everybody a few weeks ago, and first thing you know she's got a litter. Plenty of field mice to keep them all busy. If I can capture the cats while they're in the toying-with-their-prey stage, sometimes I make them fork over their catches for Speck. Comes in handy for feeding him on a drizzly day like this. It means momma cat has to go find another mouse. That's what I like."

"Oooh, I wish we had one of deeze baby kittens," cooed Mitzi.

"Will she bite if we hold one?" Gregory stroked a fat male that appeared to be the largest of the litter, while Taylor supported him from below.

"I think momma might like to give the other kittens a chance to get a drink while the big fellow takes a break with you." Taylor set him down on the floor and showed him how to cradle the kitten next to his chest for warmth.

Jake had been studying Johnny. "Say, I know where I've met you. Three years ago at the Sky Trials. You had a honey of a pair of breeding peregrines and a beaut of a hybrid gyr. A bunch of us talked about them all weekend. The pair went for a pretty penny, too, as I recall."

Taylor watched the light of memory slowly dawn on Johnny's scarred face.

"I don't remember but snatches of my life before . . . before I got hurt. I do remember those Trials, even which bird won, but not much else." Johnny looked around the barn. His eyes came to rest on a bedraggled, heavy leather hat with a cupped brim, fur-padded earflaps, and long cords at the neck. "Well it's damn sure been a long time since I laid eyes on a genuine copulation hat!" He reached out an arm and stroked it lovingly. "I never used the hat breeding method myself, but my uncle did."

Jake removed the strange looking hat from its peg and handed it over. "It's seen plenty of use. Couldn't part with it when I passed on my semen-collecting gear."

"Isn't mating the way two animals make babies?" asked Greg.

The barn was quiet. "Sure enough it is, only with a mating hat . . . " Jake's voice trailed away. He looked at Taylor. "Do you think we can go into the details without upsetting his mom and dad?"

"I don't have a dad and Suzanne doesn't have to know you told me." Greg held the kitten near his cheek where it happily molded itself around his chin. "Talking about sex kind of bugs her."

The men chuckled.

It was out. Taylor wondered if Pops would put two and two together and spell Ingram. Yep, his bushy, white eyebrows raised, lowered, and his eyes rolled right around to rest on Taylor with a big question mark in their gray-blue depths.

"*The* Suzanne?"

"Yeah, Pops. Our Suzanne. These are her stepchildren. She's a widow now."

Jake nodded and grinned, keeping his thoughts to

himself, but Taylor figured he knew full well what they were and how he was pleased as punch.

Greg stood waiting. "So are you going to tell me about that mating hat, or not?"

"Well you see, Sonny, I put on that hat Johnny's holding, tie it on good and tight, encourage a male falcon to get all excited and when he deposits his semen into the rim around the crown here, I use a syringe to collect the liquid. Then I deposit it inside a female so she can lay eggs and make baby falcons." He looked at the men for approval.

"Well done, Pops."

Greg appeared less satisfied with Jake's explanation.

"Yeah, well how come you don't just let the male and the female falcons mate without the hat? Why do they need you?"

"Smart little fellow, aren't you?" Jake ruffled Gregory's hair.

"He reads books and watches a lot of nature shows on TV," said Taylor.

Johnny handed the copulating hat back to Pops, who finished his explanation: "There are two ways to manually collect semen from the male falcons, Gregory. Both mean the breeders like Johnny here, and me in my day, we picked out which males and females to breed together for the strongest, healthiest, most beautifully marked offspring. That's how we're saving the peregrine falcon species from extinction. DDT bug spray made their eggs too fragile to come to term and hatch properly."

"Oh, that makes sense." Greg handed the kitten back to be returned to its mother. "I didn't know how people saved the falcons and helped them make their young. I remember falcons are like people, at the top of the food chain."

"That's true," said Jake. "The peregrine is a specialist. If peregrine falcons are present in a canyon, then the ecosystem balance is in order. You'd make a fine falconer candidate," he added, glancing over the boy's shoulder in his son's direction.

Taylor got the hint.

"Let's go visit our robin egg and see if there's a baby in it," coaxed Mitzi.

"Oh, the picture is becoming more clear every minute," chuckled Pops. "The little neighbor girl . . . uh huh. Come along to the nursery, folks. Seems to be a lot of things developing and hatching everywhere."

They trooped after Jake to the hatchery, watched as he retrieved Mitzi's egg and held it to the light for her and Greg.

"Now, let's put the egg back in its warm place to give the baby bird time to finish getting strong enough to break through the shell and hatch," said Jake. "It takes 21 days, and we don't know how long it was in the nest before the storm toppled that tree in your yard."

Greg was enthralled. "It sure was cool to hold the egg to the light and see the dark shape of the robin embryo, wasn't it, Taylor?"

"It sure was. Why don't you two go play with Radar or the cats for a few minutes while Pops and Johnny and I talk hawk business. When we're ready to visit the falcon mews, we'll call you."

"My grandson's bike is in that empty horse stall over there," called Jake, "and there's a trike your size there too, Mitzi."

"All-l-l right!" Greg raced the length of the barn and emerged on the bike, tearing circles around barking Radar. "Boy, would Alex ever love *this* place!"

Taylor felt a sense of pleasure and anticipation knowing these kids would one day soon be his own, and they'd come to love this old barn and this old man as he did. His life had taken on a shape and a direction that though new, felt as comfortable and familiar as the barn and its mews. He'd returned to Suzanne's glove by choice as surely as Speck ever returned by training. The rain stopped. Sun poured in through the windows and made light and shadow roads for the children to ride on.

The Wind Remembers

***

The rain carried in weighty clouds headed farther up the eastern canyons to Wyoming. Where the sunshine beat down, the pavement steamed. Taylor returned the kids to the Price home. Gravel stones in Suzanne's driveway appeared to quiver in the heat. He noted the camping gear the twins were organizing had been making its way in neat stacks down the porch steps. They'd left a path to the door, and Greg and Mitzi hurried up bursting with news to be shared.

He stretched, feeling the tiredness from little sleep and all of it on an unfamiliar sofa bed, racing thoughts of love for Suzanne, thoughts of Doug, anger, and frustration. He'd wanted to beat the shit out of Doug, yet pitied him for his pathetic approach to convincing Suzanne of his desire for her. He struggled with desires for Suzanne himself, all tossing him hour after hour between night noises and anxieties for her well being and an urgency to make her his wife, so her safety would be more within his power. For his right to hold her, too . . . and more.

He looked around the yard, once haven for another man coming home to her, observed the orderly cords of wood he'd cut, split and arranged by size against the garage, life-signs of himself. Who would have thought a felled tree would bring them back together after all these years? Life was mysterious to him. But life, in spite of all its unexpected happenings of late, was also rewarding.

Suzanne loved him. He loved her. That was more than all the years he'd tried to find a satisfying fit in a job, or with a woman. It was because home for his soul was with Suzanne, wherever that turned out to be. She and these kids were more than his business and maybe even more than himself. Perhaps they'd have children of their own in a year or two. He waved to her through the window and backed out of the driveway to go get some work done before lunch.

Where would their babies be blessed? He thought of a

scripture from the *Book of Mormon,* in "Alma", concerning the soul. Something about the state of the soul between life and death and being taken home to God who gave life. Had Heavenly Father meant them to be together? His scripture study was rusty, but the words 'happiness, paradise, a state of rest from all troubles, care and sorrow' came to him, 'the reuniting of the soul with the body.' That was how he felt, reunited with himself, not just with Suzanne. *Strange and pretty damn wonderful,* he concluded.

Up in Malan's subdivision, he climbed out, ready to prune the riddled native oaks. Randy was already trimming the street-side trees. It would be satisfying to work at something that showed progress. Dealing with the unknowns around the Price home sapped Taylor, made him feel inadequate. Considering churches and deeper spiritual commitments disturbed and comforted, leaving him somewhat bewildered with inadequacies on those topics, too.

Suzanne Price

~ Thursday the 19th of June

When Taylor entered, Suzanne set a plate of sandwiches on the table. She smiled up at him. "Thought you'd need some fortification before you go back to wielding that Pulaski for the afternoon."

"I think pruners will do it for today, but I am hungry. Thanks." He washed and dried his hands, sank into a chair and reached for a tuna-salad on rye.

She brought him a glass of milk. "Greg is the happiest in months. He loved visiting Jake's barn, the falcon, the kittens, riding the bike. I thought he'd be angry and withdrawn. I don't understand him. Maybe you had something to do with his mood."

"Hope so," he mumbled, his mouth full.

"Did you tell your dad . . . about us?"

Taylor gulped milk, "Not exactly, but he's onto us."

"Hope it's okay, me being a gentile." She put plates out for the others.

"Oh, I think he just expects me to work a little harder on your soul's conversion."

She laughed. "That should keep you busy for the rest of your life, especially since you might have to start with yourself." She fluttered her lashes in a tease. He grinned.

Dierdre and the kids, still bubbling about the barn, joined them.

"I just called Alex and told him about Speck," blurted Greg. "Taylor, can we take Alex to the hawk barn, I mean the mews place, sometime?"

"Sure we can." Taylor wiped his mouth on a napkin, grinned at Suzanne. They were content to share the same table, the same people, and the open doors of their future.

※※※

A couple of hours after Taylor left, Suzanne was filling plastic-lidded storage boxes with snack foods when she heard a vehicle in the driveway and looked out the window. The rusting hulk of a metal camper truck rumbled to a stop in front of the garage door, open since she and Dee had been hauling gear out of storage and organizing it on the porch. The driver's-side door of the old cab opened with a rasping, scraping noise and a burly, good-looking man in a cowboy hat stepped down. He surveyed the contents of the garage before he limped toward the house. *Bo Rodman?!*

Suzanne locked the back screen door and dead-bolted the heavy-oak inside door, hooking the chain lock into place. "Dee, come here!" she called in a loud whisper, glued to the spot, wishing for Taylor, even for Doug.

"What is it? You sound . . . Oh, m'god, it's that creepy loser, Bo."

"I forgot it's Thursday, the day Rehma wants the kids to go camping for the weekend. But she hasn't called back. After talking with my attorney and everything else that's happened, I put it out of my mind." Suzanne was frantic. "What shall I do? If she wants the kids for the weekend, the least she could do is to come along to pick them up herself, so I can talk her out of it."

"Tell him they aren't going. We've made other plans. Where's Rehma anyway?"

"Go get the rifle out of my closet; key's in the jewelry box on my dresser."

The man stood at the bottom of the stairs looking over the camping gear, his heavy-lidded eyes shaded by the brim of his battered hat, a smile playing about his full lips. He examined the sleeping bags, his finger rings catching the late afternoon sun, sending flashes of light along the aluminum tent poles.

"Suze, I . . . I don't know anything about guns," Dierdre stammered.

"Just get me that rifle!" Suzanne's riveting look underscored her insistence, "Go! Get it now! Tell Greg to keep Mitzi and himself out of sight, while you call Officers Reed and Lopez. The number's on the pad by the kitchen phone."

Bo Rodman

~ Thursday the 19th of June

Sliding his hand up the rail of the Price woman's porch, Bo climbed the stairs, skirting tent packs, folding chairs, a Coleman stove, a can of fuel, a coffee pot, stacks of mismatched pots, mugs and plates in a box packed with rolls of toilet paper. Another held sweatshirts and kids' clothes. On the step above it, towels and blankets were crammed into clear-plastic zippered bags. Four sleeping bags, coiled and tied, lined the porch railing opposite the door.

Why four bags? She wouldn't pack for Rehma and me

and her kids would she? Broads I know ain't that good-hearted. Bo looked around and out into the yard, saw no sign of another car, only the blunt statement of the cottonwood stump, evidence of his destruction, its rings of resin beads drawn to the surface by the sun's heat.

The reality that he and Rehma would never claim the house and property as married parents of her kids, as he had often bragged to her they would, gave him a moment's disappointment. But his pressing reason for being at the house in broad daylight uppermost in mind, he rapped his ring fingers on the screen door—polite like.

He waited, grew impatient, rapped more sharply. *Damn it, bitch, answer this fuckin' door! I ain't got time to hang around here all day and risk gettin' caught by your cop boyfriend.* The deadbolt released. He pasted on one of his best smiles. The inner door parted the width of a safety-chain. The Price woman's face appeared in a vertical strip of soft skin and big brown eyes. If he wasn't mistaken, someone had punched her for him. He broadened his smile.

"Howdy, Ma'am." He doffed his hat. "My Rehma couldn't get off work in time to pick up her kids for campin' this weekend, so she sent me." Sweeping his hat by its brim over the piles of gear, he added, "No need for you to go to all this trouble to pack for us. Me and Rehma can take care of everything they'll need." *What's the matter with her? Why ain't she answerin', just starin' at me like I'm some freak.*

"'Course you probably don't know me and Rehma are gettin' hitched real soon. My name's Bo Rodman. Pleased to meet cha, Ma'am. The kids ready now? I'm in kind of a hurry to pick up Rehma and head up the canyon. Want to set up camp before dark."

He had run out of things to say and struggled for more, to get her to bring the kids out where he could take them. He wanted the brats to be easy to take off in the truck the way he'd told Rehma to say when he stood by her that day on the phone. A noise behind the Price woman caught his attention. She unhooked the chain. The door opened wider to her body.

He grinned. "Well now, don't you look just as fresh as a daisy, like one of them shampoo commercials on TV." He bowed, straightened and slapped his hat onto his head, shoving it back the way the girls always noticed when he posed for pictures with them on the rodeo circuit. She didn't seem to notice.

"We have camping plans of our own," she said. "Gregory and Mitzi won't be going with you and Rehma this weekend—or any weekend." She had one hand on the door, the other out of sight behind the frame of the doorjamb.

His impatience getting the best of him, the gruff he felt crept into his voice. "My woman's got her legal rights to her kids, so there's no use you and me gettin' fussy about it. You got that letter from her lawyer man. Just get them kids of hers out here and I'll . . . we'll have 'em back Sunday night." *She ain't lookin' away for an instant. Keeps her damn eyes on me like the falcon does.*

Instantly, with that thought, Bo saw the Price woman as more than an obstacle on the path to what he wanted. She was his enemy. He sensed in her the steely resolve of a fighter, nothing like Rehma who had been weak and fearful of him. The woman's swollen lips parted to speak. He tried to gage her power, seeking a vulnerable spot while he listened to her words and watched the way she handled her clean, pretty body.

"My children will *never* spend time with you and Rehma." She licked her lips and drew a breath.

He watched her eyes, steady on him. *She ain't givin' herself away at all.*

"Tell Rehma my attorney assures me I'll have full custody of Steve's children very soon. You'd better go now." The door began to close. She lifted the chain to hook it back into place.

"Just a damn minute! Rehma has the law on her side to take her kids campin' this weekend if she wants to. No sense you and me taken on hasty and ruinin' a fun little weekend for them kids and their *natural* mother." He tried opening the screen door, found it locked. *Damn it.*

"Get away from that door and get on out of here!" The bitch's voice was strong, firm; she sounded fearless, angry. He was more surprised when she brought her other hand into view around the barrel of a rifle, quickly raised, and aimed at his gut.

Bo stepped back and into a bedroll, nearly losing his balance. He grabbed the porch rail to steady himself.

"Son of a bitch! What you want to threaten me with a gun for? I ain't caused you no trouble."

"I've already phoned for help," she said, matter-of-fact like some clerk at the bank. He hated her calm, business-assed attitude.

"You'd best be on your way down the driveway, unless you want me to use this rifle to slow your progress and show you how serious I am."

"Don't get your feathers ruffled. I'll go peaceable, but you and I know you ain't called no cops. You and me been talkin' the whole time I been here. You probably don't even know how to shoot that huntin' rifle." He eyed the scope and backed down to the next step, his plans slithering away between them at screen-door level, his fury mounting.

"I've done the calling for her," said a woman's voice behind the door. She stepped into view. *The big-titted beauty from Rehma's shop! What in hell is she doing here?* His mouth went dry.

No longer behind dark glasses, the Lilly he recognized said, "Believe me, my sister shoots skeet and knows how to hunt with this rifle. Get on down the road, Bo. I've seen the bruises on Rehma. If you think for a minute either one of us will let you take these kids out of our sight, we'd sooner see you shot dead right here in the driveway and explain it to the police when they get here."

Sister? Jesust H. Christopher! The Price woman leveled the gun at his chest and cocked it. Bo turned and hurried down the steps, making little jumps over the gear, hippity hopping to his truck. He hiked himself up and switched on the engine. His anger raged, choking him; everything blood-red and black. Tracker, startled, barked at him. Bo cracked the dog across the nose to shut him up and threw the truck into reverse. Roaring to the end of the drive, he careened in a squealing turn onto the pavement without looking to see if anyone was coming, then tore down the mountain.

Finding out that the woman who'd claimed she was in town to look up Frank was the Price woman's sister had thrown him as much as seeing the barrel of the rifle aimed at him with authority. Little Mrs. Price was nothing to mess with. Maybe she was extra pissed after he'd ransacked her house last night looking for Rehma's money.

The measly $50 bill he'd found in the fancy-leather travel bag wasn't going to go far, but he'd make damned sure to find out where they'd be camping. *I ain't done yet.*

CHAPTER FOURTEEN

SOLSTICE SOJOURN

Suzanne Price

~ Friday the 20th of June

"Wouldn't it be cool if those puffs of white smoke up ahead were signals made by Indians on the war path?" said Greg, straining to the extent of his seatbelt in the rear of the Blazer. "Then we'd be on a real adventure. What's the smoke from anyway?"

Suzanne, at the wheel, chuckled, sighed. "Life's been enough of an adventure lately. I could only handle friendly Indians today. Let's just let it be farmers burning ditch banks to keep the irrigation water flowing."

"Oh, that's no fun." Greg sat back, pretending to pout.

"Sure she can be fun, Greg. We just have to get your mom out of town long enough to help her remember how to relax and use her creative imagination for having a good time." Dierdre, in the passenger seat next to her, folded up the map.

"Think we can find something more like maps that I'm used to than this geophysical one of Steve's? Who cares about elevations and terrain?"

Suzanne explained, "We can pick up a regular map, but the roads will just end in designated wilderness areas. I brought that one because it shows all the paved and dirt roads the Bureau of Land Management is in charge of. The Sun Tunnels seem to be off of paved roads in the middle of no where."

"Mommy used her 'magination last night when Randy's dogs barked and woked us up." Mitzi's voice bubbled behind Suzanne. She was belted in next to her teddy bear.

"They went nuts you mean. I bet they heard more robbers," Greg added.

At the smell of skunk, Suzanne rolled up the automatic windows and turned the knob for the air conditioner. "The way those hounds carried on I was happy Taylor and Randy were there for the night."

"Improved the scenery too," said Dierdre. Suzanne whapped her shoulder.

"Mr. Armfrong got Daddy's gun and scared them quiet, really good." Mitzi replaced a crayon in the box and picked another. She held the pink one she knew was named 'Raspberry' under Bear Lovin's nose for a pretend sniff.

Dee tucked the map into its folder. "What do you say we save the cooler-packed sandwiches for later at camp and stop at Maddox's for a family-size box of fried chicken for today's lunch? See the billboard? I haven't been there for years. I'll buy. No arguments."

Suzanne smiled, signaled, changed to the inside lane. "Since this Friday traffic is already a pain, we might as well take Aunt Dierdre up on her offer, kids. After all, this solstice adventure was her idea."

"I still don't understand what's a stole sis, Aunt Dreedra." Mitzi colored a princess picture purple across all the lines.

"Mitzi, Love, it will make sense when I get us up while it's still dark."

"This I gotta see!" Suzanne laughed, waiting for her chance in the traffic to turn, adding, "Anybody need a potty break while I'm ordering the chicken and colas?"

Suzanne caught Greg's eyes in the rear-view mirror; he shook his head and grinned. She pulled left off the highway into the parking lot. A stream of cars and trucks pulling boats and motor homes flowed on by. She parked in the shade and waited until the others stepped out before locking up. The hot, dry breeze ruffled her hair. She pinned up loose strands and involuntarily shivered, looked around, studied cars, people's faces.

"I saw that shiver, Sis. How did you get a chill in this heat?" Dierdre asked, herding the children ahead of them.

"I had a spooky feeling for a minute, as if I were being watched. Can't explain it, but it gave me the creeps," she whispered.

"Oh, Honey, you really do need a vacation." Dee's spontaneous arm around her waist almost chased the chills.

Johnny Carlisle

~ Friday the 20th of June

A field of last year's teasel skeletons, here and there speared with pushy, tight green heads of new growth, bordered the ditches. Cattails had already come to brown seed heads and shattered into ragged white fluff.

When Bo's dusty truck made an abrupt stop at a vacant fruit stand just beyond the Maddox restaurant, several car lengths ahead in the traffic, Johnny signaled and pulled off on the right shoulder, coasting to a stop. He waited for what seemed a long time wondering if the mean bastard was going to hop out and cross the road for some take out. Then amid the middle-aged and elderly patrons pulling out of the restaurant parking lot, he was surprised to see young Suzanne Price, her sister and the two kids leaving in her heavily loaded late-model truck. He wasn't finished puzzling about seeing the dead policeman's wife way out here away from Farr, when he saw Bo whip into the stream of traffic a few cars behind Mrs. Price's, nearly causing a collision with an on-coming motor home. Its horn blared.

Johnny eased back onto the highway too, and followed, sweat breaking out on his forehead with the effort of puzzling out the connection between Bo and the Price car. What he didn't understand agitated him. Johnny dug around on the seat with his free hand, feeling for his pills, just in case his nerves got the best of him.

Rat

~ Friday the 20th of June

Inside the largest sheep-camp wagon, gang headquarters, Rat studied Tangie in the dim light sifting in through the tiny dirt-encrusted window above her head. In his eager mind, she was his reward for risking getting caught tagging the Price garage, the tree-company truck, and the cop's cruiser.

He'd thought he'd have to bargain for a piece of her bum with Big Blue, being she was their leader's woman. But with Blue in jail for what Rat had done, and drug charges on top of that, Rat sensed his deserved power over Tangie and his brothers in the Blue Tattoo Gang.

She pushed up her wild orange hair with both hands, motioned a come-on to him and to Sky, breathing heavy behind him. Rat wet his thick lips, drew his eyes an inch at a time over Tangie's skinny-strapped T-shirt and perky-nippled breasts, to her long legs, and followed them to the V of her short cut-offs. She laughed and spread her legs.

"I've got enough for everybody, if they have the bucks or some toot," she cooed.

"Line forms behind me," said Rat, unzipping his jeans.

"I'll wait my turn," squeaked Sky, slumping onto the other creaking cot and opening his sketchbook. He didn't take out his colored pencils.

"You bet your sweet ass you'll wait." Rat bent over her.

Tangies fingers played at the top snap of her shorts, then his jeans.

Little Rat was throbbing inside her when Rat heard the cop's bullhorn out in the shrub. Sky lurched past him for the door, yanked it open, and slowly raised both hands.

Dierdre Ingram

~ Friday the 20th of June

Dierdre's turn at the wheel came after their fried chicken picnic at a roadside park. Suzanne allowed Greg to take the passenger's seat up front, so she could play a drawing game on Magic Slates in the back with Mitzi.

Giant concrete and metal electrical towers marched north into the distance like disciplined soldiers along the west, lakeside of the highway. Orderly rows of fruit orchards climbed the east benches. Rough bricks of yellow-green hay dried acre upon acre in the fields below the peaks that stretched to reach the highway.

"Why do horses wiggle their ears and swish their tails when they eat grass?"

"I think they don't like flies buzzing in their ears any better than we do, Greg."

"Is that yellow flower what they make mustard out of, Aunt Dierdre?"

"No, I think that's dyer's woad," she said. "It's surprising, but the yellow flower isn't the dye color the pioneers used for their clothing. When I was your age we learned how they mashed up the plant to make greenish-blue dye. But the plant's leaves make cows sick and the woad takes over the natural vegetation, so farmers try to get rid of it."

"Wow! Look at those long-horned cattle, just like the kind in cowboy movies." Greg craned his neck to keep them in view, while they whizzed by the window.

"Looks funny to see them next to a split-entry home with satellite TV dishes and paved launching pads for boats and RVs, doesn't it?" Dierdre checked her view mirrors and set the cruise control at 75. Except for some distant vehicles, way in front and behind them, the traffic pressure had eased off soon after they passed Willard Bay's marina and the golf courses at Brigham City. The afternoon passed on pleasantly, even in the above-90-degree heat. "We'll be needing gas soon. What's the nearest place for it?" She handed the map packet over her shoulder to Suzanne and waited while she heard it being unfolded.

Suzanne checked the map. "Looks like the Snowville Truck Stop exit at Route 84. We should see signs any minute."

"Those big sprinklers on wheels would sure be fun to play in," said Greg. "Those wheels are way bigger than the ones on Taylor's truck. What's all that green stuff growing there?"

"Potatoes, I think." Dierdre loved how her nephew had come alive again, full of curiosity and questions, more like the happy little boy she remembered than the angry, sullen child he'd behaved like when she arrived a few days ago. Ironic because he'd lost not only his father but his best big friend Doug. What a jerk that Doug was. *Good riddance to your blocked chakras.* Suzanne was well rid of him and happy with Taylor back in her life, handsome as ever, and with a new sensitivity that made him twice as desirable. She rejoiced in their re-blossoming love, yet envied them.

"That sign we just passed said 'Next services 29 miles'."

"Thanks, Greg. I missed it. Guess I let my mind wander. You artists in the back finish up and pack your drawing stuff. We should be able to gas up in 15 minutes."

"We be almost finished with our pictures, Aunt Dreedra."

"We *are* almost finished, Honey," Suzanne corrected.

"Good for you two." How she adored her little niece and wanted to protect her from Rehma. She sometimes ached for a child of her own and the one she'd lost, and like now, crushed the thought as automatically as she would a cigarette in an ashtray full of distasteful butts.

"I'm hungry," Greg announced.

"Just like a man," she said and smiled while she ran her fingers through his cowlick. He didn't shrink away. She tapped the gum pack on the seat between them. He opened it and handed her a piece, unwrapped two for himself, and folded them into his mouth. She stroked his cheek. He blew a bubble, happily absorbed in the now.

Taylor Armstrong

~ Friday the 20th of June

A promenade of linden trees, weeping their sweetness from golden blossoms, formed an impressive archway up both winding driveway entrances, to the pair of magnificent '20's houses that commanded the brow of the bench. Catalpa trees towered above Taylor, their huge heart-shaped leaves and white, orchid-like blossoms arranged in conical clusters, which hummed with bees and flitting birds. Spent blossoms, drifted by canyon winds into a thick carpet, were scraped through where his men had dragged pruned branches down the lawn to his trucks parked at the river-stone retaining wall. Expensive, healthy grass lay exposed like pathways. The old-money family who owned the adjoining estates hadn't asked how much it would cost to clear debris, or trim, shape, and treat some thirty wind-damaged trees. They'd just demanded it be done in two days before their daughter's engagement-announcement garden party—if he wanted the job.

The Wind Remembers

Taylor had given them a high bid for the rush job and been surprised when they took it. He hired temporary workmen to assist and now the job on both properties was nearly finished. In half an hour they'd all be on their way, everything raked and cleared to perfection. The lawns resembled meticulously maintained golf greens.

He was pleased. Invoice in his pocket, the charges were substantial enough to meet payroll for the temps, Randy, Griff, and himself, and to make two months worth of truck payments on both vehicles. That would leave $850 for the cash box. Taylor'd taken to paying himself a salary, then doubling it and banking it in an investment account for when business was slack in the off-season. That decision, and keeping his commitment to do it all during last year, had impressed Pops. Taylor was glad something had, something besides being back in love with Suzanne. He wanted his dad's approval for himself as a businessman and a man first. The right wife thing could come later.

Randy came to him when the shuttle for the temps, mostly Spanish-speaking migrant workers, pulled away. The men joked and smiled, knowing they were going back to pick up their paychecks and buy beer in downtown Farr. Taylor'd jotted down the names and contacts for the best workers, the ones who had a sense of the importance for careful, hard work around living trees. He handed the list to Randy, who folded it in his pocket and patted it like insurance for the future, which could be tomorrow, the way storm and word-of-mouth business was going.

"Took a call for you from officer Doug what's his face. Says it's an emergency that he needs to know what route Suzanne's taking to camp at the Sun Tunnels."

Taylor flipped open his cell phone. "The only emergency that S.O.B. has is somewhere between his hat brim and his zipper. None of his damn business what route she took this morning. He leave a number?"

"Here, use my phone. Hit last call." Randy moved off to load tools and lock down safety hatches.

Taylor listened through the rings and waited for Doug to pick up, while he held equipment lock-up doors for Randy and looked around to survey their handiwork. He felt professional pride in a job superbly accomplished on short notice. A truck with rental tents for fancy occasions drove up the hill to set up on the immaculate lawn, a caterer's van close behind. The phone was picked up.

"Armstrong? That you this time?"

"Jensen?" His cheek twitched with the unresolved anger of what the man had done to Suzanne and how far it might have gone if he hadn't intervened. "What's up with this emergency of yours?"

"We went looking for Bo on his nephew's tip up at that Makris sheep camp above Suzanne's place. Fat little fart we picked up squealed on Big Blue, that's Bo's nephew's name. You remember the wise-ass we nailed for spray-painting our vehicles? Well, we were wrong. This kid named Rat admitted he did it to get Big Blue in trouble so he could have his girl and the 'brothers' to himself. I was mad as hell, cuffing him to take him in while Lopez helped him get his pants on and read him his rights . . . "

"Look, Doug, I haven't got time to . . ."

"Hear me out, Armstrong. As I was saying, we caught this Rat with his pants down, literally. He had a story to tell to stay out of jail, afraid we'd put him in with Big Blue and the head of the Blue Tattoo Gang would kill him."

"That mean, huh." Taylor climbed behind the wheel and prepared to return the phone to Randy, just climbing in next to him in the passenger's seat. "I've got to . . ."

"Bo cut down Suzanne's tree, broke into her house looking for money. This Rat claims he was there window peeking night before last and saw him."

Taylor started the engine. "So go pick the bad cowboy up. Now that you've got a witness; do your job. You've sure as hell proved your talent for the mean-assed stuff."

Randy grinned his encouragement, thumbs up, while he cranked up the volume on a country ballad.

"Rat took us to the body of Rehma Price. Strangled, maybe a couple of days ago. Says he watched Bo stuff her into the rocks, heard him mumbling on about taking the Price woman's kids for some money. Bo's probably following Suzanne right now. Tell me which route they planned to take. I've got to get to them before he does."

Taylor floored the engine and motioned for Randy to cut off the radio. "Not alone you're not, Buddy. You're going nowhere near Suzanne without me on your tail—real tight! Get that straight. I'll be at your office in ten minutes. You better be there waiting for me. You don't comply, as a witness I'll press assault charges on you, even if Susie lets you off. Get a copter and have a map ready. They've got a three-hour start and without stops could be close to setting up camp already!"

Suzanne Price

~ Friday the 20th of June

Suzanne directed Dierdre to the exit for the Snowville Truck Stop. They drove in and took their place in one of the eight long lines of cars waiting their turn to use the self-serve gas pumps. Heat shimmered off the pavement in waves that distorted the line up of distant cars into hazy zig-zag shapes like something out of *Star Wars*.

"Wow!" Gregory released his seat belt and rose to his knees to see over piles of gear out the back window. "Look at those cool trucks. Must be a hundred of 'em."

"I'm glad they're in a parking area of their own," said Suzanne. "We'd never get gassed up if we had to wait for them to fill up their big tanks first."

"I *got* to go potty," said Mitzi. "I'm all out of waiting,

The Wind Remembers

Mommy. Come wif me *right now, please*." She tucked the crayon box between Bear Lovin's paws and climbed out into Suzanne's arms.

"Can you handle everything from here, Dee?"

"Sis, if I can't figure it out, I'll find a man who can. You run on ahead with the kids. I'll fill up and park, then meet you inside—if I don't melt first."

"Try not to draw a crowd," Suzanne teased. She hurried the kids into the sweltering heat of the noisy parking plaza, insisting on holding their hands. Vans, trucks, campers and cars, many pulling expensive horse trailers or racks of motorbikes, wove in and out of line. Dogs on leashes, too long confined, tugged and barked to run free and investigate other dogs with similar inclinations. Kids raced to be first for cold drinks, Creamy bars, bathrooms and video games.

Inside, the air-conditioned urban-style oasis swarmed with tourists and truck drivers eddying in and out of aisles of snack foods; camping, hunting and fishing supplies; auto parts; leather work gloves and stay-awake tablets. At the far end a food court wafted its smells to entice the hungry to its choices of 24-hour breakfast, ranch-hand style including bacon, sausage and hash browns; Mexican burritos; Chinese egg rolls and Italian pizza. A darkened video-game room at one side held a sea of machines, their bells ringing and interplanetary weapons zipping and zapping.

"Stay close, you two. It's a mad house in here." Suzanne opened her handbag and counted out coins to Greg who'd decided food could wait when video games could be played. "I'm taking Mitzi to the restroom. If you finish before we do, stay here by this drinking fountain or with your aunt. Promise?"

"Okay already, okay." He ran off to claim a video machine and had crammed quarters into the slot before she and Mitzi got in line.

Mitzi danced around, studied the lowest shelves nearby, and at last held herself. "Betcha somebody's baby's going to have uh accident."

"As long as it isn't *my* baby," Suzanne said, bending to kiss her curls. "Try to be patient, Sweetheart." She saw Dierdre through the window, at last having her turn at the gas pump. She'd already solicited the aid of a smiling father, child clutching his shorts and tag-along wife pouting her disapproval, to explain the complexities of the pay-at-the-pump gas-card machine. Her chuckle at her twin's predictability choked in her throat at the sight of a beat-up truck making a screeching swing turn into the fill-up area for long-haul semi tractor/trailer trucks. Perhaps she had only imagined it was Bo Rodman's rusty camper pick-up, or was it possible he had reason to be out here hours out of Farr, too?

She looked around, reassured herself Greg was nearby zapping robot invaders with laser beams and Dee had the gas nozzle feeding the Blazer. The idea her son would be alone in the crowded place for a few minutes, and Bo was perhaps entering the building contorted her edginess to urgent.

"My little girl is desperate to use the restroom. It's a real emergency!" Suzanne interrupted the teen conversation. "Could we go first? Oh, thank you so much."

Bo Rodman

~ Friday the 20th of June

Bo drove in and parked between rows of high-profile, long-haul trucks queued up for diesel fuel and water. More than a few noisy generators in refrigerator trucks kept Utah and Idaho beef, lamb, cheese, and produce cool for thousand-mile trips to urban markets. He felt like a damn fool carrying one of Frank's aluminum falcon bath tubs to get water, but he knew if he didn't let the hawk cool down she'd die in the heat of his camper shell and he'd be out his next-to-last hope for quick money. Good thing the Price truck had turned into the truck stop too. *Where in hell is she headed? Glad it's north, I'll only have to go east to be in Montana on time to make the Canadian border transfer of this damn hawk.*

He set the bath water on the ground and opened the tailgate. Then he lifted the big pan inside and set it down by the block perch, lengthened the tether on the falcon and took off her hood as quickly as he could before she could bite his hand. She smelled and spied the water, eyeing it cautiously, but with interest. He offered her a chunk of chicken breast. Probably going bad by the smell of it. She pecked at it, uninterested, descended to the cool water and stepped around and around in it, making throaty sounds to herself, fluttering her feathers and snapping at the water. Bo scooped water onto the towel-covered perch to soak it and shut the tailgate. He left the window hinged up for the air to circulate between it and the side windows, while he let Tracker do his business in the back lot and, when he whistled, return at a lope.

Opening his can of chew, Bo pinched a wad and stuffed it in his cheek, wishing he had full use of his body like he used to, so that nabbing the kids for ransom right here in this crowd would be easy to pull off. A man and woman, driving partners he figured by their matching truck-company T-shirts and tattooed arms, passed by close enough to see into the camper shell. Bo lifted his hand in a subtle wave, gave a big smile and they walked on, talking about a steak sandwich they'd enjoyed in Idaho. Relieved that he didn't have to bullshit them to cover himself with the falcon, he felt around on the floor of his truck bed a safe distance from the falcon's talons and beak, for a bag of chips he'd ripped off from the Price kitchen. His hand touched the transmitter gear Frank'd loaned him weeks ago. A new idea formed. He took the device and its remote out, closed the tailgate window a bit more, shut Tracker up front in the cab and took his neckerchief from his back pocket. He dabbed the sweat from his neck and under his hatband, a smile playing about his lips.

Limping around the building to the auto/RV parking lot side of the complex, he stood in the shade of the overhang chewing his tobacco for a few seconds, until he spied the Price truck. *Nobody inside it.* He spat and moved off, coming up on the rear bumper of the Blazer from behind. He squatted down. People moved on around him, busy with their own activity, their minds on vacation fun. His hands felt for the right place to fit the transmitter where it would be out of sight. He gave up on the bumper area, explored too close to the hot muffler and burned his hand raw through to the flesh. *Son of a bitch!*

Looking around, Bo stood and ran his hand behind the spare-tire bracket. *Perfect.* He tied the transmitter securely with his neckerchief, backed away, blended with the crowd and returned to his truck. He tested the receiver, waited for the signal. It worked the way Frank showed him it did.

Breaking a cold beer out of the cooler, he poured some in a thermos lid and let Tracker lap at it. "Well, Ol' Boy, Mr. Frank Simmons gave us a little edge up on the competition with that falcon-tracking gadget. We can follow them women and kids wherever they go for ten miles or more back. Who says ol' Bo ain't as smart as that fancy-assed lawyer!"

He sat petting his dog, eating the Price woman's chips and drinking beer, congratulating himself, until the transmitter signal on his receiver indicated the Price truck had moved farther away. He drove around to the unleaded-gas pumps to fill up, still chuckling to himself about how he could follow at a longer, safer distance without being spotted, now that there wouldn't be so many vehicles to hide behind heading north and west. He was so caught up in being smart he didn't notice the man in the special-needs car two rows over, who pulled a new ball cap over his hair and put on a pair of dark wrap-around safety glasses he'd just cut the price tags off of with his teeth.

THE WIND REMEMBERS

Suzanne Price

~ Friday the 20th of June

Her mind on the possibility of Bo Rodman heading in a similar direction to her own, maybe even following her, Suzanne regularly checked on her rear-view mirror, but kept her concerns to herself in front of the kids. There'd be time enough to tell Dee, if she needed to. But why would he be following them? He surely wasn't so dumb as to think she'd carry $50,000 with her on a camping trip. It made no sense to her, unless he meant her harm for vengeance sake. She wouldn't put it past him. Was Rehma with him? Suzanne hadn't seen her, but Steve's ex-wife had certainly been pushy on the phone. *Perhaps she's not wanting to let me off the hook with the kids about this camping idea of hers, no . . . surely not.*

A bedraggled van with a pop-up tent putted along behind them in the distance, but now that they were well out of Elko, Nevada, vehicles other than local farm cars and machinery were rarely spotted. Suzanne took a main road that turned back across the desert into Utah, the only way with paved roads to approach the Sun Tunnels when coming from Elko. Mitzi had fallen asleep and Greg contentedly flipped pages in his insect book, only occasionally clicking his fingernails, which early on had driven Dee to bribe him with chocolate bars to stop it until they were out of the car at the campsite.

Dierdre turned on the radio. "More local grain reports, weather, country tunes and static," she said. "How do people stand living way out here? I'd be bored silly."

"Sorry the old tape player is shot," said Suzanne.

"There must be something to listen to since there's nothing to look at but cattle and sage brush for as far as the eye can see." She turned the knob in earnest.

"Nary a skyscraper or a sail boat in sight is a tough call for you, no doubt." Suzanne laughed affectionately, at last glad for her own reasons to be away from Farr and to have time alone this evening with her twin. She did regret turning Taylor down on coming with them, in spite of the fact it would have meant bringing both his truck and hers. His being there lately to take care of them had made it possible for her to start sleeping again. "The next turn will take us to the Lucin railroad cut off and shortly after that the road will go to gravel, if this late '80's map is up to date."

With intermittent static, the radio broadcast snatches: "Police have not released the woman's name pending notification of family, but say her death was a homicide. Her assailant is being sought. Be on the lookout for . . ." Dierdre twirled the knob. "Gad, murder mysteries even way out here," she said. "By the looks of this sorry looking landscape, probably nothing better for the locals to do than plan a murder."

Suzanne reached over and switched off the radio. "Let's stay positive, shall we?"

In the evening light, at the old railroad cut off, a combination-locked, lone out-building housing mysterious equipment stood guard by the single pair of shiny railroad tracks appearing and disappearing through the weeds in both directions. When the Blazer bumped over the tracks and descended the little road, a jackrabbit hopped away. Weathered wooden signs on rakish hand-hewn posts appeared to have been there for generations, pointing the way to a homestead long abandoned. Its blackened foundation remained the mute evidence of a fire. A few fence posts still supported tangles of rusty barbed wire. An ancient telephone pole that once carried electricity from somewhere to a twisted metal farm light, now served as roost for a magnificent horned owl.

"Can you believe it?" whispered Greg. "I bet it has a mate somewhere near here. There it is! — up there in that big old cottonwood above the pond. I wonder where they have a nest. Bet their wing spread is as tall as me or more."

Other than a dilapidated outhouse, minus its door and roof, and an ancient pump, the yard hosted only waist-high weeds, rusty junk and jackrabbits.

"Hey, there's some old steps going down to a door in the ground," Greg went on eagerly. "What do you suppose they go to?"

"Look's like an old root cellar," said Suzanne, delighting in his recaptured enthusiasm. "Rattlesnake heaven probably."

"What a spooky place," added Dierdre. "The map indicates this was the water station in the days of the steam engine, until the train connection was completed across Great Salt Lake." She pointed to the cottonwoods surrounding the pond. "These trees are massive. The trunk of that one is bigger than the one-room Park Valley Post Office in that crossroad's excuse for a town we came through a while back."

"If you had your roots in a pond, you'd suck up enough water to get huge too." Greg grinned with spunk.

"Aren't we the little expert?" Dierdre examined the map while Suzanne concentrated on seeing through the clouds of fine dust ballooning from their tires. "Keep the windows rolled up or we'll choke to death."

"I was told the Tunnels are big concrete tubes laid out on the desert in a sort of plus sign lined up with north, south, east and west. They're big enough to stand up and walk in, so they should be easy to see."

Dierdre didn't sound convincing to Suzanne, who focused on not bottoming out in the ruts at dusk. She had no idea if they would find the Tunnels or be forced to pitch their tents in the dark. "If this solstice event is such a big deal to you New Agers, shouldn't we be able to see other campers by now?"

"There's some little bitty cars way out there," Gregory pointed.

"Dee, shall I try that rutted track breaking off here? It heads in that direction."

"Funny, there's no posted sign. Try it. By the map it should be right here. Nothing else looks promising. Good eyes, Greg."

The Blazer jostled down into a steep dry wash where the rusted hulk of an upside-down sedan from their grandmother's era sprouted thirty-years worth of tamarisk out its broken windows. Suzanne steered erratically to avoid it, tires spinning stones behind them as the wheels dug their way forward up the other equally steep side of the wash. Flushed from the brush, a prong-horned antelope scuttled up the bank ahead of them, its tail and hooves flashing in its panicked flight.

"Wow! We could be in the Serengeti!" squealed Greg.

"Who's in bisquetti?" Mitzi wriggled to a sitting position, rubbing her eyes. "Are we lost, Mommy? It's awful bouncy for a real road. Bear Lovin's head flopped over."

"Are those gray hotdog things the Sun Tunnels?" Greg looked dejected. "I thought they'd light up or something. They look real boring."

"God lights them up with the sunrise," said Dierdre. "Tomorrow morning on the solstice, you'll see."

Suzanne was touched by the awe in her twin's voice. "Did I hear you use the G word, sister of mine?" She switched on the headlights and drove slowly out to the gathering of people, wondering with each lump in the terrain what strange solstice nonsense she was in for. She half expected to see little people in hooded, brown *Star Wars* robes appear out of the dust shrieking jibberish and brandishing pointy weapons.

"Look, somebody just lit a campfire," announced Greg. "This is going to be fun!"

Johnny Carlisle

~ Friday the 20th of June

Johnny jounced along behind Bo's truck in the distance, following its taillights, distinctive because the left one hung loosely, causing it to bob and wink in the dark. He had no idea

333

where he was going and felt light headed from a combination of heat, fatigue, adrenaline rush and medication washed down with Gatorade. Being cooped up in the car all afternoon and into the night had gotten on his nerves. Whatever advantage he'd hoped for with Bo might be negated now in the dark where the bastard could turn even being sneaked up on to his advantage. But no matter what it cost him, day or night, Johnny determined to leave him alive long enough to find out what he'd done with Felon.

It'd been risky waiting for Bo at the truck stop, but Johnny felt relieved when Mrs. Price and her sister drove away with the kids, especially when Bo made no attempt to follow them. The only break in the boredom of following him had been paying a teenager to buy two pieces of sausage pizza, a giant-sized cola, a ball cap, and a pair of sun glasses at the truck stop, so he wouldn't have to get out of the car with Bo around. After he drank the cola, he peed in the cup, snapped the lid back on and dropped it out the window into a drive-up waste can at the gas pumps. He didn't care where Bo was going. It didn't matter. Now that he was close, Johnny had no intention of letting him escape.

Deep in his healing bones he felt that this night Bo Rodman would pay for every broken one of them, and for his lost wife and sons. He was glad he didn't have to worry about the Price family while he took his revenge, but he'd only take it after learning what happened to his gyrfalcon. Depending upon what Bo had to say—as he bled and begged for mercy—Johnny would decide whether to finish him off or leave him to die the way he and his dog'd been left. Seeing camp lights in the distance, he headed in that direction.

The Wind Remembers

Bo Rodman

~Friday the 20th of June

Coming to a campsite, twinkling in the night, Bo thought, *Hell of a place to camp. No mountains for trail hikes, no rivers for fishing. What'd bring the Price bitch out here; sidewinder target practice?* He'd watch for snakes and scorpions. Nothing out here you'd want to step on in the dark. Bo cut his lights and pulled over near a shrouded pond and parked his truck nose-deep in the brush with his tail-end to the dirt road. Car lights approached behind him. He ducked down. They drew even and passed.

Taylor Armstrong

~ Friday the 20th of June

Taylor sat hunched in the little four-seater, squinting out the window at the puny landing strip in a field on somebody's ranch near Elko. He had to give Doug credit for the idea of flying closer to the Sun Tunnels, when a helicopter couldn't be arranged for on short notice, without a certifiable life-threatening emergency. They'd wasted two hours on gear and transportation. Wild fires near Provo and a search and rescue operation for some stranded cliff climbers in Little Cottonwood Canyon, meant all Utah choppers were engaged in more heroic and well-televised efforts. The whirling red and blue lights of the waiting state trooper cars moved in as the plane's propellers spun to a stop. Somebody doused the landing flares. Doug hopped down first, in charge and loving it.

Taylor stayed close to the jerk, trying to keep the disgust off his face at how pompous Doug treated the off-duty officers

335

who had shown up to help. Whatever it took to get along with Doug and not be left out of the police action, he just wanted to hold Suzanne safely in his arms. He knew Doug wouldn't have agreed to let him come if he hadn't been so short-handed and threatened by Taylor with assault charges, which would cost him his badge.

Trouble was, only one of the three officers, the one near retirement age, had ever been to the Sun Tunnels. It upset Taylor at how little attention the old guy was getting for information no one else had. Doug, chewing on his mustache and busy stashing rifles and boxes of shells in the trunk of the lead cruiser, barely listened to him. Taylor checked the batteries in his flashlight for about the tenth time, making it his business to pay very close attention to everything the older fellow had to say to his own team.

Taylor had asked him if there was a way to fly in to the Tunnel site and land close enough to cut out some cross-country time. The older fellow'd said the only thing "anywheres close" was an abandoned landing strip for crop dusters, and it was beat up and unpredictable with weed-grown broken pavement.

"Wouldn't be safe to land, 'specially in the dark with no runway lights and nobody on the ground to set flares. Besides, startin' a prairie fire with flares in the dry scrub with a good breeze is rightly frowned on around here." The old fellow chuckled and moved off to give orders about the cars with Taylor on his heels. Doug spread maps on the hood of a volunteer officer's Jeep.

THE WIND REMEMBERS

Suzanne Price

~ Friday the 20th of June

Dierdre's suggestion of setting up camp by the light of the Blazer low beams worked out well. The two tents, perhaps twenty feet apart, door flaps facing each other, were pegged taut, one farther away from the campfire than the other. Sleeping bags were fluffed out inside, awaiting four tired bodies who'd soon stretch out for a few hours of sleep before the dawn of the summer solstice on the 21st of June.

Suzanne hoped the kids would turn in soon, so she and Dee could sit by the fire and let their hair down a little. Greg, pouting because he wanted a tent to himself or a chance to sleep with his Aunt Dierdre, was making do with an extra after-dinner smore. By the campfire, he licked his ego wounds, along with the chocolate. Mitzi, drowsy with marshmallow sugar and a day more full of new experiences than she was used to, leaned against her aunt by the fire, fighting to stay awake.

Dierdre called, "Susie, how about a mug of brew? I'm too excited to sleep anyway, might as well enjoy some camp coffee."

Suzanne knew her twin had brought a flask of brandy for a nightcap and agreed without letting on she understood the real reason for some strong Columbian. She hauled out the Coleman, the pot and a jug of water to begin the campfire ritual they'd last shared alone on a few weekends years ago in college.

Dierdre washed Mitzi's face and fingers with a damp cloth and helped her take off her sneakers in the tent and climb into her sleeping bag. "You, little missy, are going to bed, so you'll be perky as a porcupine in the morning." Mitzi allowed herself to be zipped in with a lullaby about rocking horses and, cradling Bear Lovins, dozed off before the song ended. Dierdre returned to the fire and the cook stove and unpacked ground coffee, the pot and mugs.

While the water came to a boil, Suzanne put an arm around Greg's shoulders. "Thanks for agreeing to share a tent with me tonight, I know you really wanted one all to yourself. I'm glad I don't have to sleep alone. It is kind of like the Serengeti isn't it?"

"That's okay. It's cool just to come out here in the desert. Wasn't that antelope awesome? Wait 'til I tell Alex." He hugged her back. "Are we really going to eat breakfast with that gypsy woman in the motor home over there and her boys?"

"That's the plan, but I don't think she's a gypsy, she looks Indian with those high cheek bones and deep-set eyes. She is quite exotic looking with leather fringe and feathers. I can imagine how stunning she must have been as a young woman. Wish I could ask her to pose for a painting. Greg, you know your aunt. She's introduced herself to half the people here in the hour since we set up camp. I'm glad she took you and Mitzi along while I got unpacked and spread our sleeping bags to air out in our tents. She thought you'd enjoy meeting kids your own age."

Suzanne enjoyed being affectionate and talking with Greg like old times. This new closeness eased a great deal of the misery of the last few months and recent days. "Now, time for bed, *if* you've had enough smores."

She walked him to the door of the tent farthest from the fire, the one he'd chosen because it felt like the most adventuresome to be more away from everyone else in camp. Greg flashed the light around the interior and into the sleeping bag, the way the woman with the braid's showed her boys and him to check for snakes, tarantulas and scorpions. Satisfied all was clear, he handed the flashlight back to Suzanne.

Greg smiled up at her in the glow of her flashlight. "I'm glad you liked my idea to use the front bumper of the Blazer to tie the tent pole for Aunt Dierdre's tent, since we were short that stake Doug and I lost last summer." He didn't move from her touch, in fact he snuggled against her.

She realized with a rush of tenderness that he didn't want the moment to end any more than she did. Her face broke into a smile. She hugged him close.

"Goodnight Mom . . . Suzanne."

"Oh, Greg, I would love it if you felt comfortable calling me Mom." She fought the tears of gratitude forming at her lashes. "Goodnight, Sweetheart." She zipped him safely inside the tent. They touched hands with the webbed screen between their palms.

"I love you," she whispered.

"Me, too," he said.

Returning to the campfire, she was surprised and instantly disappointed to see her twin had invited someone else to share the evening that for six months they'd planned for themselves, once the kids were asleep. She recognized Johnny Carlisle. *What's HE doing here?* Behind him the woman in a fringed-and beaded-suede dress approached their fire.

Dierdre Ingram

~ Friday the 20th of June

Dierdre poured a splash of brandy into a fourth mug and looked at Johnny, still amazed to see him.

His words came out slow and deliberate. "God a mighty this coffee smells delicious." He sipped. "You put some liqueur in here?"

She watched him in the firelight. From scarred brow to misshapen jaw line the shadows played over his smiling face, in bad need of a shave. *Handsome. One incredible body. What a will to survive this guy must have.*

"You mind?" Dierdre asked brightly. *He would be some fine addition to a woman's tent who knew how to make a man forget every terrible thing that ever happened to him.*

"Not a bit. Been a long drive, a hot drink of coffee with some zip was a long shot."

At the sound of her sister, Dierdre turned. "Suzanne, look who dropped by for a fireside chat." She handed her twin a mug. "Brandy?"

"Just a titch. Hello, Johnny, I didn't imagine you'd be here to celebrate the solstice. It's a new thing for me." She prepared to sit and realized the chairs were taken by their two guests. "Dee intends to make its significance clear to me this evening." She turned to the woman. "I'm Dierdre's sister Suzanne, and you are?"

"Cosma, Cosma Stargazer." Her silver earrings danced against her deeply tanned neck. She moved closer to Johnny by the fire and left room for Suzanne.

"A stage name?" Suzanne asked. She heard Dee sputter coffee.

"No," Cosma said, "but I'm of Paiute heritage; it's a business name. I'm a licensed massage therapist. I also do healing work with herbs and give spiritual readings with animal cards, and read sign of various types."

Dierdre said, "I was about to ask Johnny about his solstice interest myself." She touched his hand. He looked up at her. She could tell he was pleased. "We'll be able to walk in the Tunnels and explore the area in the morning after the light burst at dawn. It's a shame we arrived too late to let the kids walk through them this evening."

Suzanne took a sip and thought about where to sit, wondering how long it would be until she could reoccupy the canvas chair she'd brought for herself and so looked forward to using. "I'm sure the light burst will seem all the more magical in the morning for not seeing the technology that makes it possible tonight."

"There isn't anything magic about the solstice lights," said Cosma, "but it will be more dramatic to experience it for the first time without walking the Tunnels first."

"I don't know a thing about this place and what goes on here tomorrow," said Johnny. "I . . . uh, came to meet a man . . . about my stolen falcon. I walked around the camp, but I didn't see him and his friends anywhere. That's when I spotted the Price family." He'd struggled to remember Dierdre's name and given up. His mind was more on the Cosma woman with the single, thick dark braid over her plump, beaded left breast.

"Oh, do you think you've found someone to care for your falcon when you find it?" Suzanne's voice was so genuine Dee wagged her head in wonder that anyone could be quite as oblivious to hormones raging in her vicinity as her own twin. *How can we even be of the same gene pool?*

Johnny shifted in the folding chair, propping his cane against the cooler. "We arranged to meet here. When I was walking around getting familiar with the layout, I thought I saw your kids by the fire, so I locked up my gear and came over to say hello. You ladies have everything you need, I mean to be safe and everything?"

Suzanne nodded.

"My people believe the hawk is a messenger of Great Spirit," Cosma said. "Hawk medicine teaches us to observe our surroundings to see what is obvious and what is not. Those who travel in the company of hawks are twice blessed, for the hawk makes the choice to be your brother or sister. Hawk's commitment to a human is an honor."

She bowed to Johnny with her hands folded, as though he were a holy man. "Woe to the one who took your falcon, for the hawk can perceive evil clearly with the eye of Great Spirit."

Suzanne Price

~ Friday the 20th of June

Something in Johnny's voice made Suzanne nervous, and it wasn't the brandy talking. He was here for more than his falcon; she felt sure of it. The reason was serious, not that his stolen hawk wasn't, but this felt bigger, more sinister. Everything nasty that had happened in recent days made her wary, as she'd never been in her entire life. She intended to be patient enough to get to the bottom of it. Listening to the laughter and camp songs from nearby groups, she looked up and tried to identify constellations in the perfect night. The moon was out, only occasionally slipping behind thready clouds, which drifted off toward the Eastern cliffs where Cosma said dawn would break through a cleft in the rock and spill light across the valley and into the Sun Tunnels.

They discussed the chances of the sun being obscured by cloud cover in the morning and ruining the light show through the Tunnels. With prickly apprehension giving her shivers, Suzanne stopped trying to be amiable and let her gut feelings take precedence over the moment. Those feelings returned her to the truck stop and her glimpse of the camper truck she thought might be Bo's. Then she remembered the day in her living room when Bo Rodman had been the one Doug and Johnny suspected of beating this man by the fire within an inch of his life. If she really had seen Bo at the truck stop, was it possible, perhaps even probable that the jerk was also somewhere in their vicinity and that Johnny suspected it—or even knew it for sure?

His concern for our safety seems more than casual, Suzanne thought. *I think it's time to pin him down to his true reason for being here. It makes no sense that a man as physically vulnerable as he is would come out to a place he'd never been before in the dark—even for his falcon. Is Bo following him to finish the job of killing him?*

"Mother was fifty and over-committed," Dierdre was saying, perhaps on some imaginary stage, or so it appeared to Suzanne. "I thought she had a feeling of having come full-circle like rain on a pond, then fearful that her time was over, kept repeating herself in wider worry patterns until . . . she had a heart attack and just went quiet." Dramatically, Dee drained her mug and set it down, as if on blocking cue.

"What a strange way to talk about Mom's death," Suzanne interrupted. "Let's change the subject, shall we?"

"Oh, Susie, you're always wanting to change the subject

to something more comfortable for you. Johnny and Cosma and I are just getting acquainted. Divulging our true selves is important to a good trust level."

"How about I change it to an even *more* uncomfortable topic, then?"

Dee's surprised expression made Suzanne chuckle, but only for a moment.

"Johnny, it seems to me you're more than casually concerned for our safety out here tonight. Why don't you tell us why you really came out to the Sun Tunnels—alone? What do you fear we need to be kept safe from?"

"Well, you know, you two women out here on your own with these kids in this wilderness, I . . . I'm just concerned like any man would be. You can't be too careful."

"You sure that's all, Johnny? I'm all out of patience with surprises because some man thinks I need protecting from the truth."

"Well, if you don't mind, I'll just sit here with you ladies a while to make sure that you're safe and comfortable for the night."

Dee interrupted. "Sister of mine, why don't you toddle off to bed and let us talk for a while." It wasn't a question. Suzanne felt stung by her twin's dismissal, irritated and weary of Dee's drama games for an audience. She thought it unfair of Dee to take advantage of a man so hungry for female attention and so ill equipped to take emotional care of himself and a strange woman who was perhaps out of her depth. This evening also came at a moment that supposedly belonged to the twins—and only them.

"But you *must* prepare yourselves for the solstice!" Cosma Stargazer insisted. "This isn't a tourist attraction, it's a planetary event about to happen. Surely, Suzanne, you want to be part of it at the highest and deepest levels possible for your soul."

My Soul?! Suzanne had trouble masking her skepticism and could think of no response that wouldn't make everyone around the campfire feel even more awkward.

The Wind Remembers

Dierdre handed Johnny a refreshed mug of their hot-brandied coffee, waited until he had a good grip on the handle, handed Suzanne hers and offered one to Cosma.

"Thank you, but no. I don't partake of alcohol or anything else before I smoke the sacred pipe. I'll begin the cleansing and preparation ceremony at my campfire in just a few minutes, then I won't speak until the Sun Tunnel blessing in the morning. My boys love it when I'm quiet for that long." Her rich laugh bubbled through the night air.

"Of course, we understand," Dierdre said. Suzanne wondered if her twin really did know about such New Age things or if this too was an act. Dierdre continued, "Why don't you perform the ceremony here? We have more room around our campfire, and we'd love to share in the . . . preparation. Do you have a drum, too?"

Suzanne wanted to stifle her sister with the sweatshirt brought to pull over her tank top. *What is she thinking? What happened to our sister thing? A drum? Get real!*

"Johnny, Suzanne, you'd like to experience a blessing ceremony, wouldn't you?" Dee's tone was insistent. "Of course we would, Cosma. Please get your pipe and bring your boys too. I can't believe we have a practicing shaman to lead us." Dierdre gushed her enthusiasm and cleared a flat place near the fire—for what—Suzanne wasn't sure.

She sat her mug in the weeds while she folded her sweatshirt for a seating pad and eased herself to the ground. *Well, this should be spooky interesting*, she thought. *I'll just chalk it up to free entertainment, since I can't have my sister to myself.*

"Well, if you really want me to . . ." Cosma adjusted the ribbons on her long braid, obviously waiting for Johnny or Suzanne to add their encouragement. She kept looking from one to the other in the flickering light, lingering longer on Johnny.

"I don't know a thing about this place or about smoking pipes, except what I've seen in old cowboy movies with warring Indians," said Johnny. He laughed and blew on his brandy. "But I'm willing to learn." His scarred face broke into a smile.

Suzanne realized what a handsome man he really was. She was certain Cosma had drawn that conclusion much faster than she had.

"You'll have to stop drinking once I start the ceremony," Cosma said. "But just until it's over." Her hand brushed his broad shoulder in passing toward her own camp.

That private little gesture gives me some hope this won't take all night. Suzanne sipped her brandied coffee and let the tiredness of her body from driving and making camp sink into the dusty, white-clay ground around her.

"Oh, Suze, isn't this the best? I couldn't have planned it better!" Dierdre brought out more blankets from the truck and arranged them around the fire. "Wait until I tell my cruise ship friends about this. They've been teasing me for being so 'airy fairy'. I'll have a story to blow their minds after tonight and tomorrow."

Cosma returned with a skin drum the size of a serving platter, and about four inches deep, cradled in the crook of one arm and a red parcel tied with cord in the other. She carried them like she was going down the center aisle in church with the sacraments.

"My boys are already asleep, so I'll let them rest now. I'll meditate with them in the morning." She laid her items on the blanket Dee had spread closest to the fire. Cosma removed her shoes and set them off of the blanket in the dirt. "Do you have a little more of that brandy?"

Dierdre nodded, handing her the mug she'd offered her earlier.

Suzanne was confused after Cosma's refusal of a drink and was surprised Dee didn't offer to add coffee to heat it up or to dilute it.

"We'll make an offering to the spirits." Cosma lifted the mug to the sky and the four directions, then dribbled the brandy into the dirt around her blanket.

Oh, brother. Here we go. Lord, protect me and my family from whatever she conjures up! Suzanne took her place cross-legged on the blanket where Cosma gestured for her to sit, next to Dee and across from Johnny, whom she was glad to see remain in his chair.

"There are many rituals you will not understand," she nodded to Suzanne, then to Johnny, "but please remain reverent. I'll explain as I go." Cosma placed her drum in her lap and using the fingers of both hands, tapped out a rhythm that began softly and built to a crescendo with her palms. "The drum is the heart beat of the people." Abruptly, she set the drum aside.

"Great Spirit," Cosma called. "Grandfather, Grandmother, all the Spirits of this place, Spirit of the drum, Spirit of the pipe, we come before you humbly and ask you to prepare us to receive your blessing. We would be one in spirit with you at this solstice time." She reached for the red bundle.

Suzanne feared she'd burst into giggles or simply confront the woman for being a fraud. Dierdre sat quietly, as erect as a monk. For her sister's sake Suzanne struggled to control her resistance to this blasphemy and silently thanked Jesus that her children were not present to be brainwashed, especially Greg who would've been overly impressed with all this nonsense. Johnny stirred in his chair, leaning forward on his cane. To her he seemed quite taken with the buxom woman. He wasn't just watching her hands and he seemed to have lost interest in Dee altogether. That in itself was most unusual.

Cosma lifted the red bundle in both hands, well above her head. In a husky voice she spoke, "Great Spirit, we call upon you to dwell with us as we smoke the pipe of peace and seek the common ground of goodness with one another." She lowered the bundle to the blanket and untied the many cords around it.

"This red cloth is an old Indian trading blanket, a special relic of my mother's people." Her teaching voice was hushed but normal. "It and these cords that bind it, the pipe in its bag, and everything in this bundle have been blessed in sacred ceremony. Wait patiently while I perform each ritual." She unwrapped the blanket and laid out its contents one at a time, waving her hands over each in the four directions, then toward the sky and toward the earth, before moving on to the next item.

Suzanne catalogued them with her artist's eye: a small unglazed clay bowl; a packet of wooden matches; what appeared to be a bunch of dried weeds; a palm-sized tin of something; a beaded wooden pick; a thin black cloth rolled and tied with cord; and a most beautiful fringed and beaded deer-skin pouch tied with leather thongs. Suzanne hadn't seen such craftsmanship outside the locked cases of Plains Indian treasures in the Cody, Wyoming Museum of History. *Maybe I'm here to learn something I didn't expect*, she thought. *Holy Spirit, open my mind and my heart to your wisdom while you guard me from evil.*

With her hands moving as gracefully as a ballerina's, Cosma crumbled the dried plants into the bowl and lit a match, bending her head to blow gently until the plant crumbles turned amber and the flame produced a fragrant spicy smoke. She took the bowl in both hands and lifted it to the sky. "Great Spirit, we burn the cedar and the sage for smoke to cleanse this place, to carry our prayers to you, to honor you, to remember always that you have a great plan that moves in the directions of the four winds beyond time. We are grateful to be a part of your plan, even in our imperfection. We thank you for your miracles, the big ones we see and the small ones we neglect to notice. Forgive us and remain with us even after your light moves through the Sun Tunnels at dawn—if you are willing to bless us and clear your sky of clouds so we can watch your sacred dance."

Cosma inhaled the smoke from the bowl, blew it in the direction of each of them, set it back on the blanket and with both hands scooped the smoke over her head, over her shoulders, over her long braid. Dropping her hands, she closed her eyes in silent prayer.

Dierdre reached Suzanne's hand and squeezed her fingers. Widening her eyes she smiled and mouthed, *This is fantastic!* Suzanne nodded. Johnny was with Cosma Stargazer somewhere off the planet, his face transfixed with something inexplicable.

The Wind Remembers

Cosma took a long time unwinding the leather thongs of the pouch and pulled out a carved and polished red-stone peace pipe in two pieces. She blew cedar smoke over them, then lifted the short bowl and the long stem of the pipe above her head and fitted them together. "Welcome, Pipe Spirit," she breathed in a whisper, yet they heard her clearly. "We ask your abiding peace to come upon us and erase any evil in this vast space. Let this time be a celebration of the greatest good of our Mother Earth, our Father Sky, and all of the good spirits you may bring to join us to increase the power of this solstice when planets align for your dance."

Cradling the pipe with the bowl of it in her hand and its stem resting on her forearm, with her other hand she removed the lid of the tin, took a pinch of something brown and stuffed it into the pipe's bowl. With each pinch she waved her hand in the four directions and to sky and earth. Three times she tamped the tobacco material into the pipe with the wooden pick. When it was full and firm, she used a dainty branch of cedar to carry a flame from the sputtering clay bowl to the pipe. Inhaling deeply with one hand cupped around the pipe's bowl to control the air and keep the breeze from extinguishing the tiny flicker of flame, she sucked the tobacco bark to glowing embers. She exhaled fragrant smoke until from Suzanne's view her head was swathed in white vapor. The breeze carried the smoke around them and upward on its way to the moon. Suzanne shivered. Cosma lifted the smoking pipe skyward.

"Great Spirit, for whatever reasons in your all-knowing plan you brought this group of strangers together, we thank you and ask your blessing upon us, upon our families, and on all those we love and have not brought to this place. Be with us this night; be with us when you dance your dance of light in the morning. Let us leave behind all trials that are not healthy in our lives, let us send them up to you in smoke to blow away upon another time. Take each of us home safely filled with your spirit. We seek now and always to walk beyond our own understanding in your love."

She turned the pipe in her hands in a complete circle and handed it to Johnny, giving him time to lean his cane against one knee. "You may smoke the pipe or not, say anything or nothing, but before you pass the pipe turn it completely around to embrace the spirits of North, South, East, and West, and send it whole to the next person."

Johnny's chin worked as if, as Suzanne feared, he might cry and feel embarrassed in front of three women. "I've come a long way in a broken body," he said, surprising her. "My purpose in coming was not entirely the best. But I am here and it's bigger than my dream. It's a miracle. I am a miracle . . . of yours." His eyes were as warm as glowing coals, their heat focused on Cosma who smiled a benevolent smile just for him. Carefully, awkwardly, but with determination to do it right and not drop it, he turned the pipe all the way around and handed it to Dierdre, then used his cane to tumble another log into the fire. Embers glittered above them until they dropped to earth as ash.

Drawing deeply on the pipe, smoke puffed from both sides of Dierdre's mouth and her nostrils. She sucked until her cheeks made hollows beneath the bones around her eyes squinted tight shut against the smoke rising in her face.

A piece of cake for her, Suzanne thought. *I am NOT going to smoke that thing!*

"Great Spirit, I'm thankful for learning about these Sun Tunnels, for coming here with my twin and her children, for meeting Johnny again, and Cosma Stargazer for the first time. I'll never forget this sacred time with you and all of us. Thank you for healing past hurts and sending us your power to make better choices in our lives and leading us to learn from each other." She rotated the pipe with reverence and passed it to Suzanne.

Taking the exquisite pipe in both hands, Suzanne touched the smooth hand-polished-stone surface, the beaded leather fringe, noted the exquisite carving of animals, stars, and moons on the stem that extended the pipe from her chin to her knees. Against her earlier thoughts, Suzanne brought the mouthpiece to her lips. She sucked gently, filled her mouth with smoke, tasted the strange flavors and—choked. Recovering her voice, she whispered, "Great Spirit, if you are the same as my Holy Spirit Father in Heaven—because I believe there is but one God—I thank you for revealing yourself in a *new* way to me. Forgive my eagerness to judge. Give me a heart of love and a mind of wisdom to preserve my family." Suzanne turned the pipe hand-over-hand in a circle and returned it to Cosma who smiled as serenely as a Madonna and received it palms up.

Relighting the pipe with cedar and sage several times, Cosma smoked and blew a cloud of vapors on each of them, each time pointing the bowl toward heaven, then she smoked alone until the pipe would light no more. She lifted it to the sky and took it apart. Bringing it back down to the red trading blanket, she popped the bowl section against her palm a few times to remove the remaining ash. Unsatisfied, she unraveled the black cloth and took out a length of heavy-gauge wire and reamed the pipe bowl until it was clean. She rewrapped the wire and filled the clean pipe bowl with pieces of juniper and cedar, "to keep the sacred pipe from being invaded by unhealthy spirits when it's resting in its bag," she explained.

"Great Spirit, I thank you aloud for the final time before I greet you in the morning. Watch over us and keep us safely under your awesome wings."

Cosma Stargazer brought her hands together and bowed over her belongings. She bundled each piece with gestures to the four directions as before and wrapped them all in the trading blanket. She tied it snuggly and picked up her drum. For another half an hour she tapped out a variety of rhythms, then without saying a word she stopped and rose with the drum and the bundle and walked out of the firelight to her camper, her beads and jewelry jingling softly to the swaying of fringe as she moved. Johnny watched her go, his heart in his eyes.

Soft clapping came from nearby campfires. Suzanne felt moved to tears, strangely connected to those at other campsites in the dark that had listened to the drum. She expanded her connection to embrace them, the stars, the moon, and Taylor. She felt as if she had been to church. Slowly, as if in a dream, she realized with a new understanding that church, like God *is* love, just as the Bible says. *Love and God are truly everywhere.*

It isn't about buildings and dogma, she thought. *God is simple, available to us all, in the wind, in strangers, in our hearts—even in my sister! I've judged her as Godless, felt superior to her. I was the one who needed to open my heart to love.* She looked at Dee as if seeing her for the first time. Her anxiety about how the two of them would preserve the new level of trust so recently forged evaporated. She carried the intuitive feeling further and knew she and Taylor would resolve their denominational differences. A weight lifted. She sighed contentedly, ready for what remained of a good night's sleep. It seemed as if there was no need to say to anything to Dee and Johnny. She rose without a word and left them sitting in silence by the glowing coals of their campfire.

After using the porta-potty set up behind the folding screen on the far side of the Blazer, Suzanne moved off by flashlight to the tent she shared with her son. She unzipped the tent and climbed over Gregory's sleeping bag, being careful in the dark not to put her full weight down on any part of his bag that might hurt him. Once undressed and settled into her own goose-down bedroll, she reached a hand across the dark space between them and patted what she thought was her son's shoulder. It wasn't. She patted further, then everywhere. His bag was empty!

Calling out, "Gregory, Gregory!" she yanked her shorts back on, panic rising. She brushed the far side of their tent and discovered the waterproofed wall had been slashed from top to bottom and spread wide in a triangular flap.

Dierdre came running. "Susie for heaven's sake, people are sleeping. What are you carrying on about?" Dee played her flashlight through the screen on her face.

"Gregory's gone. He's been kidnapped. Check for Mitzi!" She rammed her feet into her sneakers and tied them quickly.

"Really, Suzanne, get a grip. He's so fearless he's probably hunting tarantulas in the dark." But then her flashlight illuminated the slashed tent wall. She sucked in her breath and let it out in a whoosh. "Who would do such a thing?"

"Bo Rodman!" Suzanne and Johnny said in the same breath. He'd followed Dierdre at the alarming call for Gregory. Now he spun on his cane in the dust and hurried off to his car for more bullets than he'd planned on needing.

Taylor Armstrong

~ Friday the 20th of June

The camp was in an uproar about something when the cruisers and the rancher's Jeep bounced caravan-style across the desert from the dirt road they'd followed in from the two-lane highway. In the distance, Taylor could make out that lights were on, campfires blazed, people carrying flashlights were shouting and running everywhere.

"Must be a hell of a party," snapped Doug.

His bad-ass attitude was getting on Taylor's nerves, but he held his tongue, grateful the older officer from Nevada actually remembered how to find the damned tunnel sculptures in the dark. *Now to find Suzanne and the children in the middle of this fracas,* he thought.

"Looks like something more serious than a party," said one of the officers. "A couple of those guys have rifles. 'Course who doesn't in this part of the country?"

Doug barked an order.

"Better be prepared. Keep your weapons ready. We might have broken up a meth blast or worse. These folks could be wild as bear cats, high on God knows what."

It was the first rational thing Doug had said, in Taylor's opinion. In his gut he knew something was terribly wrong and it had to do with Susie. He just prayed to God it had nothing to do with Bo Rodman. For hours he'd been kicking himself in the mental ass for letting her out of his sight. *Why in hell didn't I come with her and the kids? What was I thinking? Worrying about making money, as usual. If anything happens to any of them it'll be me to blame.*

Heavenly Father, I haven't talked to you in a long time, but if you're listening, please, please don't let anything bad happen to Suzanne's family. You come through for me, and I'll come through for You from here on. I promise!

Suzanne Price

~ Friday the 20th of June

"You women stay here," Johnny commanded, hurrying off stumping three-legged on his cane through the soft dirt to his car. He hollered in his deliberate way to everyone in camp, "A child is missing! Wake up and help us find the boy!"

Cosma in the nearest camper climbed out to see what the commotion was about. The couple in the tent beyond her came out too. They asked her what it was about. She didn't answer but hurried to Suzanne.

"My son's been kidnapped by a vicious man!" Suzanne, called out, loud and frantic.

"Your little boy?" called the wife, pulling on her shoes.

Suzanne hurried on, flinging an urgent, "Yes! Please help me find him."

"Get the rifle, Ralph. I'll stay with the girls," the woman stoked their campfire back to a blaze.

The sisters found Mitzi safe in her tent, waking up in a

sleepy haze to all of the camp noise.

"Thank heaven!" Dee said. "Oh, my God, you're here and safe." She sank down cradling Mitzi, sleeping bag and all.

"I thought I saw Bo at the truck stop. He must want the children's money as ransom for Greg."

"Why in hell didn't you tell me?"

"I wasn't positive. I couldn't see any connection to us even if I was right about it being his truck. Besides, Dee, I didn't want to worry you unnecessarily when you'd looked forward to being here for so long."

"Now look who's making assumptions that somebody else can't handle the truth or be inconvenienced! You're sure good at laying guilt trips, Suze. Why didn't you tell me earlier you thought you saw him at that truck stop?"

Lights came on in most of the other tents and vehicles, particularly the campers and RVs powered by their own generators. Men shouted orders, women gathered children inside the protection of vans and campers. Flashlights were turned on; fires and camp stoves helped the moon light up the night. The air was alive with Gregory's name.

"Dee, stay with Mitzi. Don't leave her for *any* reason, not even for a *second!*" Suzanne unlocked the back of the Chevy Blazer. She rooted around inside for something to use as a weapon. There wasn't time to undo the cords to the main pole of Dee's tent from the front bumper or to move Mitzi out of it so it wouldn't collapse if she did.

"Just what in the hell do you think you're going to do, Suzanne?" Dierdre called from inside the tent. "Let the men handle this. That guy next to us was on a cell phone getting professional help already. Bo can't get far, there hasn't been time."

Suzanne tossed towels and bags, toys and ponchos, felt around on the floor of the truck, folded back the carpet while she held a flashlight in her mouth. She pulled up the jack equipment and removed the cranking bar. With the flashlight she hurried off behind the tent where Greg had been sleeping. With a sweeping motion she located one set of tracks coming and two going in the creamy dust. Her son must be awake, otherwise Bo would have carried him and there would only have been one set of tracks.

Oh God, please don't let him hurt Gregory. Please help us find him safe. How can this be happening to my little boy, after all he's been through? God, oh, God help us! You want me to count on You; You better come through for us this time! All my prayers about beating cancer went unheeded. I lose my son; I lose my faith in You!

Someone in an old open-backed truck roared past her, the men yelling and waving at her to go back, obliterating the tracks she was following, driving in circles that only stirred up clouds of dust that settled slowly back to the earth. Furious, she began to run, estimating where the tracks would pick up again in the dust so soft it felt like talcum powder on her skin. Her hunch was right. In between a brave stand of pickle weed and a scattering of antelope scat she found the cowboy boot prints, one worn oddly and always with a drag edge to the heel. *Bo for sure.* The others were barefoot and small. *Poor darling, your little feet will be in shreds from sand burrs and nettles. What has he done to keep you from crying out? Why didn't I go to bed when you did? Somehow I could have kept this monster from taking you.*

She renewed her efforts to run, keep her balance and eat up a yard or more with every stride. Her breath was soon ragged with unaccustomed effort and anxiety. The headlights of a car bumping behind her, the driver refusing to get over when she motioned to the side, blinded her momentarily. When it pulled along side her, the driver turned out to be Johnny.

"Get in," he ordered, in that deliberate voice that seemed to her like something out of a movie playing in slow motion. The whole night felt like a surreal play, a nightmare. He slowed to let her in and they continued, with her hanging out the window adding her flashlight to the way, low along the ground. The tracks veered toward the old road.

"There, way up ahead. That's Bo's truck, we've got to catch him," Johnny gasped.

"How can you tell its him in the dark?"

"Bo's got a bad left tail light. I followed him here by it."

Suzanne strained to see in the direction of the highway far across the desert opposite the camp and saw whirling lights approaching. "The police are here already. Oh what I'd give for a cell phone to tell them they're going the wrong way!"

Johnny was driving much too fast for the terrain and they could hardly talk for the bouncing ride. "Get your head in here and hang on."

"But the truck's taillights aren't on. How do you know it's Bo?"

"See how it's swinging free on its wires?" said Johnny. "It's him alright."

She sat back down in her seat, then lifted herself as she realized the lump on the cushion beneath her was a handgun.

"Be careful, it's loaded."

"Good," she said, clutching the jack bar between her knees, both hands holding the gun pointed to the door side of her bouncing feet.

CHAPTER FIFTEEN

COMING INTO THE LIGHT

Bo Rodman

~ Friday the 20th of June

Eve of the Summer Solstice

    Half dragging the barefoot boy along, Bo poked him with the shotgun barrel to remind the kid it wouldn't be wise to try and make a break for it. They made it back to his truck hidden in high weeds. Once he got the boy in the cab and tied his wrists together with a strip of shirt flannel, he climbed in the driver's side next to Tracker.
    "Do what I tell you kid, and I won't hurt you none. Don't—and you won't see your step mama or your little sister again."
    The boy wriggled against the filthy rag in his mouth, tasting grit and worse, gagging on the peculiar man/dog stink in

the truck. He held himself against the door, away from the huge smelly dog roughly sniffing him.

"Scared of a big dog, ain't you? He's mean and hungry enough to tear the meat off your bones, so don't get no ideas 'bout tryin' to get away."

Bo put his truck in reverse, backed out onto flat ground, turned around, and headed back the way he'd come. He drove as fast as he dared, knowing bald as his tires were, he wouldn't be able to press his luck too far in the rough brush and cactus. His plan was to get back to the Snowville Truck Stop and make his ransom call to the Price house. *The sisters are here. It'll be a while before they git home and pick up my message. I'll have plenty a time to get rid of the boy and lay low 'til I can pick up the ransom money.* He laughed out loud at how well his plan was working.

"Good thing you was in a little tent of your own, hey boy? Sure made you easy pickin's. Trackin' yer ma by that falcon-finding gadget worked out pretty good, too. Bo's a lot smarter than they give him credit for."

He turned sharply, headed around a curve in the dirt road, and switched on his headlights. The beams swung ahead of him beyond the curve. Too late, Bo realized he'd forgotten about the dry wash. Before he could hit the breaks, the truck banged to the bottom of the arroyo. The pop of his worn front tires sent the boy into the dashboard. Stunned, Greg slid to the floor of the cab, groaning against the rag.

Bo cut the lights. "Damn it to hell! Wake up you little shit! I need your ass. I'm not about to carry you to the main road on my back."

Throwing his weight against the driver-side door, Bo lowered himself to the ground. Moving through brittle, shoulder-high weeds, a little at a time to make sure of his footing, he growled, "Come, Boy."

Tracker leaped down and shuffled to his side.

Feeling his way around to the kid's door on uneven footing, Bo hauled the dazed boy out to the ground, but lost the grip on his knife. It clattered down the embankment and landed somewhere in the dark under the trash and brush.

"Son of a bitch!" Bo smacked the boy to bring him around. "Shit! You a little woozie, kid? You stay right here and clear yer head while I get the falcon. Then we'll find us a place to hide. Stay Tracker. Keep our money-ticket company."

He moved through tangled brush and weeds, scaring off some small animal that scurried away to the silver trickle of spring water below.

Rammed into the bank, the truck listed at an angle on top of something else. It turned out to be another car, belly up. Brush grew out its broken windows glinting here and there in the moonlight that eddied in the shadows of the waving trees. *Must've been here fer years. No use lookin' for my knife down there.*

Bo climbed back up the bank along side both vehicles gripping his truck chassis to leverage his weight until he could get to the tailgate. He pulled himself toward it and shoved the window up and away. Steadying his knees on the creaking tailgate, he stretched inside and unclipped the hooded gyr from where she'd fallen off her post. He rolled her in what was left of the shirt he'd stripped to tie the boy and used the sleeves to make a bundle of her. He let her hooded head stick out the shirt neck so she could breathe. He grabbed the box of ammo, put the falcon and the box on the far side of the tailgate, eased himself to good footing on a fender, and let himself down carrying both items. He forced the ammo box into the boy's tied hands. "Hold onto it, I got enough to deal with."

Bo picked up the shotgun and one-armed, nudged the barefoot kid with the barrel, holding the gyr against his chest with the other. There was no choice but to climb out of the wash and go up and around to the road. *Unless we can make it to the highway, we'll hafta hide in the shrub 'til I can sneak back and steal one of them campers' vehicles to make our getaway. I'll bargain for one with the boy if this goes bad.* Bo didn't want to think about that right now.

Tracker scrambled up the bank ahead of him and went to snuffling in the barley grass along the road. Bo prodded the boy up the side of the wash, stones and dirt crumbling away at their every step. They made their way along the embankment side of the road, working toward the pond he'd passed coming in. He had to find a place big enough to hide the kid, the falcon, himself and Tracker, or several places, until he could steal a truck or figure out a way to get to a phone and lay a story on Frank to come and get him and the falcon. It was hard for Bo to make a change of plans so fast. He liked time to work things out in his head because it generally took a while. He wouldn't have to tell Frank about the boy. They'd never find him. That decision was easy.

"You hang onto that box of shells, boy. Don't you dare drop it or I'll sick Tracker or this here hawk to take a big bite out of yuh and sell what's left o' yer skin back to yer step-ma."

Bo yanked the stumbling kid through the weeds, the gyrfalcon's hooded head bobbing outside the shirt at his elbow. Where the gravel road forked to follow the bank of the spring-fed watering pond, they took the road that split off toward the burnt-out homestead.

They reached the foundation boulders vomited to the surface by decades of frost heaving. Bo's gun barrel poked the boy in the back to move off the road and onto the hard-packed clay. Its silky layer of cream-colored dust rose at each step and settled back to earth like so many moths. In the distance, lights from cars searching the undulating landscape bumped over the flatland circling as they came. Two police cars, their lights flashing, bounced off the dirt road onto the desert floor moving away from him, followed by a Jeep. Cops must be after somebody else, 'cause nobody knows ol' Bo's here," he muttered to himself and the dog.

The only structure standing was the old outhouse. It wasn't big enough for both of them and the dog. Likely it had plenty of vermin. Bo needed time to think without the trouble of the boy and carrying the shotgun, keepin' an eye on the kid and the ammo, and the hawk. Straining his eyes around the outhouse's dark interior, with the stock of the shotgun he cleared dry leaves from the corner. He laid the bundle of gyrfalcon in the spot, then kicked a crunch of leaves back over it. Shoving the boy to the outhouse floor, he pushed him against the seat of the toilet hole.

Bo leaned the rifle against the wall, unbuckled his belt, slid it out of the loops on his jeans, and pulled it free. He grabbed the boy by the back of the neck.

Gregory Price

~ Friday the 20th of June

Greg bit the rag and braced himself to be whipped like in the movies, so fearful of the mean stranger he could hardly keep from wetting his snagged pajama bottoms. He felt his arms pinned to his sides and watched the belt get looped through the broken hinge where the door once hung. The man tightened it with the plate-sized buckle, shining in the moonlight high beyond his reach.

"Tracker'll see you don't go no where. Wouldn't disturb that hungry hawk neither, if you know what's good for yuh. Just sit tight 'til I find a place to hide your sorry ass. Stay Tracker."

The limping man moved off with the shotgun. The dog settled down to wait.

Tracker's thick body blocked Greg inside the outhouse. The smell of the dog and his panting was frightening, but not as bad as when the dirty mean man was with them. Greg inhaled air and wished he could take the gagging cloth out of his mouth and clear his throbbing head. He wished even more for his Dad, for Suzanne, for Taylor, and his Sunday-school Jesus. Wished for anybody to save him the way things happened in Bible-story videos and cartoons on TV. He wished himself back home safe in his Dad's big recliner. Wished for the remote in his hand so he could change a channel and make this night disappear.

On the way to the outhouse Greg had tried to forget about his raw feet and the jabbing pain in his back ribs from the gun barrel by thinking about how he could be smarter than the man. The clinging dust made the heavy shell box slippery in his aching fingers. He held it against his bumping chest to keep from dropping it and maybe breaking his bare toes or causing the man to hit or shoot him. Hearing the rhythmic thud of the man's good leg and the scrape of his drag boot behind him had made Greg feel like they were moving in a strange dream. He feared the dream would go on and on until he floated away up to his Dad in the sky with Jesus.

He wondered if Jesus really answered prayers from kids because praying hadn't worked for him yet. He'd doubted since he'd prayed so hard, even on his knees, for his Dad not to die and for Doug to marry Suzanne, so he could have a dad to take him fishing on this side of heaven. It got confusing when Doug turned out to be a jerk. But now it occurred to him, *Maybe Jesus knew Doug was a jerk the whole time. Maybe he didn't answer my prayers so Doug couldn't be mean and hurt Suzanne anymore and maybe even hurt Mitzi and me even worse 'cause we're just little kids.*

Greg wriggled, helpless to free himself. His hands, feet, and legs could move but his arms were pinned against his sides. The dog growled, deep and low. Greg tried to think of what heroes on TV and in the Bible did when there was trouble. When he thought of the boy David who killed the giant Goliath with a stone, probably like the ones around the dog on the ground, the idea came and gave him hope.

With his feet he scootched the box of ammunition between his ankles, squatted over it, down low in the man's belt as far as he could reach. He opened the box lid with a foot, toes, and the tips of his fingers. Tracker growled and his hackles stood up, but he stayed where he was.

A few at a time, Gregory dropped the shot-gun shells through the broken floor boards of the shanty, hearing them thwuck into the reeking outhouse sludge below. With his toes he grasped stones and refilled the box. A movement caught his eye. A tarantula emerged in the moonlight walking over the wrapped falcon. Its delicate legs scaled the side of the gun-shell box and entered the space with the stones.

Gregory closed the lid and sat back to wait with the smelly man's dog. Missing Murphy and his room back home, he decided to pray, just in case somewhere above him in the stars his Dad told God to listen to his little boy and help him.

Bo Rodman

~ Friday the 20th of June

Scouting the area, Bo discovered an abandoned root cellar for a hiding place. There wasn't any place else big enough. He headed back for the boy and Tracker, muttering his plans to himself. He'd waste Frank, keep the lawyer's fancy Ford truck with the king cab, and use Frank's cell phone to call in the ransom offer for the Price boy. He'd hide the falcon until he could head to Montana. If he'd even bother with the hawk or the kid once he had a shit load of money from sweet Mama Price. A lot depended on if he could hide out until she'd move on to the highway in search of the boy. He could back track to his truck, get his grub and hike to the road, where he'd hitch a ride to Elko or steal a car from the nearest farm. He might have to waste a few more losers in his way before he figured out how to get himself to a phone. He came around the barbed-wire fence. Tracker and the boy waited for him. Bo's rodeo buckle glinted in the moonlight from the outhouse hinge above the boy's reach.

THE WIND REMEMBERS

Dierdre Ingram

~ Saturday the 21st of June

Before Dawn of the Summer Solstice

Cosma's sons opened the camper door and peeked out at her in the firelight. Cosma shooed them back in to don warm jackets. She remained outside, stoked their fire, and set a pot of water to heat on the Coleman stove. Her deep-set, kind, dark eyes like enormous bruises in the firelight, she trained them on Dierdre's camp while the pot came to a boil. At other campsites word about Greg spread. Men in cars and trucks had already joined the search.

At the sounds of the rising commotion, Mitzi scrambled out of her sleeping bag and into Dierdre's waiting arms.

"Here, Sweetheart, let me help you get your shoes on."

"Is it time for soltis lights, Aunt Dreedra? Me and Bear Lovins are too sleepy."

"No, Love, it's only 2:00 in the morning. Y-your brother has . . . Greg must have wandered away from camp. Everybody's looking for him." Dierdre packed up the dinner things and began folding and unfolding sweatshirts, biting back panic.

"Even Mommy, is she finding our Gregory, too?"

"Yes, she's looking, too. Help me roll up these sleeping bags, will you, Dear? Just stand on that end and keep it from unfolding, while I roll it up and tie it."

"Why we be putting our stuff away? Do we have to leave before the lights, and the tunnels, and the hot chocolate wif marshmallows s'prise you promised?"

Dierdre took the little girl in her arms and sat on a folding chair, cradling, rocking, praying to the universe's Force for Good. Her tears gathered and trickled down her dusty cheeks.

"What's a matter, Auntie Dreedra? You got lots of tears, *real big* ones!"

The Wind Remembers

"Mitzi, does your Mommy pray with you?" Dee fingered the little curls, covered the small hands with her own, still rocking, the rhythm somehow making the incredible pain and terror easier to bear.

"She prays wif me every night and some other times, too. Want me to do one for you? Mommy says I do good prayers from my heart. They make her feel better real fast."

Dierdre could only nod, overcome, not daring to release all that she was feeling and thinking to a three-year old—even perhaps—to herself.

"God bless Daddy in heaven. Be wif Mommy looking for Gregory, so she can find him. Bring Mr. Armfrong to help us. God bless Aunt Dreedra and fix her tears, and me so we can see the soltis lights before we got to go back home. I love my family until morning and always. Amen."

Mitzi patted Dierdre's cheeks and wiped her tears. "Did my prayer make you feel real better?"

"Dee, where's Suzanne?" Taylor stepped into the light of the campfire and touched her shoulder. "They tell me Greg's missing."

"Mr. Armfrong! See, Aunt Dreedra. God listens to little girl's prayers, just like Mommy said." She hopped down from her aunt's lap and hugged Taylor's knees.

Dierdre tried vainly to pull herself together, regretting too much brandy—fuzzy thinking. "Oh, Taylor, thank God. Where did you . . . ?"

The look in his eyes forestalled a pause for explanations.

Stumbling to her feet, still holding Mitzi's hand, Dee managed, "Susie's following the tracks that lead from Greg's tent over there. It's slashed in the back."   Crying, her make-up running, she didn't care, nothing mattered but her sister and Gregory. Gripping Mitzi's hand she tagged along behind Taylor to the tent.

"I tried to stop her. She's only got a flashlight and a car jack. Find her! Johnny Carlisle went after her in his car. He can't move fast enough to keep up with her on foot."

"Carlisle's here?" Taylor voiced over his shoulder, but he didn't wait for whys. Moving off at a run, he signaled with a sweep of his arm for what appeared to be Doug in uniform, who waved, a rifle cradled barrel-down in his other arm. The men swung up and into a noisy battered Jeep that roared away from her in a cloud of white dust.

The moon illuminating the campsite made everything more dreamlike and unreal. Dierdre pinched her arm to make sure the whole thing wasn't a nightmare and felt new anguish at the reality of what was happening . . . and wonder for a child's prayer.

Where did Taylor and Doug come from? How did they know? What's really going on here? Dierdre's knees gave way. She sank to the ground. *Oh God, oh God in Heaven help us!*

Feeling like every hurt she'd held inside for a lifetime bubbled forth to drown her, the tumult couldn't be stemmed any more.

Mitzi squatted next to her. "Auntie Dreedra. I'll stay wif you; don't be scared. Mr. Armfrong will bring Gregory and Mommie back to us."

Cosma, her boys bundled in warm jackets, made a pot of hot tea and carved a loaf of crusty bread. Seating her boys back to back, she wrapped them in a blanket, closed her eyes and raised her hands in the air—palms to the stars. Her lips moved in silent supplication to Great Spirit.

Suzanne Price

~ Saturday the 21st of June

At the sharp turn in the road, the moon and Johnny's headlights flashed on the aluminum strip of a camper shell too far below road level to make sense.

"Hold on!" Johnny pulled the lever on his steering-wheel brakes and skidded, fish-tailing to a stop sideways, just in time to avoid piling into the dry wash on top of Bo's camper truck. Its headlights apparently smashed, it blocked the road but couldn't be fully seen until they'd nearly created a pile-up. "Stay here, Mrs. Price." He grabbed the gun. "I'll check the cab. It may not be pretty."

Suzanne was out the door, jack bar in one hand, flashlight in the other, plunging down the wash before Johnny had gotten fully out from behind the wheel. She heard him descending laboriously behind her. The lights of his car and the moon above dispelled the darkness around Bo's truck. Their moving bodies cast long eerie shadows in the tamarisk and across the labyrinth of cracks in the rocky bed of the arroyo, to the thin wiggle of silvery water below.

"Gregory! It's Mommy. You be brave. We're coming to help you."

She switched the jack bar to the other hand and came up on the open passenger door from the back, bar raised over her head ready to clobber Bo. Afraid of what she might find, yet hopeful, she swept the interior of the truck cab with the beam of her flashlight. Empty, except for a crushed potato chip bag, what looked somewhat like a remote control or keypad, and some beer cans. There didn't seem to be any blood. Her heart pounded with a mixture of relief that Greg wasn't lying in a broken heap from the crash and dread that he'd been taken somewhere else. She feared they might not find him in time to prevent putting him through something even more frightening. She squelched her terror that Bo would hurt or kill him, praying continuously in the back of her mind as steadily as she breathed.

"They're gone, Johnny!" She studied the bank ahead of her, swept the flashlight, saw where recently dislodged dirt had cascaded down the embankment, and started to go.

"Hold up a minute, let's check the back end." He reached it first and steadied himself against the waist-high bumper. He handed his cane to her. Chest heaving, with powerful forearms he hoisted himself onto the tailgate and drew his gun.

Suzanne joined him, ready to use the jack bar. She

squatted next to him on the tailgate, her legs burning from exertion and scratches where she'd climbed through bracken. The acrid smell of the enclosure assaulted her nose. Suzanne froze in horror that something unspeakable had been done to her son. *God prepare me.*

"Oh, Sweet Jesus," whispered Johnny. "Maybe she's still alive." He reached in as she watched. Her flashlight shown on the truck's camper bed littered with a whitewash of hawk droppings. The roosting block had gone over in the crash and tipped into a round birdbath, still sloshing with water and floating litter as they shifted their weight. There was evidence the spilled bird had struggled, entangled by its jesses in its tether and the perch. Among the debris, Johnny discovered several cast pellets, some old but one not more than a couple days old. "Falcons disgorge a pellet 12 to 24 hours after eating. This is a hopeful sign!" He spoke over his shoulder. Felon, so he hoped the hawk to be, was gone. So was the boy. Climbing down from the tailgate with renewed hope, crashing through brush, Suzanne and Johnny hurried back to his car.

While Johnny drove, Suzanne took the gun again and held it in both hands, nozzle down between her feet while they backed away from the dip of the wash and rambled across the flats a few hundred yards to an old metal culvert. Far in the distance, a straggly line of cars and campers, including a police car's whirling lights came steadily across the desert toward them in an undisciplined attempt at a military sweep formation. She felt a surge of hope. *Lord, you know our need. Soften Bo's heart toward Greg. Keep him safe. Help us find him before . . .*

Johnny's car bumped across the expanse of culvert and back up onto the unpaved road, fog lights on, Suzanne straining her eyes to see any tracks. "The gravel is too heavy here to hold footprints."

"We'll find the dirty bastard and my Felon," Johnny said. "And your son, too. Sorry about the cursing."

"There, by the pond, through those trees, I thought I saw something." She swung the flashlight into the cottonwoods. A

THE WIND REMEMBERS

raccoon, blinded in the light, gripped a frog in its paws. Her heart sank. Then, something in the weeds caught her eye. A shiny gum wrapper. "They've come this way. Greg had gum this afternoon; he's leaving a trail for us."

"Don't get your hopes up, that wrapper could have been there for weeks, dropped by anybody."

"No, Johnny. It wouldn't be that shiny in this dusty place, not so close to the road. They had to come this way, it's the only easy route for a crippled man along the pond." She kept the gun barrel down and opened the door. "Stop the car and let me out. I'll follow them on foot from here."

"No way!" He reached for the loaded gun. The gas-feed control of the special-needs car at his hands instead of at his feet, Johnny's hesitation was all she needed. With the drop in acceleration, she was out of the car as it slowed, following a hunch, running from tree to tree, beyond the canopy of the cottonwood grove, along the pond bank. The moon lit up the terrain. *Thank you, God, for moonlight!*

She turned off the flashlight, jammed it in the waistband of her shorts and focused her attention on keeping her bearings. Her senses acute with fear and anticipation, she seemed to see and hear uncountable details in the pickle weed and the high scrub that whipped at her legs and scratched her face.

Making her way around a rusted irrigation pipe, she crossed the old homestead yard through the foundation rubble toward the metal sprout of the well's hand-pump. She remembered that other than the giant cottonwoods by the pond, the only hiding places big enough for a man and a boy were the outhouse and the root cellar. If Bo had come in the dark as she supposed, then he wouldn't know about the stairs to the cellar until he searched them out, which would take some time, she certainly hoped he'd be less likely to get very far with Greg.

She headed first for the protection of what remained of the outhouse, watching everywhere for a sign of Bo, who probably possessed not only her son, but a loaded gun or at least the knife he'd slashed the tent with. At the dirt area around the little privy, there were plenty of prints in her flashlight beam. Boots, big paw prints of a dog, and yes, *Thank God*, little bare toes! Nothing inside the doorless outhouse but a mound of rags and leaves. She hurried on.

Johnny Carlisle

~ Saturday the 21st of June

Johnny's energy wired on adrenaline and urgency, he followed Suzanne. Knowing Felon was still alive and probably nearby, spurred him on. He cut across the shortest route to Suzanne, her white blouse and shorts a glowing blur in the moonlight, where she ran, crouched, paused, jumped, leapt obstacles among the tall weeds. She had his weapon. He had no choice but to catch up and talk her into handing it over. It took all of his determination not to weep with the frustration of a woman out-maneuvering him and taking his gun—*a woman for god's sake! I should be taking care of her and her boy not the other way around!* His bitterness nearly choked him.

Suddenly, the air cracked with the muffled sound of a gun going off. He took cover in a dilapidated outhouse, the only cover for a hundred yards in any direction. A second shot. He dropped to crouching position. He dare not move out into the clearing, where he'd be an easy target. Suzanne had disappeared, but where could she go? It seemed the earth had swallowed her. He stood gasping for air, straining to hear, afraid to go—afraid to stay. *That first shot didn't sound like my 38. It sounded more like a rifle going off in a pickle barrel.*

Listening . . . listening . . . his own heart a hammer in his ears. A rustling sound at his feet suddenly made his skin crawl. Imagining poisonous snakes with lethal fangs at his ankles made him freeze in place; he wouldn't move and make it strike. He feared for Suzanne and the boy, yet feared even more moving out into the open where he would be a mighty big target for Bo, or staying where he was for a snake or scorpion bite.

His eyes were darting, lively things searching every crevice and moonlit spot around him. He studied the warped floor, the gaping holes harboring blackness where missing boards could hold a viper. Movement in a pile of leaves and ragged clothing caught his attention. He steeled himself to whack the imagined coiled rattler with his cane or try to spring free of the dilapidated nasty-smelling latrine before it bit him. But the moving pile exposed a metal clip capturing a flicker of moonlight for just a moment, something familiar about it. He nudged it with the tip of his cane. The shirtsleeve fell away, revealing the clip's leather loop, then the clutched yellow talons of a hawk grasping and releasing air—cause for the movement he'd detected.

It took him a moment to fully comprehend what he'd discovered. Perhaps his own Felon, stashed like a cast-off piece of rubbish, by a man with bigger evil on his mind.

For the moment Suzanne and her boy, the gunfire, even the sounds of crashing cars and distant voices, were a million stars away in importance. Probing gently, Johnny brushed back the leaves, lifted the bundle of bird—too light for a hawk of this largest breed—the gyrfalcon. Yet the yellow-orange scales of its feet would be right for a gyr. He brought it into the moonlight of the doorway, turned the metal leg band to the moon. It was too dim to read the serial numbers to be sure.

Yet he knew it was her. With his fingers and teeth he undid the strings, pulled off the plumed hood to reveal Felon's head and the yellow-orange arc of her beak cere. Her eyelids blinked in the pale moonlight, her head swiveled. She took him in with her golden-rimmed black-eyed stare. He fingered along the nostrils of her beak for obstructions or breakage, relieved she could breathe comfortably. He cooed to her, stroked her. The fear of snakes out of mind, he straddled the space next to the toilet hole so he could lay her across his knees and undo the binding of the old shirt. He unwrapped her like a newborn and with parent-love assessed her condition inch by inch.

She needed water and live meat as soon as he could find it or he would lose her even now that he'd at last found her again. He cried tears of joy and tears of anguish for her terrible condition. Bringing her to his stubbled cheek he listened at her breast for what he hoped would be a steady heartbeat. She rewarded him with throaty stirrings the way she had greeted him months before in their mews.

"My Felon, my Felon," he whispered fiercely. "Somehow I'll see you healthy again, you brave old girl. By God, I will! Bo bastard's going to pay for nearly killing us."

Johnny hooded her again to keep her stress to a minimum and to assure she wouldn't shriek and endanger them. The leather hood would calm her until he could get her to a safe place for water and nourishment. He feared she might be too weak to ride his free arm anyway. Besides, he reasoned he couldn't risk being less mobile with her and the cane. He opened his jacket part way, stuffed the bottom of it in his pants and tucked Felon inside, zipping her in against his heart, a welcome burden of precious bones and feathers from his belly to his chin.

Sobbing with emotion, he gritted his teeth and stepped back out into the night in the direction he'd last caught sight of Suzanne. Now it was time to find the boy, get his gun back, and help Mrs. Price. If time allowed, Johnny planned to end Bo's pitiful life one vengeful inch at a time.

Suzanne Price

~ Saturday the 21st of June

Before Dawn of the Summer Solstice

Pausing for breath, Suzanne listened with her whole being to discern the slightest movement of where Bo might be hiding Greg. The sounds of on-coming vehicles a quarter mile away were followed by a crash, then another. *The dry wash must be filling up with cars. Unless those campers find the culvert and have narrow axles, they'll be forced to come to our aid on foot. That will take too long to be much help.*

She looked back for Johnny and saw he'd parked as close to the old barbed wire fence along the pond turn-off as he could. In the moonlight she noted his heaving progress on a cane, perhaps a quarter mile away, his shadow reaching out ahead of him. Then he was lost in the shadowy expanse of the pond trees. He emerged and hurried on. Far ahead of him, the metal outhouse roof shown silvery between her location and his. He was too far away and her need too urgent to wait for him. She crept forward fifty paces to the base of what few rocks and crumbling mortar remained of the blackened chimney, startling a scurry of scorpions. Shuddering, she moved on toward the mounded earth indicating the homestead's abandoned root cellar.

She remembered Greg pointing out the place where stairs went underground. Reasoning the cellar seemed most likely to be where Bo would take him, she hurried toward a clump of tamarisk taller than a man. It obscured the stairwell and the cellar entrance. A horned owl hooted above her. Its mate answered from not far away. Her heart pounded in her ears. *Do owls that huge attack people?* She wondered. *God help me, I must find Greg before something terrible happens to him. He's with a mad man. You know Bo's mind is selfish and evil. Please help me, please . . . or am I forgetting again to have faith, dear Jesus?*

Her eyes searched the moonlit landscape for any other place large enough that Bo could be holding her son against his will, perhaps bound and gagged. Weeds and boulders posed like silent witnesses in the trash-strewn yard, but none of sufficient size to hide more than a jackrabbit. The hot air stirred the hair on the back of her neck. Sweat ran down her throat between her breasts. She moved on. An old tractor tire's inner tube and a pile of salvage wood forced her to skirt their perimeter in case she dislodged the boards and the noise gave her location away to Bo. *Is Rehma here, too? Is she helping him kidnap Greg, since I wouldn't let her take the children camping?*

The Wind Remembers

Listening with intense concentration, she could no longer hear Johnny approaching and wondered why. Frogs croaked from the pond. Distant car doors slammed, raised voices called indistinguishable words. Insects hummed and buzzed. She moved to the shadows of the tamarisk. Within a pace of the top step a sound stopped her. . . insects . . . but not exactly. She forced herself to focus. A clicking noise, insistent, familiar . . . *Gregory!* His insect signal she'd heard a thousand irritating times.

Oh my Dear God, he's alive! Bless you darling. Oh, Steve, how could I have fussed at you for teaching him how to do that! Mommy's coming, Gregory.

She stepped down onto the first railroad-tie stair. Underground, behind the sagging wooden door, a dog growled deep and menacing. By that sound and the size of the paw prints she'd followed—a very big dog. Her hands steadied the gun, one underneath the other, practicing the way Steve taught her. The great horned owl swooped closer; its broad wings cast a kite-sized shadow over her. It settled without a sound onto the woodpile above her. Head swiveling, it watched her progress.

She descended the rough-hewn relics of stairs to the door below ground level, cautiously to keep her balance, quietly to not give Bo a warning. She risked switching on the flashlight, studied the hinges to know which way the door would swing—in or out.

Out. To my disadvantage. Make your insect noise, Greg. Make me positive you're in there before I open this door to that awful man and his dog. She willed him to click his fingernails. . . and he did, a steady little pattern that gave her great comfort. The dog barked a deep barrel-chested woof. The clicking became more frantic.

She propped the flashlight on the top stair so its beam would reveal the inside of the cellar. With her free hand, she pulled the door toward her. It creaked open. Quickly she repositioned both hands on the gun. The dog barked furiously but remained out of her view somewhere in the dark behind a pile of caved-in shelving.

Why doesn't it come after me? Will I have to shoot it? Where's Bo? Is he holding Greg to keep him quiet or is Greg tied up and Bo is out here—behind me—somewhere? With the heel of her sneaker, she shoved the door. It scraped across the stone threshold and wedged to a stop.

The flashlight cast her silhouette into the cellar, which smelled earthy and dank, but felt cool. Greg, hands tied to a hook on a support beam, lifted his head—a gag in his mouth. His eyes squinted into the flashlight. At his side, Bo's eyes were narrow slits, too. Glint of metal, a shotgun barrel. She heard the clicking. It wasn't Greg's fingernails.

At their feet, amid loose boards and broken bottles, a sizable coiled rattlesnake shook its tail. Searching head raised, it flicked its tongue, testing the air. Her son's eyes squeezed shut. She aimed the gun, descending into the cellar, realized she might accidentally shoot Gregory and swung it instead at Bo.

"Well ain't you just the little heroine, bitch! I got this loaded shotgun at your boy's throat, so you'll want to hand *yer* little hand-gun weapon over."

The snake shook its tail more insistently. Its rhythmic head held high—ready to strike.

"Or you could finish off that rattler before it bites your boy, and we can talk about you handin' over that $50,000 to get him back safe and all . . ."

He does know about the money. No wonder all this . . .

Suzanne lowered her aim to the rattlesnake's weaving head moving in and out of the flashlight's beam. The angle was bad. She didn't feel skilled enough to hit a moving target. The steady click of the snake's rattle magnified in the little earthen and stone room. The dog's menacing growl sent shivers up her arms. If she missed, the snake might reach Greg instead of Bo. *If I don't shoot, the snake will likely strike anyway and maybe move closer to Greg.*

She wavered in dilemma, then kicked bottles and debris to distract the rattler, hopefully to a place where she could take better aim. The snake struck in her direction, too far short to reach her shoe. It recoiled quickly, raising its head again. The flashlight beam on the steps behind her glittered on its eyes and its searching, forked tongue.

She swung the gun toward the snake as Bo aimed and fired his shotgun. When the shell exploded, the spray of pellets broke glass canning jars and punctured metal-can rubble on the floor. The snake whipped into the post that held Gregory. Its head blown clean away, its long body convulsed in a writhing whorl, as if still alive. Greg's eyes expressed shock and followed the rattler's death throes in fascination.

Suzanne's ears heard nothing. The concussion of gunfire had winked her hearing to absolute silence. Commanding with words of her own she couldn't hear, she shouted, "Untie Greg. I'll be happy to talk about money for letting him go." *Crap, Bo probably can't hear any better than I can.* She felt foolish and frustrated.

The smell in the room was acrid, overpowering. Suzanne repositioned Johnny's gun aim on Bo's chest. She didn't want to miss if she got the chance to shoot. She saw Bo's mouth move, though she couldn't hear anything and could barely read his lips.

"Bitch. Got this barrel on your boy's throat. Drop your gun or hand it over." She saw his mouth open in laughter and his lips form, "Get her, Tracker Boy!"

Suzanne caught on just when Bo released the collar on the snarling beast. The massive dog came at her, huge paws seeking purchase in the debris, launching itself at her with powerful haunches, knocking her down. Its jaws gaped like the smile of Satan himself ready to sink hideous fangs into her throat.

Suzanne couldn't hear herself cry out in fear. She raised the gun and fired at the dog's chest. The recoil of the 38 slammed her back against the stair steps. Her face and arms stung from the gunpowder spray, her shoulders and hips bruised from the stairs. The acrid smell of cordite burned in her nostrils. The instant silence deepened in her head—amazing—like nothing she'd ever experienced. Steve had told her when teaching her gun handling that if she took off her ear protectors she'd be deaf for a while. Now she understood.

The momentum of the dog's lunge had made the bullet pass further back in its body. The bleeding dog struggled up the steps dragging his useless hindquarters. At the top the tipped flashlight rolled down the stairs and came to rest against the doorsill. Half the light was cut off, lowering the quivering beam to the floor.

Though she could hear nothing and was further disoriented by the second gun blast, Suzanne, her face and lips on fire, detected Bo moving, stumbling toward her. With both hands, she steadied the gun in his direction to fire again.

Bo moved out from behind the post where Gregory hung limply by his bound wrists from a rake hook.

In the semi-darkness, Suzanne imagined her son's eyes, wide with fear and his deafness as acute as hers. *Perhaps a blessing that he can't hear all the horrible things Bo is probably saying.* She struggled to regain a standing position amidst the junk on the floor. In the slash of light across Bo's boots coming for her, she saw blood streaming from his pant leg and knew a moment of triumph. Her bullet had passed through his dog and lodged somewhere in his body. She had no idea where he'd been hit. *Thank God I missed Greg! What a shame I didn't hit Bo in the heart or the head to stop him completely.*

Just before she could fire again without endangering Greg, Bo wrenched the pistol from her. He grabbed a handful of Suzanne's hair and yanked her to her knees. She screamed in pain and fear, wished she could hear because being totally deaf made getting her bearings nearly impossible. Imagining Bo couldn't hear any better was little comfort.

Suzanne felt the stairs giving with something's weight moving above and behind her. She prayed it wasn't the wounded dog come back to attack her. Bo's face was inches from hers. She knew that in the dark and unable to hear, Bo was unaware his dog or perhaps Johnny had joined them above on the stairs of the root cellar.

Bo was saying something because his breath moved in spittled spurts on her cheekbone. Deaf and without light on his lips she couldn't figure out what he wanted her to do. The flashlight beam moved. *What made it do that? Johnny or the dog?*

Bo turned, the 38 at Suzanne's jaw. She'd been struggling against his grip on her hair but ceased moving so as not to make the gun go off accidentally. If only she could hear. Suzanne felt the round pressure of the gun barrel against her pulse, smelled the disgusting sweat and horrific breath of Bo in her face, as sickening as the gunpowder smell and worse. She thought of her terrified Greg gagged and helpless, tied to the upright beam on the rake hook. Willing herself to keep her wits about her for her son's sake, she determined to be more like Dee and just do whatever had to be done without wavering. *I've got to do something he doesn't expect.*

Bo pulled Suzanne around to where he could line the hand gun up with the stairwell again, toward whatever was making the stairs give and the flashlight beam move, without taking the barrel from where he'd pressed it to her throat. The hand that held the gun experienced involuntary tremors. Suzanne feared he wouldn't be able to control his trigger finger and the gun might go off. Worse, she knew Johnny had no weapon, nothing but his cane. Impaired as he was, he'd be no match for the wounded madman holding her captive with Johnny's own gun.

Though she couldn't hear herself, she said, "Bo's got a gun!" to warn Johnny. She couldn't tell if he answered.

The flashlight beam raised and descended the stairs in a bobbing motion.

It has to be Johnny! What can I do? Lord, Johnny will die trying to help us. Help me think of what to do. I must save Greg.

Suddenly, Greg kicked the rubble at his feet. The light beam switched to some sound Suzanne couldn't hear. Bo wheeled with the light, giving Suzanne the chance she needed.

She put her knee behind Bo's and pressed in hard and quick. He lost his balance. With her elbow she knocked him hard in the ribs, shoving with all the fury she wished she'd given Doug when he attacked her.

Bo lost his grip on her, but not on the 38. Recovering, he staggered to his feet. Before he could raise the pistol again and fire, she threw her body at him with all her might, not caring if the gun went off in her stomach. She kicked, punched, screamed, and knocked him off balance. His legs appeared in the flashlight beam.

Suzanne saw on his thigh a spreading dark, wet patch. She guessed she'd hit his femoral artery. He was losing blood fast but not fast enough to stop him. She grabbed his gun arm with both of her hands and pulled down hard. He hit out at her with his forearm, but when she ducked, he lost his grip, dropping the gun. He fell to his knees, kneading his throbbing thigh with his hands. Beads of sweat stood out on what she could see of his face. In their struggle, they'd moved in and out of the flashlight beam. Frantic to locate the gun before Bo could come around and beat her to it, she kicked at the debris, praying not to disturb more snakes if there was a nest.

Then everything happened too fast to make sense. Bo pulled her to him by the hair. Upended, her butt toward the ceiling, her searing face smashed into Bo's shirtfront. He let go of her hair. She felt herself smacked against a timber roof support, knocking the wind out of her. Gasping for air, rage surged through her like a living thing.

The fury of being taken advantage of by Doug; the outrage at Bo slashing open their tent and snatching her son and putting him through yet another fearful experience; the powerlessness she'd felt against Steve's cancer; the anger at his dying and leaving her to fend for herself; even her anger at God—all coalesced into a power that filled her with determination to never be vanquished again by anyone or anything in her life—most certainly not by this vile-smelling, willful, evil man. She vowed to outwit him, defeat him, become a wild thing if she had to. She would save Greg if it cost her own life.

She righted herself in the boards and rubble and mounted the stairs, scrambling for the flashlight to free Johnny's hands to defend himself and them—everything happening like a silent film. Flashlight in her grasp, she spun the beam around and around the little room as if it were a strobe light in a disco scene, while she tried to figure out if Greg was unharmed and exactly where Bo was.

There among the debris. Johnny's cane tip was at Bo's throat, his free hand pointing her to his handgun on the dirt floor where none of them could reach it. He was shouting at her but she could only catch snatches of sound to make it out. *Good, my hearing is returning!*

Bo's thigh oozed blood through his jeans, while he struggled to rip the cane away from his Adam's apple and get it free of Johnny's grip. His face an expression of pain and confusion like something in a horror film, the two strong men rocked with their efforts, one above the other, both physically impaired. Johnny protected his chest by hunching his back. The bleeding man had the advantage if not the superior strength.

Suzanne crawled through the rubble for Johnny's gun. Just as she got her fingers on its barrel, Johnny's body crashed past her. Swinging the flashlight with her left hand, she fumbled for the handgun with her right and glimpsed Bo lunging for his shotgun at Gregory's feet.

Not able to hand the 38 over to Johnny, who struggled to a standing position beyond her reach, and fearful of losing the gun again if she tossed it and he missed the catch, Suzanne aimed the flashlight into Bo's eyes to make him as blind as he was deaf.

Bo, fighting the shudders, growled, "Bitch! You probly killed my dog. You hurt me bad. I don't need to see to load my shotgun and blow you all to hell."

I heard that alright, she thought.

Squinting in Suzanne's light, Bo's hands located the gun and hauled it to himself. With shaking fingers he dragged the ammo box within reach and opened the shotgun's empty chamber to reload. Tugging at the box of shells until he could slide the fingers of his free hand into the overlap of the lid, he rambled on, now clearly understood by Suzanne.

"Yes sir, by god, ol' Bo's just gonna make this a real farewell party and take y'all with me." He ground out the words, "Come on, Carlisle. I want to finish you off like I thought I did, if it's the last thing I do, 'cause I sure as hell ain't goin' back to the pen. I got nothin' to lose."

Suzanne felt she had nothing to lose either and backed toward Greg, putting herself between him and Bo. While Bo gripped at the shelves to pull himself to his feet with his rifle and struggled to stand, she unhooked the loop of Greg's wrist ties from the rake hook. She let the boy lean against her while she worked the filthy gag out of his mouth.

"You're so brave and so smart to cause that distraction!" Suzanne soothed him.

"Mommy," he managed, choking and crying.

Bo sputtered, "As for you, bitch, you and yer boy are gonna pay for what you done to me and my dog."

"No, Bo, please. Please let my little boy go." She shoved Greg behind the wooden beam. "You can hold *me* here. The folks on the way from camp can get you to a hospital. You were a little boy once, your mother loved you, wanted to keep you safe. Do a good thing for this boy, Bo. Please." All her love was in her voice, a prayer for a shred of compassion for Greg.

"I ain't got no carin' for anybody's boy. Thanks to you, all I got time for now is a little satisfaction." He held the shotgun barrel down to reload, opened the ammo box, and reached in for a shell. His fingers felt for shells and brought out stones. "What the hell?"

He kept scrambling his free hand in the box. It came out flinging a tarantula. The spider crawled on his arm and scurried up his neck. Bo screamed in horror. The empty shotgun rattled to the floor.

Suzanne saw her advantage, kicked the gun away and

held Johnny's 38 and the flashlight on Bo.

Johnny reached her side. She handed the 38 over, held the flashlight out for Greg to hold and picked up the shotgun. She turned it in her hands to use the stock end as a club and held it above Bo.

"I'll crack him good if he moves a muscle." Her voice was shrill with exhaustion and the emotion of wanting to get her son out of the cellar and away from the evil man.

"Move and I'll smash your head in," she hissed. "It would be a pleasure after what you've put my boy and all of us through."

Greg clutched the flashlight in his fingers and trained its wavering beam on Bo and his mom.

Once Johnny stood over Bo with the 38, Suzanne leaned the shotgun against a shelf full of web-draped canning jars and propped the flashlight to light more of the room. She gathered her son into her arms. He crumpled against her. She kissed his hair, kissed his cheeks, crooned to him while untying his hands. Once his hands were free, Greg held on to her as if she might disappear. She rubbed his arms and hands to restore the circulation, keeping a constant banter of comfort going in loving whispers.

"You two okay?" Johnny sounded edgy, his stressed emotions barely in check.

"Yes, we'll be fine," Suzanne said. "Now that *you're* here, and *if* there aren't any more rattlesnakes or tarantulas." She caught sight of the bobbing hood of the bird at his throat inside his shirt. "You found your falcon!"

"He dumped her like trash in that old, dry outhouse," he said, adding in a rough whisper to the man on the floor. "About time you paid up, Rodman."

Suzanne guided Greg to the stairs, paused. "Johnny, did you see the dog?"

"It's dead, gut shot. Safe for you two to go on up. The men from the camp will be here any minute. Leave the flashlight on that shelf aimed our way." He took a steadier stance. "Me and

Bo got some unfinished business."

"Kill me, you son of a bitch, just shoot me dead." Bo struggled to stand, but collapsed to the dirt floor amid rat droppings, old boards, and seasons worth of shed snake skins. "I ain't goin' back to the pen. Kill me quick before the cops get here. I saw 'em. I know they'll be here soon. Quick, damn you! Or gimme the gun. I'll do it myself."

Johnny held the gun steady on Bo. "He hurt you, son? If he hurt you, I'll kill him now, like he's begging for, but I'll let you and your mother leave first so you won't have to watch him die."

"No, sir, Mr. Carlisle," Greg said, his voice quavering. "He tied me up, but he never hurt me, not for real, except where he poked me with his gun, and my hurt feet."

"Lucky S.O.B. ain't you, Rodman?"

The suffering man writhed in a heap on the floor.

"I thought you'd wasted my gyr like you thought you did me. I've lived through hell to make you pay for what you did to me . . . my family . . . my dog, and Felon here."

Suzanne heard voices at the top of the stairs. Men's voices, saw many flashlights. The cellar and its jumbled debris lit up as if someone had turned on the single broken bulb dangling from the center beam.

"Johnny has everything under control," Suzanne said.

Doug bent his head and entered first with his rifle drawn, Taylor right behind him.

Suzanne, stunned to see them both, backed down the stairs and held Greg by the shoulders. She looked from one man to the other, trying to fathom how they could be among her rescuers from the Sun Tunnel camp. Police officers and fellow campers crowded on the stairs, all their flashlights and eyes trained on the cellar.

How could Taylor and Doug know to find us and rescue Greg?

"Let us take it from here, Carlisle." Doug's rifle cast a slice of shadow across Bo's sweat-darkened shirt and the spreading bloody blotch that bubbled from his thigh.

"Susie? Greg?" Taylor crunched through the mess on the floor separating them. "You two okay?" He clutched them to himself, sharing a three-way hug, as best he could with a rifle and a fat lantern flashlight in his hands. He stepped away and played the square-faced lantern over them both. He saw Greg's bloody bare feet. "We've got to get those cleaned up and disinfected." He looked at Suzanne. "Who shot that dog up in the yard—you?"

Suzanne nodded. "How'd you know we needed you?" she breathed, smiling up at him, feeling safe at last.

"Later." He handed her his rifle and the lantern. He examined the soles of Greg's feet, then hiked the boy onto his back. "Let's get you two out of this hell hole."

"Everybody just step back and take it easy," said Johnny, to the crowd. "We'll let Mrs. Price and the boy get by up the stairs, then I want this low life to know what a good beating feels like with the butt of this 38. No mercy, just the way he did me." He spun the chamber open and let all but one bullet fall to the dirt.

"Let him get in a few good licks," said one of the men. "Serve him right for takin' the boy and scarin' hell out of all our families."

"Not while I'm in charge," said Doug. "Rodman's going to stand trial for murder, and if I know juries, the only break he'll get is his fair choice of how he takes his death sentence. Death row'll be too good for him. He deserves a few mean lifers to rough him around a bit first. The'll have a little sport with this weasel."

"Greg's seen and heard enough, Doug," Suzanne said wearily. "Let us take him out of here, please. Bo's been shot; he's bleeding fast. I think I hit an artery."

"Well, *I* didn't die," said Johnny, looking at Doug, "who'd he kill to be accused of murder?"

"His girlfriend," said Doug quietly, giving Suzanne a knowing glance.

She sucked in her breath and looked up at Taylor, who nodded assent.

Rehma?! Oh, my God. Suzanne couldn't grasp it all at once. *Then, he'd already murdered Rehma when he came to get the kids for a campout. He intended to kidnap them then!* It occurred to her the time would come when she'd have to tell Greg about his mother, unless he'd figured it out already. *How will he take the news?*

She looked anew at the pathetic man on the floor and felt both outrage and shock that he'd had an opportunity to kill her and her boy, and somehow had not. Their brush with death shook her profoundly. She struggled with pity, anger, and relief. *God forgive me for my lack of faith!*

Bo's body twitched uncontrollably. "Just shoot me now. No way I'm goin' back to no pen. Get it over with."

"Dying is too damn good for you!" Johnny bent low and whipped him across the head with the butt of the 38. Blood oozed into his eyes. Bo sagged against a broken shelf on the floor. He laughed, a hollow racket in his chest.

"That's enough!" Doug yelled. "One of you officers read Rodman his rights, while we get him to a hospital. Taylor, give a hand with holding Carlisle back."

Taylor moved up the stairs with Greg on his back. "I don't take orders from you, Jensen."

Eyeing the headless rattler, Johnny said, "Raw snake meat is just what Felon needs."

Nobody moved to pick it up and hand it to him. Johnny opened his shirt, took the hood off his falcon, and let it get purchase with its talons on a canning shelf. "She's underweight and hungry, too long confined to fly for prey in the morning. Not enough flight feathers left to soar or stoop."

"I'm not getting close to that big hawk," said a patrolmen. "You're so high and mighty, Jensen, you restrain Carlisle. I'll hold your rifle." Several men laughed.

"Do what you have to do," interrupted Taylor. "I'm taking Suzanne and her boy out of here. They've seen and heard too much already."

"Johnny," Suzanne touched his arm as she passed, "let Bo get his justice by the law and from God. You and Felon come back to camp with us. You've been through enough, too. If it hadn't been for you, Bo would be long gone with my son. Don't put yourself in jail over him; he's not worth it. You have Felon back. She needs you."

The officers hauled Bo to his feet, his bloody face inches from Felon's dark eyes and her razor beak. Her wings lifted and settled, lifted again. She shrieked a piercing call and flew at Rodman. Her talons closed on his face, rupturing an eye that sputtered blood. She pecked at him viciously, with the dispatch she'd use on a roughed grouse or a pigeon.

In fear of their own safety, the officers let go of Bo who scrambled on the floor screaming in terror, covering his face with his bare hands. Felon persisted, bloodying his fingers, his scalp, exposing bone, shrieking between savage, hooking bites.

"Get it off me! Get it off!"

Johnny's scarred face strangely peaceful, his eyes downcast on Bo, he let out a long sigh. His big shoulders slumped. "I don't know if this screetching and misprinting can be extinguished or not." He handed the 38 to Doug Jensen. "Time will tell. God willing my Felon survives this low-down rat."

Greg, his face averted, covered his ears from Bo's cries and the shrieking of the gyr. Taylor eased the boy down against his mother and pulled off his jacket. He moved to the falcon, covered her swiftly, talking to her, smoothing her back feathers where he felt them through the fabric.

"It's a rare thing for a well-trained falcon to behave like it's misprinted on a poor handler," he said. "But gyrs are highly intelligent. She's been confined and starved. She remembers Bo's indifference and neglect."

Her body covered, Felon calmed in the enveloping jacket's darkness. She released her hold on Rodman's scalp and allowed herself to be lifted away.

Bo whimpered, his blood running through his fingers. His

one eye socket a ragged hole. The cellar dirt room was pungent with the cool smell of decay and Bo's warm blood. Amazed curses whispered from those crowding in the doorway for a better look.

"God a mighty, what a gory mess that hawk made of him."

Johnny Carlisle's tired and shaky voice broke the tension. "My bird's mighty hungry. Hand us that dead rattler."

Taylor returned Felon, jacket and all to Johnny. He lifted Greg onto his back and tucked the boy's bloody feet around his waist. Suzanne heard her son crying into Taylor's shoulder. Someone passed Johnny what was left of the rattler. Behind them on the floor, under Doug's direction, the officers labored to save Bo's life. In the light of half a dozen flashlights, Bo lay sobbing like a child, afraid to live, afraid to die.

When he lost consciousness, his ranting stopped. At the top of the stairs, Suzanne turned, heard Doug calling Elko for a medi-vac 'copter on his cell phone. Noted that the officer with his fingers at Bo's throat, shook his head.

Doug nodded. "Never mind the rush on code blue. Take your time boys, Rodman's gone. We'll get him up to a clearing. Tell your pilot to take a rest, you can come in a few hours when it's light."

Suzanne mounted the stairs behind Taylor carrying Greg. A new family forged underground emerged in the moonlight. They waited for Johnny to catch up.

"Taylor, I'm mighty happy to have Felon back," said Johnny, his cane handle managing the rattler's drooping loop of body. "Think your dad would help me find a good home for her, where I could visit, you know, see she's cared for?"

"Pops has some empty mews, now that Speck's his only falcon. Felon can stay there until she's regained her strength and her flight feathers. Worst comes to worst, or maybe best to best, Johnny, you can help Greg and me care for her. It's time I taught my boy the art of falconry."

The big man's shoulders shook.

Greg lifted his head, peered around Taylor's shoulder. "Really? You'll teach me to be a falconer? Wow!"

"You can count on it. Rest now, son."

Doug and the officers used an old cellar shelf for a makeshift stretcher to carry Bo's body out on. Suzanne, Taylor, and Johnny stepped aside to let the four officers pass, reminding Suzanne of pallbearers at Steve's graveside service. She shivered, skirting the body of the dog she'd shot. *Did I really kill it, and Bo as well? Oh God! Forgive me. I don't believe in killing.*

Johnny squatted in the dust and took Taylor's jacket off Felon. He let her rip into snake flesh, turning and hooking ravenous bites. When she was sated, he hooded her and tucked her back into his shirt. He draped the remainder of the snake over his shoulders for another meal in an hour or so. He rose to his feet, steadied himself with his cane. Near exhaustion and in need of his meds, he fought to stay focused.

Johnny was surprised to find the Price family had waited for him. A few campers stood about with flashlights to show the way, kindnesses he was unprepared for. His tears came again. This time they flowed unheeded. He walked among his new friends, under the moon and stars with 'the wind' near his heart once more.

~Saturday the 21st of June

Dawn of the Summer Solstice

Few wound-up campers returned to their sleeping bags after the excitement settled down. Finding Greg and preparing the spot where Bo Rodman's body would be lifted off in a medivac helicopter as a certifiable 'death emergency,' brought a sense of unity and relief to those assembled for the solstice Sun Tunnel light-burst.

The Wind Remembers

Under Doug's direction, trips were made to the dry wash to help stranded searchers return to the campsite. Cell phones on roaming charges were in evidence lining up wreckers and tractors from nearby farms. Plans to remove three vehicles from the arroyo by mid-morning, meant everybody with an axle too wide or a rig too heavy to navigate the irrigation culvert would have a way back to the main road by noon.

Campfires were stoked and stoves pumped into service under pots of tea and coffee, hot chocolate mixed up for the kids, coolers opened and their contents shared. Four-in-the-morning communal breakfasts at tailgates and camp stoves attracted campers like magnets to get the story straight on what had happened and where. The general mood was one of genuine kindness and mutual concern as though all had pulled together to assure a good outcome. They reassured themselves that all was well with Greg and his family before the universe lined up its illuminating power east of the cliffs. At dawn the solar dazzle would delight them with its annual summer-solstice performance through the constellation holes in Nancy Holt's concrete Sun Tunnels.

When Suzanne and Greg returned to camp, Dierdre held onto Suzanne with Mitzi, Bear Lovins, and Greg in a family-reunion hug that would have made the fallen cottonwood at the Price home proud. Cosma Stargazer brought a basket of herb packets and a basin of warm water. In gestures, she communicated her insistence that she be allowed to care for Greg's feet.

The woman with the husband named Ralph brought her first-aid kit. She and Cosma, who still had not spoken since her firelight ceremony, applied anti-bacterial ointment and wrapped each raw foot in sterile gauze. Greg had no choice but to sit in a camp chair with his bandaged feet propped on a bedroll. He was tired and sore all over but happy to be safe and the center of attention.

"I'd have a tetanus shot as soon as you're back to civilization today," said Ralph's wife. "Don't even drive beyond

389

Elko without getting one. I wouldn't take *any* chances with puncture wounds from who knows what in that filthy cellar. Ralph says they buried that brute of a dog you shot, ma'am."

"Everything happened so fast," Suzanne had so many questions for Greg, like the stones and the spider in the box and the gum wrapper, but they'd have to wait. She had a million questions for Taylor, too. Like, *how did Bo follow us out here when I didn't see his truck behind us even though there was hardly any traffic?*

"Ralph said you were damn lucky that dog didn't go for your throat."

"He did. That's why I shot him." Suzanne thanked her profusely and offered payment to restock their camper medicine chest.

"Not on your life!" the woman said. "There was so little any of us could do. We're just happy you and your boy are safe."

Suzanne returned to the Coleman and washed up in hot water. She helped her twin pass out goodies to the kids, her own and those from nearby camps who'd come to visit Greg and get a peek at the hooded falcon.

Johnny rested in the other folding chair. Cosma offered him steaming herb tea. Her boys and Greg watched the hawk's slightest move, indicated by the quiver of the plume on his stitched-leather hood.

Taylor stood chatting with the retiring Nevada officer who'd gotten him to the Sun Tunnels, and would have done so in time to help Suzanne, if Doug hadn't needed to be so almighty important that nobody could move without his every say so. Taylor was grateful Doug and the others were staying out away from camp with Bo's body where they'd staked out a landing spot for the helicopter that would arrive after sun up.

He looked at Suzanne while he talked, beautiful in her dirty clothes and rumpled hair, handing out sweet rolls to strangers like it was her life work. Her genuineness, her happiness in spite of the red rash on her swollen face and neck from a combination of Doug's slap and the gunpowder filled him with a tenderness he couldn't have expressed in words if he'd tried.

Suzanne looked up, met his gaze, and smiled. Handing the box of pastries to her sister, she came toward him with her hands clasped behind her, as awkward as if they were meeting for the first time. He excused himself from the men to join her.

A step apart, they opened arms to each other and clung together long and fast, their hearts beating to one rhythm, aware through their whole beings that nothing but death itself would ever separate them again.

"Mom, it's time for the show," called Greg. "Sit down, Mitzi, by me on the cooler. There's room for Bear Lovins, too."

"See the streaks of pink on that far ridge? It's almost dawn." Dierdre carried Greg's folding chair to be closer to the pair of Sun Tunnels aligned for the summer solstice. Suzanne propped his bandaged feet. Everyone in camp hurried to find a place to view what some came every year to experience. Fine creamy dust covered the cars, the people, and their clothing. All agreed the dust was worth what nature and Nancy Holt had prepared for them. Bundled against the chill, their breath showed white in the air. They whispered to one another and waited for the light.

"Know what's going to happen, Mitzi?" Taylor lifted her to his shoulder so she could see above people's heads and turn Bear Lovin's eyes toward the Tunnels.

"Nope." She zipped his lips shut, bending forward over his head. "But I be ready for it. Auntie Dreedra says we needs to be bery bery quiet." Taylor laughed and patted her pants leg against his cheek.

Johnny kept to the chair Dierdre offered next to Greg. Felon, center-of-attention with many of the kids and most of their fathers, perched at his elbow on a tire pump wrapped with a hand towel. Johnny removed her hood. She shook herself several times. No longer hungry after a feast of half a crop of the snake meat and as much water as she wanted, she settled with her master handler, sated, her feathers tight to her body with contentment. "She's on the come," Johnny explained to Greg in a whisper. "Her eyes are shiny and her keel bone will flesh up soon. She cast a good pellet an hour ago."

A hush fell over the assembled campers. Only the chirping of insects and the delicate sounds of the breeze riffling through pickle weed, rabbit bush, sage brush and barley grass—for as far as they could see into acres of distance—could be heard.

"Why is everybody being so quiet?" Greg whispered.

"To many of us, and certainly to Cosma," said Dierdre, "this is church, a sacred planetary event. With all the excitement, there hasn't been time to explain it to you this morning. You'll just have to watch as it happens."

"Here it comes!"

The expectant energy of the people grew until it was palpable. Light reached out through a V in the cliffs opposite them. Like the finger of God it moved with laser swiftness across the land and into the first Tunnel. Shafts of brilliant light burst through hole after hole in the constellation arrangement that pierced each of the Sun Tunnels. As the sun rose over the cliffs, it crossed the space between the Tunnels and entered the second concrete tube. The awesome starburst effect grew and grew until a magnificent halo of light embraced the Tunnels, extending far out into the surrounding space.

A chorus of coyote yips floated across the desert, sending shivers through the crowd. "Wow!" Greg exclaimed, only to be shushed lovingly by his Aunt Dierdre.

Felon shrieked and fell silent.

At Johnny's elbow, Cosma broke her silence in a whisper to Johnny. "The Ancient ones believed hawks bring messages on the Good Red Road from the world of the grandfathers and grandmothers for our Earth Walk. Hawks have keen eyes and bold hearts for they fly close to the light of Grandfather Sun. They remind us that all our gifts are equal in the eyes of Great Spirit. Hawk's cry means we are to receive a message."

"I think we already got it," answered Johnny. He smiled

at her. She touched the ribbons on her braid, then his shoulder, and nodding, smiled back.

For more than fifteen minutes, the play of light beamed in moving halos while video cameras recorded and people whispered. Restless children wiggled, until the morning was fully realized, and the sun moved above the openings of the Sun Tunnels and the cliffs. Transformed to gray concrete, innocuous sausage-link forms like butterflies reversing the process of metamorphosis, the Sun Tunnels rested to await the next equinox or solstice gathering, when if the sky is clear they will again glow brilliant with dawn's first light.

For some time the camp was busy with people packing their gear and sharing space until their cars and vans could be made operable. They stood shaking hands and chatting about the natural spectacle they'd shared, the relief that Greg and his mother had returned to camp unharmed, and the shocking story of Bo Rodman and his dead girlfriend, Greg's mother, they expected to read about in the papers back home.

The pulsing whir of the helicopter taking Bo's body away, with Doug still in charge, had made the event more than memorable because the resulting creamy dust cloud took a few minutes to settle back to earth. By noon, all of the vehicles and Bo Rodman's truck had been hauled out of the arroyo. Cosma and her boys, Johnny and Felon, Suzanne and Dee, the children and Taylor, remained after the last RV departed the campsite.

Johnny seemed restored after a hearty breakfast, his medication, and a great deal of attention from Cosma, which appeared to please them both.

Everything about the arid spot fascinated Cosma's sons and Greg, who asked Taylor to take him to view the center point of the four tunnels' convergence marked by a disk in the white dust. "It's like we're explorers or something," Greg exclaimed. "Come on, Mom, you've got to see this."

Nearly dizzy with fatigue, Suzanne did follow, if not as

quickly as he wanted. She said to Mitzi, "Run and ask your Aunt Dierdre if there are any shots left in her camera. If there are let's get everyone over here by the Tunnels for pictures to remember this summer solstice."

"We won't forget, even wifout pictures in our scrapbook," said Mitzi. "Wait 'til I tell Leesha everything. It's bigger than a s'prise. But lots of it's not so bery good." Her curls bobbing, she turned and ran kicking up wisps of white dust back to the campsite, calling, "Aunt Dreedra, bring your camera real quick!"

After a hasty photo session, they packed up ready to leave. Taylor took the last box from Dierdre and set it inside the Blazer, which was already heating up. Dierdre moved to Johnny's car while Taylor closed the tailgate. He was about to walk around to the driver's side when his eye caught the flutter of something red.

He squatted down to view it at eye level, a cloth stuck in the housing of the extra-wheel on the back of the truck. *A dirty old bandanna?* Taylor tugged on it, realized it was knotted and felt around behind the wheel to a boxy shape. Light in his mind dawned on a familiar form. "Hey, Johnny," he called. "What do you make of this?"

With Johnny at his elbow, Taylor used a pocketknife to cut through the bandanna knot. He pulled out a falconry telemeter and handed it to Carlisle.

"So that's how he tailed this truck from miles back!" Johnny spat the words, shaking his head. "I should have suspected something like this."

Taylor patted him on the shoulder. "Don't be hard on yourself. The guy was such an amateur, who'd have thought he was up on falcon-tracking tech? Let's keep this between ourselves for a day or two."

"Let everything settle a bit, you mean?" Johnny stuffed the gadget in his windbreaker pocket. "Fine by me," he said.

They turned back to the women and children.

Dierdre walked over. "How about I ride back with

Johnny so Taylor can drive you and the kids."

Suzanne thought her twin's orchestrating was perfect. She didn't want to be separated from Taylor, though she'd thought he'd ride back with Carlisle and the gyrfalcon, since they wanted to get Felon to his Pop's mews and a restorative bath.

"We'll stop at the clinic and get Greg's tetanus shot," said Taylor. "Johnny's had a workout; maybe you can spare him some driving, Dee."

"Doubt she'll want to drive a hands-only special-needs car," said Johnny.

"We'll manage just fine," Dierdre said. "We're following Cosma's RV to Elko for lunch together before Johnny and I get Felon to your dad's mews. I've told Johnny to make plans for a little cruise vacation in the Caribbean. I can get him a deal they can't afford to refuse, maybe even a honeymoon suite."

Suzanne burst into laughter. She snapped Mitzi into her seat belt and handed her a Magic Slate. In the desert heat of the longest day of the year, it was refused. Suzanne tucked the slate back into the travel bag.

"Mommy, Bear Lovins says his tummy can be a pillow for Gregory's owie feet."

"That's really nice of Bear Lovins," chuckled Suzanne, adjusting Greg's bandaged feet on the mound of brown fluff. She gave him a loving pat on the leg and a delighted smile.

"Mom," said Greg, "could we stop some place for a strawberry shake? It's hot as blazes." He buckled his seat belt.

Taylor and Suzanne settled in up front.

She looked over her shoulder. "Honey, if they'll serve this rowdy bunch of dust-covered campers, our brave boy can have all the ice cream he can hold!"

"I'll buy," added Taylor, "enough for everybody including me." He buzzed the windows up and switched on the air conditioner.

"Goody," sighed Mitzi, fighting drowsiness. "Wake me up for mine wif a grizzar and a kiss."

They hadn't driven all the way out to the main road

before both kids were asleep.

"That twin of yours is quite the matchmaker," quipped Taylor.

"Do you suppose Dee really will get Johnny and Cosma to take one of her honeymoon cruises to the Caribbean? I suppose they'd get married first, but heavens, they've just met."

Suzanne ran her fingers through the thick hair at the back of Taylor's head, eager to touch him and content to feel comfortable enough between them for such intimacies.

"Wouldn't surprise me at all," Taylor chuckled, patting her lovingly on the thigh. He looked over at her and winked before turning his eyes back to the road.

"Penny for your thoughts, Susie, *if* they're about you and me. If not, I'm not interested."

He swallowed a laugh.

She swatted him playfully on the shoulder, and with both hands in his hair, pulled his head toward her and stretched to kiss his stubbly cheek.

"Right this particular minute, Mr. Ruggedly Handsome Lumberjack, *all* my thoughts are about you and me."

The End

THE WIND REMEMBERS

ACKNOWLEDGMENTS

My sincere thanks to supportive writer friends and professional experts who have made the authenticity of the scene action in The Wind Remembers *plausible:*

Howard Brinkerhoff, NAFA falconer, captive-breeder, co-originator of competitive falcon-meet Sky Trials and Master of Ceremonies in Utah, South East Arabia's country of Oman and other locations of these events worldwide. His manuscript draft review for falconry facts and revision suggestions was invaluable.

Dave Peterson, NAFA falconer, raptor expert, U. S. Bureau of Land Management in Utah and Oregon, falconry consultant to European royal families and the falconer friend who first took me to the Sky Trial competition that inspired my passionate appreciation for falcons, gyrfalcons in particular, and falcon breeders.

J. Lynn Peterson, (wife of Dave) fellow-artist friend and falcon expert, bird and wild animal rescuer for research assistance and accompanying me to Utah's west desert Sun Tunnels for our first summer solstice, light-burst event.

Steve Chindgren NAFA, Steve Hoffman, expert falconers, research support.

Ogden Nature Center, Utah for allowing me to volunteer as a raptor feeder to gain experience with birds of prey and their habits in protective captivity.

Hawk Watch International staff members for phone support in my research.

Doan Kemp, Guy Lebeda, Peter Wilks, hand-gun and shot-gun expertise.

The late Craig Slater, forestry, tree-management and 1990's equipment expertise. Kenneth Kardong, rattlesnake strike-behavior biologist.

Consulting editor Steve Price, Prentice-Hall, for his enthusiastic encouragement.

JoLynn Smith Fowles, friend and widow of police detective, remarried to tree expert whose example prompted the plot beginnings for this book.

Nancy Holt, sculptor who created the Sun Tunnel installation on 43 acres of west desert, Box Elder County land she purchased in Utah. I am many dramatic, Sun Tunnel solstices happier.

Feedback supporters: Kathy Lloyd, Sally Lindsay, Lynn Champagne, Karen Foster, Peter Wilks, Lynda Scott; CRAMP members: Kendra Fowler, Cory Webb, Chris Miller, Kenneth Lee, Christy Monson, Janette Wright, Margot Hovley; SWAP members: Barbara Anderson, Christine Perkins, Prudence Bice, and Linda Lowe.

Kimbra Quinn Sullivan for key stroking the early concept manuscript from my handwritten notes. Sally Lindsay, Shannon McBride Blomgren, Robert McKanna for their unending belief that my "suspenseful adventure-love story" should be told.

Author/Publisher David W. Smith, Synergy Books.

Beta readers: Howard Brinkerhoff, Keith Spahr, Kimbra Quinn Sullivan.

About the Author

Caroll Louise Shreeve is an author, editor, illustrator, art and writing educator. Over the years, Caroll has been a workshop leader for Asilomar Writer's Conferences, *Reader's Digest, Writer's Digest*, University of Utah, Weber State University, and at the Eccles Art Center in Ogden Utah. She is a former in-house editor for Peregrine Smith Books, Karen Foster Scrapbook Co., Vice President of Publishing 1984–1994 for Meridian Intl. custom magazines & books, and Editorial Director for Chapelle Sterling, packager.

Caroll is the author of Sterling Publishing's *Victorian Details*, interior and garden design, *Life Is Good*, a guided gratitude journal for Walking Stick Press; and co-author of *Celebrate Your Stories* for Watson-Guptill. Her "Tell Your Story" journaling for scrapbook columns appeared in *Memory Maker's* magazine. She has written and illustrated interior design books for Sterling on a ghosting work-for-hire basis.

In addition, Caroll is co-owner and painting instructor at the Blue Raven Art Studio in Coyote Gulch Art Village located in the community of Kayenta in Ivins, Utah.

She is an award-winning writer and a board member of Heritage Writers Guild chapter of League of Utah Writers, where she currently serves as secretary of the state board.

Caroll also writes for children under the pen name: Susie McGruder McGlish.

The Wind Remembers

Coming Soon by Synergy Books Publishing:

Caroll Shreeve's Newest Novel,
Secrets of the Diary Goddess

A Young-Adult Fantasy Romance

Secrets of the Diary Goddess

Diana's mystical diary channels a Spirit Woman

When teen adventurers Diana and her BFF Sunni, ride horses up a forbidden canyon, a secret cave is discovered. Journey with fifteen-year old Diana as she plunges through a mysterious portal within the cave. Ancient Indian pictographs, a shape-shifter, and dangerous pit falls tumble her back in time.

A Spirit Woman of a long-ago tribe, welcomes Diana. She meets a young Indian brave who stirs her mind and heart. To join his tribe she must surrender a piece of her Self. Will she? Heroes and Sheroes merge on the pages of Diana's diary. Promises made, pledges broken—peel away veils of secrecy, revealing how Diana's and Sunni's lives will be changed—forever.

Also by **Synergy Books Publishing**: Read the top-selling and award-winning novels, **HIDDEN MICKEY** and **In the Shadow of the Matterhorn**. Also read two of the top-rated tennis instructional books, **TENNIS MASTERY** and **COACHING MASTERY** by David W. Smith.